Take It
To
The Limit

The most exciting account of air terrorism ever written! A European Baron dealing in international illegal arms loses an important nerve gas shipment on the Mediterranean Sea. His ship and its deadly cargo are captured during an action-packed US Navy SEAL commando raid. To save his family fortune, the Baron takes even more sinister work. He agrees to plant a bomb aboard a Boeing 747 bound from Chicago to London. The Baron hires a disgruntled airline employee and they develop a devious and clever way to plant the bomb. The horror of the disaster for those on board is depicted as the bomb detonates during flight over Canada. FBI Agent Sally Stein and CIA Agent Nick Barber continue a tumultuous romance as they track the air terrorism to its evil source. Will they be in time to prevent a second bombing attempt on a flight originating at Los Angeles International Airport? Closing scenes find Sally and Nick in a desperate firefight at a gangster's plush north woods hideaway. Follow the breathtaking action on the high seas and in exotic locales across Europe and North America.

Take It
To
The Limit

Mike Hatch

Empire Publishing
Empire, WI

Empire
Take It To The Limit

Printing History
First Printing 1998

ISBN: 0-9657225-1-1

Empire Publishing
N5432 Dondor Drive, Empire, WI, 54935

PRINTED IN THE UNITED STATES OF AMERICA
10 9 8 7 6 5 4 3 2 1

Works by Mike Hatch:

FICTION

Horseshoes & Nuclear Weapons, H&A, 1997
To order: 800-507-2665

Take It To The Limit, Empire, 1998

NONFICTION

*Production & Inventory Control Handbook -
Manufacturing Resource Planning*,
McGraw-Hill, 1997
To order: 800-444-2742

Visit us on the internet:
http://www.atlasdesigns.com/hatch

To Dotty
Ma and Editor

"Hell hath no limits, nor is it circumscribed
In one place; for where we are is hell,
And where hell is there we must ever be."

*-The Tragical History of Doctor Faustus
[1604], act II, sc.i*

PART ONE
THE HERO

ONE

April 5, 1944, 9:00 A.M.

Roaring through the sky at nearly two hundred miles per hour the massive formation of aircraft created man-made thunder. Man-made lightning would soon rain down over the German Empire, the Third Reich. U.S. Army Air Force Captain Gordon Halvorsen was flying right wing support for the bombing mission in a P-51 Mustang. The compact fighter plane, known as the "51", was considered the fastest machine in the air. Over an hour earlier Gordon had eased the control stick back and climbed into the sky at Steeple Morden, England. He was a member of one of several fighter groups that had assembled over the North Sea with two hundred and sixteen heavy bombers. The fighters were to escort them to the day's targets at Kiel and Harburg, Germany. They had, as often done, flown a circuitous route planned by Army Intelligence. This was supposedly to avoid detection by the enemy until the latest possible moment. As the big twelve cylinder engine in front of him kept up it's constant roar, Gordon wondered, as most of the pilots did, how good that intelligence really was. Most of the Army Intelligence information, it was rumored, came from German girls that the American OSS and British DI5 agents were fooling around with on the European continent. How good could it be, he thought? It seemed only to waste fuel and time, forcing the fighters to carry the dangerous auxiliary fuel tanks below the wings on nearly every sortie and mission. But then, whatever intelligence planned they followed.

Tomorrow was Gordon's birthday. He would be twenty-three.

Flying at twenty thousand feet the formation approached the west coast of the Jutland peninsula on an east-southeast course just north of the Danish border. German airspace was just beyond. Gordon reached down and turned the fuel selector from "R.H. COMBAT DROP" to "MAIN TANK R.H.". He reached to his left and pulled the bomb salvo handles to release the auxiliary fuel tanks. As the tanks fell away to the sea the plane gained speed and altitude slightly. He adjusted with stick and throttle. The auxiliary tanks were partially full, but to hell with regulations, he thought. He was not going to fly into German airspace with two gasoline bombs under him. Better to get the pilots and planes back for another mission, he rationalized. He knew most of the other fighter pilots were doing the same. Of course, there were always a few Polish recruits and other crazies who would expend every available drop of gasoline getting a few last licks in on the Germans. But if the drop tanks were hit by the ubiquitous flack, it would be all over.

Cloud cover was very heavy now as they approached the coast. He looked over to his left, through the wisps of mist he could see the wing of the P-51 to his left. He adjusted his altitude and air speed to line up with the wing. In the center of the formation were the heavy bombers; American B-17s, B-24s and British Liberators. The fighters keyed on the positions of the heavies and leveled accordingly to the outer edges.

Now feeling a bit safer, Gordon's mind drifted to the events of several days earlier. He and some of the other pilots had been making the rounds of a few English country pubs when they were off duty. It was strictly forbidden for pilots to do this. They were told by their superior officers that they were an elite corps and that they should not be socializing with the locals. Actually, there were German spies in England. The pilots knew too much about plans and strategies and aircraft and weapons technology. And about the number of planes at their bases. The Army Air Force Command didn't want drunken young pilots shooting their mouths off in public places. Therefore, they furnished nightclubs on base for them. But these were not as much fun as the pubs frequented by the local women. He remembered the Red Horse Pub from a couple of weeks earlier. Her name was Elizabeth. How they had danced! The tune "Chattanooga Choo Choo" began to play clearly in his mind now as he remembered.

> You leave the Pennsylvania station
> 'bout a quarter to four,
> Read a magazine and then
> you're in Baltimore,
> Nothing could be finer,
> than to be in Caroliner....

The music in his mind was seemingly in beat with the roar of the powerful engine.

The proprietor of the Red Horse had turned in Gordon's group to the MP's after that visit, or so they thought. They had decided to get even. A few days later, during night practice maneuvers under a moonlit sky, a team of six P-51s including Gordon had buzzed the Red Horse Pub. They had flown in low over the English countryside and dipped one by one over the roof of the pub. Then they had pushed their powerful engines to full throttle and climbed into the night sky. On the ground later they had joked about shattering every bottle, glass and window in the place. One of the pilots had bragged about scraping the chimney of the building with his air intake scoop. They told him he was full of it. But when they inspected his plane he was as surprised as they were to see a scratch on the underbelly scoop of his plane.

The next day it had been announced that all leaves were canceled and sorties and missions would be stepped up. Rumors were that this was in anticipation of the impending Anglo-American invasion of the European continent.

Now Gordon's life would be in grave danger again and he felt pangs of guilt about buzzing the man's pub. They might have destroyed the proprietor's livelihood. Why in the hell had they done it?, he thought. At least it wasn't as bad as the stories he had heard about reckless behavior at other bases. Supposedly, a pilot had swooped down at night over a railroad track flying at twenty feet and switched on his landing light. The engineer of an oncoming freight train mistook it for the headlight of another train coming at him at high speed. In a panic he applied the brakes and reversed the locomotive engine's truck wheels. The engineer and the fireman were killed in the resulting wreck. Recollection of this story only sent more chills of real fear through Gordon. Once again, he dreaded that he would not come back. He recalled the words of the Army Chaplain the evening before, "If I can't make believers of you, the Germans will." Gordon prayed.

Suddenly, the radio crackled in his ear. He adjusted his oxygen mask and listened carefully to the coded message. The heavies would be turning back! That meant the cloud ceiling had dropped to twelve thousand feet. The bombers relied on visual sighting and at altitudes below that they would be sitting ducks for enemy antiaircraft fire. But Gordon's worst fear was then realized as he listened to the remainder of the message. The fighters were ordered to reform and go in anyway. They would be the main instruments of the attack rather than guards. One target was the naval shipyards, the canal, railroad and roads supplying them at Kiel. The other was the shipyards at Harburg, an industrial suburb just south of Hamburg on the Elbe River. Gordon was assigned to Kiel. Both sites were near the limit of range of the smaller planes. The fighters, armed with small rocket bombs and large caliber machine guns would do little damage compared with what the heavy bombers could do. Somebody up there wants to worry Hitler today at all costs, Gordon thought. Again, the tune "Chattanooga Choo Choo" returned, playing clearly in his mind. This time the chugging, wailing sound of the brass instruments seemed to take on an ominous tone that he could not put from his head.

The fighter wings reformed and increased their speed as they crossed the Jutland peninsula. They followed the route mapped out by Army Intelligence. They banked due south, over the dairy farm country of Schleswig-Holstein, west of Flensburg, Germany. Then they made a wide arc to the east toward Kiel. Several squadrons peeled off, headed for

Harburg. Gordon stayed with the others, completing the great arc and approaching Kiel from the south. Perhaps Intelligence was right this time he thought; they had seen no flak, yet. Gordon heard the crackling radio message, they were going down at a heading of 80 degrees to strafe and rocket bomb the submarine shipyards along the inlet. Gordon dived the P-51, he watched the altimeter, still heavy clouds at twelve thousand feet, and ten. Finally, he broke through the clouds at nine thousand feet, the city was below, just to his left, the inlet ahead. He increased his speed. The P-51 could dive in excess of five hundred miles an hour. But, there was the point of no return; an altitude from which one couldn't pull up in time at high diving speed. Gordon glanced at the altimeter and airspeed gauge nd did a mental calculation. Fighters to his left and right peeled off, beginning to strafe and rocket the supply lines on either side of the inlet.

Black flak began to burst in the cloudy sky.

As Gordon pulled back on the stick, he compressed the trigger switch on the front of it, strafing the west bank of the inlet with the six .50 caliber guns. He could barely hear the clattering of the powerful guns over the roar of the engine. The submarine shipyard came into view. He held the button at the top of the stick, releasing his rockets in train, then pulled further back on the stick. He climbed at full throttle as shells began to burst everywhere in the surrounding skies. In less than a minute he was in cloud cover, out beyond the inlet over Kiel Bay. He would do one strafing run at the west rail lines, then head back. He banked left and came down out of the clouds above the inlet mouth.

Suddenly, a Messerschmitt 109 came at him from the west, machine guns and cannons blazing, flying belly up for a fast dive away escape. This tactic was usually reserved for use at high altitude against bombers. His plane jerked and shuddered, he had been hit. Gordon sucked breath as he felt a sharp pain in his lower back, shrapnel had entered his right kidney. He was dazed for a moment, his plane continued to dive. He lost the feel of the plane briefly. Then he came to, the vibrating airborne machine an extension of his body again. He pulled the stick back, managing to bring the plane level only twenty feet above the water of the inlet. The city was dead ahead. Huge anti-aircraft guns thundered in the hills surrounding the inlet, spitting exploding shells up everywhere in the skies. He banked to the right and began to climb. Suddenly, out of the mist and smoke a cone shaped mountain of coal loomed in front of him. He pulled back hard on the stick. With his left hand he pushed the throttle all the way forward, past the gate stop, breaking the safety wire. Take it to the limit, he thought as the engine RPM's increased to the absolute safety limit called: "war emergency power". In a moment, the plane jarred for a split second. The belly of the plane had scraped the top of the pile, but he was still airborne. The engine was screaming now, as he continued to climb toward the west. As he gained altitude, the black flak bursts were everywhere again, some so close he could see the red-yellow flash as they detonated. He was climbing steeply now, abruptly there was a bright flash and burst to his left, then to his right. Oh God, he thought, the antiaircraft guns are sighting me in! He thought of bailing out but the cloud cover was dead ahead. As his plane entered the clouds he banked quickly to the right and heard a shell burst somewhere behind.

As he continued to climb at full power, he noticed the needle on the temperature gauge was beginning to rise. He thought for a moment. The cooling system may have been hit or, more likely, the coal clogged the cooling air intake on the belly of the plane. He throttled the engine down, leveled off and slowed at fourteen thousand feet. He radioed his squad leader and explained his situation about the overheating. The leader replied that they were reforming and going back at full speed; that Gordon would have to make it back as best he could.

Out over the waters of Kiel Bay he cruised along in the clouds on a northwest heading. The temperature gauge needle continued to move to the right. He slowed to 200 miles per hour, the gauge seemed to stabilize for a while, then move again. Gordon realized he would not be able to stay in the air for long, he would probably have to ditch. He wanted to avoid German territory. The pain in his back was excruciating now, he could feel a cooling dampness that was a mixture of blood and sweat. He banked to the right taking a more northerly course. He hoped to make it to Danish soil. Denmark was occupied by Germany, but certainly he would be safer there. The temperature gauge continued to climb gradually as he crossed Kiel Bay. He cut the airspeed to 150 and began to decrease altitude. The altimeter read nine thousand feet now and he was still in heavy cloud cover. It was becoming terribly hot in the cockpit. Gordon's flight suit was soaked with sweat. He cranked the canopy open a few inches for cool air. The cool air was a blessing. The deafening rap of the engine and propeller roared in his ears and after a few moments he cranked it shut again.

The minutes ticked by, it had been nearly thirty minutes since he left Kiel. He judged he was over Danish soil by now, at least the southern islands. He dived out of the heavy cloud cover at six thousand feet. It was foggy and there appeared to be only water below. The temperature gauge needle was all the way over on the right stop pin now and beginning to vibrate, bouncing off the pin. He heard a 'pop' and hiss and he realized that a coolant line had blown. It was only a matter of minutes now before he would have to bail out or land. Steam was escaping from beneath the plane as the glycol engine coolant sprayed into the atmosphere. Then, far in the distance to his right he saw land, but it was a deep forest. He brought the plane down to two thousand feet. He could smell the engine oil boiling away. Then suddenly, the engine seized. The huge propeller stopped abruptly forcing the plane to momentarily lurch down on the left. Instinctively, he reacted with stick and rudder to level the plane. He then feathered the prop quickly for more glide distance and better control.

Suddenly, it was quiet, except for the rush of air and the hissing of the boiling oil. He decided not to bail out, thinking he might not be able to make it to shore from a distance in his condition. He glided the fighter down toward the tree lined shore. He had memorized the P-51 pilot's manual. The sentence about ditching over water flashed in his mind, "It will go down in 1-1/2 to 2 seconds." Flaps down and elevators up he brought the tail down first into the water, the fuselage splashing down gently after. The plane settled into the water only twenty feet from shore.

As the plane began to take water he unlatched his seatbelt and reached to his right and pulled the canopy emergency release handle. The clear canopy popped up and back. He began to crawl out, slipping out of his parachute straps as he did so. The right wing was already submersed and steam was rising into the mist as the sea water cooled the overheated engine. He got onto the nose and as it sank kicked himself off toward the shore. He dogpaddled for a few moments then felt solid ground under his feet. He was standing in reeds in four feet of water. He walked with difficulty toward the shore, the pain from his wound surging over him. A rock ledge jutted out into the water only a few feet away. He walked toward it and grabbed the rocks to steady himself. He was standing in three feet of water. Breathing hard, he rested. After a few minutes he heard voices, and then a truck engine.

He peered over the top edge of the rock through grass and weeds. To his right was a small castle-like stone structure half in ruins. Through the green foliage growing on the ledge he could see a large gray truck come around from behind a hill on a gravel road. Then another behind it. The trucks were obviously heavily laden, the rear bumpers nearly touching the ground, the rear wheels plowing the gravel. They were German trucks. They stopped in front of a large hill. Now he noticed there were guards moving to positions through the trees up in back of the hill. They were wearing nondescript dark clothing and carrying rifles. The door of the lead truck opened and two men stepped out, each wearing a dark suit and trench coat. The taller of the two turned and surveyed the area. Gordon looked in amazement at the familiar flaccid face with small wire rimmed spectacles. The man was a dead ringer for Heinrich Himmler, the Nazi SS Chief, head of Hitler's personal state police. Himmler was known to have raised chickens before his association with Hitler, Gordon mused.

Other men were moving around on the other side of the trucks and, Gordon was astounded to see the side of the hill in front of the trucks open up. Some sort of huge door was built into it. The men climbed back into the trucks and backed into the opening. It closed behind them. Gordon turned and looked the other way along the shore, he wanted to get away as quickly as possible. He began to walk in the water, keeping his head down in the reeds. He walked along the wooded shore for one half hour. It was quiet and there was only the mist now. He crawled up on dry land and stood. It had been easier to walk in the cool water. His right side was becoming numb as he began to walk inland through the dense woods.

After another half hour he was winded and weak. He leaned against a tree and could see a clearing ahead. There was the outline of a church steeple in the mist. He went on toward it. As he came closer he saw the small white church surrounded by a low stone wall. He approached the wall and leaned over it. A neatly kept graveyard surrounded the church. He crawled over the wall and fell to the ground, pain pulsing throughout his body from the exertion. He sat up against the wall and pulled a wax coated packet from his shirt pocket and opened it. Inside was an envelope addressed to his mother. He hadn't written the letter yet. He pulled the blank, flimsy yellow paper from the envelope, picked up a flat rock from the ground next to him and scrawled a letter. He placed the letter in the envelope and sealed it and put it back in his shirt pocket. Then he died.

PART TWO
THE VILLAINS

TWO

Langley, Virginia, Wednesday, June 8, 1994, 9:00 A.M.

Nick Barber was in his late forties. His still dark brown hair was parted at the center and touched only slightly with gray at the temples. His wide, high cheekboned face was tanned and bore a hard look as though chiseled from stone. Crow's feet at the corners of his piercing green eyes and a few furrows in his forehead belied his age, if the color of his hair did not. At six foot and one inch he was above average in height. His good physical condition was betrayed only by a slight paunch at his mid-section. He held the rank of Brigadier General in the U.S. Marine Corps and had spent most of his career in the employ of the Central Intelligence Agency. Barber was not his real name. He had been born and raised in upstate New York. He received his degree in psychology from Ohio State University in 1965, with a minor in Indo-European language studies. It was the minor that interested the CIA when they interviewed him on campus. He had studied the Indo-European language base vocabulary and realized that he had a talent for quickly learning any of the languages spoken from Scotland through Sri Lanka. After basic and specialized training with the Marines, he did three tours in Vietnam. He had worked for the CIA all over the world since then, mostly in Europe and usually where unpleasant jobs had to be done. Now retired from the field, he was assigned to overseeing the training of other agents and analyzing security at government installations.

He walked the halls of the Central Intelligence Agency's expansive headquarters building. He was thinking, as he always did just after passing through the foyer of the building, of the inscription there: "And ye shall know the truth and the truth shall make you free". He knew this was a biblical quote, from the New Testament, Book of John, chapter VIII, verse 32. He also knew just how difficult it sometimes was, to obtain the truth in the real world.

He looked into the retinal identification scanner next to the door of the outer office of his immediate superior, CIA Deputy Director for Operations, Joe Ronzoni. The door buzzed and he opened it and walked in. Joe's secretary, Leslie Jackson, waved Nick into Joe's office. Joe sat behind his large desk. Behind his head on the wall was a giant executive geochron. It was an electronic map of the world, the sunlit area illuminated in a curve that slowly crawled west, marking time.

Ronzoni was a heavyset balding man with graying hair that had once been jet black. His five o'clock shadow, heavy black eyebrows and dark brown eyes gave him a serious, almost ominous look. Joe had attended military schools in Virginia as a child and later was graduated from Annapolis, commissioned as an Ensign. He had planned to make the Navy his life. He served as a lieutenant on a battleship off Southeast Asia during the early stages of the Vietnam War. A routine physical had revealed mild color-blindness and he was asked to resign from active duty. This had been a devastating blow, dashing his hopes to command a battleship someday. He was accepted by the CIA in a minor administrative position and had been with the "company" ever since. The move had uniquely allowed him to maintain his military rank, at increasing grade levels as he was promoted in the civilian classifications. Now, as one of the Deputy Directors of the CIA he was a Naval Rear Admiral. This meant far more to him than the Deputy Director title.

He was not one for amenities.

"Got an assignment for you, Nick." Joe said in his usual abrupt, to-the-point manner. "You're free for a while now, right?"

"Well, I just finished my three-month stint as commandant at Camp X. I don't go to Camp Y until next spring. Nothing now but a few security installation inspections that I can handoff to someone else." Camp X was a secret, CIA training camp in the northeastern United States; Camp Y was a similar facility in the Bahamas.

"Good. Got a project for you. Cushy one for a change, just like a vacation junket." Joe handed a file in a manila folder across to Nick.

"I'm all ears," Nick said.

"You know the stories about the massive Nazi Treasure that SS Chief Heinrich Himmler supposedly stole and hid during World War Two," Joe continued. "Gold bullion plundered from France and other countries, valuable paintings and other art treasures. Even jewelry and rings taken from the concentration camp victims, the precious metals melted down into bars, for chrissakes. The evidence that he amassed the treasure was always pretty solid, but where did the bastard hide it? Some has been found in caves in the Bavarian mountains, but the bulk is still missing. People continue to search there, of course. Himmler was captured near the German-Danish border at the end of the war, you recall. Committed suicide by biting a phial of sodium cyanide before he could be questioned. He was obsessed with the Scandinavian gods and myths and the Arthurian legends, philosophical mysticism. He decorated his Wewelsburg Castle headquarters at Westphalia in those themes. He had a lot of contacts in Denmark and he apparently told people he wanted to retire there. And, there's a theory that he hid the treasure in that country. It's supported by some evidence. Two Danish farmers observed some unusual activity near the south coast of Fyn, Denmark's central island. Heavily laden trucks moving toward the coast in the spring of 1944, guarded by Germans in plain black suits. Those farmers' testimonies are in the file. One of them, a Jens Anders, is still alive. If it was the treasure there wasn't enough detail to locate it. Our government and the Danish government tried and failed."

"We try again?" Nick asked.

"Only because new evidence has come to light. A few days ago a woman named Charlotte Halvorsen died in Ohio. She was ninety-seven. Had a son, Gordon, who was a P-51 pilot during the war. During an air raid on Kiel, he was apparently hit by German antiaircraft fire and disabled. He flew north and probably ditched the plane in the sea near the south coast of Fyn. He made his way to a small churchyard and died there. The minister of the church reported that Halvorsen had taken shrapnel in the back, apparently bled to death. In any case, a letter he wrote to his mother was found in her belongings, never opened. Gordon's brother, a retired Army Intelligence officer, forwarded it to us. There's a copy in the file, have a look."

Nick opened the file. Pages containing the testimonies from the Danish farmers were on top. He flipped past them and found the letter. He read it:

Dear Ma,
I have been shot down and wounded but I think people will find me and take care of me. Came down in water and found a churchyard. This must be a dream but I think I saw the old Chicken Farmer himself unloading trucks into the side of a hill at the shore near a small castle ruins. I feel weak, must go. See you as soon as I can.
Love, Gordie

The closing words and signature were written with an increasingly unsteady hand. Nick could barely make them out. He looked up from the letter. "The 'Chicken Farmer' is Himmler himself, right?"

Joe nodded and said, "That's a strong possibility. That was supposed to have been his occupation before he became one of Hitler's NAZI henchmen."

"Where did Halvorsen come down?"

"That's what I want you to find out. His plane was never recovered as far as we know. And, he may have gone a long distance on foot. Or, he may have found a boat and traveled along the coast."

Nick looked down at the letter, "Castle ruins? Doesn't help much. There are stone ruins all along the coasts of Fyn, southeastern Jutland and the islands all around the area."

"The Danes were supposed to report when they found planes, but some were just cut up for scrap without any reporting. If we can find out specifically where he landed, we might be able to zero in on the loot."

"And if we find it?"

"That's up to the politicians, but I would think we would work with the Danish government and attempt to restore it to the rightful heirs in some way."

"So I go to Denmark?"

"As soon as possible. You'll need a disguise, I don't want any of your old enemies causing trouble."

Nick sat back in the chair and scratched his chin. "How about a British professor?" he said, lapsing into a perfect English accent. "An 'istory professor doing research on war artifacts. First though, I have a wake to attend. Vito Votilinni, head of the Chicago mob, died yesterday. My FBI buddy Sally Stein asked me to escort her. It's in Wisconsin, we're flying out Friday morning."

"Oh yeah, I remember, she knew him personally from the time she was a kid. Is this business or pleasure?"

"Business for her, I think. She's on an investigation that involved Votilinni in some way. I don't know the details."

"I know a few and this is strictly top secret. Seems some representatives from a middle eastern terrorist group have been shopping around for some special services. They want someone to hijack or sabotage an American passenger plane. Old man Votilinni was approached, he turned them down. Stein's going to talk with some of his people, see if she can get some more information about this."

"I see. They're looking for someone else to do their dirty work. What about that arms shipment Tommy Garcia's been tracking?"

"Tommy's on board posing as a crew member. They've left Lisbon for Benghazi, Libya, today we think, to load more weapons. We're formulating plans to capture the ship in the Mediterranean after it leaves Libya. By the way, you're to see Thom McCormick before you leave. He's got a little going away present for your trip to Europe." Joe was smiling.

Thom McCormick was in charge of CIA experimental technology. His department's offices and labs were in the basement levels of the headquarters at Langley. At six foot four and two hundred and fifty pounds, he was a large man. He had a square face and wavy brown hair. His easygoing, countrified manner was genuine. He had been raised on a farm in Indiana. He held bachelors' and masters' degrees in mechanical engineering from Purdue University.

Nick, having passed several security checks on the way to the basement levels, stood at McCormick's door and rapped on the metal surface. The big man opened it and, smiling down at Nick, held out a ham-sized hand. "Nick Barber, I'll be damned. Haven't seen you in a while. Why the hell don't you stop by when you're in town?"

"You know how it is," Nick said, "no time. I hear you've got a present for me and it isn't even near Christmas yet."

"Follow me, you're gonna love this. You are a biker aren't you?"

"I still take a vacation trip on my bike when I can. Remember what Arlo Guthrie sang, 'I don't want a pickle, I just wanna ride my motor-sickle.'"

Laughing, Thom led Nick down a wide hall and rolled open a garage door. There were two motorcycles there. The fenders were chrome, the gas tank and trim painted black. The windshields were small and curved back in the style of the high speed "crotch rockets", so popular with young riders.

"These are experimental units", Thom began. "They're powered by a new type of gas turbine engine, designed by Jet Propulsion Labs. Runs on kerosene or either type of diesel fuel. They threw out the idea of simply compressing gases and windmilling a single turbine wheel and started over." The engine side cover was off the closest bike. Thom crouched down and pointed to the front of the engine. "You can see that the side covers make it look like an ordinary four cylinder Japanese engine. What appears to be the radiator is actually a lubricating oil cooler, uses the transmission for a sump. The engine is a two-stage turbine. The four cylinders at the bottom in the front, that look like air intake horns are actually small jet engines. Their exhaust gases drive four turbine wheels inside the engine. The gases expand against the ceramic blades on the wheels, converting the energy to mechanical power more efficiently and positively than traditional turbines. As you're probably aware, both acceleration and deceleration were problems with gas turbines. You'll find that this design solves the acceleration problem. In normal operation, the acceleration is equal to or better than any piston driven bike on the road. For a little extra kick, they've added a liquid oxygen tank to feed the jet engines. When you open the throttle all the way the oxygen feed effectively converts'em from jet engines to rocket engines temporarily. The new ceramics technology makes it all possible. All of the parts in the high temperature areas are made of high impact ceramic or coated with it."

Nick was smiling and shaking his head, "How fast?"

"Well," Thom continued, enjoying his own explanation, "the power is transmitted from the turbine shaft through a torque converter and a four speed transmission, then through a shaft to the rear wheel. The shifting is easy to remember. Second gear at fifty miles an hour, third at one-fifty and fourth at two-fifty. The optimal engine rpm range is thirty to sixty thousand. The top speed? Well, your guess is as good as mine, but certainly in excess of three hundred miles per hour."

"Yeah, and how do you keep it on the ground at that speed?"

Clinically, Thom continued, "For that purpose we have fold out spoilers above the front and rear fenders." He pushed a button on the right handlebar and a spoiler slid out of its glove on each side of the front fender in front of the forks and from under the rear fender in the back. They were small black wings. "We recommend you use them above one-seventy-five."

"I don't mind testing this for you," Nick said, "but don't look for me to be running at those kinds of speeds."

"All we want is a nice average road test. A report on how it handles under normal driving conditions. A couple of them are being tested at high speed in Utah."

"And the deceleration?"

"Still a problem. When you close the throttle there's little drag or braking effect as with a piston engine. Scary, especially at high speed. Just try dropping your motorcycle or car for that matter in neutral at high speed and using only the brakes to slow down. Chrysler and others experimented with variable position nozzles to slow the turbine wheel on deceleration. Didn't work very well. Harley-Davidson built the frames for these and put in a super heavy duty braking system. Dual multi-pad Hayes brakes front and rear with carbon fiber discs. That's what's there to stop you. We'd like to know what you think."

"Mind if I try it out in the garage here, just to get the feel a bit, before I take it out on the road?"

"Go ahead. The second one is ready to go, key's in it."

Nick walked over and turned the key to "on" and pushed the starter. The engine whirred to life with an almost silent "woosh". He climbed on and let it warm up for a minute. The dash sported electronic readout gauges and a Heads Up Display, or HUD, as well. The HUD was a bright orange, light emitting diode image of the tachometer and speedometer readouts, embedded right in the small windscreen. There was a simulated analog needle gauge and digital readout for each. This allowed the rider to check the gauges while keeping his head up and eyes on the road; a critical feature for high speed operation. There were automatic, load leveling controls. He pulled in the clutch and pressed the shift down into first gear. He let out the clutch slowly and rode the motorcycle out into the hall and around the open garage area a couple of times. He rode it back in and parked it.

"Smooth and quiet," Nick said, "this trip could be fun."

"That's not all," Thom said as he unzipped the tank bag and pulled the flap back. A video display screen was there built into the top of the tank. He flipped a switch at the side and the screen came on. "This is our latest in communication/navigation computers. Works on the ground position satellite system or SATCOM GPS. It locates a position on earth with a programmed error of 15 meters or about 50 feet, good enough for navigational use. The error is programmed in for national security purposes so that potential enemies using the system can't have pinpoint accuracy. The software on the bike's computer corrects for the programmed error, bringing the position location to within fifteen centimeters or about six inches. The software is highly classified, only us and a few key military units have it. Make sure this one doesn't fall into the wrong hands," Thom warned.

On the video display screen was a color map in hues of yellow with streets and buildings detailed and labeled. It was apparently the immediate Langley area. A bright red "X" began to flash on the screen. "The "X" in the display indicates your position," Thom said. "The maps are stored in compact disk read-only memory units. Same CD ROMs used on computers. We have several that work with this unit now, including the United States and Western Europe. We're developing others. The U.S. disk is in the drive under the screen and the Europe disk in a storage slot just below. Just switch them when you're in Europe. You can zoom in and out with this wheel on the side and pan with the small track ball next to it." Thom rolled the wheel and the red "X" got progressively larger as the picture zoomed directly on the CIA headquarters building. Then he rolled it the other way and as the "X" became tiny. Nick could see the Potomac, then parts of Washington. Arlington National Cemetery and other landmarks came into view. The yellow hue turned to shades of brown showing land elevation as Thom backed out of the Potomac Valley. He then panned around the area using the track ball. "There's a second track ball for locating the cursor and a button just above it for marking points." He demonstrated by marking two points. "Notice at the readout top of the screen. It gives the shortest distance by road and outlines the route. And, there are transmitters that can be planted on others so they can be tracked." He opened a small case with five black buttons. "Activate them and the battery should be good for several days."

Nick played around with the unit for a few minutes. "And," Thom continued, "all of this can be done by voice commands with voice response in the helmet headset. It's still speaker-dependent technology so you'll have to practice with it until it can consistently recognize your particular voice pattern. There is a microphone and receiver built into the helmet. I'll send it with the bike. You can make phone calls and speak on the radio by voice commands." He handed Nick a small pamphlet marked "Top Secret." "It's all in here."

Nick took the pamphlet then turned off the unit and zipped the tank bag flap over it. He said, "You don't happen to have any machine guns and guided missiles for this baby, do you?"

Thom smiled craftily, "As a matter of fact I do. Of course that's highly confidential information. As you may have guessed, these units are part of a major experiment involving mobility, navigation and high tech weapons. Hell, I've got a list of weapons for you to select from," he joked.

Nick smiled, "Not on this trip, thank God. Have a rack for removable Samsonite side bags installed and send the bags to my office." Nick was studying the electronic calendar on his watch. "Put it in a crate and have it delivered to the King Frederick Hotel in Copenhagen by Sunday night. Now, I want to ask you a favor. My weapons, can you hide them in the bike? Much easier than a diplomatic pouch or some other arrangement." Nick pulled the Heckler & Koch caseless ammunition pistol out of his shoulder holster and handed it to Thom. Then he reached down and took his double-edged

Fairbairn-Sykes commando knife from its ankle sheath and held it out.

Thom was scratching his chin, looking at the motorcycle. "I suppose I could put them in the seat padding. Of course if they happen to decide to open the seat at customs, there's going to be a lot of red tape." Thom shook his head, "Hell, they'll probably put you in jail for a while, General."

"I'll take that chance."

"How do you like the new pistol?" Thom said looking down at the automatic in his hand.

"I've used it only in target practice so far, but I like it. It's small, accurate, powerful, quiet and fast firing. Holds sixty rounds. More than any other pistol I know of. No ejected shells to worry about either."

"I've got more to show you about that helmet that goes with the bike."

Nick followed Thom down another level to the target range. They walked down a long hall and entered a booth. In the target area thirty feet from them was a black, full coverage motorcycle helmet with the smoke-tinted, eye shield flipped down. Thom handed Nick a thirty caliber semi-automatic rifle. "The shield", he said nodding toward the helmet.

"You're kidding. That eyeshield won't stop this."

Thom nodded toward it again. "Hit it to the side so the bullet doesn't ricochet directly back."

Nick put on the safety glasses and earmuffs that were there. He aimed at the side of the shield and squeezed the trigger. As the explosion of the shot cracked, he felt the kick of the powerful rifle at his shoulder. The helmet, obviously secured down, shifted slightly. There was damage on the right side of the shield, but the bullet had bounced off and rattled into the collector box in the target area. Nick aimed at the other side shield and fired again with the same result. He flipped open the dutch door and they walked in to examine the helmet. Each side of the shield had a dent about a quarter inch deep, the plastic-like material around it cracked in a spider web pattern. Nick flipped up the shield. It was light, about a quarter inch thick. "It's like transparent Kevlar", he commented.

Thom was smiling, "You're close. It's a special composite recently developed by a private company trying to make a better hockey mask."

"It'll stop a hockey puck."

"It's too expensive for use in sports. But they leased us the technology and I couldn't believe it myself, when we first tested it. Until now the best thing we had that you could see through and was this light, would barely stop a light handgun. It's not yet possible to make one completely clear, but this isn't bad."

"Of course the helmet is bolted down. What happens when you're wearing it? Your head comes off?"

"Actually, that's your problem. My job is to supply the equipment. But if your head should come off, rest assured whatever's inside the helmet will be undamaged," Thom said, chuckling.

"That's a comforting thought."

They walked back to the firing area and adjusted their earmuffs. Thom had stuffed the HK pistol in his pants' pocket. Nick motioned to it and Thom handed it over. It was smaller than a .45 automatic. It had a black plastic case that made it look much like a toy. But it was no toy. The weapon was a smaller version of the HK G11, caseless ammunition assault rifle. The pistol fired a 4.73 mm 50 grain bullet in excess of three thousand feet per minute. The bullets came imbedded in a solid block of propellant explosive and were fired electronically by a capacitor discharge ignition system. They could penetrate a steel helmet at 400 yards. It fired a full, three-round-burst in seventy-five milliseconds. Nick clicked off the safety and took a couple of single shots at the shield. The pops of the shots were quiet in comparison to the rifle. The smaller bullets made respectively smaller dents. With his thumb, he slid the selector lever to three round burst and squeezed the trigger twice. A succession of pops resulted and surface pieces of the shield were blown into the air, but the shield was not penetrated. He slid the selector to full automatic and sprayed the shield. Finally, it disintegrated in the hail of small, high velocity bullets. The helmet itself was undamaged, except for a few surface dents and furrows.

He handed the pistol back to Thom. He took it and said, "Your composite pistol, I suppose you're going to carry it on the plane?" He was referring to the small, .22 caliber, supermagnum automatic that Nick carried in a special padded pouch at the back of his pants. The pistol and its ammunition were made of non-metallic composites that could not be discovered by x-rays or metal detectors.

"We have to test the security systems, sometimes", Nick said.

Thom smiled and shook his head, "Be sure and write me from jail, General."

Frankfurt, Germany, 4:00 P.M.

Baron Soren Ingemann Von Kloussen sat at the desk in his second floor office. He leaned back in the chair, his notebook computer on his knees. He was a tall, thin, wiry man. At fifty-two his blonde hair held only a hint of frost at the temples. His pale-blue eyes and pallid skin told of his Scandinavian ancestry. He was a man of expensive tastes, who liked to gamble. He had gambled and spent extravagantly throughout his adult years, until his inherited family fortune was nearly gone. He had overextended himself with both personal and business loans. The banks that held both his short and long term debt were already asking questions.

He keyed in the password to call up the data for his personal spreadsheet accounting system. He entered a number. It was a secret key which converted the data mathematically to the actual numbers in his accounts. He had double protected the data to keep it private. He rolled down through the rows and columns of numbers. The gross income, costs, expenses, loan payments and net income from both his personal and business sources, legal and illegal were merged. It didn't look good, at least not until the weapons shipment arrived at El Ladhiqiya. He would net five million on the deal. He would need that, plus another several million to keep his head above water for the next year. He paged to the top of the spreadsheet and removed the projected income from the current shipment. He was doing a "what if" the ship was lost calculation. Then he paged down to the bottom line. The information was distressing. His losses would probably mean the forced sale of his factories, one in Philadelphia and one in Odense, Denmark and his homes in the United States and Ireland. There was even the possibility of liens against his ancestral castle and grounds on the southern coast of the Danish island of Fyn, his main residence. At best, he would be reduced to selling passes to tourists to visit his castle. He would do absolutely anything to restore his wealth.

His two factories were in the legitimate business of supplying various types of storage tanks to chemical and petroleum processing companies throughout the world, mostly to the Middle East. He owned the factories through a series of paper holding companies to insulate himself from the operations. When his funds had begun to dwindle a few years earlier, he purchased them using the remainder of the money to leverage the buyouts. Occasionally, he visited them or attended their management meetings. He did so incognito, posing as John Barrington, a British accountant, representing the ownership interests. The storage tanks and the accompanying crates of piping and other loose parts, used to install the vessels, were good places to hide the illegal armaments. The deals with customers in the Middle East, Ireland and other places were organized by his partner, Arun Rashidii. After all, there was nothing unusual in shipping petroleum storage tanks to the Middle East.

Von Kloussen leaned back in his chair and looked out beyond the park, across the street at the Rhine River valley. He could see barges and ships crowding the waters, moving slowly in both directions, framed by the rolling green banks that sloped down to either side of the river. The phone rang. He sat forward abruptly and picked up the receiver, "Ja?"

"CT here," the voice said in English. It was Arun Rashidii, CT was for another name he was known by: Cha-Turgi. "I am at my hotel here. We must meet, right away!"

"Come to the office."

"No, no for this, the park. I'll be there in ten minutes." Rashidii hung up.

Von Kloussen stood and selected a pipe from the rack on his desk. He filled it with his personal blend of African tobaccos from the humidor. Holding the flame of his gold lighter over the tobacco he took small puffs as he walked over to the window. He leaned against the window frame and stared down at the green park, studded with trees. There were numerous colorful park benches and a children's playground at one end. Eight minutes later, a black BMW motorcycle stopped across the street in front of the park. Von Kloussen went down to meet Rashidii. He crossed the street and gestured to the motorcycle, "You're too old for that, those things will be the death of you yet."

Rashidii chuckled as he clipped his helmet to the side of the bike. At thirty-four he was a muscular man of less than medium height with a round face, black hair and coal-black eyes. Born of a German mother and Palestinian father, his skin was of medium tone. He wore sunglasses as usual to avoid being recognized. He smiled at Von Kloussen's comment. In his twenties, Rashidii had ridden in motorcycle races all across Europe, including the grueling, almost suicidal, Isle of Man Tourist Trophy race in the U.K.

He thought of that race now as he walked toward the Baron. It was a thirty-seven point seven-three mile course around the perimeter of the island. He had ridden in the 750 cc Formula 1 class. They ran at average lap speeds in excess of one hundred and twenty miles per hour, touching two hundred at some points. He remembered the buildings and low stone walls along the macadam road whizzing by in a blurr. They zipped by so quickly one couldn't even be sure they were ever there at all. To leave the road and collide with such a structure was certain death. And these could only be seen in the peripheral vision. At those speeds one never, ever took one's eyes or one's concentration from the road ahead. The rider, in fact, had to plan his moves and throttle adjustments well in advance. Always, the rider fixed on evaluating the road a quarter mile to a half mile ahead. Leaning into each curve at just the right angle and rolling the throttle off and on at the right times was literally a matter of life and death. The low coastal stretches were usually dry and one could take the high powered Japanese racing bike to its limit there. The twisting road course took them gradually up into foothills, then the mountains. There were often streaks of fog as the riders climbed to higher altitudes. Intermittent rain sometimes wetted the road surface. This reduced dramatically the coefficient of friction that applied to the tires and road surface. At the highest altitudes, after the fourteen hundred foot winding climb up the eastern face of Mount Snaefell there had even been sleet and slush on the road at times. The rider slowed to below one hundred miles per hour and plowed through, tires planing, hoping the gyroscopic effect of the wheels would keep the machine straight up. Many had died on the course. Still, anxious competitors, the crazy and the brave and the crazy-brave had come every year to race.

Rashidii had been cautious the first year he had run the race. His elapsed time had put him among the last place finishers, but he finished without mishap. The second year he had been more aggressive. He remembered approaching a wide turn in the foothills. The light rain had just begun but the entire surface of the road was wet. He rolled the throttle off and leaned left. The last thing he remembered was the speedometer reading: one hundred and sixty miles per hour. The bike had gone down, skidding along the slick road in a spin. He stayed on until it left the road and bumped through the low ditch at the edge of the road. The cycle bounced away and Rashidii had flopped through an open, grass meadow like a rag doll shot from a cannon. He was lucky. There were no obstacles in his path. His tight leather suit, heavy boots, gloves and full coverage helmet kept his injuries to a minimum. He had suffered only a broken wrist, dislocated shoulder, sprained ankle and slight concussion. These were considered very minor injuries indeed for the Isle of Man race.

Another rider in that race had not been so lucky, Rashidii recalled. He had also lost control at high speed and skidded feet first through a muddy field on his belly. The chin guard of his full coverage helmet had scooped in the mud. The force packed it tightly and under considerable pressure in his mouth and nostrils, in front of his face and around his head. The man had suffocated trying to remove the helmet. Rashidii shuddered at this thought. The third year he had taken third place. This was a major accomplishment in the motorcycle racing world. Was it courage or insanity, he pondered as he walked silently through the park with the Baron.

Von Kloussen's concern for Rashidii's safety was business, not personal. It would be difficult to find someone else with the right Middle Eastern and European contacts to make the arms deals.

As they walked Von Kloussen said, "Why have you come here? You're supposed to be supervising the loading in Benghazi."

"I will be, my plane leaves for Libya in two hours. I have a message from El Alamien, that I can deliver only in person and out of range of any electronic surveillance." They selected a secluded park bench and sat down. Von Kloussen puffed on his pipe anxiously. Rashidii looked around suspiciously. He spoke under his breath, so the Baron could barely hear, "They want an American passenger plane destroyed during an international flight which originates in the U.S."

Von Kloussen thought for a moment, tiny clouds floating momentarily from the bowl of his pipe, then whisked away by the breeze. "Absurd to ask us this...we have no means to do it. We'd be hunted down to the ends of the earth."

"They offer ten million in U.S. dollars. Five upon agreement to arrange it and submission of the plan. Then five upon successful completion. Gold bullion or deposit in your numbered accounts, whichever you choose." Rashidii was a ruthless man who wanted money and didn't care how he got it. He was trying to sell the idea to the Baron.

"And where do these people get that kind of money?" Von Kloussen asked.

"If you ask them they will say, 'We have ten million followers and each contributes a dollar'. I do not necessarily believe this."

"And this is the Liberation Army of the Holy War making this offer?"

"They don't tell me that, but I would wager the group you have named will claim responsibility," Rashidii responded.

"And why are they not doing this with their own people? Why hire someone else?"

"They have hired others in the past, I believe, such as Carlos the Jackal. He is nothing but a gun-for-hire. Perhaps this is to insulate themselves from these activities. Perhaps there are other reasons as well. I have contacts with these people but even I don't know who they really are. There are rumors, you know, about a well-funded group of Russian officers and former officials...," he shrugged.

The Baron pondered all this for a moment. "No, absolutely, no. Let them find someone else. This conversation never took place."

THREE

U.S. Army Special Forces Major Tommy Garcia was
a member of the material handling crew on the Portuguese
registered bulk cargo ship Cabal. Now the ship was docked at
the Libyan port of Benghazi. Tommy stood five feet eight
inches tall with broad shoulders and a muscular body he had
inherited from the German ancestry on his mother's side. He
had dark eyes and black hair like his Mexican father and a
round, ruggedly handsome face with a dark beard. The
perpetual hint of a smile belied the rugged warrior that he
was. Tommy had graduated from West Point in 1987 and was
commissioned a Second Lieutenant. He had immediately
applied for Special Forces training and after a short
assignment in Army Intelligence in Germany, he was

accepted. He completed the Q course at Camp Mckall in North Carolina late that year and went on to take advanced training in weapons and demolitions. He received the coveted Special forces shoulder tab in early 1988. After serving on several Army Intelligence assignments, he applied for the CIA's advanced intelligence and espionage training school. He was accepted and went to the CIA's secret Camp X for training. There he met Nick Barber, the camp commandant, who was his instructor in covert operations activities. They became friends and Tommy came to consider Nick his mentor. Nick considered Tommy his protege and encouraged him to go on and complete the grueling British Commando training course in Scotland, which he did.

Tommy had seen action, leading advance ground troops in Panama and the Desert Storm war. For the past few years, he had often been on loan to the CIA working on special assignments. This time he was working with Eli Goldberg of the Israeli Mossad Intelligence group. With the help of the Longshoremen's Union, the two had boarded the Cabal in New York as crew members.

It was nearly dark. Several shrouded trucks had pulled up on the secluded dock. The shrouds were removed and the ship's crane swung out over the first truck. The crew there secured a pallet of four barrel sized, seam-welded canisters to the crane and gave the signal. The crane hoisted the pallet up over the edge of the bow. Tommy, on the front deck, signaled the crane operator and helped guide it into the gaping, dark opening to the hold below. Eli was below helping the small crew make the final placement in the hold.

When Tommy saw the shroud removed from the first truck his greatest fear was realized. Chemical weapons, perhaps nerve gas, would be loaded. So far the ship had been loaded with crates and steel vessels containing handguns, assault weapons, anti-tank weapons and ammunition for all of them. It was suspected that nerve gas would be loaded in Libya, but Tommy and Eli had no way to confirm this to the Navy, too risky. Tommy had only been able to place an ultra-low frequency homing device on the ship, so it could be tracked. He had been distressed to see the guards augmented. A fresh platoon of Libyan guards had just boarded, armed with AK-47 assault rifles and sidearms.

Tommy noticed a man about his own size coming up the gangplank. He had a round face, black hair and wore steel-rimmed dark glasses. He wore a dark suit. Apparently a man of importance. The Captain came out immediately to greet him. The man followed the Captain up the exterior metal staircase into the superstructure. Later, as the last of the pallets was being loaded, they emerged and walked over near where Tommy was working. Checking down in the hold, they walked around without speaking and then the man left the ship. The Captain gave the order to sail immediately.

The U.S. Navy aircraft carrier *Forrestal*, waited in the waters of the Mediterranean. She was accompanied by the missile-equipped, U.S. Destroyer *Spruance*. The Radar Officer on each ship picked up the signal from the Cabal as she sailed northeast from Benghazi. On the deck of the *Forrestal*, Navy SEAL assault troops were boarding three CH-46 Sea Knight helicopters. Fighter pilots were on alert. As the massive anchors were weighed, the giant carrier began to move forward. The *Spruance* was also moving to the north. Wisps of fog passed around the ships and a bright moon was rising in the east. The *Forrestal* was capable of 33 knots and the *Spruance* nearly 40, it was unlikely that the Cabal could outrun either and if so, she couldn't certainly outrun the aircraft.

On the Cabal, Tommy busied himself on the upper deck behind the superstructure near a stairway. A Libyan guard passed occasionally. An hour after leaving port, Tommy heard the chopping of the helicopters faintly in the distance. He went cautiously down the stairs. Halfway down he could see Eli checking the load stability, staying in sight of the stairs as planned. Tommy glanced around, there were deckhands and guards moving about in the semi-darkness of the hold, but none seemed to notice him. He caught Eli's attention and nodded, then went quickly up to the deck. The helicopters were louder now. Would the Cabal crew have been searching for aircraft with the radar? Tommy wondered as he climbed the exterior superstructure stairway to the bridge. He pulled his CIA issue .22 supermagnum from the pouch at the rear of his pants. He reached the well-lit glassed-in bridge area two stories above the upper deck. He peered in through the window at the starboard door. The pilot was seated on his stool at the steering controls. Next to him stood the Captain, leaning forward on the console. Tommy was relieved to see that the radar screen was unmanned.

Holding the pistol out of sight he opened the door and entered the bridge. "Captain," he said excitedly in English, "I have something to report." Surprised, the Captain turned, his dark eyes squinting with suspicion. Tommy came around behind the console, approaching him rapidly. The Captain's right hand went for his sidearm, but Tommy was there grabbing the man's wrist in both hands and forcing the hand up behind his back. The Captain winced in pain as Tommy forced him against the console and held the barrel of the small pistol to the man's eye. Tommy gestured toward the pilot who was now looking over his shoulder at them, his eyes filled with fear, "Tell him to stop the ship. NOW!"

The Captain struggled, but Tommy held his wrist up behind his back with an iron grip. "No", came his reply as he looked into the barrel. Tommy relaxed his grip, letting the man stand back, a puzzled look came over the Captain's face again. Then Tommy squeezed the trigger. The silenced weapon coughed like an air rifle. The bullet entered the Captain's head between his eyes. A small, blood-spattered hole instantaneously appeared in the metal wall plate behind his head. His hands reflexively went to his face, as his body crumpled against the wall behind and slid to the floor. Tommy's attention was already on the pilot.

He held the pistol to the man's head and said in English, "Stop the ship. NOW!" The man, terrorized, shrugged and shook his head. Tommy repeated the order in Spanish, then in Farsi. The man nodded, he seemed to understand. He pulled the throttle control back down through its arc. In a moment, Tommy could hear the ship's giant steam turbines slow. He could also hear the helicopters overhead. Tommy pulled the man from the stool and shoved him around the console toward the starboard door. "Get out", Tommy shouted at him in Farsi.

Lights and gunfire came from above and ropes swung down to the deck, as the helicopter blades chopped the night air. Navy SEALs festooned down to the front and rear decks. Their HK G11 assault rifles were peppering the deck with gunfire.

As the pilot lurched for the door it swung open and two Libyan guards were there, AK-47s pointed in. They opened fire, bullets tearing the pilot's body apart, as he danced backwards into the console. Bullets, blood, fatty flesh and bits of bone were flying, spattering and ricocheting everywhere. Tommy crouched down behind the console in an instant. He felt a numbness, then a burning in his right calf and realized he was hit. He held the small pistol, ready for a hopeless battle against the heavily-armed guards.

Below in the hold between two crates, Eli had clubbed a Libyan guard with a wrench and was pulling the AK-47 out from under him. He could hear the gunfire from above and he knew the raid was on. He peered around the crate toward the front of the hold. He knew he had to prevent the scuttling of the ship if anyone should attempt it. The Libyan government might have ordered the guards to do so to cover the trail of the chemical weapons sale. He made his way toward the front in the dark hold, slipping between the pallets until he could see the canisters stacked. He heard some activity to the port side. Covered by the noise of the battle above he climbed to the top of the crates and looked over the edge. It was difficult to see in the near darkness between the stacks of crates. Two guards were applying what appeared to be plastic explosive to the hull of the ship. One of the men pulled a detonator cap from his pocket.

Above in the bridge, Tommy crouched behind the console, waiting. A pool of blood was gathering around his right foot. The burning in his calf becoming more intense. Suddenly, there was a roar from the port side of the bridge, as the windows began to disintegrate. Glass flew everywhere, some in pieces and some blown to dust. Bullets pierced the metal panels on the starboard side. The guards that had fired in the door and killed the pilot were now dead themselves, in a hail of gunfire from the SEALs, positioned on the port side.

The SEALs rushed in and Tommy, seeing one of the dark blue helmets yelled, "Garcia Here, U.S." He could hear the firing on deck continue as two men stepped behind the console. A white man on his left stepping over the Captain's body and a large black man on his right, positioned themselves on either side of him. Each crouched down and grabbed one of Tommy's arms and lifted and steadied him, behind the protection of the console.

"Good to find you alive," the black man said, "we've got'em at bay now. We better get you on the ship to get that leg fixed."

"Radio your ships," Tommy said frantically, "reasonably certain there's nerve gas aboard and the Libyans may attempt to scuttle."

The black man spoke into his microphone, relaying the message and ordering the troops to search the hold and prevent any attempt to scuttle. The gunfire died down and they lifted Tommy with them as they stood, the three of them looking out over the front deck. They could see the Destroyer *Spruance*, from a distance, approach at starboard, its bow reflecting the moonlight across the water.

In the hold below, the guard set the timer on the detonator and pushed it into the plastic explosive material on the wall. Eli nosed the AK-47 over the edge of the crate and squeezed the trigger, spraying both men in the darkness below with a stream of bullets. As he repositioned the weapon and pulled the trigger he was himself hit by a stream of bullets from behind, fired by a guard. The bullets snapped into Eli's back along his shoulder blades, creating small spouts of blood and flesh. Aided momentarily by the force of the bullets he flipped to his back, holding the still firing rifle in front of his face, neck and chest for protection. The flash from the barrel of the rifle cut brightly into the darkness, as bullets pinged against the metal interior of the ship. The AK-47 in the guard's hands had "walked" its barrel up and away from Eli. The guard released the trigger and as he swung the barrel back down to reposition for more firing, he noticed the bright flashes from Eli's weapon and hesitated. Eli rolled into the crevice between the crates, falling directly on the dying guards he had just fired upon.

The Libyan guard watched him, then suddenly, several bright lights flashed around the hold. The SEALs were coming down using the powerful flashlights on their rifles. A light shone directly in the guard's face and he fired blindly. A SEAL behind him opened fire with his HK-G11 assault rifle. The guard was driven forward by the momentum of the slugs; his back arched and his belly was forced out, being ripped open by the successive exit wounds. He landed in a crumpled heap on top of the crates.

In the crevice below, Eli discovered he couldn't use his arms. His upper body still numb from the gunfire, he forced himself up on his knees. Using only his legs, he worked his way off of the still quivering bodies and toward the plastic on the wall. He struggled for several moments. The gunfire above had died to nil now. His head fell against the wet metal of the ship's wall, his nose nearly in the plastic explosive. His knees were in a couple of inches of filthy water at the base of the wall. His chest was against the wall. He searched around in the plastic using his nose and lips. He located the detonator and pried it loose with his teeth. He spat it into the water at his knees then collapsed back onto the floor.

The SEALs searched and secured the freighter. The all clear signal was radioed to the navy vessels. Twenty minutes later, light poured over the deck of the captured ship with an eerie glow. The *Forrestal* had pulled up on port next to the freighter, the great arc of its towering steel gray bow reflecting the moonlight down onto the deck of the smaller ship.

* * *

It was nearly dawn on Thursday morning, when the phone rang on the Baron's desk. He was on the bed in the sleeping room next to his office. He slipped on a robe quickly and walked through the open door and lifted the handset. "Ja?", he said groggily.

"CT here, no deal. Cargo is taken. Transaction is dead."

Von Kloussen suddenly came awake, frantic, "No, impossible." He was speaking into a dead phone, Arun Rashidii had hung up. Von Kloussen switched on both the radio and television and began to twist the radio dials and punch the television remote control, searching for news. He nervously lit his pipe and half filled a small snifter with Gammel Dansk schnapps.

Eva Van Damme, his beautiful German secretary and mistress, had arisen from the bed also. Arms akimbo, she stood naked in the doorway and watched him stare at the television set in front of his desk. He sloshed down the Gammel Dansk in one gulp and poured another.

"Soren, what is it?" she said. He turned abruptly, his bloodshot eyes wild like those of a cornered animal. She backed into the bedroom at the sight of him.

"Someone has taken the ship," he hissed under his breath, "unless that goddamn raghead has his information fucked up."

Eva knew that the Baron lapsed into such American vulgarities only when extremely agitated. "I've always said you can't trust them." She offered this in hopes of soothing the man somewhat.

He turned to her again, now approaching a rage, "You stupid kraut bitch, put some clothes on and find the news on that goddamn radio."

The words were hurtful, Eva thought. But then, men of royal blood are allowed the privilege of an occasional outburst, she reasoned, immediately forgiving him.

As they searched for and scanned news programs, the sun rose above the horizon and light flooded in through the east office windows. Finally, at 8:00 A.M. they found a German radio station that carried news of a ship bearing illegal arms, taken the prior night northeast of Libya. When the Baron heard this he slumped back in his executive chair and stared at the brown Gammel Dansk bottle in front of him for an hour.

Eva considered trying to comfort him but decided to let him brood. She loved the man and dreamed of the day, when he would divorce his wife as promised. Then she would become a Scandinavian Baroness. She believed she had royal blood flowing in her veins and would do anything to attain what she considered her rightful position in European royal society. Eva had studied history and knew that her family, the Van Dammes, had historically been a part of the German nobility. The two world wars during the twentieth century had obscured those ties. They had also wiped out a family fortune that had survived until the late 1930's. Her father owned a small factory and had done well financially, but had never again attained what Eva considered the family's rightful social status. She had hoped to marry a German nobleman, but there were few such men remaining. Her world view was that the central Europeans, Germans in particular, were members of a master race that would yet rise to dominate the world militarily and politically. She believed herself to be a prime member of this superior race of people. She believed that they would inherit the legacy of the Roman Empire. She had fantasized for years about being the queen, the first lady, of such a dynasty.

As a youth and young adult, she had been involved with the New National Socialist movement in Germany. She had read their literature, attended meetings and later written and spoken before the groups. She became a popular, attractive young neo-Nazi crusader for a while. When she first joined in the early eighties, the movement had been more secret, largely covert. With the rise of the skinhead faction during the eighties came more and more overt criminal activity and violence. Eva became disgruntled during that time and ceased to be active. This was not because she no longer believed in the white Aryan supremacist philosophy and other National Socialist notions. On the contrary, it was because she believed such activity would damage the cause. In the real world she had spurned many handsome young suitors, some from inside the movement, some not, while she schemed to land a man with royal blood and wealth. She had lived in several German cities working in various jobs, trying to make contact with such an individual.

Then, during yet another job search two years earlier, at age thirty, she answered an ad for an administrative assistant to manage the Baron's small office in Frankfurt. During the first interview she discovered he was a Danish Baron. She was thrilled at the prospects. She had read that some German race theorists in the early part of the century had considered the Scandinavians to be the purest of people even within the Aryan master race. Hitler had often spoke of the pantheon of nordic heroes. He had ordered the use of Scandinavians along with Germans in his human breeding experiments. She knew from history, that the Goths and other Germanic peoples from whom she was descended, had originally migrated from Scandinavia more than two thousand years ago. And, after all, the party symbol, the swastika or broken cross was based on the swinging hammer of Thor, the chief Scandinavian god. Denmark had a complete royal family. Von Kloussen was nearly twenty years older, of course, but he was handsome with his blue eyes, blonde hair and pale skin. Eva felt she had reached an age, where she would have to make her move or resign herself to the life of a commoner. She decided she had her man of royal blood. They became intimate within two weeks of her employment. She began to travel in Europe with him and even to the United States. After a year they began to discuss marriage, but there was the Baroness. Fortunately, there had been no children. And the Baron had hinted at divorce. Meanwhile, she tended all the Baron's needs when he was traveling. She became an intimate advisor and a clever accomplice in planning the arms deals. But she was not fully aware of the dire financial straits into which the loss of the ship had plunged the Von Kloussen estate. Now she went out for food as the man brooded.

Later, Von Kloussen shakily got dressed and returned to his desk. He sat there for several hours, puffing his pipe, thinking. At 1:00 in the afternoon the phone rang. It was Rashidii, back in Frankfurt. Von Kloussen told him to be in the park in ten minutes. Looking out the west window he watched Rashidii pull up and park the motorcycle. When the man had selected a park bench, Von Kloussen went down. He looked about as he walked, a bit unsteadily, across the park. He sat down next to Rashidii and under his breath, said angrily, "What happened?"

"The Americans," Rashidii said nervously, "they tracked the ship and captured her. A helicopter raid. Spies aboard, no doubt."

"The bastards," the Baron said, "they'll pay for this in many ways. Tell El Alamien that we'll do the job for him. I have a plan. But I want fifteen million in U.S. dollars. To be put in escrow accounts when you present the plan one week from now."

Rashidii sat back, surprised at the quickness of the Baron's decision, "And my share?"

"One third."

Five million would be nearly enough to disappear and retire in the style he desired. "And how will we do this?"

The Baron looked around the park suspiciously. "I have some ideas. Be at my estate in Denmark on Tuesday morning. I'll have more chance to think before then. We'll review the plan during a small game hunt where no one can eavesdrop."

FOUR

Friday, June 10

FBI Chief Inspector Sally Stein was forty-two, blond, nearly five foot six, wore wire rimmed glasses and was considered plain looking by most of the men who had known her. She had been married, had two teenage sons who lived with their father Sam, an attorney in Washington. They were divorced, virtually an occupational hazard in the Bureau. She had been born Sally Warbrasac in Grand Falls, Wisconsin, a paper mill town located in the center of the state. After high school, she went on to the University of Wisconsin, where she received her degree in accounting. She spent a couple of years in the employ of a large accounting firm auditing companies' books, a task she considered exceptionally boring. At twenty-five she applied for and was accepted to the FBI's training program. They were always recruiting accountants, due to many bank fraud and embezzlement investigations. Over seventeen years she had been promoted up through the ranks and was based out of the central office in Washington.

In Grand Falls, she had grown up with James "Diamond Jimmy" Votilinni, grandson of Chicago crime boss, Vito Votilinni. In the 1930's Vito had selected Grand Falls as his retreat away from the big city. He built a mansion on a small lake just south of town. Now, at eighty-seven he had died of heart failure. The Votilinni family had built a hotel/office complex on the grounds between the mansion and the highway. Vito's Friday wake and Saturday funeral were to be held there.

It was late afternoon. Sally rode with Nick Barber in a car they had rented in Chicago. Nick had set the cruise control at an easy fifty-five and they enjoyed the scenery along the way. As they headed north on Highway 13, the sun was dropping quickly in the cloudless sky. The shoulder on either side of the blacktop road was of sandy red clay and just beyond, row upon row of neatly planted evergreen trees marched by as they drove. In little more than a week, the solstice would signal the official onset of summer. In the sand country of central Wisconsin it was already hot.

Sally turned to Nick, "Before long it will be ninety degrees or more out there every day. You can SEE the heat rise from the sand everywhere. We always said that in the summer this is the hottest place in the world and in the winter the coldest."

Nick nodded then returned the conversation to business. "So you don't think there will be any gang wars as a result of Vito's death?"

22

"Hell, during the last three months Jimmy's had all his rival bosses eliminated, including some in his own organization. His biggest competition was the Spaboski mob. Two weeks ago the Spaboski brothers were gunned down in a Chicago restaurant. Two head shots each, while they were spooning in their borscht. Their bodyguards just backed away, while guys in ski masks came in and did the job. The triggerman dropped his gun on the floor and left."

"Gangland style, just like the movies."

"And we think Diamond Jimmy himself pulled the trigger. The arrogant bastard flipped an ace of diamonds into the mess on the table, before he left, a public warning to others. That's the way he is. Always liked to have a hand in the action. Of course, up until now, grandpa was always there to pull big strings and bail him out. We're going to be his biggest problem now. The U.S. attorney is close to indictments on Jimmy and a number of his people for extortion, gambling, RICO violations, probably murder. I don't think he's aware of how close he is to being put away and never seeing daylight again."

"If you're so sure he was the shooter in the restaurant, why can't you just nail him on that for starters?"

"Because he has a good alibi: he was having dinner with a Cook County Assistant District Attorney at the time of the murders. We think she figured she could get some information from him by agreeing to go to dinner with him, it's an old mob trick. Jimmy and his bodyguards have some drinks and a big meal with her, then some more drinks and Jimmy goes to the bathroom. The others keep her distracted, she remembers Jimmy being gone about 8:00 P.M. for fifteen, maybe twenty minutes. The murders occurred about 8:15 P.M. We figure it's possible to race across town to the restaurant, kill the Spaboski's and be back in twenty-five to thirty minutes. Our people ran the route a couple of times. Traffic conditions would have to be ideal, but that can be arranged by having a couple of cars along the way to help clear the route. That's the way we think it happened. Our agents and the cops told Votilinni this when they picked him up on suspicion of murder later that night. Naturally, there was a so-called witness who said Diamond Jimmy was in the bathroom sitting on the pot. I understand that during the interview Jimmy offered to stand and drop his pants, so they could dig some shit out of his ass and compare it to what was in the toilet drainpipe at the restaurant."

Nick laughed, "This guy sounds like a real sweetheart. And you dated him?"

"Yes, in junior high school", she sighed. "He was good looking and popular. The boys didn't take much interest in me, but I think he was trying to date every girl in town at least once."

"What about Diamond Jimmy's father? There seems to be a generation missing here."

"Killed in a mob hit back in the early fifties. Some rival mob trying to take over. Vito defeated them. Jimmy was only a toddler when it happened. His mother and grandfather tried to raise him straight, but it didn't work. He got in trouble on his own and Vito decided on a mob apprenticeship for him. Jimmy's been indulged all his life, beyond anything you can imagine. The word spoiled doesn't even begin to describe it. As a child and teenager his every whim was satisfied immediately. Instant gratification. He had a new Corvette when he was twelve years old. Vito had blacktop roads built on his farm near Grand Falls, so Jimmy could drive it. Naturally, he drove it on the public roads, anyway. Vito took care of it with the locals when he was stopped. Hell, as kids we thought that was kind of neat, but I see the result of it now. As an adult, Jimmy became an extreme, grotesque epitome of our 'me' generation. For over twenty years he has been literally allowed to get away with armed robbery, murder, any crime you can name. He's done a couple of stints in prison, of course, but even that is a pampered experience for someone like him. Vito has been able to use his connections to fix almost anything over the years, but not any more."

Vito Votilinni had come over from Sicily in 1929, as a young bodyguard with a Mafia group, as a result of a gang war on the island. He rose through the ranks of the mob in Chicago, to the position of Capo, over the next several years. He selected Grand Falls, Wisconsin, as his home away from his Chicago activities and built a mansion there, in 1935, with bootlegging and gambling profits. The big house was situated on Lake Vesper, back in the woods off Highway 51. It had five levels, massive living and dining areas, bedrooms with fireplaces, a library, tennis courts and a private beach. It was a resort for Vito and he spent most weekends there over the years. James Votilinni had grown up in the mansion. Even as a youngster, he had hosted elaborate parties for his friends and schoolmates. Sleigh riding parties in the winter, beach parties in the summer, parties for every holiday with presents and prizes for everyone. Sally Warbrasac Stein and Mac McGinnis were among those friends. In the late fifties, Vito built a small hotel/resort complex on his grounds close to the highway. He called it, simply enough, the Vesper Lake Hotel. By that time, Vito was the undisputed head of the west Chicago mob.

Mac Mcginnis sat in the Venus Lounge at the Vesper Lake Hotel. The bar was U-shaped. From the base of the "U" he could see the shimmering, clear Lake Vesper, and beyond the bridge where Highway 13 crossed the narrow end of the lake. Across the bridge was the Wisconsin River into which the lake waters slowly flowed. The setting sun was visible through the windows as it cast a dazzling, silver streak across the waters of the river and lake. People had been arriving all day to pay their respects to the Don, Vito Votilinni.

Mac wanted out now, he wanted to retire. He had been Consigliori to the Votilinni family, since they put him through law school many years earlier. He had been married to Jimmy Votilinni's sister, Mia. Their two children, a boy and girl, were now in college. Mia had been killed in an automobile accident ten years earlier. With Vito running the show things had been fine. He had been a man of wisdom who thought things through before he acted. He kept himself well insulated from the day-to-day activities. Jimmy had inherited only the old man's charisma, none of his wisdom. Now the handwriting was on the wall. Mac knew Jimmy would go down, it was only a matter of time. But Jimmy refused to believe it. He also refused to cooperate in any way with the FBI, against Mac's advice.

Nick drove the car up the hill and into the parking lot on the north side of the hotel. He and Sally went into the lobby and he followed her past the front desk into an inner lobby with a cloakroom. There, a short dark-haired man with very broad shoulders, his mouth hanging open, nodded a hello to Sally and said, "No weapons inside."

Sally said, "How you doing, Danny?" as she pulled the Beretta nine millimeter automatic from her purse and handed it over.

"Ok." He looked at her for a moment. "Sally. Lot'sa people come today ta' see da' ol' man."

Nick took his Beretta from its shoulder holster and handed it over. Danny placed both weapons on the cloakroom counter. Nick then pulled a pen from his shirt pocket and said,

"You better take this too. It's a special weapon. Whatever you do, don't push the button on top and DON'T drop it." Danny took the pen cautiously with both hands and carefully set it in a silver tray on the counter. He then patted them down briefly, missing the composite .22 magnum automatic at the back of Nick's pants. With a jerk of his head, he motioned them toward the inner door.

When they had stepped through into the bar area, Sally looked up at Nick, "That was just an ordinary pen, wasn't it?"

"Yeah, just havin' a little fun with the gorilla. He looks tough, but he seems a bit weak between the ears."

"You got that right. He's one of the Bakers. Local family, eight kids. The Votilinni's employ some of the boys as bodyguards around here. They're not rocket scientists, but they're good shots and have no fear of personal harm if called into action, I hear. Couple of the brothers are doing hard time. Danny's one of the younger ones. Actually," she said, smiling, "Danny's one of the first in the whole family to walk upright."

Nick laughed at this remark, "This I can believe."

She turned serious, "Don't mess around with these people. They'll kill on a whim." Then, she remembered that Nick was also an expert at killing.

They entered the bar area. The haunting brass crescendo of "Wonderland by Night" was playing in the background. Nick looked around. Sally pointed down a hall to their left. A large set of doors was angled off of the hall. "That's Vito's, well, now Jimmy's office," she said. There was a big, ominous looking, man with a pock-marked face standing next to the doors. "That's Johnny Grimm, Diamond Jimmy's personal assistant", Sally whispered.

Nick followed Sally over to the bar and she tapped Mac's shoulder. The heavyset man turned abruptly, his eyes wide. He seemed relieved that it was Sally.

"The Feds have arrived," Mac said.

"And you know Nick Barber," she said, "you met briefly earlier this year." Mac and Vito Votilinni had provided information to Sally and Nick on a terrorist case months earlier.

Mac slid off the barstool and shook hands with both of them. He was as tall as Nick, but with broader shoulders. At one time, a muscular heavyweight prize fighter, Mac had gone partly to fat over the years.

"Where's Vito?" Sally asked as though the old man were still alive.

"Laid out right in the office," Mac said motioning toward the hall with his head. "Jimmy's there. You want to pay your respects now?"

"It can wait. I think I'll have a drink first. Nick?"

He shrugged and nodded. "It's your party," he said, smiling, "I'm only the escort."

Mac waved the bartender over and Sally ordered a gin and tonic, Nick a bourbon and water. Mac leaned against the bar in silence. He looks tired, Sally was thinking. When the drinks were served, Sally looked at Mac and said, "I want to know about the offer Vito received. About the airliner."

"You get right down to business, don't you? Any discussion I have with you I'll have to clear with Jimmy. Preferably when we're all present. When we go in I'll ask. You know how it is."

Mac seemed frightened and he was not the kind of man to frighten easily, Sally thought. She knew that there had always been a tension between Mac and Jimmy, ever since they were kids. They had grown up together and worked for

Vito all of their adult lives. They had even served time together in their early twenties for a botched robbery. That was when Vito had taken them both under his wing. She tried to imagine how working for Jimmy Votilinni might be. It wasn't a pleasant thought. The penalty, for even the appearance of crossing him, would certainly be death, likely preceded by torture. She feared for Mac, actually felt sorry for him.

Sally glanced across the bar. She took in the panoramic view of Lake Vesper and the wide river across the bridge beyond. The sunlight on the surface of the water, that had been a silver streak only an hour earlier, was now blood red as the sun dropped in the western sky. She looked at Mac again. They had been friends, good friends as she liked to remember it, when they were fourteen, fifteen or so. Fate seemed to throw them together in a lot of classes in school. How would one describe it? she asked herself now. They had goofed around with each other. Yes, that was about it. They laughed and joked and kidded around in a way, that had none of the bitterness or nastiness that often was a part of relationships between the sexes at that age. They didn't date or even often see each other outside of school and so none of that heavy, dating baggage was there either. They had just gotten along well, she remembered fondly. She actually got up in the morning, looking forward to the banter with Mac in those days. A tear formed at the corner of her eye. He had kissed her a couple of times at the movies. And she thought of all that had happened since those seemingly carefree days. Her college years, her marriage and children. Her struggle for recognition and promotion in the Bureau. The heartbreaking divorce, for which she blamed herself. She traveled too much, she had been too ambitious. Sam eventually took an interest in another and that was it. All of this, all the years seemed to pall, beside the sweet, brief relationship she had with Mac as a teenager. And then they had gone their separate ways.

She dabbed her eye and forced herself out of her reverie. The two men, oblivious to her, were engaged in talk about boxing.

"Hell," Nick was saying, "you were one of the toughest fighters I ever saw. I remember that fifteen rounder with Alverez. Saw it on TV in Vietnam. Jesus, what a fight! Knocked him out in the last round. Those last two fights? You can't shit me, you threw'em man!"

"That's what the boxing commission thought too," Mac said. "But they could never prove anything. It doesn't matter now. Jimmy set it up, with Vito's financial backing, of course. I took out a few bums, then a couple of ok fighters. Then we paid off a couple of pretty good contenders to dive, including Alverez. I don't know what motivation Jimmy told offered'em besides money, but they never said a word so I can about imagine. Anyway I built up a record, you know? To build up the bets on me. Then I took a coupla' headers. Jesus, Jimmy and I cleaned up for a couple of young bastards. I went back to college. I knew damned well I wasn't good enough to go up against Muhammad Ali. Besides, I wanted to keep my brains."

"Ready to go in?" Sally said as she set her empty tumbler on the bar.

They finished their drinks and Mac led them down the hall into the office. It was a huge room with a large horseshoe-shaped sunken area at the center. The sunken area was surrounded with a built-in black leather couch, broken only by two aisles with steps. Near the rear there was a huge black desk positioned at the upper level, so that the occupant could look down on all others in the room. Jimmy Votilinni was at the back of the sunken area talking to two men. Vito's body lay in an ornate casket in the center of the horseshoe. It was ringed by elaborate, free standing, flower arrangements. The three approached the casket and stood in front of it for a moment. The old Don lay there in his best tux, his hair done in the jet black of his youth and his prominent hook-nose powdered heavily. When the two men left, the three of them walked over to Diamond Jimmy.

Votilinni was over six feet tall and very slim at forty-two. His coiffed black hair was slightly gray at the sides. He wore a tailored dark silvertone sharkskin suit. Its shiny surface was a bit gaudy for a wake. Unquestionably, he was "wearin' it": the look of a mobster. He had the same prominent hook-nose as his grandfather and dark, almost black, foreboding eyes.

Sally stepped up to him and offered her condolences. He nodded, obviously not happy with her presence. She introduced him to Nick and Nick stepped forward to shake his hand. The hand that reached out to Nick was cold, bony and meatless with a grip that Nick felt was surprisingly weak. Even Nick, who had faced some of the most merciless men on earth, felt a shiver as the black, seemingly lifeless eyes looked right through him. You cold-blooded bastard, Nick was thinking. Diamond Jimmy Votilinni was thinking exactly the same thing as he looked into the piercing green eyes of the man facing him.

Looking at Jimmy, Mac broke the silence, "Ok if I fill'em in on the info Vito got?" He paused, "Then that'll be it."

Jimmy nodded and said, "Then that better fuckin' be it." He turned and reached up to the desk behind him and took a cigarette from a pack there and lit it. He didn't turn toward them again as they left.

When they had gone he reached up to the desk again and pushed a button. In a moment, Johnny Grimm entered and walked up to Votilinni. They were alone. Votilinni looked up at the taller man, "I don't trust that goddamn, fuckin' pinky ring McGinnis any more," he snarled, referring to Mac's non-Italian ethnic background. "That mick bastard's gonna flip and rat us out. I want the son-of-a-bitch followed every fuckin' place he goes from now on, twenty-four hours a day. Get the best fuckin' guys you can find on it. Bug his goddamn house, his car, any fuckin' place he stays." The big man nodded and turned to leave. "And see if you can get a goddamn bug in the car those feds are usin'. I wanta' know what the fuck they're talkin' about when they leave. That goddamn bitch Warbrasac," he growled under his breath, referring to Sally by her birth surname.

Nick and Sally collected their weapons and walked outside with Mac. At Mac's suggestion, they drove into downtown Grand Falls and had dinner at a small steak house on Main Street. Nick was impressed with the meal, one of the best fillet mignons he'd ever had. He ate in silence as Sally and Mac made small talk about the days of their youth in the small town. Eventually, they turned to the subject at hand.

"A man calling himself El Alamien visited Vito a week ago," Mac explained. "Said he'd pay ten million dollars if Vito could arrange to sabotage a U.S. airliner enroute to Europe."

"You were present?" Sally asked.

"No, the man insisted on seeing Vito alone. Vito later relayed the conversation. I picked up the man at O'Hare Field, though. He was tall, about six feet. Dark, Middle-Eastern features, broken nose, scar below his right ear."

Sally was making notes, "How did Vito respond?"

"You know how he is, 'er, was. Calmly gave the man the impression he might consider it at first, listened to the proposal, then said no. The man talked about upping the offer but Vito refused. I'm sure the only reason Vito agreed to meet with him was to get information and evidence. Probably to use in bargaining with you people or somebody at some point. He was always figuring angles like that. Never missed an opportunity to gather information that might later be useful."

"We know that all too well," Sally said.

"The guy flew in from London, States Airlines, flight 723, on June third. He apparently flew back there on June fifth. That's all we know. But, we did get a video tape of him talking that he doesn't know about. Vito had it set up. He figured it might be useful in a trade with you people at some point, I suppose." Mac was smiling as he handed Sally a small cassette tape from his side suitcoat pocket, "We use technology too."

Sally sighed audibly, "That's what wakes me up in the middle of the goddamned night."

Sally was surprised to feel Mac's hand grasp hers. Into it he pressed the tape as he squeezed her hand. Stuck to the back of it, she felt a folded piece of paper. She put the tape in her purse and said, "If you get anything further on this, just call me at my Washington office. Anytime."

"Of course we may ask a favor in return," Mac said, rolling his eyes skyward and repeating a sentence Vito Votilinni had used many times.

"Of course."

Mac relaxed back in the chair and sipped his wine. He looked at Nick, who had been paying more attention to his steak, than to the conversation. "So, Mr. Barber, Vito told me that you're a knight."

Nick stopped chewing. He frowned and looked across the table at the man. "Excuse me?" he said.

Mac turned to Sally, "In ancient kingdoms, throughout the world, the king always had a personal army. The knights were the elite warriors of that army. Loyal to the king above all and willing to do anything at his bidding. The same thing exists today. The CIA is the President's private army and the top agents are secretly considered knights. Today's knights perform the same function as in ancient times, to destroy the enemies of the king without hesitation or remorse. Slay the designated dragons, so to speak." He turned back to Nick. "In return, the President is sworn to use all his powers to pardon and protect you, whenever and wherever necessary, just as the ancient kings did."

Nick continued to stare for a moment, then he swallowed his last bite of steak and smiled. "You have a very poetic way of looking at a plain old government agency, Mr. Mcginnis. In any case, I'm pretty much semi-retired. To a desk job, you know. I guess they think I'm too old to travel much at my advanced age." The three of them laughed at this remark.

An hour later, Sally and Nick were on the highway headed toward Chicago. As soon as they left, Sally pulled out the paper Mac had given her. She studied it and replaced it in her purse without speaking. She looked over at the man next to her, his face barely visible in the darkness. She remembered Mac's words. She knew for certain that Nick could kill human beings without hesitation or remorse. It seemed as though it was just a job to him. She had met him many months earlier. She remembered the sketchy dossier, the FBI had obtained on him, most of it blacked out. What little was there, and the high-level Washington rumors, indicated he had acted as a CIA assassin. She and Nick had been involved in an investigation of a terrorist plot to detonate a nuclear weapon in Chicago. They had successfully thwarted the attempt. Then Nick's superiors had assigned him the task of putting together a small covert force to finish the job. The president of a small Central American country was among the terrorist plotters. They were to enter the country and destroy the remaining bombs and the factory where they were made. Sally had gone along at Nick's request to help plan the mission. She was to stay on a ship offshore, while the teams went in. As they were preparing to go in, one of the team members backed out and Sally had volunteered to replace him. With some hesitation, Nick agreed. She had performed bravely and the mission was a success, albeit with the loss of a couple of the covert team members. Later at their meeting place near the coast, Nick dressed down one of the junior officers. This was for not destroying the teeth and fingertips of one of his own men killed in the operation, so that the body couldn't be identified. Nick himself had done this with the other downed man. Nick treated the incident as matter-of-factly as if the man had not shined his shoes properly.

Sally had thought the mission was over at that point. Then, to her surprise, Nick and a young officer named Tommy Garcia had returned to the capital city. To assassinate the president, she later came to believe. Nick never talked about it, but the man was dead when they returned. Later, he had gunned down the other terrorist leader right in front of her eyes. This was done without a call, and minutes later, Nick calmly asked her to dinner. She and Nick had dated a few times, they had been intimate a couple of times. He seemed so normal, polite, even sweet on a day like this. She harbored powerful, mixed feelings toward him. She liked him, maybe even was beginning to love him, God forbid? But she was apprehensive, even fearful in his presence at the same time.

He had always treated her well, they had some fun...but...she thought of an old cliche', the man had ice water in his veins.

Nick reached over and put his hand over Sally's and she awoke from her thoughts abruptly. "I'd like to spend some time with you again," he said. "It's been a long time since we've been together. This assignment I have in Europe will take a couple of weeks or so. Then you could fly over and meet me, say in Paris. I'll send you the plane ticket. Take some vacation. We could spend a week or so touring."

She put her other hand over the back of his and squeezed it, "I'd love to, it sounds wonderful. But, I know I'm not going to be able to take any vacation for at least a couple of months. I've got agents working all over the country investigating critical cases, not the least of which is finding out who is shopping for a saboteur. Now something else has come up, that I'm sure will take more of my time. Could we postpone the trip until fall?"

"I guess...Europe is beautiful in early fall. But if you can break away sooner."

"Call me sometimes, while you're away."

"I will."

They picked up Interstate 90 at Madison, Wisconsin and less than forty-five minutes later, they crossed the Illinois border. They drove through the flat plain of northern Illinois and on southeast toward the Chicago area. Nick had a plane bound for London to catch the next morning and he knew Sally had a plane ticket to return to Washington. He hadn't asked her yet but he hoped she would spend some time with him that night. Nick pulled into the Ramada O'Hare parking lot and turned to her, "You'll join me for a drink?"

"Sure, why not?" she replied matter-of-factly.

Nick entered the lobby and walked to the front desk. He checked in. Unsure of Sally's plans, he asked for a single.

He came out and drove around to a rear entrance door. He pulled his suitcase out of the trunk. He was surprised to see Sally reach in and pull out her overnight case. They went up to the room. Inside, Nick put his suitcase on the stand and Sally set down her case. "Nick, we have some unfinished business from today," she said.

"Oh?," he said, turning to her.

She put her finger to her lips. "Shhhh. Just wait a few minutes," she whispered. She went into the bathroom and closed the door. Nick shrugged and sat down in a guest chair, next to the table at the window. He put his elbow on the table and put his cheek in his palm. He waited nearly ten minutes.

The bathroom door opened and Sally stepped out. She was naked. Her small body was firm and muscular, her breasts perky. In each of her hands was a small, folded piece of white paper. Nick looked her over, grinning like Christmas morning, his eyes twinkling. She walked over and sat in the chair on the other side of the small round table. She looked around in mock suspicion, then reached across the table and handed Nick the paper in her right hand. He opened it and read:

I have information that can only be discussed out of range of any bugs. Diamond Jimmy is very cautious these days. He may have put a bug somewhere in my clothes so I left them in the bathroom. Before we can talk though, well, he might have a bug in your clothes too. So, well, you know what to do. *You are* a spy, aren't you?

Nick was laughing, he loved her sense of humor. He got up and went into the bathroom. Several minutes later he came out. He was naked also, a towel in his hand. Smiling, she took in his hairy chest and muscular upper body. He bent down and made a big production out of stuffing the towel under the door of the bathroom. A couple of times he looked at Sally and put a finger to his lips. She was giggling and giving him the "ok" sign with her thumb and forefinger. Then he walked over and handed Sally a note. He sat down in the other chair again, a big smile on his face. The note was written on toilet paper. Sally read it:

> Yes I *are* a spy. You can tell this by the way I cleverly found something to write this note on. People who are not spies obviously would not have been so resourceful. Actually, I think I'm being had and I think I'm going to enjoy it.

Sally handed him the other paper. He looked at it:

> The handwriting is on the wall. I'm ready to talk. I'll call you at your office Monday.

This wasn't in Sally's handwriting, it looked like a man's scrawl. Nick looked at her. Her face was serious now. "Mac?" he asked. She nodded. "Jesus," Nick said, "he's turning state's evidence. Quite a coup for you." Then, he looked at her and laughed, "The clothes? You didn't really think..."

Sally laughed hard now, tears came to her eyes. When it subsided she shook her head, "No."

"Oh you are the evil one," he said with mock slyness.

"But seriously," she said, "I didn't want to say anything in the car. Diamond Jimmy might have had it bugged." She held out her hand and he handed the paper back to her. She stared down at the paper. "I'm sure Mac has never pulled a trigger, but I'm equally sure he knows where all the bodies are buried."

"Speaking of bodies," Nick said, "why don't you come over and sit on my lap?"

"All in good time," she said as she picked up the matchbook from the ashtray. Holding the paper by the corner she lit it and let it burn, the ashes floating down to the ashtray. She dropped the still burning corner in and did the same with the other notes. Nick watched her sparkling, blue eyes dance behind the flames. When she had dropped the last flaming piece into the ashtray Nick walked over and scooped her up out of the chair. He laid her on the bed and they embraced and kissed with a pleasure that neither enjoyed often.

FIVE

Nick Barber had taken a tourist's flight from New York to London and then, the train from Heathrow to the small airport at Southend. There he boarded a Maersk Airlines taxi flight bound for Copenhagen. His hair was done in white. He wore wire-rimmed, rose hued glasses and the tweed suit and hiking boots of a British professor. Neither the walk through metal detectors at O'Hare Airport nor the hand held detector probes at Southend discovered the .22 composite automatic. From the airport at Copenhagen, he took a cab to the King Frederick Hotel and checked in. The next afternoon, Sunday, he was told that the crate had arrived and was downstairs in the hotel garage. He went down and opened it, tossing the wooden pieces in a trash barrel. Thom

McCormick had put red wax sealer on the inside joints of the crate. It hadn't been opened. The motorcycle was there, looking undisturbed and ready to go. Nick decided to leave the weapons in the seat for the time being.

After dinner that evening he visited the hotel bar on the lower level. The rectangular bar in the center was surrounded by dark hardwood booths on the outer walls. There were ornate, masculine carvings of Nordic forest scenes on the dark, oak walls. Deer and wild boar charged out from among the trees. Antlers and tusks surfaced from the panels above the booths, creating the illusion of motion, of action. A complete medieval suit of armor was displayed in a corner, a lance in the hand. Nick had a couple of shots of Gammel Dansk, the traditional Danish Schnapps, chasing them with Carlsberg beer. Then, he walked outside and down the ancient cobblestone street. It was warm and there was still subdued sunlight, even though it was late evening. It was so good to have an assignment like this, he thought. No danger, no worries. A chance to pay a visit to old familiar places. He arrived at what the locals called the "walking street". It was an ancient, open mall where only pedestrian traffic was allowed. The shops were closed and only a few people were about, their footsteps clacking on the old stone. He walked up to an ancient building that was said to be the world's oldest stock market. The wide, massive stone steps were worn in great concave arcs from hundreds of years of use. He wondered about Himmler, the amassed treasure, if there was anything there to find. If so, could he find it?

Later, in his room on the third floor of the ancient hotel he lay on the bed. He had opened the window and the summer night breeze was warm. The big city was quiet. There was only a murmur of audible activity in the distance. He thought of Sally. He had thought of her more and more since he had met her, when? Months ago now. He longed for her company. He had not been so taken with a woman in years. He had never married, but there had been a couple of women he had proposed to. One had accepted, for a while. Neither relationship had worked out because of his career. Now Sally's career stood in his way. The breeze lifted the sheer inner curtains into the room like ghosts. She was too busy for him. You could usually tell how well a person liked you by the amount of time they were willing to spend with you, he thought. Then he felt a pang of guilt about his own inability to spend time to make his former relationships work. Was she sincere about a trip this fall or was she putting him off?

On Monday morning, he had breakfast in the dark, wood paneled dining room of the King Frederick. He dined on fried eggs, spegepolse and toast with juice and coffee. He had ordered a double helping of the spegepolse, a raw, red Danish sausage with a unique taste that he loved. Then he carried his bags down to the garage. He clipped the bags in place at either side of the motorcycle and locked them on. It started with ease, the engine producing only a quiet whirring sound. He rode through Copenhagen and then out onto the South Highway E4. He followed it to E66 and then west headed for the ferry port at Korsor. The turbine-powered machine purred smoothly all the way. He arrived just as a ferry was docking. He got in line behind a car and rode the motorcycle into the large lower hold of the ferry. He clipped the helmet to the side and slung his black, leather jacket over his shoulder. He went up to the main deck. It was hot now as the sun stared from above, the heat only slightly broken by a mild breeze coming across the water. There were sailboats moving about everywhere in the Harbor at Korsor. Nick knew how much the Danes savored their few weeks of good warm weather during midsummer. Most took their holiday during that time. By the time he reached the upper deck, the ferry was already moving. A hazy mist sparkled in the sunlight above the dark waters as they left the dock.

It was approaching noon. Nick went into the restaurant and ordered sol over gudhjem, the traditional roeget sild Danish lunch. It was smoked herring on a small piece of rye bread, topped with two raw eggs and garnished with onions, radishes and chives. It was a delicacy few Americans liked, but Nick enjoyed the dish. The ferry rolled almost imperceptibly as it made its way west across the Store Baelt for the central Danish island of Fyn. It was hot in the restaurant. The old wood of the interior creaked with the slight rolling. Little more than an hour after leaving Korsor they docked at Knudshoved.

Nick resumed his journey on the motorcycle and followed traffic to highway F8 which cut diagonally across southern Fyn toward the southwest coast. As he moved away from the coastal area, the traffic began to thin out. The traffic was moving a little faster than usual for Denmark, a country that enforces its speed limits, Nick thought. He found himself behind a low, white Lamborghini Countach. Nick chuckled to himself, "I'll bet he thinks he's the fastest vehicle on this road. Of course he's wrong."

Just then the sports car pulled out quickly and passed two cars. Nick hit the throttle hard for the first time and was surprised as the acceleration literally jerked his body forward. He stayed on the Lamborghini's bumper and when it pulled back into line Nick passed it, the bright orange Heads Up Display in the windshield at 115 miles per hour. Nick pulled into the lane and slowed down and suddenly, the sports car rushed by on his left. Nick said to himself,. "I can't believe I'm doing this," as he hit the throttle again, and began to pass the still accelerating sports car. His HUD read 148 this time when he pulled in again in front of the sports car. He could see traffic ahead in the distance now as he slowed again. The sports car passed him and made a right turn off the highway. Nick slowed more and followed, the cycle seemingly floating as he slowed rapidly. He followed the car and stayed with it as it accelerated. The deserted country road ahead was straight and narrow. As the HUD reached 150 Nick kept his head down behind the small windshield and shifted into third gear. He pressed the button that activated the spoilers. As they slid out of their gloves Nick felt the machine drop slightly, hugging the road. Nick kept the rocket assisted acceleration on as the readout climbed to 170, then to over 180. The machine's engine was screaming like a true jet now. He was coming up on the sports car, closing the gap so fast he couldn't believe it. Cautiously, he pulled out to pass, the readout moving through the 190's now as he whizzed past the car. Accelerating rapidly to 215 miles per hour, he put distance between himself and the car. He then began to slow down. After a long process of braking, he brought the machine to a halt and pulled off the road. The Lamborghini slowed also and pulled up next to him.

A gull-wing door flipped up and a young, dark haired man leaned out behind it. "Do you speak Italian?" he said in the language.

"Si." Nick said nodding his head.

"We took the car to the limit and still you passed. Will you sell the motorcycle?"

Nick smiled under the helmet and said, "No" and shook his head. The door closed and the sports car sped away.

Nick went back to A8 and cruised southwest at normal speed. At Falborg he turned south along the Coast Road and found the Church Road. He could see the white church at the end of the road less than a mile away. A minute later, he parked the motorcycle in front of the low, white stone wall that bordered the cemetery grounds around the church. He clipped his helmet to the motorcycle and slung his jacket over his shoulder. He walked in the front gate. Inside the wall the grounds were kept immaculately. Raked gravel paths separated islands of tombstones and markers. Each island was green with bushes and small trees and dappled with flowers in pink, red, white or shades of violet and bordered by a low hedge. The dark exposed earth among the flora was well tended and scattered with small stones. Not a single weed could be seen. The church itself was white and clean with high walls and a sharp steeple pointing the way to heaven.

Nick walked up the steps and tried the heavy oaken door. The latch clicked and the massive door opened with surprising ease. The interior of the church, bathed in sunlight from the southwest windows, was as pristine as the exterior. The fully rigged model of a sixteenth century, sailing ship hung in the center above the aisle. Nick knew that this artifact represented the journey of life. He heard someone at the front near the altar. "Undskylde mig," Nick said loudly, excusing himself in Danish as he walked down the aisle.

An old man popped his bald head up from the front row of pews. He had a white fringe at the back from ear to ear and was dressed in a white shirt and bib overalls. An unlit pipe was clamped in his teeth. He squinted through his glasses in the hazy sunlight. "Ja?" he said.

"Are you the caretaker?" Nick asked in Danish, now face to face with the man at the front of the church. The man nodded. Nick introduced himself as Cecil Bradshaw. He explained that he was a professor from the U.K. and was searching for World War Two artifacts and information. Then he asked, "Could you show me the grave of Captain Gordon Halvorsen?"

"Of course," the old man said. Then he pointed to the baptismal font. "Many years ago, shortly after the war, his mother visited and made a gift of this to the church."

Nick looked at the white marble stand with an ornate brass tray inset at the top. The man walked slowly past Nick to the side door, motioning him to come. They walked out into the sunlight and Nick followed the man toward the south wall. They stepped over the low hedge and the man stopped and motioned to a large boulder. Nick walked around the stone. The south face of it was ground flat and polished. Nick crouched and read the carved inscription:

FLYVER
GORDON A. HALVORSEN
f 6/4 1921 OHIO U.S.A.
+ 5/4 1944 FYN DANMARK
FALLEN FOR SIT LAND OG FOR VORT

"Flyer Gordon A. Halvorsen. Born April 6, 1921, in Ohio, United States of America. Died April 4, 1944, in Fyn, Denmark. Died for his country and for ours," Nick murmured to himself translating the epitaph from Danish to English.

"He died there," the caretaker said, motioning to the stone fence. "He came from toward the sea." The caretaker pointed to the stone with the stem of his pipe. "The name, he was Scandinavian. He rests through eternity in his ancestral homeland." The greenish waters of the sea could be seen in the distance through the trees.

"Do you know of any unusual activities in this area at the time of his death?"

The old man perched on the low stone fence and lit his pipe. When he was satisfied with the white wisps of smoke rising from its bowl, he began, "We were at war so, of course, everything seemed unusual. At that time, I was imprisoned at Froslevlejren Camp by the Nazis. The site is now on the Danish side of the border on the Jutland Peninsula. We were slave laborers. When I returned I heard that the Gestapo or some high-level Nazis had taken over the Von Kloussen estate for a while in forty-four. Used it for a retreat. The entire Von Kloussen family was imprisoned at Sonderborg Castle," he motioned to the sea, "just across the Lillie Baelt in Jutland. Even the present Baron. He must have been one or two years old at the time."

"What about the Nazis bringing truckloads of material in?"

"I heard there were many Nazi vehicles going in and out of the estate for a time. They all left after the allied invasion."

A few minutes later, Nick was cruising on the Church Road back to the Coast Road. He turned left, backtracking his former route and within a minute, he was turning left into the driveway of the Jens Anders farm. The house was a one level red brick with a black tile roof. It was the building closest to the road. Behind was a large barn, also of red brick and an assortment of smaller outbuildings and grain storage pits. It was a dairy farm.

Nick parked at the side of the wide driveway and removed his helmet as he walked toward the house. A middle aged man and woman stepped out the side door, wary looks on their faces. Nick extended his hand as he approached, "Bradshaw, Professor Cecil Bradshaw of Chatham, England."

The man, now smiling, held out his hand, "Jens Anders and my wife, Elsa. We didn't expect you to come on a motorcycle."

They shook hands and Nick said, "You're not...?"

The man laughed. "No, no, it's my father you're here
to see. Come in. He's on the patio. Your Danish is very
good."

They led Nick through the home, which was well kept
and filled with furniture of both modern Danish teak and
antique, polished dark oak. In front of the living room was a
large patio. An old man of at least seventy wearing denim
work clothes sat there, a glass of beer in his hand. The
younger Anders introduced them and went to get Nick a beer.
After the three men had enjoyed some small talk, Nick asked
the older man about what he had seen in the spring of 1944.
Before he could speak his son excused himself to do some
work in the barn. The old man began with a question, "Why
have you come? Is there new evidence of the Germans'
activities?" He had guessed correctly.

Nick downplayed it, "So much time has passed that
it's only of academic interest now. But you saw trucks that
appeared to be heavily laden and heavily guarded, leaving the
Coast Road toward the sea in early April, 1944?"

"First, the Germans took over the Von Kloussen estate
west of us. For a retreat or officers' quarters, we heard. This
was early in 1944, February, I think. Then, several close
neighbors were evacuated. Some were taken to the camps. My
parents and I managed to get to Odense. We stayed in my
aunt's apartment there. Sometime later, I decided to make the
journey back to the farm on foot for some belongings and
that's when I saw the trucks."

"Was it April fifth?"

"Could have been. It was about then...I've tried to
remember, but was never able to recall the specific day. We
were hiding from the Germans, the days were all the same.
Anyway, from the woods across from the estate, I saw two
large covered trucks painted in gray. They were moving

slowly, their springs were creaking as though they carried a heavy load. Several guards walked next to the trucks. They wore black suits and carried automatic rifles. They were far away, but I knew from their gait they were German. I got out of there and returned to Odense by back roads. A neighbor, Kurt Christian, saw them too, God rest his soul. He died a few years after the war. We thought they might be carrying what, weapons? Explosives? Valuables? Representatives of the Allies questioned us both and the area was searched but nothing was ever found. The Baron and his family moved back on to the estate after the war."

"Did you see or hear an American fighter plane come down that day?"

"Ah, the fellow buried at the church? No, nothing."

Nick took a swallow of the good Carlsberg beer, "My main purpose here is to find evidence of that plane, for historical purposes, of course. I'm writing a book about military activity in this area. Would you be willing to help? I can pay you a little."

"I will help and no pay is necessary. I'm just a retired old man with little to do. It would be enjoyable."

"Good. May I hike about tomorrow on your farm with my metal detector?"

"Of course."

"I may want to get some diving gear and explore undersea. Do you have a boat, do you sail?"

The old man laughed loudly and hoisted his glass, "I will answer both questions, ja and ja. All Danes sail until they die and after death, they sail throughout eternity."

Nick fended off several invitations to dinner and lodging with the gracious Anders family that evening. He rode north to Odense.

Odense was a large city in Denmark, near the center of the island of Fyn. It was second only to Copenhagen in population. He had booked a room at the Tre Roser Motel just south of the city on Highway A9 about twenty miles from the Anders' farm. The motel was of one story reddish brown brick with a gray tile roof. Four long rows of rooms formed the sides of the square complex. They enclosed a large outdoor swimming pool in the center. The pool was bordered by a concrete walk with tables and chairs. This was in turn surrounded with a grass strip, studded with small, well-tended gardens of colorful flowers and small bushes. All of the rooms had a glass wall with a patio door opening into the pool area. At one corner was a large building, which housed the office, reception desk, restaurant and bar.

Nick pulled up in front of the office and went in. He had stayed there some years earlier, and was familiar with the layout. The restaurant was straight ahead as he entered the lobby; the bar was to the left. On his right in the lobby was the reception desk, a long, light brown counter of polished wood. Behind it stood a short, young man with jet black hair and goatee. "Professor Cecil Bradshaw," Nick announced, "I believe you have a reservation for me." The use of such titles was common in Europe and Nick was playing the part to the hilt.

The man smiled and examined the book in front of him. He nodded and handed Nick a small, white card to fill out. Nick completed it and then looked around slyly. He motioned the clerk closer as though he were about to impart some great secret. Under his breath he said, "The connecting room next door. Is it available?"

The clerk checked his book. "Yes," he said, also under his breath, as he also looked around suspiciously.

"I'd like to rent it also, secretly. I may have a special guest during my stay." Nick leaned closer and winked at the clerk.

"The man looked down at the plain gold band Nick wore on his left hand and smiled, "I see.   Well...I don't know." Nick wasn't married, of course. He wore the ring only as a ruse.

Nick shoved a one thousand kroner note, worth about one hundred and thirty dollars, across the counter. The clerk's eyes widened. "This is yours, and another when I leave, if you tell no one."

The clerk looked around and then quickly pocketed the note. "Yes, of course. I know nothing of you renting this room. It is forgotten."

Nick had the clerk fill out the card for the other room with a phony name and paid the next week's rent on both rooms in cash. This was a routine precaution Nick often used while traveling. At night he would arrange the bed in his room to appear as though it were occupied and sleep in the adjoining room. He was a man with old and clever enemies.

Nick parked the motorcycle in front of his room on the south side of the complex. He brought his luggage in through the outer door. The room had a teak wall desk with a radio, a Danish modern easy chair with floor reading lamp and a long couch with teak base and ends. On a low table there was a small screen television. He walked over and opened the drapes that covered the glass wall. He had a good view of the long side of the rectangular swimming pool.

Tuesday, June 14

In the morning, Nick rode into Odense and located an electronics shop. He purchased a Fisher M-Scope 1280-X metal detector. This was a unit that could be used on land or under water. He then rode south to the Anders farm.

The Von Kloussen estate was located on two hundred wooded acres on the southwest coast of Fyn. The centuries old main house was nearly a quarter of a mile south of the coast road across an expanse of beautiful green lawn. The long, curving drive was studded with giant oak trees on either side. The large house was finished in white stucco with a large, three story portico framing the front door at the center. Two large columns supported each side of the portico giving the appearance of an English country house. The first, second and third floors had long rows of latticed windows trimmed in brown. At the fourth floor level were matching windows on each of the eight dormers that jutted out of the black tile roof. At each of the rear corners was a white tower rising above the roof. The towers were turrets complete with parapets giving the house a castle-like appearance. It was, in fact, known as the Von Kloussen castle. There were twenty-eight rooms in the huge rectangular structure. On the east side was a six car garage, added in recent times. Behind was a horse barn, three servants' cottages and other small outbuildings, all in matching white stucco with brown-trimmed windows.

Above the arched front door, under the portico, was the Von Kloussen family crest. The entire achievement was there painted in black, gold and red. On the arms, or shield, at the center was a giant black claw, apparently of a predatory bird. A muscular tendon was attached to the claw. As with many arms designed in the late middle-ages the design was a punning allusion to the family name, Kloussen. Klo was Danish for claw and sene for tendon. The achievement was complete with flowing red and white mantling, gold helm and a black falcon crest above the arms. The supporters at the sides of the arms were semi-human styled black hunting hounds. At the bottom was the compartment containing the motto scroll. The flowing scroll read "FORSVARE UDEN NADE" meaning "DEFEND WITHOUT MERCY".

Kurt Kohfer had been the Baron's estate manager, bodyguard and chauffeur for nearly three years. At thirty-three, he was six feet tall with dark hair and a handsome face that was framed with a well-trimmed narrow, black beard that framed his large jaw. He was German and had been a police officer in Frankfurt, before coming to work for the Baron. His various corruptions had cost him his job and he had decided to leave Germany. Now, he stood in the Baron's office in the northwest corner of the main house. He watched out the side window as the Baron and Arun Rashidii walked a gravel path toward the woods, shotguns over their shoulders.

Eva Van Damme sat at the large, oak desk in the center of the room. Von Kloussen had given her a pile of paperwork. She was reconciling accounts on a personal computer. Kohfer saw a white Mercedes roll in the long drive and stop under the portico. One of the French doors to the office swung open. The Baroness stood there dressed for her trip to Copenhagen. She was tall and slim wearing a white dress with the hem above the knee revealing her still shapely legs. She had an attractive, aristocratic face and striking red hair that, now that she was fifty, flowed from a bottle. "I'll be leaving now," she said to Kurt. He turned and nodded.

Outside, the Baron and Rashidii had walked some distance from the house along the gravel path. Suddenly, a grouse sprang up from the brush along the edge of the path. Wings snapping rapidly, it was flying away from them. Rashidii swung his shotgun down from his shoulder clicking off the safety in one quick motion. He fired from the hip. The shot exploded with the familiar crash of a shotgun, echoing in the morning air. The bird accelerated and tumbled forward from the momentum of the shot, feathers flying, then dropped to the ground. Rashidii walked over and picked up the still struggling bird. Instinctively, he wrung its neck with a quick snap and put it in his leather quarrybag.

Nick Barber was a mile away on the Anders' farm making his way to the shore, when he heard the distant shot. He adjusted the metal detector and moved on.

"Very good!" The Baron said complementing Rashidii on the shot. "But, we have other concerns."

"Yes, your plan."

"It would be foolish to try to put anything in luggage," Von Kloussen began as though thinking out loud. "It has to be an inside job, of a sort. A small, but significant percentage of Americans are criminally insane. All you have to do is read their newspapers or listen to their television. We have to find the right person. Someone who knows his way around the airports, knows the employee security systems. Ideally, someone who has been fired by an airline recently and holds a grudge. He must have a pronounced criminal bent."

"And how do we find this man among thousands?"

"The American way, of course. We advertise. Tomorrow, we drive to Copenhagen, then fly to London. I have disguises and false papers prepared for us to use from there on. I'll fly to New York and you'll fly to Chicago. We'll each take a hotel suite." He pulled a folded page out of his pocket and handed it to Rashidii. It read:

SHIPPING SPECIALIST
We are seeking a dynamic individual
to become part of our transport team.
Airline experience a must, computer
experience a plus. The successful
candidate will receive an excellent

benefits package, top starting salary and bonus plan and profit sharing plan. Please send resume and salary requirements to:
EXPERT TRANSPORT COMPANY
Equal Opportunity Employer

The post office box and zip code in Chicago, Illinois followed.

"Eva and I took overnight flights to the U.S. last Thursday. She went to New York and I went to Chicago. We rented a post office box in each city and arranged for this ad to appear in the local newspapers. It will start appearing within a couple of days." The Baron handed him a key, "Here is the key for the Chicago box. We should start getting replies by the weekend. We'll select from the replies and interview the candidates as necessary. References should be able to give us the information we need, particularly secondary ones. That is, get additional names from the references the candidate gives. You, myself and the chosen candidate will be the only ones knowing all of the details. Eva will be involved on a need to know basis only. We must do everything with our own hands. It is too risky to have anyone else involved. When the job is done you will eliminate our 'partner'."

Rashidii looked at the Baron and nodded.

SIX

Nick Barber walked west along the seashore, moving the searchcoil of the metal detector just above the sandy, pebble strewn beach. He was wearing the unit's earphones. He stared down at the hand held console, occasionally making adjustments. He had found ships' hardware and some coins along the beach under the sand. He didn't expect to find much on land. His main objective today was to get familiar with the unit for later undersea use and to get familiar with the area. There was a reed bed in the water to his left now and a shadow. He looked up. In front of him a rock ledge jutted out over the water. He shut the machine off and removed the earphones. He set the unit on the ledge and looked over the top. The gray ruins of the small castle was there to his right.

This could be what Halvorsen had described in the letter, he thought. He could see the broad, sloping side of a hill about two hundred feet in the distance. Strangely, the facing side of the hill was bare except for shallow grass and a few stunted trees. The rest of the hill was heavily wooded all around. Below it the low grass gradually sloped down giving way to the sandy gravel of the beach.

He climbed over the ledge and walked over to the ruins. The front rooms of the structure were gone. Some of the heavy stones that had once formed their walls, were scattered about. Grass grew up between the large, flat stones of the bare floor. The walls of the back part of the structure appeared to be still intact. He pushed open a heavy, decaying wooden door. He stood in a room with bare stone walls and a partially rotted wood ceiling. There was an open doorway to his right, that opened to another, similar room. In front of him was a heavy oak door that, apparently, led to the small, three story round tower at the rear. He pulled on the door and with difficulty opened it. The stone floor was bare. The plain, gray walls were windowless, except for a couple of narrow, vertical rectangular slits near the top that let in slivers of sunlight. The ceiling of the round chamber was of stone, supported by a heavy oak framework set in the walls.

Nick left the ruins and reactivated the metal detector as he walked toward the hill. He adjusted the discrimination knob, to just below the "three" setting, to pick up iron. As he walked closer, the light-emitting diode on the small console, began to glow and, simultaneously, he heard the tone in the earphones grow louder. At the base of the hill the tone grew still louder. He turned down the power/volume knob. As he climbed the bottom of the hill the tone stayed steady and the diode illuminated, as though there were a large, metal object just below. Nick stopped and took a folding spade from his sidepack. He carved out a divot of sod and dug below. Sweating in the heat of the day, he dug over eighteen inches deep, widening the hole carefully several times. Finally, laying on the ground with his arm in above his elbow, he struck a solid flat surface. From his pack he took a tool with a carbide tip, which resembled a small screwdriver. He reached down and scraped the flat surface. Between his thumb and the tool, he brought up shavings of metal, at first rusty, then clean as he scraped deeper. He deposited them in a plastic evidence bag and sealed it, when he felt the sample was large enough. He carefully filled the hole and tamped the divots into place exactly as he had removed them.

He walked the broad, flat side of the hill with the detector. He was able to map out the edges of a large rectangular object approximately fifteen feet high by twenty-five feet wide set into the side of the hill like a large garage door. He made a sketch in his notepad and then dug another hole and took more metal scrapings. The sun was at its noon peak. He walked down toward the beach thinking this could well be it! And, imagine stumbling onto it the first day out. But, maybe the Nazi loot was never buried here or if it was, Himmler may have moved it before the invasion forces got this far, he thought. Whatever the case, if the hill had been dug up, someone had gone to a lot of trouble to cover it up and make it look like an ordinary hill again.

He looked into the low, wooded area between the beach and the hill. Surrounded by old growth forest was a path of new growth forest wide enough to be a road. He hiked through the new growth and noted several mounds, some of them five feet high. They were very likely man-made but intended to look natural. They would prevent any vehicles from entering the area and make it look like none ever had, at least to a casual observer. Nick selected a flat area between two of the mounds and dug a hole. Six inches down he struck crushed stone. Just as he suspected there had been a roadbed! He took a sample and covered the hole. The roadbed curved through the old growth, so that even when in use it wouldn't have been easily noticed. The mounds and hill were probably covered with thick grass, even small trees by the time the allies got around to searching the area.

Nick put on the earphones and switched on the detector, now hoping to find evidence of Captain Halvorsen, or anyone who had been there. He came out of the woods and walked slowly along the beach, practicing a slow, waving motion with the searchcoil. As he came close to the rock ledge, he heard a voice over his left shoulder.

"STADSE, STADSE." A voice shouted in Danish, telling him to halt.

Nick froze, startled at the sound, then remembering his training, he composed himself. He removed the earphones and turned slowly. At the top of the hill were two men dressed in brown. Each was holding a shotgun and had a leather quarrybag with its strap across his chest. The shorter man wore a cap and dark glasses and appeared to Nick to be of dark complexion. The taller man came quickly down the hill toward Nick. As he walked up to Nick he was demanding, "Who are you? What are you doing here?" in a nervous, frustrated voice. He stopped a few feet away.

Nick looked directly into the man's pale blue eyes and displayed a broad smile. In the best British accented Danish he could manage he said, "Bradshaw here, Professor Cecil Bradshaw over from Chatham College in England doing research on World War Two artifacts in the area."

"I am Baron Von Kloussen and you are trespassing on my land."

"Mr. Anders has given me permission, I..."

"His land starts there," the Baron interrupted pointing beyond the rock ledge. "I suggest you stay on it."

"Yes of course, so sorry to inconvenience you, sir," Nick said, folding his hands in front of him and dropping his head slightly in a submissive pose.

Von Kloussen was now eyeing Nick suspiciously. Finally he said, "What are you looking for?"

Trying to be as vague as possible Nick said, "Aircraft came down in this area and I'm looking for pieces and parts. No luck today, I'm afraid."

With an evermore wary glint in his eye the Baron said, "See that this does not happen again." He waited for Nick to begin moving toward the ledge, then made his way back up the hill.

Von Kloussen rejoined Rashidii and they watched Nick make his way east until he was out of sight. "Who is he?" Rashidii said.

"He says he's a Professor from Chatham College in England named Cecil Bradshaw, but there's something very strange about him. Speaks Danish with an accent that's supposed to be British."

"But?"

"But I can detect another accent below the British; it is American."

"Damn. But then perhaps he has just spent some time in the U.S."

"Perhaps," the Baron said, looking to the east.

Back at the main house the Baron sat at his desk. Kurt Kohfer and Rashidii sat across from him. He placed a call to Chatham College in England. When the receptionist answered he said, "Professor Cecil Bradshaw please," in his best British English. The Baron spoke several languages and was himself very good at accents.

There was a pause. Then she said, "He's on a research project in Denmark, sir," as she had been instructed to do. "Might I take a message for him, sir?"

He said, "No, thank you," and hung up the phone.

She immediately placed a call to London, as she had also been instructed to do.

Von Kloussen turned to Kohfer, "I have a strange feeling about this. People don't intrude without a reason. Go have a look at the Anders place, discreetly of course. See what you can find out about this man."

A few minutes later, Kohfer selected a dark brown Volkswagen Rabbit usually used by the servants from among the cars in the garage. He drove a short distance east on the Coast Road and turned into a clearing in the woods. From behind some large trees, he had a view of the Anders house and buildings without being easily seen himself. He took out a pair of binoculars and surveyed the grounds. The large, black motorcycle parked next to the house caught his interest. Within an hour, Nick Barber came out and rode away on the motorcycle. When he had gone by on the Coast Road, Kohfer pulled out to follow him.

Three hours later, Kohfer had returned and was knocking on the french doors of the Baron's office. Arun Rashidii sat in a guest chair in front of the desk reading a magazine. At his desk Von Kloussen was just hanging up the phone. "Come in," he said.

Kohfer entered, shutting the door behind him. "The man rides a large Japanese motorcycle," he began excitedly. "At least a seven-fifty cc, black, looks very fast. Probably a Honda."

Von Kloussen looked at Rashidii, "Very unusual for a British professor in the later stage of middle-age. I'd expect a motor scooter, if he rode a two-wheeled vehicle at all."

Kohfer continued, "I followed him nearly to Odense. He's staying at the Tre Roser Motel south of the city. I distracted the clerk and got a look at the register. He checked in yesterday afternoon, room twenty-eight. I waited around for a while, but he just stayed in his room."

"Good work. If he checked in yesterday, he may have come in to the country by plane recently or...more likely...by ferry, with that motorcycle. I'll make a call to Copenhagen and have schedules for the last few days checked. Have Eva come in."

Kohfer left the office and Rashidii said, "Why so much concern? No one could possibly know..."

"It's a loose end and I won't be satisfied until we know for sure."

Eva entered the office followed by Kohfer. "Eva," the Baron began, "I want you to go check in to the Tre Roser Motel in Odense." He explained what they knew about the professor. "Get to know him. Find out everything you can about him. It is important to our operations to be sure he is not spying on us for some reason. We'll think of a cover story for you. Kurt will be working with you on this while we're on our trip."

"How well do you expect me to get to know him?" she asked apprehensively.

"Be as intimate with him as you need to be." Eva looked sad and disgusted at once.

The Baron leaned back in his chair and looked at her, "This is only a job. Please treat it objectively. It's become part of our plan. Do it for me."

At 9:00 P.M., Nick was in the restaurant of the Tre Roser just finishing his meal. He had ordered fillet of sole with green beans and almonds and boiled potatoes, one of his favorites. He had a view out of the windows toward the pool and had been watching, as a beautiful blonde woman emerged from across the complex and walked toward him along the pool. She was tall and her lithe body moved with a smooth, probably practiced, seductive style. She wore dark sunglasses and a black string bikini that barely covered her firm, ample breasts. As she rounded the end of the pool and walked along the opposite edge, it was obvious that the thong bottom of the garment didn't even attempt to cover her shapely, lightly tanned buttocks. She selected a lawn chair across the courtyard, directly between Nick's room and the edge of the pool. Nick went into the bar and ordered a Carlsberg. He nursed it while he watched a soccer game on a television in the corner. Denmark's team was doing well and the other patrons were very excited about the game. Nick couldn't get his mind off the blonde.

Nick left and walked around the pool toward his room. It was 9:30 P.M. and still there was hazy sunlight everywhere. In the summer, it never gets completely dark in Denmark. There is a dusky light even in the early morning hours. She was still there as he approached her chair from behind. As he passed he looked down at her, noting her full lips and turned-up nose as she looked at him. He went into his room and opened the drapes. He flipped on the television and relaxed in the recliner. The blonde was walking around the pool now. It was almost, he thought, as if his passing had triggered her to move. She entered a room across the pool. Nick could see a light come on and she stepped in front of it. Only the sheer drapes were closed. He could see the sharp outline of her body as she slowly removed the bikini.

Nick went for a walk around the suburban area surrounding the motel. When he returned at 11:30 P.M. he stopped in at the motel bar. There were still some business people and travelers at the tables. They were laughing and talking loudly, having a good time at the late hour. Nick sat on the stool at the bar and ordered a Carlsberg. Only minutes later, the blonde came in and sat at the bar two stools down. She was wearing a gray pants-suit with baggy legs, but tight at the hips. Underneath the jacket was a low-cut black blouse. She ordered a Rose' wine and as she turned back from the bartender she gave Nick a big smile. "Guten Nacht," she said in perfect German.

"Guten Nacht," he said. Nick couldn't keep from looking her over. She had a face like a Roman goddess, ruby lips and full breasts, half exposed, that jiggled as she spoke.

"From Germany?" Nick asked.

"Yeah," she said, "Gertrude Reinhard. I am teaching school there in Bremerhaven. I am here on holiday. And you?"

He held out his hand, "Professor Cecil Bradshaw, over from Chatham College in England, doing research on war artifacts. I guess you might say I'm here on business." He quickly returned the conversation to her again. "I trust you are enjoying your holiday?"

"Well," she began, "maybe yes and maybe no. There was this man, we had lived together for some time. He left me a few weeks ago and I decided to have a change of scenery to forget." She sighed a long sigh and brought the long-stemmed glass of red wine to her lips.

"I suspect this man has made a grave mistake. You are a very beautiful woman."

"Dankashoen, Professor."

"Please, call me Cecil."

"Married?"

"Nein, but the clerk here thinks so," Nick said, laughing.

"Excuse me?"

"Nothing, Fraulein, an inside joke. Well, I must retire now. Maybe I'll see you again."

"Yeah. I will be here for a fortnight, Professor, perhaps longer."

Nick returned to his room, leaving her at the bar.

CIA Headquarters, Langley, Virginia, Wednesday, June 15, 10:00 A.M.

Joe Ronzoni leaned back in his executive chair as the door buzzed and his secretary, Leslie, ushered in Sally Stein, Jack Vanlandingham and Mac McGinnis. Vanlandingham was an FBI Deputy Director and was Sally's immediate superior at the Bureau. He was a tall lanky, balding man with a long face. He wore trifocals rimmed in plastic, brown-yellow striped frames. Joe motioned them to be seated. The door clicked shut.

McGinnis had called Sally from a pay phone. Yes, he might be ready to talk to the government about the Votilinni organization. But first he insisted on a meeting with a high ranking CIA official. Sally had gone to Vanlandingham with the request. Because of the potential vital importance of McGinnis' testimony, the meeting with Ronzoni was arranged.

Mac had been followed to O'Hare, where he caught a plane to Dulles International. A phone call from Johnny Grimm had arranged a tail in Washington also. Two men had followed him to FBI headquarters there. They didn't see Sally, Mac and Vanlandingham leave the basement parking garage, an hour later, on their way to Langley.

Joe looked at Mac, "What would you like to discuss?"

Mac looked around at all three, then began, "I said I would be willing to turn state's evidence, provide information. I could make your case for you. My take is that Jimmy Votilinni is going to go away for a lot of years. And soon. But that still leaves the two Capos, Tosco and Veldon. Votilinni can run the organization from prison, through them."

"Your boy, Diamond Jimmy, is going to be facing the death penalty," Jack reminded him.

Mac looked at him, "It'll never happen. At least, not without my testimony."

"Tosco and Veldon are going away, too."

"Hell," Mac said, "the Capos could run it from prison, through the ten lieutenants below them anyway, at least for a while. Any of the three top bosses will have me killed if they suspect I talked."

"We'll put you in the witness protection program," Vanlandingham offered.

"Not good enough. The bastards'll probably find me. You don't know what they're capable of. And, my kids..."

That goddamn Votilinni wouldn't harm his own niece and nephew would he?" Vanlandingham asked, an increduous tone in his voice.

Mac shook his head and said, "No, I-I don't think so," his voice wavering. Then he looked at Sally, "I never realized how much Jimmy hated me until Vito died. It's partly jealousy, ever since Vito took me under wing when we were younger; put me through law school. Vito respected me, appreciated the legal work I did for him, the advice I gave him over the years. He always told Jimmy to listen to my advice. When I think of the times that we bailed out that crazy, reckless son-of-a-bitch."

"So," Joe said, yawning, bored with the whole conversation, "what can we do?"

"The mob as a whole is like a monster with many heads. Sometimes, one head chops off another and takes over that operation. Jimmy's done a lot of chopping lately to protect his interests as Vito's death approached. Now is the time to chop the head off the Votilinni organization." He looked at Jack, "Number one, I want total immunity from prosecution. Number two, I want the witness protection program for me and my family." He looked at Joe Ronzoni, "Number three, I want you to eliminate Jimmy, Tosco and Veldon. The FBI can move in and bust the rest of the goddamn organization, lieutenants on down. I'll give you all you need to do that, if you agree to my conditions."

"You're talking about murder, assassination. What makes you think we would even consider such a request?" Joe asked.

"Things Vito told me. You're saying the CIA has never killed enemies of the government or the people before?"

Joe leaned back in his chair, "I'm not saying anything. If we refuse your request, then what?"

"Then I go on working for Jimmy. Help him fight any legal problems as best I can. He might kill me anyway but he'll sure as hell find a way to do it if I talk while he's alive. Even from a goddamn cell on death row." He shot a glance at Jack.

"Then, I'm afraid you'll have to do that as far as I'm concerned. This meeting never took place," Joe said. "Mrs. Stein, would you please escort Mr. McGinnis out?" Sally escorted him through the door and closed it. Joe turned to Jack, "Not a bad idea he has, huh? Of course, we have no interest here, so we can't be involved."

"Yes, well like you said, the meeting never took place," Jack said as he got up to leave.

U.S. Embassy, Copenhagen, Denmark

Nick had selected scuba gear in Odense and arranged to have it delivered to the Anders farm later that day. Then he took a leisurely ride across Fyn and boarded the ferry for Sealland at Knudshoved. On Sealland he rode into Copenhagen. He toured the city and then visited the American embassy. He checked his watch, 4:33 P.M., it was 10:33 A.M. at Langley. He placed a call to Joe Ronzoni on a safe phone.

Joe had just finished his meeting. "Joe here, Nick. How's the trip?"

"Good, I have some interesting results already." He explained the information about the hill and roadbed. "If this is what we think it is it would have taken a lot of men to lay the road bed and dig out that hill. Why isn't there anyone around who remembers some details about this?"

"That's a damned good question," Joe replied. "Investigate, see what you can find out."

"A couple of people I've talked to mentioned a Nazi slave-labor camp over in Jutland near the German border. They imprisoned Danish citizens there, used them for construction and roadwork. It's a museum now. I understand they have the records of the camp's operation there. I'll pay the camp a visit in a few days. See if I can learn anything about the work on the Von Kloussen estate in forty-four. Tomorrow, I'll start diving, see if any evidence of the plane is still there. Probably take a while."

"You say the hill is on this Baron Von Kloussen's land?" Joe asked, as he made notes on a pad on his desk.

"Yeah," Nick said, "he's a first-class prick, too. I bumped into him and another guy out hunting. He asked a few questions, then told me to get the hell off his land."

"That might explain why Chatham got a call asking for you, though they said it sounded like a British accent."

"Could be something else. There's a woman here at the motel, who seems to have taken an unusual interest in me. Checked in the day after I did. Her story is that she's a German schoolteacher from Bremerhaven, on the rebound from a failed love affair. Here for a vacation away from home. Says her name is Gertrude Reinhard."

"She any good looking?" Joe asked slyly as he made notes on the pad in front of him.

"Beautiful, blonde, tan, great bod." Joe was laughing now. Nick continued. "She approached me very directly. Unusual for a European woman, who's not a prostitute and I don't think she is. Hell, they're never this attractive."

"Sounds like this is a topic where you have a lot of knowledge and expertise," Joe said, laughing again.

"She may be working for the Danish authorities, keeping an eye on me."

"Not unless they check on every professor that visits. Only MI-5, the British counter-espionage group in London knows you're there and they wouldn't notify Denmark without telling us."

Changing the subject Nick asked, "Have you spoken with Sally Stein recently?"

"As a matter of fact I have. I expect she'll be in her office in about a half an hour. But, I have new orders for you." Joe said, now laughing harder, "You're to give this Gertrude a complete checkout forthwith." Nick could still hear the laughter as Joe hung up the phone.

Nick waited nearly half an hour, then dialed a safe CIA number in New York. The operator there connected him with FBI headquarters in Washington. Sally had just come into her office when the phone rang. "Inspector Sally Stein speaking," she answered.

"It's Nick. I'm calling from Europe. Have you been considering my offer? I should finish up here in about a week."

"I'd love to come over Nick, but it's impossible."

"Well dear, the offer still stands. Maybe, I can see you when I get back."

"Yes, please call again. It's good to hear from you. Of course, I suppose you can't talk about where you are or what you're doing."

"That's correct."

SEVEN

On the next morning, Thursday, Nick loaded his diving equipment and metal detector into the Anders family sailboat. It was tied at their private dock in the Faborg Fjord, an inlet from the Lillie Baelt waterway between Fyn and the Jutland peninsula. The boat was a wooden twenty-five footer with a center cabin. The old craft was in immaculate condition, the beautiful deck and side rails varnished and polished to a shine. It was a pleasant, almost cloudless day. The bright sun warmed the gentle breeze to seventy-five degrees. The elder Jens Anders started the small, auxiliary diesel engine and Nick untied the boat. They chugged out into the calm waters of the Fjord.

"Shall we sail?" Jens Anders said.

"Fine. Today, I want to survey the area and try my equipment. I'll start my diving search on Saturday."

The old man shut off the diesel and suddenly all was peaceful, the water gently lapping the sides of the boat. Nick helped him unfurl and hoist the fore and aft sails as the older man shouted specific instructions at him. Anders adjusted and lashed the boom on each. He then went to the rear and stood at the wheel, adjusting their course with the rudder. They sailed west following the south shore, out from the fjord out into the Lillie Baelt. Through the woods Nick saw the white church he had visited. Its pointed steeple rose above the sparse forest along the shore. Nick was studying some maps he had purchased. He marked distances on them as they sailed. The easterly breeze pushed them along slowly.

Suddenly, Anders yelled to Nick, "Cecil, get the binoculars please! Below decks stowed under the table in the center." Nick looked up at him and then at the shore. There was a beach. Naked men and women played in the sand and sunned themselves on blankets. Nick retrieved the binoculars and handed them to the grinning old man. He surveyed the beach for a couple of minutes, then handed them back to Nick. Nick adjusted the binoculars as he studied the people. He saw Gertrude Reinhard on a blanket by herself. She wore nothing but a pair of large, dark sunglasses. He adjusted the binoculars and squinted for a clearer view. Only her breasts, and a small strip at her lower abdomen, were a lighter shade than the rest of her tanned body. She rested on her elbows. She seemed to be watching them.

Nick handed the binoculars back, "Let's turn around here. I want to go back into the fjord and inspect the shore."

"Sure and I would say, it's time for a beer," came the reply.

Nick got two beers from below deck and returned to join the old man at the helm. Nick twisted open the beers and handed one to Anders, "Are you sure I'm not inconveniencing you?"

Anders took a long pull on the beer, as he spun the wheel with his other hand to turn the sailboat. "I assure you, there is nothing I would rather be doing than this."

Using only the rudder he tacked against the gentle breeze. They sailed west now, past the white steeple again and past the Anders' property. Nick was surveying the shore with the binoculars. He saw rocky outcrop and the sloping hill behind. Above the hill he caught a glimpse of a tall, bearded man. As Nick focused the binoculars to get a better look the man was gone. He had moved out of sight behind a tree. They sailed to the head of the fjord. There they anchored for an early afternoon lunch of raw eggs, marinated herring and bread, all washed down with beer. As Jens Anders steered the ship east again, Nick began to put on his wet suit. By the time they reached the shore off the Anders' property, Nick had all of the gear on and was ready to dive. They anchored and Nick made a final adjustment of his mask. He checked the diving computer on his wrist. The device would tell him how long he could stay down at various levels and even how soon he could fly afterward without danger of getting decompression sickness.

He perched on the side rail and half fell, half jumped back into the water. The water was tepid, greenish and a little murky. He swam around a bit to get the feel of the equipment. Everything seemed to work well. He switched on the light attached to his headpiece and went deeper, feeling the water grow cool. The floor of the sea was irregular, populated with swaying seaweed and studded with silt-covered rocky ridges. Herring darted about, their shiny scales reflecting his light. He swam some distance toward the shore. There were undersea ravines ten to fifteen feet deep. A fighter plane could have drifted down into one, he surmised. Could it have become hidden in the settling silt, barnacles and growing vegetation over the years? Returning to the boat he swam through a school of transparent jellyfish.   Anders saw him surface ten feet from the boat, holding up one of the jellyfish in his hand. Nick pulled out his mouthpiece and slid up his mask. "See," he yelled, "I caught something here but not what I'm looking for."

At that moment, Eva shut the door behind her in the Baron's office. Kurt Kohfer was seated at the desk. "I saw him on a sailboat today, from the beach," she said.

"Did he see you?"

"Perhaps, he was looking with binoculars."

"I saw him pass the estate on the boat. He was with old Anders."

"There is nothing suspicious. Do I have to return to the motel?"

"You have your orders from the Baron. I was able to pick the lock on the outer perimeter door of Bradshaw's room today and install a bug. It is under the wall desk near the phone. I found nothing unusual in the room. Hopefully I wasn't seen." He handed her a small, black plastic case with an earplug and silver telescopic antenna. "This is the receiver. You should easily be able to pick up the transmission from your own room."

Nick returned to the Tre Roser at ten minutes to six that evening. There was a message at the desk. He read it: "Please contact the Dean. The grant has been denied." This meant he was to call Joe using the scrambler. There was an urgent confidential message. Back in his room he retrieved his attache' case, hidden in the adjoining room. He opened it on the desk and pushed the motel phone handset into the universal modem inside. He put the handset from the case to his ear and keyed in a New York number, using the international direct dial system. He heard a beep and then entered a five character password. The call was switched to Langley. Leslie, Joe Ronzoni's assistant, answered.

It was just before noon EST. Ronzoni was just getting ready to go to lunch. The phone on his desk buzzed. "Yes," he said.

"Hello Dean, calling from Odense," Nick said. "Message?"

"Oh, yeah," Joe said. "I checked on your lady Gertrude Reinhard with German Intelligence. No such person by that name or your description, who teaches school in the Bremerhaven area. Better shoot me a photo and some prints. We'll see if we can find out who she is. Also checked on this damned Baron Von Kloussen. Seems Interpol has been investigating the man. When I mentioned his name to them it hit some hot buttons. Suspicion is that he may be involved in illegal arms shipments with our mysterious Cha-Turgi. Interpol suspects he may have masterminded the Cabal shipment. They're asking the FBI to investigate the origin of all the material loaded on the Cabal at New York. I called the Bureau and asked them to put a priority on it. Both agencies'll keep my office informed. The navy is escorting the Cabal to Charleston Naval Weapons Station in South Carolina. Should arrive in a few days. We'll take everything apart piece by piece, if necessary, to find out where the shit came from. It's just a damned good thing that Garcia and Goldberg were able to keep it from being scuttled."

"This would explain the Baron's suspicious nature," Nick said.

On the other side of the motel, Eva listened to Nick's words on the receiver.

"Be careful and keep me posted," Joe said, "I'll call if anything important breaks." He hung up.

Eva kept the receiver to her ear. She heard nothing more, except the phone handset clicking into its cradle and then, Nick apparently bustling about in the room. Something he was told on the phone would explain the Baron's suspicious nature. Perhaps the Dean at Chatham College had investigated and discovered that it was the Baron who called asking for Bradshaw. But why would they bother? Why would they be discussing the Baron's suspicions? It was unlikely that simple curiosity was involved. It was almost certainly something much deeper. Someone investigating the Baron just as he had suspected. She sat listening for several minutes. She heard the door of Nick's room close. Two minutes later there was a knock at her door. She quickly shut the receiver off and slid it under the bed. She adjusted the front of her bathrobe and opened the door.

Nick Barber stood there. "Might you join me for dinner this evening Fraulein Reinhard?" he asked in German, trying his best to apply a British accent.

Eva feigned surprise at seeing him again, "Oh! Dankashoen." She was genuinely flustered and surprised. She cleared her throat, "Yeah, I would love to go to dinner. If you could wait, uh, I'll have to get ready. I'll meet you in the bar in a half an hour, Professor."

"Fine and please call me Cecil, dear. I must ask a large favor. Do you have a car?"

"Why, yes."

"May we use it? I have only a motorcycle for transportation and I would like to drive to a great restaurant I know on the west coast of Fyn. If it should rain, well."

"Of course, we'll take my car."

She pushed the drape on the glass door aside slightly and watched Nick walk away along the pool. Quickly, she picked up the phone and dialed the Baron's estate office number.

Kurt Kohfer lay in the enormous bed in the master bedroom on the second floor of the castle, staring up at the canopy over the bed. The room was huge, paneled in dark oak with beautiful, baroque Scandinavian carvings of hunters and their quarry in forest scenes. A painted carving of the Von Kloussen arms was mounted above the stone fireplace. The Baroness Von Kloussen lay with Kohfer, asleep after another long lovemaking session. Her head was on his hairy chest and her long, thin arms were locked around his neck. The phone rang. The Baroness came awake and he rolled her aside. He reached through the canopy curtain and fumbled for the phone. He heard a dial tone and the ringing continued. He looked out of the curtain and punched the button on the phone for the office line. "Office of the Baron Von Kloussen," he answered.

"Kurt! I overheard Bradshaw on the receiver. He was speaking to someone he called 'Dean'." She told him what she had heard. "Then he came and asked me to dinner this evening. I'll be joining him in a few minutes."

Kohfer was now standing naked outside of the canopy curtain. He pulled it shut and thought for a moment. "Good, stay with him. Damn, I should have put a bug on his phone instead of under the desk," he muttered as though talking to himself. "I'll have to do it now. We have to be able to listen to both sides of his conversations. How long will you be gone for dinner?"

Probably several hours. We're taking my car to some restaurant he knows on the west coast."

Kohfer's mind raced, "I'll have to get some items together. Make sure he's not at the motel between, ah, nine and ten. Do anything you need to do to stall him."

She said, "I will." She rang off.

Kohfer crawled back into the bed and lay back on the pillows stacked against the massive, ornately-carved, oak headboard. The Baroness crawled up to him and kissed him lightly on the lips. She lay her head on his chest again and began to play with the black, curly hair there with her fingers. "What was that all about, my love?" she asked sleepily.

"Nothing, just business. Arranging some meetings for the right times."

As she began to snooze again, Kohfer thought about the subject that had been constantly on his mind for months. He was planning to murder the Baron. His relationship with the Baroness had grown strong and recently, she had confessed her love for him. He knew divorce was out of the question. But she had told him, speaking hypothetically, that she would marry him if the Baron died. His feelings for her were not particularly deep, but with the Baron out of the way, he could marry her and enjoy the estate, the wealth. She was a sensitive and somewhat frail woman and he knew he couldn't involve her in any murderous scheme.

He had developed several scenarios and gone over and over them in his mind. It would have to look like an accident or possibly a suicide. The Baron liked to hunt small game on his estate often, even out of season. A staged hunting accident was one possibility. But then, any death by gunshot is viewed with suspicion. Also Von Kloussen always used a small-bore rifle or shotgun. It would be difficult to kill him with one shot, unless it was perfectly aimed. A sailing accident was out of the question, since he always had several lads with him on his large sailing boat. Kohfer had considered various household accident schemes, but suspicion would certainly fall on him as estate manager and bodyguard. He realized that the servants, and even the Baron himself, had suspicions about his relationship with the Baroness. But then, what the hell, Kohfer thought, everyone knows he's screwing Eva. Men like Von Kloussen always have a mistress. So far, a staged one car accident somewhere away from the estate seemed best. But best of all would be, if someone else killed the man or at least put him away for a long time in some foreign prison. Kohfer knew from bits and pieces of conversations he had picked up, that the Baron and Rashidii were involved in illegal business dealings; he just didn't know specifically what. Certainly the Baron sent Kohfer on errands often enough. Errands that required him to commit minor crimes such as the eavesdropping he was doing now. Perhaps this Bradshaw really represented some authority. Or better yet, a rival criminal investigating the Baron. Kurt Kohfer needed to learn more for his own purposes.

He realized he had better get to the evening's work. He crawled out of the bed and closed the curtain again. As he began to get dressed, he reviewed the conversation with Eva in his thoughts. Then, abruptly something she had said flashed in his mind: "we're taking my car." She had taken the Volkswagen Rabbit. Of course, it wasn't her car, it was one of the Baron's, registered in his name. It would be a simple matter to get the license number and connect Eva with Von Kloussen. Damn! How foolish they had been, he thought, as he picked up the handset and punched in the number of the Tre Roser. They should have rented her a car! The phone in Eva's room rang fifteen times. No one answered. He hung up and called the motel clerk. He said the lady had left with another guest several minutes earlier.

* * *

At that moment it was just past 11:30 A.M. in Chicago. On the second floor of an empty warehouse on the west side, George Noska stared into the screen of the notebook computer on the desk in front of him. He had three more diskettes to copy and the job he had been working on for several months would be finished. He didn't relish working for these people, but it was the only paying job he could get. At age thirty-nine, Noska was five-foot-three and balding with dark, unsympathetic brown eyes and a nose shaped like an old potato. It was red with crater-like pores from years of heavy drinking. He let his thinning, light-brown hair grow long on the left side of his head and combed it over his nearly bald pate. He was an intelligent but despondent man, given to fits of anger. Clinically, he might have been described as having a sociopathic personality disorder with a napoleonic complex and a definite criminal inclination. He finished making the last diskette copy. Then he turned off the computer and walked to the office behind him. He knocked and opened the door.

Leaning against the wall next to the desk was Elmer "Ellie Winks" Veldon. He was a tall, thin wiry man, freckle-faced, with curly, red hair and a long, pointed nose. His small, narrow blue eyes had a perpetual squint that gave him the look of a sly, evil fox. The nickname came from a nervous twitch of his eyelids, that made it appear as though he was often winking. Veldon was in charge of all of the gambling operations for the Votilinni organization.

Anthony "Tough Tony" Tosco sat behind the desk. A heavyset man in his mid-forties with greasy black hair and sagging jowls. He ran The Black Olive restaurant and, through several lieutenants, all drug, extortion, hijacking and other assorted operations for Votilinni. He was giggling into a cellular phone that was cradled in his meaty hand as he waved Noska in. He clicked the phone off and set it down, "You fuckin' little bald-headed butt-lick. You finally done?" he said.

Noska nodded nervously, "These are four copies of the diskette to unscramble the databases. You can't do it without'em, so keep'em in safe places. Just like I went over with you guys and your people. If there's a problem your people just invoke the keyword, type a 'y' to the question 'are you sure?' and within ten seconds, all of your client and gambling event records are scrambled. The scrambling program eliminates the fuckin' keyword from the database then purges itself. No goddamn evidence, nothin'. When the scrambling is fuckin' complete, a spreadsheet from your legitimate warehouse rental business is brought up on the screen. Any of these diskettes will reverse the procedure and unscramble your data, then restore the scrambling program and a new keyword."

"An' nobody can read the fucker when it's scrambled?" Tosco asked.

"Nobody, well, I spose' the CIA or somebody might have a big enough computer to unscramble it. I dunno. If you got a problem, call me."

Tosco tossed a wad of soiled bills down in front of Noska. The final payment. "If I gotta goddamn problem I sure to fuck won't call you," Tosco said. "But dese goddamn computers better work da way you say or I'll have your fuckin' nuts tacked up onna wall ova' dere." He bellowed with laughter at his own crude attempt at humor as he pointed to the wall with a thumb as big around as a bratwurst.

Veldon reached over and picked up the diskettes. He put them in his suitcoat pocket.

George Noska picked up the wad of money. It was supposed to be five thousand in small bills. Afraid to count the money in their presence, he shoved it into his jacket pocket.

Outside in the alley, Noska climbed onto his Harley Davidson Sportster and started the machine. He needed the five thousand since he had spent the last of his prior earnings from the project on the bike and accessories. He also needed a job now. He picked up a copy of the Chicago Tribune on the way home to check the want ads.

* * *

Nick and Eva were on Highway E66 traveling toward the west coast of Fyn. Nick had noted the oval DK sticker and license number of the Rabbit, as soon as they approached the car at the motel. He had made small talk as he drove along the highway. They spoke in German. Finally he asked, "How do you happen to have a Danish car?"

She became flustered at the question. He noticed her tan cheeks take on a rosy hue. She thought quickly, then said, "I-I have a cousin here on Fyn. He has allowed me the use of one of his cars during my stay."

"How very kind of him," Nick said as he thought about her reference to two cars. He knew it was unusual for a Danish household to have more than one car. Therefore, her cousin must be well-to-do, he mused and tucked that factoid into his memory.

He took the exit ramp at Avlby and drove south toward Gamborg.

They drove through the small city and as they approached the waters of Gamborg Fjord, he turned in a drive. The sign at the entrance said Gamborg Kro. The restaurant was a large, white stucco building with a thatched roof. It was nestled in a wooded cove. From behind the restaurant there was a view of the Fjord. Inside, Eva and Nick were seated next to a window at the back of the building. They had a view of the calm waters. The waiter was wearing a tuxedo and had a white towel draped over his arm. He handed them menus with soft, leather-bound covers.

"Oh, the prices!" Eva exclaimed, trying to sound prosaic. Actually, cash had never been a problem since she had been with the Baron.

"My Danish friends tell me that only those who have too much money dine here. But, as a single man I have little else to spend my money on, so order whatever you like, my dear."

They discussed the menu and when the waiter returned, Nick ordered in Danish: "Vinbjergsnegle (snails) and flodelegeret aspargessuppe (cream of asparagus soup with meatballs) for each of us to start. The lady would like the Engelsk Boeuf an I will have the Fiske symfoni med sauce vin blanc smagt til med sennep (Fish symphony with wine sauce and mustard). He then ordered the wine.

Kurt Kohfer parked two blocks from the Tre Roser. He had procured the transmitter he wanted. He walked around the corner of the motel to the south side. Seeing no one in the immediate vicinity, he went into an outdoor walkway between two rooms. Nick Barber's room was on the end to the east. The view from the pool was blocked by a small, concrete block privacy wall. Across the walkway from Nick's room was an entrance to showers for swimmers. On the outside wall of his room were utility boxes. Kohfer examined them. The largest one was obviously for electricity. Next to it was a long, narrow box for the telephone lines. It had a security seal made of a loop of copper wire that was sealed with lead.

Kohfer pried the wire out of the lead and opened the box. The room number was clearly marked next to each two-terminal set. He loosened the copper nuts on the terminals for room twenty-eight. He took the black transmitter from his pocket and connected the wires. He bent a knockout plug on the side of the box and threaded the antenna through. He taped it to the side of the building next to the box. Then he switched on the transmitter, closed the box and clamped the seal back in place. The batteries should be good for several days, he was thinking.

At the Gamborg Kro, Eva and Nick had finished their meals. She had left the table to powder her nose. Satisfied she was out-of-sight he picked up her wine glass by the stem. He took a three-inch-wide strip of paper from his pocket and peeled off a plastic backing. In his lap he wrapped the paper around the glass, held it for a moment. The paper was chemically treated to pick up fingerprints. He took the paper off and replaced the backing. In his shirt pocket was a camera disguised as a pen. The tiny lens was set in a round, silver frame at the top of the pocket clip. It looked like polished, decorative stone. When he twisted the barrel into position, the pen took a photo each time the button at the top was clicked.

Eva returned and sat down just as the waiter brought the check. Nick handed him a credit card and he walked away. "I was thinking," Nick said, "I'm going out on the boat diving again tomorrow. I'll be searching for the American plane I told you about. Perhaps you'd like to join me." Nick had decided it was better to keep her in sight as much as possible while she was being investigated.

Surprised at the invitation, she thought for a moment, then said, "Yes of course, Cecil. I'd love to."

The waiter returned with the receipt for Nick's signature. Nick took out his pen and, aiming the lens at Eva, clicked it. He started to write, then lifted the pen and clicked it a couple more times, then shook the pen. "Trouble with the pen," he said. He signed his name and then stood up. As he stepped over to help Eva out of her chair, he clicked the pen and slipped it back in his pocket. He now had a profile view.

As Nick started the car, Eva checked her watch. It was just after 9:00 P.M. If she didn't delay their trip back to the motel, they might arrive before ten. She liked this man. She was curious about him. The Baron had given her the go-ahead to be as intimate as necessary, she remembered. She reached over and grabbed him around the neck with her left arm and kissed him full on the mouth. Nick put his arms around her and hugged, lifting her body out of the passenger's seat. Her shapely body was light and firm. He caressed her back and shoulders. She pulled her lips away. "Why don't we go down to the beach for a while?" she suggested, nodding toward the expanse of beach below. "I have a blanket in the back. We're not in a hurry are we?"

To Nick, she smelled like a spring flower and her red lips tasted like strawberries. Her offer was too tempting to resist. Besides, he chuckled to himself, my boss has ordered me to check her out thoroughly. In a minute they were walking from the restaurant parking lot down to the beach below. The air was a bit cool and Nick helped her adjust the blanket over her shoulders as they walked. Lights from sailboats dotted the harbor in the distance. They walked along the beach to a secluded spot, near some trees some distance southeast of the restaurant. They lay on the blanket. Eva removed her clothes and Nick his. They embraced. Then Eva broke away and, laughing loudly, sprinted across the beach into the water. Nick followed, splashing and rolling in sea water that seemed warm in comparison to the cool air. Eva swam out to deeper water and Nick followed, lunging after her and tackling her naked body among some reeds in four feet of water. Nick bent his knees and put his hands at her waist, pulling her toward him. Eva let herself float toward him, her legs apart, straddling his thighs. Her lithe body, buoyant in the salt water, moved as easily as a toy balloon in air. Her large breasts bobbed at the surface of the water, white and shimmering in the moonlight as they undulated with the waves. As he caressed her back and buttocks he pulled first one erect nipple into his mouth then the other, biting each lightly with his lips stretched over his teeth. Nick realized he was being overcome with sexual desire for this beautiful woman. Eva put her hands at the back of his neck and pulled his mouth up to hers, her tongue stabbing inside. The water lubricated their skin and she slid easily toward him along his thighs. Each felt the warmth as their bodies touched and slipped against each other in the water. In full embrace she wiggled trying to position herself on him. The end of his erection found the mouth of her vagina. He entered her, slowly at first, then thrusting fully as her eager body came into rhythm with his, sending a pulsating wave across the moonlit water.

Later, they lay on the blanket. They made love again in the twilight of the late evening, between the forest and the sea. Nick looked down at Eva then buried his face in her breasts. "For God and country," he murmured to himself sardonically in English.

"What?" she asked.

"I said God, that was good!" He said in German. He looked around and then smiled at her, "I wonder what the penalty is for sex on a public beach in Denmark."

Eva smiled and reached out to him, laughing, "I wouldn't know, but no matter what it is it would be worth it."

She tightened her arms around his neck and they kissed in a naked embrace.

* * *

On Friday, Nick made the trip into Copenhagen again and went to the U.S. Embassy. There he sealed the film and fingerprint paper in a top secret, diplomatic pouch addressed to Joe Ronzoni at Langley. Then he made a call to the Danish Bureau of Motor Transportation. To avoid an official inquiry, he told them he was a service station employee. He said he had gotten the license number, but couldn't read the name of a customer for a credit purchase. Could they please help. They gave him the name of the owner of the vehicle: Baron Soren Ingemann Von Kloussen.

By 3:00 Saturday afternoon, the Anders' sailboat was anchored in Faborg Fjord. Eva lay on the deck sunning herself in the skimpiest conceivable black thong bikini. She was on her stomach, the back tie undone and her breasts resting in the bra cups on the deck. Her bare back, buttocks and legs soaked up the sun's rays. The elder Anders sat in the rear enjoying the view, a beer in his hand. Below the surface, Nick swam about hovering the metal detector over the rocky sea bottom. The water was dark and murky and his light was not sufficient for an adequate search. He swam in and out of deep, dark ravines and over muddy areas, where patches of seaweed swayed gently in the current. With his spade he dug a bit when the tone and LED on the scope came on. He had started near the shore at the rocky outcrop and then worked his way east toward the church. He had found nothing of interest so far. He knew the detectors didn't necessarily work as well under water. But certainly, he thought, he should be able to find a wing, fuselage or whole airplane if it was there.

A mile away at the castle, the Baroness sat on Kurt Kohfer's lap in the Baron's leather executive chair. The drapes were drawn. He grabbed her thigh under the sleek, white dress she was wearing. They both giggled. The phone on the desk rang. The Baroness jumped up, still giggling. Kohfer reached for the phone. "Be quiet," he said to her. He picked it up.

It was the Baron. He was calling from a pay phone in New York, so the call wouldn't be traceable to his hotel suite. "Kurt, any news?"

"Well, the man Cecil Bradshaw definitely has an interest in you." He explained the words Eva had overheard and the eavesdropping.

The Baron was upset, "You goddamned idiot, you should have bugged his phone in the first place. Now I want to find out who he is as quickly as possible. No mistakes. He could be a foreign agent, possibly an American for God's sake. Get some photos of him and some fingerprints. In the address file on my computer, there is a phone number for a place on Rue de Hyeres in Marseille. Call the number there and tell them you are representing me and will be bringing information for identification. Someone should arrange to meet you. Take the photos and prints there personally. Be prepared to pay at least ten thousand kroners for their services."

"Yes, sir. Where are you calling from?" Kohfer asked, hoping to get some information on the Baron's activities.

"That doesn't concern you. Just do as you're told. I will call again in a few days." He hung up.

Eva called Kohfer that evening and he explained the Baron's directive. Later, she talked to Nick and invited him to accompany her on a sightseeing trip the next day. He agreed to go. The next morning they walked to her car at the time they had agreed upon. Kurt Kohfer watched from across the street, through the trees that studded the lawn, on the south side of the motel. He took some photos of Nick with a telescopic lens. All day, as they toured the island of Fyn, Eva noted objects in the car Nick handled and touched. She was careful not to touch them herself. From those items Kohfer could pick up his prints later.

EIGHT

On Monday, Nick rode to Copenhagen again. There he was able to purchase a much more powerful underwater light to aid in his search. In the afternoon he visited the Embassy and placed a call to Joe Ronzoni.

"Joe here," he answered.

Nick identified himself, "No plane yet. I'll keep searching, it's a big fjord."

"Oh, the woman. According to German Intelligence, the prints match a woman whose name is, or was, E. S. Van Damme. She was picked up in Germany a few times in her late teens and early twenties for questioning about Neo-Nazi activities. She was a card-carrying member of the National Socialists back then. The stuff's ten years old. Her name hasn't come up in any investigations of the party in more recent years as they became more open and violent. They're still investigating further to see if she's been using the name Gertrude Reinhard."

"A Nazi? I've been over here consorting with a damn Nazi?" Nick chuckled a bit. "Well, I suppose she could have changed her name to break with her past."

"Yeah that's possible. Consorting? What do you mean consorting? I think I should get a full report on this." Joe laughed.

"It's not only the different names. She dyes her hair. She's a natural blonde and she dyes the hair on her head brown."

"So what? Lots of women dye their hair."

"It's not so common over here. Especially if you're blonde to begin with."

"How do you know she's a natural blonde anyway?" Joe said, ending the sentence with a sly snicker.

"Close and careful investigation," came Nick's reply as he chuckled a bit. "My instinct tells me something is wrong here. She's going to some trouble to disguise herself."

"Well, then why don't you just penetrate this disguise?" Joe was guffawing now. "As deeply as you can." He spoke between bursts of laughter, "Pierce the veil, so to speak."

When Joe's laughter finally died down Nick said, "There's more. She's connected with Von Kloussen somehow. She's using his car. Claims it's borrowed from a cousin. She hasn't said so but maybe the Baron is her cousin."

Joe's voice became serious now, "Or maybe one of his servants is."

"Hell, I suppose I'd better just ask her. I will when the time is right."

"I don't like the goddamn smell of this somehow. I'm still waiting for more dope on Von Kloussen. I don't think your evidence is worth shit, Nick, but I do trust your instincts. You'd better come back in a few days if you don't find anything. And be goddamn careful." He hung up.

Nick stayed in Copenhagen at the King Frederick that night and returned to Odense on Tuesday. He resumed the search on Wednesday and again on Thursday with Eva along both days. By mid-morning on Thursday, they had gone east beyond the white church with no results. Nick decided to start over again searching close to the shore. Anders guided the boat back to the rocky outcrop under diesel power and anchored.

Nick dove again, this time he searched only fifteen to twenty feet from the shore. In shallow water, he swam slowly over a deep, dark ravine. He had attached the powerful light to the handle of the searchcoil. He heard the tone and the LED on the unit flashed. He kicked himself around with his swimfins. He swam deeper and hovered the searchcoil over the spot again. The tone sounded loudly in the earphones. He adjusted the discrimination knob and kicked himself down into the ravine the searchlight guiding the way. The walls of the ravine, seemed to slope together at the bottom forming a "V" shape. There was some outline on the south wall near the bottom. He shined the searchlight along the edge. It looked like an airplane fuselage! The outline was clear. Covered with mud, detritus and barnacles, but almost certainly a P-51 Mustang. The wings and most of the tail were gone, torn away by the buffeting of the wave motion during many years. He hadn't imagined it would be this close to shore. He swam down and examined the cockpit. The canopy was gone. Barnacles had long since taken up residence inside. He turned and kicked himself back to examine the tail. With his spade he dug silt and mud from under the left tailplane. He clipped the spade to his belt and unclipped his pliers. He clamped them on the serial number plate. It pulled off easily, breaking the corroded aluminum skin of the plane at the rivets.

Back on the sailboat he informed Jens and Eva of his find.

The Black Olive Restaurant Building, Chicago

That same day, James "Diamond Jimmy" Votilinni, the new Don, had summoned Mac McGinnis to his office for a 3:00 P.M. meeting. Votilinni had not spoken to Mac in the several days since Mac had returned from Washington. Mac's office was just across from Votilinni's on the second floor. They had passed several times in the halls and saw each other in the restaurant and bar below. Votilinni had not acknowledged his greetings. Mac knocked on the oak-paneled door. From inside he heard Votilinni say loudly, "The fuckin' door's open." Mac entered and with a jerk of his head, the Don sent Gary, his bodyguard, out. The short, heavyset blonde man left, closing the door behind him.

The large office was at the corner of the building. It was still exquisitely furnished in 1930's decor as Vito Votilinni had kept it. Several large windows set in dark, baroque wooden frames hung with flowered drapes, looked out onto the front and side streets. The walls were paneled with dark mahogany and near the corner, set between two windows was a large fireplace. The perimeter of the firebox and the floor in front were done in white ceramic tiles decorated with brightly colored flowers. The mantle and facing were of beautifully carved wood. Large potted ferns surrounded the room and a potted palm tree stood in the corner. The carpet was brown with a floral pattern.

At the end of the room, Diamond Jimmy Votilinni leaned back in his grandfather's antique leather chair. His feet were up on the huge, polished oak desk. He glared at Mac with a look that could kill. "Sit down, motherfucker," he said in an angry, sarcastic tone.

Mac sat on one of the guest chairs in front of the desk. A shiver of terror shot up the big man's spine and a bead of sweat appeared at his hairline. "You wanted to see me, Jimmy?"

Votilinni continued to stare at him for several moments. Mac had seen that look on the man's face before. When he was about to murder someone or had just finished. Finally, the Don spoke, "I wanta' know what in the fuck you're doin' at the goddamn Fed's office in Washington?"

Mac suspected he was being tailed. He decided to play it tough. "Tryin' to save your ass as usual."

Votilinni raised his eyebrows, "Whatta' you fuckin' talkin' about?"

"Indictments, Jimmy. I been tryin' to tell you for months. You gotta believe me now. They're gonna issue warrants for you and probably Veldon and Tosco. Maybe within a week or two. They wanted me to talk, you know, but I told'em to go fuck themselves." Mac's story was pretty much the truth as far as it went.

"If you're fuckin' lyin', they'll find you at the bottom of the Chicago River with your goddamn dick stuffed in your cocksuckin' mouth."

Mac knew this was no idle threat and the fear shot through him again. Jimmy had been extremely angry at Mac in the past, but had never before directly threatened his life. "Whatta you bustin' my balls for, Jimmy? I'm just tryin' to advise you. You oughta' get out of the country and soon, just like I been tellin' you all along."

"And if I fuckin' don't?"

"In my opinion, they've got enough shit on you to lock you up for life. Actually, there's a possibility of the death penalty. I think that's what they're shootin' for."

"That goddamn bitch Sally Warbrasac is in this, isn't she?"

"Yeah, she's involved in the investigation."

"I just about fuckin' had it with that nosy cunt. I oughta' hang her up on a goddamn meat-hook."

"Christ man, she's an FBI Chief Inspector. She's untouchable."

Votilinni stared at Mac, "Bullshit. No...fuckin'...body's untouchable. They kill goddamn presidents, don't they?"

Chicago Marriott O'Hare Hotel, 5:10 P.M.

Baron Von Kloussen walked toward the elevator carrying his suitcase. He had taken an afternoon flight from New York. His hair was now dark brown and he wore brown contact lenses. He sported a dark mustache. The first replies to the ads had come on the prior Friday. On Monday, both he and Rashidii had set up interviews in their hotel suites, in New York and Chicago, respectively. From Tuesday through noon Thursday, Von Kloussen had interviewed eighty-one people from four hundred and twenty-two responses. Rashidii had interviewed sixty-eight of three hundred and twelve. They had worked long days and kept up a hectic schedule. They each allowed fifteen to twenty minutes for each interview and a few minutes afterward to analyze their notes. They had discussions late each night about the candidates. By Wednesday night Rashidii had convinced him that he had the best applicants; or perhaps the worst, in this case.

That day, Rashidii had moved from the Ramada O'Hare suite, where he had done the interviews, to the suite at the Marriott. Von Kloussen entered Rashidii's suite. There was a living and dining area with two separate bedrooms. On the dining room table, Rashidii had laid open a packet on each of three men he had interviewed. In each was a color photo he had taken of the man, a resume and letter from the applicant. Each also contained Rashidii's notes from the interview and reference contacts. The Baron placed his reading glasses on his nose and studied the material for some time, reviewing each carefully. Finally, he said, "This Noska, Viet Nam veteran, no close family ties, worked in several airline jobs, knows computers. He has a police record and most important, was fired from States Airlines six months ago."

"Yes, his former boss told me, 'off the record', that computers and other equipment were missing on his shift. They could never prove anything, but he was the prime suspect. I called Noska and questioned him some more. It's my opinion that he still holds a grudge against them, wants revenge."

"Good."

Rashidii looked over Von Kloussen's shoulder at his own notes. "I called some other former bosses and got other names from them. Fifteen years ago, Noska shot an acquaintance in the shoulder at point blank range with a .38 caliber pistol. He was arrested, but the other man refused to press charges saying it was an accident. The police didn't believe it but the charges were dropped. He had some drug possession charges about that time also. Two years later, Noska was arrested on theft of electronic equipment and other merchandise from stores. He was sentenced to three years, spent two in the Illinois State Prison system. He managed to cover all this up when he interviewed for several of these jobs. Of course now they do more thorough background checks. Some of this came from inquiries after he was employed. Some came from people I got ahold of that knew him in years past."

Von Kloussen looked at the resume. The jobs were listed in reverse chronological order:

Jun 1992-Jan 1994 U.S Airlines. Supplies   Loading
    Specialist, Baggage Handler
Aug 1990-Jun 1992 Overnight Express Airlines.
    Shipping Clerk.
Oct 1987-Jan 1990 International Airlines.   Baggage
    Handler, Shuttle Driver...

Rashidii interrupted Von Kloussen's reading, "He apparently had some kind of trouble on all of the jobs, but not enough to prevent him from being hired on the next. Disputes with other employees, that sort of thing. Says he used the computer system at States Airlines extensively. He claims he took up personal computers as a hobby a few years ago and has been free-lancing; setting up computer networks for small companies since January. He seems intelligent enough. Somewhat unkempt though. I've met people with better personal hygiene."

The Baron looked at Rashidii over his reading glasses. "I think it's time you paid a personal unannounced visit to Mr. Noska."

"Now?"

"Now."

One half hour later, Arun Rashidii was on Interstate 90 in a rented black Toyota Corolla. Across the median the late afternoon traffic was heavy coming out of Chicago, but he had an easy drive going toward the city. He took the Irving Park Road exit, made a left at the stoplight and then turned north on Pulaski Road. He drove four blocks and there, he saw the two story apartment building to his left on the northwest corner. It was a large, old wood-frame building. The exterior was covered with gray tar paper made to look like shingles. In the first floor corner facing Pulaski was a small beauty salon. The sign in the front window proclaimed the shop's name in pink neon cursive, "The Magic Touch". The rest of the building appeared to be apartments. He made a left turn onto Elmond Street and found a metered, parking place on the street a block down. He walked back to the building carrying a large black attache' case. He tried the building's corner door on Elmond. It was open. There was a first floor hall to the right and in front of him a long, steep stairway, each gray wooden runner concave from years of unmaintained use. He was looking for 205. The stairs creaked as he went up. At the top he was faced with a long, stench-filled, wainscotted hallway. The floor was as curved and twisted as a fun-house mirror. He passed old discarded furniture, piles of dirty rags, newspapers and other debris as he walked. He passed numbers 217 and 215, then the hall turned right for another long run. Finally, after another right turn he saw 205 on the left. It was in the front of the building on the Pulaski Road side.

He could hear a television behind the large old wooden door. He knocked hard twice. No answer. Again he knocked and there was a stirring inside. "Who is it?" Noska said from inside, his voice barely audible.

"Grant Hopper, Expert Air Transport. I want to talk to you about the job some more. Looks good for you," he added loudly.

The door scraped against the old, worn hardwood floor with squawks and thuds as Noska pulled it open. He looked at Rashidii with rheumy eyes, then he motioned the man in. Rashidii was shocked as he stepped inside. The air was heavy with the smell of urine, stale sweat and rotting food. Crumpled balls of paper and crushed aluminum beer cans were strewn everywhere. There were piles of clothes and cardboard boxes, stacked along the walls and spilling into the center of the room. In front of him was an old beat-up coffee table with a television set on one end. Behind that under a set of windows was an old worn couch. There was an end table next to it and a battered, easy chair in the corner. The shades were drawn letting in only narrow planes of sunlight along their edges. The television was on, casting a glow back toward the chair. In a small room off to the right, there was a similar glow. A heavy layer of grime and dust was everywhere. As Rashidii walked in, his steps kicked up loose dirt and balls of dust from the floor. This set off a chain reaction that caused dust particles to dance and float in the glow of the television and in the planes of sunlight.

Noska motioned him in. Rashidii stepped in and scanned the front room. He stepped over to the doorway of the only other room, a tiny kitchen. He stepped in and looked around. On a small table in the center was a relatively new personal computer. It was the only somewhat clean object in the entire apartment. Its screen cast an eerie glow in the airborne dust. He checked a closet door, boxes of junk. Noska frowned as he did this but said nothing. When Rashidii came back into the front room, Noska motioned him around the coffee table to the couch and invited him to sit. Examining the couch, Rashidii brushed some dust off the end near the easy chair. He sat down, perching on the edge to minimize the soil his pants might pick up. He set the case down next to him. On the floor he noticed an upended cardboard beer case, nearly full of cans. It was next to the chair within easy reach its occupant. On the end table, was an open bottle of Southern Comfort whiskey and a tumbler, also in easy reach. Next to the tumbler was a large ash tray mounded over with so many cigarette butts they spilled onto a halo of ashes on the table.

"Drink?" Noska offered as he reached into the case. He was unhappy that the man had come. He knew, full well, that his living quarters would make the worst possible impression on a prospective employer.

"No, thank you," Rashidii said. He was doing his best to hide his accent as he had done all week during the interviews.

"Look, I know my place is less than exe-empla-rary," Noska said, garbling the last word. He popped the top of the beer can. "I was just gettin' ready to clean it up when you came," he added sardonically. Noska had lived there less than two months and it was already a terrible mess. He had been forced to vacate a rooming house, several miles south on Pulaski, that the city had belatedly condemned and was now tearing down.

"I have no concern of this. Are you still interested in our opportunity?"

"Yeah, sure," Noska said, surprised.

"We are alone?"

Noska frowned, "Yeah."

Rashidii decided to be direct. "It pays one-half million dollars."

Noska sat forward abruptly. "Huh? What the hell do you want me to do?"

"Only one thing. Place a package on a passenger airliner bound for Europe." Rashidii's hand was inside his coat feeling the butt of his pistol; he was ready for any reaction.

Noska sat open-mouthed for a moment, then fumbled out a cigarette and nervously lit it. He blew out a stream of smoke forcing airborne dust particles into swirls and eddies. He took a gulp of the whiskey, chased it with a long pull on the beer, sat back and smiled, baring a row of decaying teeth. "I suppose nobody's supposed to know about it either, right?" Rashidii nodded. "A bomb?"

"You need not ever concern yourself about the contents."

"What airliner?"

Rashidii relaxed. "That's up to you."

The ugly smile became even broader now. "How and when?"

"That's part of the job. We, I want you to figure out a way. Give me a proposal."

Noska thought for a few moments. "I might be able to get into the AOA, that is, airport operations area and put it in luggage. But, the goddamn security is tight, they use thermal neutron analysis machines on the baggage now. Some kind of particle bombardment. It can detect the nitrogen in explosives."

"Do they use the TNA on supplies before they're loaded?"

"No."

"Good, I was thinking that might be the place to put it. Are you willing to consider this?"

Noska thought for a moment. This was crazy, but the money was tempting...and so was the prospect of revenge. "The money, what're yer fuckin' terms?" His tongue was getting thick from the alcohol now.

Rashidii opened the brief case and brought out a wad of bills, held together with a heavy rubber band around it and put it on the coffee table. "Twenty thousand now, if you agree to work with us. One hundred thousand when the plan is set and the rest when the job is done. Also, you'll have to disappear for a while, take up residence in another state. I'll supply you with all of the false papers you need. One identity for travel and another for your new residence."

Noska greedily eyed the bills. He had paid off gambling debts and then placed more bets. He had bought a newer car. Nearly all of the five thousand he received less than a week ago for working Tough Tony Tosco was gone. He looked at Rashidii. "Yeah, I'll fuckin' figger out a way."

"Good. Then we'll have to do a couple of things now." He pulled several wigs and fake mustaches from his brief case. After trying several Noska selected a black set and a blonde set. Rashidii took out a camera and first took a photo of Noska wearing the blonde set. Then he darkened Noska's eyebrows with an ebony-black, cosmetic pencil and took a picture with the black set. "Any preference as to the state?"

"California. I always wanted to live in California," Noska said, slurring the words.

"I'll reserve a room in some motel that rents by the week in the L.A. area. That'll be your address on the papers. Let people know you're moving away. Tell them New York or something."

This wasn't much of a problem. Noska knew none of the tenants in his own building. The landlord, whom he had met once to pay three month's rent in advance when he moved in, lived out in the suburbs. He was acquainted with perhaps only four or five people in the neighborhood, from his visits to a small restaurant across the street and a couple of taverns. He kept to himself mostly and they knew little about him.

"You sons-of-a-bitches think of everything, don't you?" Noska said, the tone of his voice rising with a hint of drunken belligerence.

Rashidii ignored the remark and continued. "Now, one more thing. I need to be able to contact you at all times. Do you have an answering machine?"

"Used to. It went to hell. I just got the phone. It's on the modem in the kitchen."

Rashidii took a large, plain cardboard box from his case. "I'll give you this one to use."

They went into the kitchen. Rashidii unplugged the wall cord and the modem from the phone and plugged the large, black combination phone/answering machine from the box in it's place. "Now you'll always get my messages. I won't leave a name. You'll know when it's me. I'll be back tomorrow afternoon with the false papers. Meanwhile, figure out how you're going to do this."

Rashidii walked back to his car. He drove back on Elmond Street and crossed Pulaski Road. He turned around again and pulled up to the corner across from the apartment house and parked. The sun was now below the buildings across the street. Dusk was enveloping the city. He checked his watch, it was 8:30 P.M. He plugged the portable telephone handset into the receiver on the floor of the car. He switched it on and adjusted the volume. The unit he had hooked up in Noska's apartment was much more than what it appeared to be. It had two long-playing tapes in the bottom and a microphone that activated at a preset decibel level. It would record all sounds in the apartment, if the detected decibel measurement was at or above the preset level. It would also record any phone conversations or digital data communications directly. It transmitted all of this, so that Rashidii could eavesdrop, anytime he was within range. Baron Von Kloussen and Rashidii wouldn't trust Noska at all, not until he was further investigated.

He adjusted the microphone decibel control down slowly so that it would pick up fainter and fainter sounds. Suddenly, the sound came on in his phone. He could hear Noska moving about in the apartment. He sat there for over an hour, as the shadows of night began to fall across the city. Then, he saw the door open just north of "The Magic Touch" Beauty Salon. Noska came out and walked north on Pulaski. After Noska had walked a block, Rashidii started the car and turned right on Pulaski, hugging the curb, following slowly. Noska turned left at the end of the second block onto Monreal Avenue. As Rashidii cruised slowly by, he saw the man turn into the entrance of the B&B Tavern. This was a small, wood-frame building, three hundred feet off Pulaski just past a large, brick building on the corner. Rashidii turned around and turned onto Monreal street. There was a small, apartment house parking lot, elevated by several feet, across from the B&B. He pulled in and parked at the rail, facing the tavern door directly across the street. From this vantage point, he could see Noska at the bar a few stools from the open door.

"Wanda, you goddamn fat ass," Noska growled drunkenly, "I want some service down here!" He banged an aluminum ashtray on the bar.

Down the bar, a heavy, bleached-blonde thirtyish woman turned from some other customers and yelled, "How about ya' gimmie a fuckin' minute, huh Noska?"

When she came down, he said, "Comfort and a beer." He looked her over. Under her soiled, pink blouse one large breast stuck straight out, the other sagged to her stomach. Frumpy green stretch pants covered her lumpy, misshapen buttocks and as she turned to serve him, he looked at the black, hairy mole next to her mouth. He laughed.

"What's so goddamn funny," She said as she put the drinks in front of him.

"You."

"Fuck you."

"How'ed you like to fuck me tonight?" He flipped a quarter on the bar.

"You're so goddamn funny I forgot to laugh."

He then pulled a wad of bills out and counted ten hundreds onto the bar. "How about for a grand then?"

Her eyes widened with greed at the sight of the money. Then she said, "I ain't sleepin' with no goddamn dirty, diseased rat. Not for no amount a' money." Another set of eyes staring from down the bar was also on the pile of money. She took one of the hundreds and made change.

Three hours later, Noska was barely able to keep his eyes open. The other customers had gone. Wanda came over and said, "Closen' up. Get your ass out." Noska looked at her through the slits his eyes had become. "Com'on or I'll have Denny stuff you inna' garbage can out back again. 'Course maybe you like sleepin' with them goddamn rotten fish scraps." He managed to get off the stool and then lurch toward the door. As he began to stagger down the street toward Pulaski, Wanda slammed the door and locked it.

A man, wearing dark clothing, stepped out of the alley next to the building, as Noska approached it. Rashidii had watched the man come out of the building and mull about the area. He suspected the man had seen Noska flash cash around and was waiting for him. Rashidii reached up and removed the dome light bulb. His stiletto was already in his hand. He pushed the button and the thin, razor-sharp blade snapped out. He silently crawled out of the car, letting the door come to rest on the latch. The man stepped out of the darkness of the alley between the B&B and the brick building. He leaned against the corner of the building. Noska, oblivious to his presence, staggered slowly by.

Rashidii crouched unseen in the shadow of his car. The man poked his head out of the shadows and looked about the area. There was a tavern up the street a half-block further from Pulaski. Light poured out of the front door of the tavern into the street. Loud country and western music could be heard from the door, but no one was about. Apparently satisfied he wasn't being watched, the man fell in directly behind Noska. As soon as the man's attention turned to Noska, Rashidii was crossing the street. Covered by the music and traffic noise from Pulaski, he crept up quickly behind the would be mugger. In the man's right hand Rashidii noticed the glint of a knife. He moved swiftly and without hesitation. He brought the stiletto in his left hand up over the taller man's left shoulder. He drove the thin blade into the soft flesh under the man's jaw with a quick, practiced motion. As he did so, he pushed his forehead into the back of the man's neck, to provide a backstop as he drove the knife in. Simultaneously, he grabbed the man's right fist in an iron grip to prevent any reflexive use of the knife and keep it from falling to the pavement. The man struggled silently, for a moment, as the tip of the narrow knife severed the top of his spinal cord. Rashidii pushed the head forward with his chin to minimize the bleeding. The man was already being dragged into the alley as he died.

Noska, thinking he heard something, stopped and put his right hand up on the brick to steady himself. Just as the man's feet passed the corner of the brick building into the alley, Noska turned his bobbing head back to look. He squinted, peering back under his right armpit. Seeing nothing, he spat droolingly on the sidewalk and turned back. Weaving about, he continued on toward Pulaski.

In the alley, Rashidii removed the stiletto from the throat and wiped it on the shirt of the corpse. There was little blood, none on the sidewalk. He quietly scooped debris away from the wall of the building next to the B&B Tavern and laid the body down quickly and silently. He covered it with cardboard and papers, until it couldn't be seen then, weighted them down with bricks and pieces of broken mortar. He checked the street, it was dark and empty. He walked across and got in the car and quickly drove away. He circled the neighborhood for a while and saw no unusual activity. He then parked where he had before, with a view of the front of Noska's apartment building. Rashidii arrived in time to see him enter the front door.

Rashidii put the receiver to his ear, keeping watch for any police activity in the area. He heard Noska banging about in the room, then he heard the man's voice, loud and raspy. "The goddamn sons-a-bitches. I got'em by the balls now. Them fuckers'll pay, especially that fuckin' Richards. An' I'll be fuckin' rich!" John Richards was the man, who had fired Noska from his job at States Airlines. "Yeah, I'll fix those bastards...," the slurring voice trailed off.

It was silent for ten minutes, then he heard the sound of Noska's snoring, faintly at first then growing progressively louder. After another twenty minutes, Rashidii was about ready to leave, when the snoring stopped and he heard banging around again. Then a sound like rain spattering on a tent. Noska had gotten up. Staggering about, had leaned over and wedged his head into the corner. He was urinating into a pile of clothes there.

NINE

Back at the Marriott, Rashidii woke the Baron. It was 3:00 A.M. He explained the events of the night. Von Kloussen was distressed at the killing. He rubbed his eyes, "You sure no one saw you?"

"You can never be sure, but it was too dark to recognize anyone."

"The car?"

"I dropped it in the lot at the airport. Rented one from another agency down the road."

The Baron sighed relief. They had different identities for such things as car rentals. There wouldn't be any traceability.

"I probably should have let the mugger have him. Noska's a psycho. No sane person would live the way he does."

"Sounds like just the man we've been looking for. Get back on him in the morning. If he tries anything funny, get rid of him. Then we'll go to New York. I interviewed a couple of possibles there. I'll see about getting some California documents for him. I should be able to find someone to do it. I understand these street people can get it done in an hour. It's said the place to look is near a social security office in the right neighborhood." The Baron abhorred doing this work with his own hands. But, if he hired others, they would have to be killed. All links to himself, would have to be cut, when it was over. He was pondering killing Rashidii and even Eva, once he had the money in his accounts. The whole thing had to be a limited-risk gamble for him, personally. He was, after all, the Baron Von Kloussen, defender of his own without mercy.

* * *

On Friday morning, Nick was on Highway E66 traveling west from Odense. Before leaving, he had called Langley but Joe wasn't in. He reported the P-51 serial number to Leslie. Now, he was on his way to visit the Froslevlejren, the labor camp used by the Nazis during the war. At the motel, he had studied the verbal commands for the communications/navigation computer on the motorcycle. After switching on the unit and cruising away from the motel, he experimented with the commands. "Nav," he said loudly into the microphone in the helmet chin-guard. This was the abbreviated command, that was supposed to provide access to the navigation software.

"Yes." A synthesized female voice responded. The "yes" was known as the prompt to the system user. This meant the computer had interpreted the last command and was ready to accept the next command or data.

"Route-to-Froslevlejren," he said slowly and carefully.

"Destination not understood." The voice was in English, but it seemed to have a bouncing Scandinavian brogue.

"Froslevlejren."

"Destination not understood. Options are repeat, spell or cancel."

Was his pronunciation off or was the damn thing a piece of junk? He wondered. It was a complicated Danish word. "Spell," he said.

"Yes."

"F-r-o-s-l-e-v-l-e-j-r-e-n."

"Route to Froslevlejren." The voice nearly sang. "You are at (pause) Highway E66, five-point-six kilometers west of Odense. Continue on E66. Thirty-four-point-three kilometers. Cross bridge at Lillie Baelt from Fyn to Jutland. Zero-point-four kilometers. Continue on E66. Eleven-point-nine kilometers. Merge to E3. Continue on E3. Sixty-six-point-eight kilometers. Exit at Froslev. Turn right at Padborg Gade. Continue on Padborg Gade. One-point-three kilometers. Froslevlejren. (long pause) Would you like trip monitoring, confirm yes or no?"

Nick was impressed. He had checked the route and the computer's response was accurate. "Yes," he said. The trip monitoring would warn him a kilometer ahead of oncoming turns. Supposedly, it would also warn him if he missed a turn or made a mistake.

He traveled through open, rolling green territory dotted with well-kept farms. Nearly all the houses and buildings were of red brick. Trees were a scarce and precious resource in Denmark. As he approached the west coast he cruised through dark, cool forest. He crossed the long bridge across the Lillie Baelt from Fyn to the Jutland Peninsula on the European mainland. At each end of the bridge were marinas crowded with sailboats. After several minutes, the navigation computer announced, "One kilometer ahead. Merge to E3. Continue on E3. Sixty-six-point-eight kilometers." E66 merged with E3 which took him around the city of Kolding and south toward the German border. He took the E66 exit to the west and had gone nearly a half kilometer, when the voice came in his ear, "Warning. You have left planned route to Froslevlejren. Return to E3. Go south." He turned around and returned to his route. He rode along through an open, grassy flatland south of Kolding several miles. Then he cruised through the marshy lowlands of southeastern Jutland for forty minutes. He took the Froslev exit and found the camp.

He parked the motorcycle and paid the museum entrance fee. He entered the camp area on an asphalt path. There were several, plain clapboard buildings painted in a flat red. Their roofs were tarpaper. They had served as barracks for slave-laborers fifty years earlier. The only windows in the long structures were at the ends, facing the center of the camp. Those were neatly trimmed in white. The buildings were immaculately maintained. Between the buildings were beautifully manicured lawns, studded with trees and flower beds. The only obvious evidence of the camp's wartime use was a tall, white guard tower in the center. Through one of it's open windows Nick could see a large black machine gun mounted on a tripod.

He inspected the first of several buildings. There was a long hall down the middle of the building. On either side was a row of doorways to the rooms that had been the prisoners' living quarters. Nick peered in the first one. It was plain, bare wood with several sets of bunk beds crowded in. Under the lower bunk of one was an open trap door. A manikin dressed as a prisoner was crouched in the hideaway below the floor. A 1940's vintage radio earphone set was on his head and a microphone held to his mouth. A brave radioman working literally underground, communicating with the other underground agents or perhaps directly with the allies. The penalty for this activity would surely have been death, Nick thought.

He looked at the other similar rooms that had been prisoners' quarters and then went on to explore the other buildings. In one, there was a combination ambulance/bus used for transporting prisoners. In another was a manikin outfitted as a fully uniformed German motorcycle messenger. The helmeted dummy was on a vintage BMW complete with sidecar and machine gun. In many buildings, were cartoons and drawings the inmates had made, mocking their Nazi captors. On display were numerous carvings, drawings and ceramic sculptures incorporating frogs and spoons made by the prisoners. Froslev, from the name of the camp could be interpreted as meaning "frogspoon".

On the walls were pictures of the camp's exterior when it had been in use. The buildings were drab and gray, the grounds barren.

Outside, Nick walked to the camp's office and went in. Inside, there were two desks separated by a small partition. A young redheaded woman sat at the desk on the right. A man sat at the desk on the left. On the front of his desk, was a placard indicating he was the curator. As Nick approached the desk the man put his reading glasses down and stood. He was a small, older man with a full beard that was salt and pepper in color. Although it was a hot summer day, he wore a dark wool suit. Nick introduced himself as Professor Bradshaw of Chatham College doing research on World War Two for a book. The curator greeted him warmly.

"Are records of the camp's operation during the war available?" Nick asked.

The man smiled broadly. He almost laughed. "The Germans kept detailed records of everything. They were, are actually, absolute fanatics for record-keeping. After all, Hitler's Third Reich was supposed to last a thousand years, was it not?" He stepped to the side of his chair and pointed to the wall behind his desk. There was a large line graph on the wall. It showed the population of the camp from late 1943 to early 1945. The title at the top was lettered flawlessly in green ink and the graph label key was in red. The graph itself was stylized to look like a landscape. The line indicating the camp's population showed a bumpy, but steady rise from left to right. It appeared to be the profile of a dark mountain range. Above was a surrealistic sky, painted in darker shades of blue, as one looked from the line to the top of the graph.

On the wall next to the graph was an organization chart of the camp's officers. A large black swastika and silver eagle with wings outspread was at the top. In its talons, the eagle carried an enemy prisoner. The boxes representing the administrative positions were boldly lettered in red and blue. The curator waved his open hand at the wall, "And, as you can see, when they finished recording everything in journals, they graphed and charted the data."

Nick looked the documents over. He had seen similar graphs and charts posted in the other buildings. "Very elaborate and well done."

"Oh, yes. The Germans did it first-class or they didn't do it at all." The curator said with a sardonic grin.

He escorted Nick to a room in back of the office. There were bookshelves with rows of bound journals. "As I have told you the Germans are sticklers for detail. These are all of the records of the camp's operation from the day it opened, until liberation by the allies in 1945. These are public documents. You're welcome to browse, research and copy all you like. The names, status and disposition of all prisoners are here. Each transaction was recorded as it happened. Someone was brought into the camp, someone committed an infraction of the rules, someone was assigned to a work project or released from one, someone died, it's all here. Dates, names, comments. Do you read German?"

"Ja," Nick said. "I noticed a list of names of individuals sent to...it said 'the east' in the other buildings."

"Oh, yes. Some prisoners from here were sent to the death camps in the east, Auschwitz mainly, and other camps. That was the penalty for what were considered serious offenses; attempting to escape, anti-German subversive activity, assaulting a German." A knowing smile came to the man's face. He shook his head and said, "I've worked for the government a long time. I've learned a lot about bureaucracy in that time. Whether you were shipped east or not probably depended as much on the mood of the officer in charge that day as it did on your actual offense."

Nick nodded, "I know exactly what you mean."

"In any case, it will all be in the records here. Very few of those sent east ever returned." The man waved his open hand about the room. "Perhaps we didn't need bombs to win the war. I should think the Germans would have withered away, if someone had deprived them of their quill pens and recording books."

"Actually I'm interested specifically in work projects starting in January, 1944."

Without speaking the man led Nick down between the two closest rows of bookshelves. He stopped about halfway down and studied the back binders of some journals for a moment. He put his index finger to the top of one and tipped it out. He held the heavy volume out to Nick, "This is the January work log. February is next on the shelf. If you need any help just call us." The man walked away between the shelves.

* * *

Several hours later it was nearly 10:00 a.m in Chicago. The sun was visible through hazy clouds. Arun Rashidii parked a car-length behind a delivery truck on Elmond Street facing Pulaski road again. He had a view of the apartment house front door from around the side of the truck. He was driving a dark green Dodge Intrepid now. He listened in, playing with the volume knob on the receiver. For over an hour, there was only the sound of Noska's snoring. Finally he awoke. For nearly another hour, Rashidii heard noises in the apartment. Then the door squawked and slammed. A minute later Noska came out the front door north of "The Magic Touch" Beauty Salon and crossed Pulaski Road toward Rashidii. As he crossed he disappeared from view behind the building on the corner. Risking a parking ticket, Rashidii got out of the car and went to the corner. He saw Noska turn into a small, greasy spoon restaurant. Rashidii walked down the sidewalk toward the place. In the dirty front window a red neon sign burned, shaped to spell "Ed's". The brim of Rashidii's hat was pulled low over his forehead as he walked by. He shifted his eyes to glance in. Noska was at the counter, his back to the street.

"Coupla' eggs, sunnyside up, hashed browns and a double order of bacon," Noska said to Ed, the heavy, balding man at the grill behind the counter.

Down the counter a homeless man and woman, each of whom had ordered tea, were stirring ketchup into the hot water to make soup. Ed was thinking he should kick them out, but he didn't have the heart. What the hell he thought, they paid for the tea. He looked into Noska's bloodshot eyes. "Jesus, do you look rough," he said as he set a mug of coffee down in front of the small man.

"Had a party last night. Fuckin' good time," Noska said, feeling nauseated. "I screwed that fat assed Wanda last night, too."

"From the B&B Tavern?" Ed asked. He eyed Noska as he slopped a scoop of air-whipped government surplus butter onto the greasy grill. "I seen better lookin' faces in the warthog cage at the zoo." He laid down strips of bacon and shoveled a pile of potatoes onto the grill. It all but floated on the grease as it began to sizzle. He shot a sly glance at Noska, "She any good?"

"Nah, she's a stinkin' pig an' you can tell the bitch I said so."

"Why the party?"

"Movin' to New York, got me a big job out there."

With one large hand, Ed cracked two eggs simultaneously over the grill. "Yeah? Doin' what?" He asked with a sarcastic tinge to the words.

"Government job. Fuckin' top secret, you know. Can't say nothin'."

"Yeah, right," Ed said as he turned his attention to the grill.

Across the street, Rashidii noted that Noska was eating. He went back to the car. Later, he watched Noska walk around back of the apartment building and drive out of the alley behind in an old dinged-up brown Chevrolet Celebrity four-door sedan. Rashidii followed him south on Pulaski road and then, onto Interstate 90 northwest toward O'Hare Field. Noska exited at 294 and took Des Plaines River Road north. As Rashidii followed, he noticed the right side of the road was lined with a deep stand of trees. There was even a forest preserve with a park and small lake along the way. To his left he saw alternating residential and commercial areas as he drove along the busy, bumpy street. About three miles after leaving the expressway, Noska turned left into a parking lot and quickly came out, heading back south. As he passed a large, long brick building on the right, he slowed and crawled by in the right lane, hugging the curb. Rashidii swung around and followed him, then continued on by to avoid being recognized. He made a quick left and found his way into a pharmacy parking lot across the street from the brick building. There were about twenty-five cars in the lot. He pulled up between some cars facing the street and the north end of the brick building across it. Suddenly, Noska pulled in and parked at the north end of the same lot.

Fifteen minutes passed and then a tractor-trailer rig bearing the logo of a paper company flashed a turn signal to turn into the drive at the north end of the large brick building. Another followed behind. Noska's car was on the move. Rashidii watched him pull out and nearly hit a car crossing the street. He let it pass and then pulled across and parked in what was, apparently, an employee parking lot north of the building. A long, chain-link fence gate topped with razor wire opened in front of the first truck. The front end of the rig pulled just inside, the brakes squeaked as it stopped next to the guardhouse. The other queued up close behind. Noska got out of the car and walked close along the right side of the two semis, where neither driver could see him. Inside the security fence, he went quickly to a long row of large dumpsters north of the gate. He opened the first one and looked in. He let the top down easy and ran to the second and opened it. He reached inside and pulled out several small, light blue boxes. Then black smoke poured from the exhaust stack of the first rig as it pulled forward. Noska hid between two of the dumpsters. The second tractor-trailer rig pulled up to the guardhouse and squeaked to a stop. Noska walked briskly out of the gate and back to his car. Rashidii could see now that Noska had waited until the trucks were in the drive. This allowed him to get into the secured area unseen and blocked the guard's view of him and the dumpsters.

Noska was back in his car in seconds. He threw the boxes in the back and slid into the driver's seat. The truck in the drive began to roll forward just as Noska pulled back into traffic. Rashidii followed him south on Des Plaines for a mile. Then he pulled into the parking lot of a small diner on the right. The sign in front read: Peter's Kitchen. It was obviously a stopoff used by traveling sales people and delivery truck drivers. A half hour later, Noska pulled out of the lot and Rashidii followed him back to his apartment.

Back at the Marriott, Von Kloussen laid the documents out on the table. There was a social security card, California driver's license and Los Angeles County birth certificate for each of Noska's two new identities, David Kowalski and Fred Hamm. His face squinted out of the photos on the driver licenses, one with the blonde mustache and wig and one with the black. Rashidii stared down at them shaking his head. "These Americans are efficient," the Baron said, cackling. "It took a couple hours of driving around, but only an hour to get the false documents made. I finally made a contact right on the sidewalk near a social security office.

They had these within an hour. Now, you'll meet with Noska this evening. See if he came up with anything."

An hour later, Rashidii cautiously took a seat on the old couch in Noska's filthy apartment. Noska was alert and agitated. He sat in the easy chair and nervously lit a cigarette. Rashidii showed him the false credentials, then put them back in his pocket, saying he would keep them until they were needed.

Noska showed Rashidii two plain, light blue boxes, each slightly crumpled. One was marked "napkins," the other "facial tissues" in black letters. "States Airlines uses these," Noska said, "will your package fit in one of 'em?"

Rashidii looked them over and nodded. "How?" He said keeping his voice down.

"The caterer the airline uses is out on Des Plaines River Road about five miles north of the airport. They've been planning to move it all into the airport operations area for security purposes. Started work on it while I was still there, but they haven't moved yet. I was out there today, got these goddamn boxes out of a dumpster."

"Oh?" Rashidii said, feigning surprise.

"For security purposes, everything comes in to Des Plains Road loose and is packaged under close supervision. Food, utensils, everything. Even paper products like these are delivered to the caterers in the flat," he said, holding up the tissue box. "Then, the scissors box trucks are backed in and loaded with rolling carts, also under close supervision. Then they roll the truck's back door down and the supervisor puts a bar-coded plastic and wire seal on the padlock brackets. He records the seal number, work order number and truck number in the computer. The work order number keys it to the flight number in the computer. I don't think the bastards at the caterer's even have access to the flight the truck is being loaded for. They only have a work order number, packing list and delivery time. Then they drive the truck to the AOA at O'Hare. The trucks unload from the front, but they have to open the back and get in before they elevate the box. The jerkoff in charge of loading the plane records the seal number with a portable bar-code wand and breaks the seal. He wands the work order number and types the truck number and flight number in his data transmitter. It's sent to the main computer system. With each transaction into the computer the time is recorded also. Any number mismatch or anything unusual in the timing of the transactions causes a warning message on the computer screen of a supervisor. Sometimes, the security people come out and check everything. I've seen it happen." Noska went into a momentary coughing fit.

When the fit subsided, Rashidii said, "So, neither the driver nor anyone else can open the truck, between loading and unloading?"

"So the bastards think," Noska said, baring his rotting teeth in an ugly smile. He reached over to the coffee table and picked up a heavy, curved wire bent in inward angles, at the ends and a broken, thin transparent plastic case about two inches square. It resembled a padlock. "This is a busted seal."

"Where did you get it?"

"I stole the son-of-a-bitch a long time ago, when I worked for the airline. I got a couple more, found'em in my junk today. They were supposta' be destroyed, but I fished'em outta the trash. Ta' seal it you press the ends of the wire into the plastic case. You can see'em through the sides. The bent wire ends clip in behind the plastic stops. No way to get them out without bustin' the plastic all to hell. But, I figger I can open the seal and put it back on, between the caterers and the airport without anybody knowing shit."

"Where could you do this?"

"There's a little cafe called 'Peter's Kitchen' a little way south of the caterers. The drivers sometimes stop there for a coffee break or for lunch. There's a fence around part of the lot for cover and the drivers always back in the stalls. I saw a couple there today."

"A very weak link in security," Rashidii mused aloud. He looked at Noska, "The airline allows this?"

"I don't know if it's against the rules or not. Might be. But a guy I knew was a driver for a while. He mentioned it and now I know they still do it. If they move the operation inta' the AOA later there won't be any problem with it. Anyway, I think I can cut the wire, get inside and plant the fuckin' package, an' reweld it all in a few minutes."

Rashidii picked up the curved wire, it was about three sixteenths of an inch in diameter. "Why not just put a new seal on?"

"How we gonna make a new seal with the right goddamn bar code in a coupla' minutes?"

"Of course. How can you weld the wire without melting the plastic?"

"By letting it hang in a can of ice water, while I clip two electrodes to the wire and spot weld it back together using a battery."

Rashidii was impressed by the man's ingenuity. He picked up the wire and examined it. There was no rust, only a thin patina of dark corrosion on the silverish color. "Possibly stainless steel of the four hundred series or a similar alloy. Maybe even an alloy with a unique formula for security. Do you know how to set up a circuit with adjustable amperage?"

"I think so."

"Then set it up and practice on these pieces." Rashidii drew on his knowledge of welding from his motorcycle racing days. "The red-hot nugget at the center of the weld will have to grow to join the metal, all the way out to the edge of the wire. Then polish it with an abrasive cloth. Make sure there's no line or slag visible. Apply an acid in paste form, that should restore the surface uniformity. And bring a can of compressed air to dry it, even a few water droplets in the plastic case could cause suspicion."

"That is the easy part."

"What do you mean?"

"If you want an international flight goin' to Europe, I have to figger out which goddamn truck is loadin' one."

"Of course. You have an idea for this?"

"Yeah, maybe. States Airlines' main computer system is upstairs in one of the buildings at the airport. All the scheduling is done there. The schedulers input and maintain the flight schedules. But before they can do anything they have to sign on to the main host computer from their PC terminals by sending a password across the line. Anyway, then they coordinate the schedules with the other airlines. Then they run computer programs to generate the maintenance and supply schedules from those, including outside suppliers like the caterers. The data is sent to them over phone lines. Let's see, goddamnit, EDI they call it: electronic data interchange. I used to use some of the output screens. I kinda' know how the system works."

"It is possible for you to access this data, their passwords perhaps?"

Noska smiled thinking of revenge and riches. "Prob'ly too many protections these days to hack in from an outside line. But, if I could get inside for just a coupla' minutes, I could install a wireless transmitter on the input/output port of one of the schedulers' personal computer terminals. Let's see, Airlan I think it is, makes a wireless. Um-cost? Off the shelf, they'ed stab ya in the ass about four large. They use the bastards for local wireless networks. It would transmit all data sent and received in a half-mile radius for as long as the fuckin' battery lasts. I could pick up the transmission in the general area using a notebook PC with a receiver unit. We'd get the security password." He took a long pull on his cigarette and wheezed out the smoke before he continued. "They change the goddamn passwords at random intervals about once a week, but it should be good for a few days. With the password and the dial-up phone number I can access the schedules remotely. From right here if I wanted to," Noska said, nodding toward the PC in the kitchen.

"Don't do it from here." Rashidii said firmly, as he shot a glance toward the door of the small kitchen. He had his wallet out. He counted four thousand dollars in cash onto the coffee table. "And how will you get in to install the transmitter?"

"Officially, the area is outside the AOA, but you still need a security card to get in. I been thinkin' I could pose as a computer repairman. CINC is the name of the company that handles their service. I'd need a laminated card to get in. I've seen'em before." He made a sketch on a piece of paper. "The photo on the left, CINC in dark blue block letters like this on the right and a name typed below. Fuckin' simple." He sketched in some dark vertical lines. "Bar-code at the bottom for CINC's use, States Airlines don't check it. Should get me in for a few minutes. Can you get one made?"

Rashidii studied the sketch for a moment. He nodded as he folded it and slid it into his inner jacket pocket. Trying to think of a way to simplify the operation, he asked Noska, "Why not just change the bar-code number once you are in the system. This could avoid all the trouble of welding."

Noska snickered, "Because, the passwords the goddamn schedulers have won't allow that change. Only the internal security programming group has the password level required to set those numbers. An' I don't have the slightest fuckin' idea how to get that."

"I see," Rashidii said, then he asked Noska, "Do you have a gun?"

"Yeah, bought it for protection last year." He reached behind him and brought out a nine millimeter automatic from under the seat cushion. "Cost me over four hundred bucks." Rashidii was holding out his hand. Noska reluctantly handed the pistol to him.

Rashidii examined it, a Taurus PT92AF manufactured in Porto Allegre, Brazil. Cheap and easily obtainable. "You have a shoulder holster?" Noska shook his head. "Then I suggest you get one."

Noska replaced the weapon and stood up. "Christ, I gotta wring it out," he said. "Be back in a minute." He went to the door and Rashidii heard him walk down the hall to the bathroom.

Rashidii seized the opportunity. He went into the kitchen and snapped open the bottom plate on the answering machine. He removed two audio cassettes and shoved them in his jacket pocket. He replaced them with new ones. Later, he could listen to the tapes to see if Noska had said anything to anyone by phone or while in the apartment. When Noska returned, Rashidii was standing by the door. "Try to get everything you need tomorrow morning," he said. "I'll see you early tomorrow afternoon." Noska nodded and Rashidii walked out.

TEN

Saturday, June 25

Noska had hunted around hardware stores in the morning and purchased wiring, brass clamp electrodes, switches, a small transformer and a couple of six-volt lantern batteries. At an electronics store, he purchased a male/female twenty-five pin connector with an auxiliary port and the wireless transmitter. He also purchased a receiver unit and a notebook computer. At home, he constructed the circuit and experimented with spot welding the pieces of wire together.

Rashidii arrived in the early afternoon. He handed Noska the Fred Hamm credentials and an airline ticket for a one-way trip to establish his residence in California later that day. He instructed Noska to buy his return ticket separately to avoid suspicion of being involved in drug deals or money laundering. Short term round-trip tickets often aroused such suspicion and airline employees sometimes reported them to authorities. Rashidii also gave him the CINC employee card, that the Baron recently had made. The name on it was Al Johnson. Then Rashidii helped Noska fine tune the circuit to get the desired seal wire weld on the practice pieces. Then, they fashioned a nylon belt out of an old backpack and some duct tape. Fastened to it were the electrodes, wiring, transformer, and a small, covered can for the cooling water. They agreed that Noska would attempt to pose as a serviceman and get the password on Monday morning.

Late Saturday afternoon Noska boarded a flight from O'Hare Airport to Los Angeles International. That night, he checked into the Crescent Moon Motel there and paid an additional four weeks rent in advance. For the trip, he was wearing his black wig and mustache and using the name Fred Hamm. He stayed the night in the motel, polishing off a liter of Southern Comfort and most of a case of beer. He was finally up and around at 1:00 P.M. on Sunday, feeling sick. Now, he was having serious doubts about doing this. Hundreds of lives would be taken. Yet the bastards at the airline had fucked him over, he thought. He wrestled with these thoughts in the pain and depression of his terrible hangover. Finally, he made a decision. He would get the password and read the schedules, but would follow through only if, somehow, John Richards would be made to suffer. Or better yet, be killed. He caught an evening flight back to Chicago.

Marseilles, France, Monday, June 27

Kurt Kohfer sat at a small table in the waterfront restaurant. He was waiting. Nervously, he checked his watch. It was nearly noon. He had made the call a week ago. The man he reached agreed to meet with him on Friday. Kohfer had driven to Copenhagen and then flown to Paris. From there he had taken a taxi flight to Marseilles. At noon on Friday, a man wearing a beret and filthy sport coat had met him at the same restaurant. A messenger, no doubt, Kohfer thought. He gave the man Nick's fingerprints and photos in a sealed envelope along with five hundred dollars in U.S. currency as agreed upon. The man told him only that it would take a few days and that he would receive a call at his hotel. He had waited it out in a stuffy room for three days and finally received a call on Monday morning. He was to meet someone at noon.

A tall, balding man in a black suit approached the table. He studied Kohfer for a moment and sat down. He looked around suspiciously. "Are you the man from Denmark?" he said in broken German. Kohfer nodded. "You have something of great value here", he said, pulling a sealed envelope out of the breast pocket of his jacket. "For one thousand in U.S. currency it is yours."

"We agreed on five hundred more," Kurt said.

"Yes, but now that I know the value of this information, the price has gone up. Believe me, it is a bargain."

Five hundred was all Kohfer had in U.S. dollars. The man agreed to take the rest in francs and kroners. He handed over the money. The man counted it and put it in his pocket. He stood and held out the envelope. Kohfer grabbed it. Before the man let go of the other end, he said, "Call me if you decide to collect. I will negotiate the best price for you." The man walked away.

Kohfer looked around and began to tear open the envelope. What did the man mean by the best price? He removed the typed page and read it:

Man identified usually uses the name Nick Barber. Known in European circles as "The Barbarian". His real name is not known. He is a top level CIA operative and holds the rank of Brigadier General in the United States Marine Corps. Speaks German, French, Spanish, Italian, Russian, Scandinavian dialects. During and since the Vietnam War era he has served as a captor, interrogator and assassin of enemies of the United States. He has hired, trained and directed others in this work. He is believed to have killed communist leaders Martino Cervantes in Cuba, Pierre Andre' in France and Major Krenski in East Germany and others. He was captured in Lebanon in 1984 and escaped, rescuing another CIA agent. It is believed he allowed himself to be captured. He is said to act without fear of personal harm when necessary. He is unerringly persistent in pursuit of his assigned objective. Consider this man to be extremely dangerous. A price of at least one half million U.S. dollars has been offered for him dead, perhaps more if he is captured alive. He is believed to have been retired from field work for about one year and living in the Washington D.C. area. He is disguised in the photos. His hair is dark and it is believed he does not wear glasses.

Kohfer was incredulous. He folded the paper slowly and put it in his pocket. Could the Baron be a target for assassination? If so, it was ideal for Kurt Kohfer.

Chicago, 8:30 A.M.

In the alley next to the B&B Tavern, Chicago Police Detective Sergeants Tanya Williams and Francis "Fritz" Grinke squatted and examined the dead man's body. They held handkerchiefs over their noses and mouths to filter out the awful odor and wore latex gloves on their hands. They picked the debris of bricks, mortar, cardboard and other trash from the corpse. It was the beginning of another hot, humid day in the city.

Tanya was a short, attractive black woman with a gregarious smile. She had been on the force for six years. At twenty-nine she was among the younger detectives. She held a bachelor's degree in criminology and was working part-time on her master's degree. She had been promoted to detective six months earlier. At forty-three, Fritz was a twenty-one year police veteran. He was a heavy-set white man, balding and once very muscular, but now getting a bit flabby with age. His nose was flattened from his boxing days as a youth and that, with his heavy jowls and dark foreboding eyes, gave him a look of intimidating toughness. He had been through just about every experience and hard knock a big city cop can have in a career, both professional and personal. He and Williams had been working together for less than a month.

A uniformed officer stood in the alley near the sidewalk. With him was Denny Belongia, one of the two owners of the B&B. He had found the body that morning while picking up trash around the Tavern. Another uniformed officer came in from the street and announced that the medical examiner was on his way.

The several day's growth of black, scraggly beard on the dead man's face stood in contrast to the pallor of the skin.

Gravity had long since pulled blood and other body fluids to the lower levels of the body. There was slippage of the livid, blistered skin over the bones of the skull and the skeleton-like left hand. The fingers and thumb of the right hand were still wrapped around the handle of a dagger with a six inch blade. One eyelid was nearly closed. The other eye was wide-open staring lifelessly at the sky, the dilated pupil so cloudy it was nearly white. There was a brick under the back of the head, elevating it and forcing the chin down over the throat. Tiny maggots were visible moving in the nostrils and between the lips. Swarms of flies buzzed about above the corpse.

Grinke stood and backed away. "Jesus," he said, "what a goddamn stench. Been here three days. I don't see no wounds."

Williams continued to examine the body. "Dried blood, I think, at the throat." She slid the brick from beneath the head. Slowly, the head moved down and rested on the pavement as though the man were still alive and was lowering his head slowly to avoid injury. "Rigor mortis nearly gone," she said. A dark patch of dried blood around the wound was visible now. She scraped it with a flat wooden stick exposing a gash one-half inch wide at the top of the throat. "Knife wound." She measured its length with a scale. She leaned over and examined the right hand of the corpse. "Knife held tight in his right hand. A cadaveric muscle spasm; the victim was holding it at the time of death."

"I better get up to goddamn speed in my official terms." Grinke said, "We usta' jus' call it a death grip."

"Usually indicative of suicide," she commented.

"Case solved," Grinke said sarcastically, "the son-of-a-bitch stabs himself in the neck, lays down, covers himself up with garbage, and dies."

Tanya sighed, "I didn't say that. The throat wound is only twelve centimeters long, much too small to be made with his own knife. This is a homicide. Probably a murder." With another stick, she scraped a few maggots out of a nostril. She stood and held her scale near the end of the stick. Closing one eye, she carefully measured the lengths of several of the tiny fly larvae. The millimeter length of the largest maggot plus two would approximate the number of days since death. "He died about seventy-two hours ago," she announced clinically.

"Like I said, three days," Grinke commented. Pencil and notepad in his hands, he turned to Belongia and asked, "Know who this guy is?"

"Nah. I think I seen the sombitch aroun' a coupla' times. I think my bartender, Wanda might know'em." Belongia stated her last name and address at Grinke's request.

Fritz was making notes. "You see or hear of any fight or anything out here, uh, let's see, Thursday night, Friday morning?"

"Nope, Wanda was workin' that night. We ain't open in the mornin'"

"I doubt if it was a knife fight," Tanya said. "It would be unusual to inflict such a precise wound in that spot during a struggle."

Fritz Grinke looked down at his partner. "No shit, Dick Tracy," he said.

* * *

At the same time at O'Hare International Airport, George Noska walked along in front of the ticket counters in one of the main corridors. The bright rays of the sun flowed through the high windows to his right, bathing the interior of the building with light. He had cleaned himself up and was wearing the blonde wig and mustache Rashidii had given him. He wore a white shirt with the sleeves rolled up and a narrow black and red striped tie, loose at the collar. When he put the tie on that morning he was vaguely aware that it was out of style. But then, he reasoned somewhat correctly, that should be ok for a computer jock. He carried a black attache' case and the fraudulent CINC card was clipped to the pocket of his shirt, dangling as he walked. He was unaware that Rashidii had followed him to the airport.

He passed a busy restaurant on his right, then entered the next building through a walkway. He was a long way from the parking lot. What if he was discovered and chased or worse yet, caught? He had made up a story about a man coming to him and paying him to install the transmitter and nothing more. If questioned he wouldn't have any idea why. The story was true as far as it went, he reasoned. He entered a doorway and walked up three flights to the U.S Airlines office area. He didn't want to take a chance on getting caught in an elevator.

He entered an open reception area. It was plush with a thick gray carpet, the gray walls trimmed in horizontal soft pink stripes. He walked up to the receptionist's desk. "Here to check on a problem with one of the computers in the scheduling department," he said. He pushed the ID card out to her. She had him sign the register and escorted him down the hall. He went through a door, only to be faced with a departmental receptionist. He repeated the purpose of his visit. She examined his ID card and had him sign another logbook. He signed "Al Johnson" again, the name on the ID card. She looked at the signature, then at the card and stated the name to make sure she had it right. Noska was concerned about this. He was feeling queasy and his mouth was dry. She waved him through the door into the scheduling department.

When the door closed, she immediately called CINC and told them serviceman Al Johnson had arrived. This was a routine security procedure. The receptionist at CINC recorded it in her computerized activity log. She didn't recognize the first name, but then, she was relatively new on the job and there was a Johnson in the employ of the company. She was going to check it right away, but then the phone rang and she forgot.

Noska looked around the scheduling department. There were at least a dozen men and women seated at PC terminals busily clacking away at the keys. A few glanced up at him then returned their gaze to their monitor screens. Nothing unusual in a visit from a CINC serviceman. At the far side of the room was a long set of windows that overlooked one of the many airline boarding paddocks. He shot a glance toward an open office door to his left, apparently the supervisor's. It was empty. Damn Monday morning meetings, he thought and smiled with slight relief. After surveying the heads he selected an unattractive young woman with dishwater blonde hair. She was seated at his right near to the door. He noticed that she wore no wedding ring. He knew that a homely, unmarried woman would be the most cooperative and least suspicious.

He leaned over her and said, "Hi, I'm from CINC. We've got some problems with the network lines we need to check out. I'd like to look at your PC for a few minutes."

"I haven't had any problems," she said matter-of-factly.

He looked down at the ID card at her waist, "Mikey LeFay" was her name. "If you could just sign off and take a break, I'll check the line and be done in a few minutes."

She shrugged and said, "Sure." She made a note on a pad next to her and clicked "EXIT" with her mouse to end the program she was working in. Then she typed "LO" for logoff and stood up.

"Fifteen minutes," he said. He thought quickly, the phone number! Why not just ask? "Oh, by the way, do you have the dial-in number you use when you work at home? I'll need it to make sure the communications line is working, that the signal is correct."

Her face flushed with red. Quietly she said, "I don't work at home, so I've never used it."

Noska was worried about getting the phone number. But, he could see he had the woman at a slight disadvantage.

Before he could speak, she pulled open the top desk drawer and said, "But, I think it's here." She shuffled some cards for a moment and handed one to him.

He sighed in audible relief and said, "Thanks." She nodded and left.

Noska wrote the number on a slip of paper and put it in his pocket, then replaced the card in the drawer. He set his case on her chair and opened it. He took out the connector and transmitter and a small roll of cellophane tape and went immediately to work at the back of the machine. As he worked, he imagined in dread, some authoritative person stepping up behind and asking what he was doing. With a tiny screwdriver, he unscrewed the main communications line from the back. He plugged his connector into the computer and the mainline connector into it. The transmitter dangled on a wire from his connector. He taped the transmitter to the rear, lower corner of the machine's base. He unrolled the wire antenna and secured it along the base with a strip of tape. All of this was under a tangle of wires behind the machine, where no one would look unless servicing it. Then, he switched on the transmitter. The battery would have the capacity to transmit the line signal for twenty-four hours or more in the immediate area.

Noska, a rivulet of sweat rolling down the middle of his forehead, stood and looked around as slowly and casually as he could manage. The keyboards clacked away. No one took any unusual notice. He left the room quickly. He was required to sign out at each reception desk and he did so without incident. Two minutes later, in a public restroom three floors below the office, he was in a stall tearing the mustache off. He put the mustache, wig and white shirt in the case. He was wearing a tan T-shirt underneath. He combed the long strands of hair over his bald head and put on a pair of wire-rimmed glasses with smoke lenses. He walked out to the side of the building facing the boarding areas. People were lined up at a metal detector across the wide walkway. In the center was a small gift shop. He selected a black and chrome waiting chair in a group next to the shop. He judged he was directly below the scheduling offices. He took the notebook computer from the case, flipped up the screen and switched it on. He initiated a word processing software package.

The transmitter he had installed contained a small modem to convert the digital American Standard Code (ASCII) output from the PC to an electrical analog signal. It broadcast that signal in the area over a specific frequency. Noska had the receiver in his case set to that frequency now. The receiver amplified the weak signal and demodulated it back to digital on his computer's input line. He had written a small computer program to read the signal, character by character, into a word processing file. A blank word processing screen up now, he reached in the case and switched on the receiver.

As power surged into the unit a couple of random characters appeared on the screen, then nothing. "Com'on

LeFay you bitch, get back to work," Noska said to himself, under his breath. He adjusted the frequency knob on the receiver, first one way, then the other. A few random characters appeared on the screen from odd signals picked up here and there. He returned the knob to its original setting. What if she doesn't return? he thought. What if someone were up there looking over his handiwork right now? He could imagine the area being cordoned off; a net of security officers tightening around him. His intestines wrenched with a spasm at the thought. He waited.

Crowds of travelers marched by on either side of the island of seats. Their bustling movement created a clamor of noise that melded into a constant loud din. Men and women carrying briefcases, pulling wheeled suitcases behind. All in a scrambling hurry. To Noska, the minutes seemed like hours. Suddenly, characters began to appear on the screen in rapid succession. "TYTYTY52984973". Probably the header and terminal number. Noska narrated mentally to himself, "74298371TAB(10)States Airlines System Active[CR]TAB(10)LOGON AT 072594 1022AM[CR]TAB(10)USERID:29872984. Header number, request for user identification and trailer number. She inputs her name to sign on, her computer adds header and trailer incrementing by tens and transmits:52984983Mikey Lefay73081294. 74298381Password:29872994. Password request. She inputs the password, server computer adds header and trailer and transmits: 52984993I78B373081304".

He leaned forward, squinted at the screen, the password is I78B3! A menu of selections appeared on the screen. She's in the system, Noska said to himself, as he reached into the case and switched off the receiver, then saved the data he had captured.

Rashidii was waiting impatiently in his car on Elmond Street. It was nearly noon. He listened to the receiver, Noska's apartment was quiet. Then, he saw Noska turn into the alley next to his building in the old Chevrolet Celebrity. Rashidii pulled up behind him as he got out. He motioned for Noska to get in the passenger's side. Noska opened the door and got in, laying his case on his lap.

"How did it go?" Rashidii asked as he pulled out of the alley.

"Perfect, I got the fuckin' password and the goddamn phone number," Noska said triumphantly. Then he was struck by sudden fear. This strange man had always been calm and professional and yet, there was a sinister foreboding about him. "Where we goin'?" Noska asked nervously.

"Just to try it out at a phone booth. I have a universal handset modem with me. Will that do?"

"Should," Noska said, calming a bit.

Rashidii drove west to Cicero Avenue, then turned left and cruised along south for several miles. He turned into a gas station with a drive-up pay phone and pulled up next to it. He took the modem from a box in the back seat and put it on his lap. He pushed the payphone handset into it. Noska had taken the notebook PC out of his case and connected it to the modem. He switched on the PC and fished out the paper with the number and handed it to Rashidii. Rashidii reached out the window and depressed the switchhook for a moment, then dialed the number. After a few moments, characters began to appear on the screen:

States Airlines System Active
LOGON AT 072594 1236PM
USERID:

Noska smiled and typed "John Richards," thinking of implicating his former supervisor in this. The system responded "Password:". He typed "I78B3". The system responded "ACCESS NOT AUTHORIZED" and printed two options, "Abort or Retry?".

"What's the problem?" Rashidii asked.

"Probably just an ID and password mismatch. Some systems check for that." He typed "R" for retry.

"USERID:", the computer responded.

He typed "Mikey LeFay".

"Password:", the computer responded.

He typed "I78B3". In a moment, a menu of options came up on the screen.

"We're in," Noska said. "It's a goddamn good thing it's the noon hour. This fuckin' system probably checks for a double sign-on an' she's probably signed off for lunch."

"Then we better get what we need now."

Noska nodded and began to hit keys. He worked his way around in the flight schedule inquiry screens. After several minutes he said, "There's a regular daily flight to London, number 283. A goddamn milk run, a 747 scheduled to take off at 2:40 P.M. Rashidii nodded, staring at the screen. Noska keyed up the supply schedule screen. After a few more minutes he said, "This is perfect. The supply trucks are scheduled to leave the caterers starting at 11:30 A.M. Some of the drivers will probably stop for lunch." The work order numbers, truck numbers and lists of materials to be loaded in each truck, for the next several days were all there. He captured them in his word processing file and added some notes. He logged off.

Rashidii pulled into the alley to drop Noska at his apartment. Noska had sat silent on the trip home, staring forward, his case closed on his lap. When the car stopped, he quickly swung the door open toward his building and put his right foot on the ground, as though ready for a quick escape. He turned to Rashidii. "We have a problem," he said nervously. "There's somethin' I need done."

Rashidii remained calm. "And what is that?"

"I'm not doin' this unless John Richards is taken care of."

"This is your former boss?" Rashidii said, hiding his anger. "Do you mean he is to be killed?"

"Yes."

Rashidii looked through the windshield into the debris-filled alley. "There might be a way. Tentatively we'll target for tomorrow's flight. Just wait for my call."

Von Kloussen pulled into the parking lot at the Marriott just after 6:00 P.M. The prior morning, he had driven a rented car from Chicago, to his factory in Pennsylvania. There, in a storage shed behind the factory was a wax-coated, cardboard box marked "Personnel Forms". It contained over six pounds of C-4 plastic explosive. He had arranged for the delivery, through his contacts in New York, the prior week. He left the package in the trunk of the car and went up to the suite.

Rashidii was on the couch watching television, a can of beer in his hand. Von Kloussen noted that he didn't look pleased.

"You have it?" Rashidii asked, frowning.

"Yes. There is some problem?"

Rashidii explained the day's events and Noska's demand. "I think it's more than killing this man," he added. "He may be afraid to go through with it at all."

Tiredly, Von Kloussen lit his pipe. He sat in an easy chair for a while, thinking, puffing on the pipe. A cloud of bluish-haze had grown around him by the time he spoke. "To ensure Noska's full cooperation, we must put this John Richards on the flight."

Rashidii was staring across the room at him, "But how?"

"The man must have a boss. He may be requested to travel to emergency meetings on short notice at times. Something like that. Airline management people travel on business junkets all the time, as sure as my butcher's personal freezer is always full of the best cuts of meat. With the proper motivation, Richards' boss might order him to take a trip." Rashidii nodded. "Go see Noska. The two of you ought to be able to come up with something. Meanwhile, I'll go buy tickets for you and Noska to go to California."

"Me?"

"That's right. If he's getting this upset, you better stay right with him. Kill him at the first opportunity after you get there and make it look like a suicide. We're changing plans a bit. We'll no longer try to cover Noska. His name will almost certainly come up in an investigation, anyway. Let the authorities find him. Make everything look as though he acted alone."

Rashidii left to meet with Noska. When he returned to the suite it was nearly midnight. Von Kloussen sat in the chair puffing on his pipe. "When I got there Noska was drinking again. I got rid of the booze and we made a trip to the suburbs," Rashidii began. "To see the house of Don Stafford, John Richards' boss."

ELEVEN

Tuesday, June 28, Mt. Prospect, Illinois

At 6:20 A.M. Don Stafford backed out of his driveway into the street and turned south. At forty-eight he was a heavy-set man with dark hair and graying temples. He drove a late model Cadillac DeVille, navy blue in color. He was unaware of the old brown Chevrolet that pulled out, following him a block behind. Noska was at the wheel wearing the black wig and mustache. He hadn't wanted to use his own car, but Rashidii had insisted. It would be big trouble if they were caught. He now wished he had never mentioned John Richards. A golf course was coming up on the right, a stand of trees and bushes lined the road along the edge. On the left were meeting halls, Knights of Columbus and American Legion, their parking lots empty at this time of the morning.

Rashidii was becoming concerned. What had appeared to be a straightforward operation, at first, was now becoming complicated. First the killing of the mugger and now a kidnapping in broad daylight. He had argued with the Baron that they should simply kill Noska now and Rashidii himself would plant the bomb in the truck. The Baron had said no, only Noska was familiar with the items in the truck and knew exactly how to do the job. And, he said, he didn't want Rashidii handling the bomb in the open. Rashidii realized the Baron's main concern was insulating himself from the operation. If Rashidii were caught they might be able to link the Baron to the bomb.

"Now." Rashidii said.

Noska pulled out and passed the Cadillac. Then he slowed and stopped directly in front of it. Stafford slammed on his brakes and honked the horn. Rashidii was out of the car, his automatic pistol in his left hand, shoved into his left pants pocket. In his right hand, he carried a hatchet, the handle and blade formed from one piece of steel. The hatchet was hidden behind his right thigh as he walked quickly to the passenger's side of the Cadillac. He checked the street quickly. A car was passing going the opposite way, the driver was paying no attention. Another vehicle was approaching three blocks behind. The perturbed look on Stafford's face turned to horror as Rashidii swung at the passenger's side window with the hatchet. Rashidii kept his back to the oncoming car to shield the action. He hacked a couple of blows across the top and then, a couple down the front of the window. Stafford attempted to regain his composure. He was being robbed, he thought quickly. With the hatchet in his right hand and his left forearm Rashidii slammed against the window, using the weight of his body to push it in. The shattered glass flopped down against the inner door panel. Stafford had put the car in reverse and was pressing the gas pedal.

"Stop or I'll shoot." Rashidii said loudly, holding the automatic low, aimed at Stafford. He hung onto the door as the car began to move backward.

Stafford looked into the barrel of the pistol and in the panic of heightened fear slammed the brake. The car jerked to a stop with Rashidii leaning in the window. The vehicle coming from behind, a service truck, passed them without slowing. Rashidii already had the door unlocked, he got in the passenger's side, the pistol leveled at Stafford. The man stammered, "Wha-what do you want?"

"Just follow that car. If you do as you're told you will not be harmed. If not, you and your family will be killed!"

They drove south to Algonquin Road and went east. In Des Plaines, the Chevrolet drove into a large, discount store parking lot. There were a few employee cars parked at the edge of the lot at the side of the building. They parked the Cadillac there and Rashidii said to Stafford, "You have a cellular phone?"

"Y-yes, in my pocket."

"Give it to me." The man handed it over. "Now, get in the back seat of that car." Rashidii had Stafford lay face down on the floor of Noska's car and placed a peach-colored adhesive ocular bandage over each of his eyes. He kept the barrel of his pistol at Stafford's head.

They drove to Noska's apartment house and parked in the alley on Elmond Street, next to the door at the corner of the building. They marched Stafford in. Noska was in front checking to be sure that first the street and then the hallway were clear. Rashidii was behind their captive with the automatic at his back. In Noska's apartment, Rashidii secured Stafford's hands and wrists behind him with duct tape. He then sat the man down on the filthy couch and taped his ankles. He removed the ocular bandages. Noska had protested bringing the man to his apartment, but again, Rashidii had insisted. Rashidii now explained to Stafford that he would first make a call to his secretary explaining he would be out for the day. Then he would place a call to John Richards. Rashidii wrote a script for each call on a piece of paper as he elicited information from the terrified Stafford. Occasionally, he turned to Noska for agreement or verification of some point.

Stafford shifted uncomfortably on the couch. He strained to think who the small man with the dark hair and mustache was. He was familiar. He was wearing a wig. Stafford studied the eyes, the mouth, the ugly red nose.

"What the hell are you lookin' at?" Noska said in the first words he had spoken to Stafford.

The features, the voice...the thief they had fired. He struggled mentally to recall the name. He had met the man briefly a couple of times and had conferred with Richards on his firing. "Noska," Stafford whispered hoarsely.

"Shut the fuck up," Noska said.

Rashidii frowned at both of them. Then, he realized he could use the man's recognition of Noska to his advantage. He could tell Noska he was going to kill Stafford to prevent Noska's identification. Noska would then be locked into a murder and kidnapping and would have nothing to loose.

Rashidii had rewritten the phone scripts with different wording to eliminate any codes Stafford may have used in his words or phrasing. Such precautions were sometimes taken for airport security purposes. He asked Noska for help with the rewording. Then, he went over them with Stafford. "Your house is being watched," Rashidii lied. "If you do not do exactly as we have said, your wife and son will be killed and then you will be killed."

The heavy man, sweating profusely now, nodded. He was thinking, could this be a bombing, sabotage? How many lives were at stake if these people were successful?

Rashidii handed Noska the cellular phone. Noska checked his watch, it was after 8:00 A.M. He dialed States Airlines' main number and asked for Stafford's secretary. In a moment, she answered, "Operations, Patty Warrener speaking."

Noska held the phone at the side of Stafford's head. Rashidii held the script in his left hand in front of Stafford's face and kept his left thumb poised over the hookswitch button on the phone.

"P-Patty, this is Don. I'm going to be on some errands today. I-I may not be in at all. Minor emergency. Cancel my appointments, please." Rivulets of sweat were racing down his forehead.

"Is something the matter?"

Watching Rashidii frown and shake his head Stafford said, "No, nothing of importance."

"Ok, see you tomorrow for sure?"

He was reading the script carefully as a drop of sweat fell from his chin. "Yes, I'll be in at noon. 'Bye."

Rashidii pushed the button down. He motioned to Noska. A minute later, Noska was there with a towel mopping Stafford's face. Stafford recoiled at the smell of the towel but Noska got the man's face dried off.

Rashidii said, "Now, calm down. Do this properly and you'll be released unharmed, in a couple of hours."

Stafford caught his breath and tried to calm himself by thinking of his release. Noska dialed the number again and asked for John Richards. A phone rang several times and then, the receptionist came back on, "Shall I page him, sir?"

"Yes," Noska said.

After a few moments a voice answered, "John Richards."

Noska put the phone to Stafford's head. "John, this is Don," he said nervously in a higher than normal tone. Rashidii frowned. Carefully controlling his voice Stafford said, "I'd like you to catch number 283 to London today. I know this is short notice, but there's a problem with the supplies handling procedures. They're using the same software as we are now and they're not getting the hang of it." As he concentrated on the words, Stafford's voice became more calm.

Richards was out in the baggage handling area. There was background noise, but he thought, at first, that he could hear an unusual nervousness in Stafford's voice. When he heard the rest his thoughts became engrossed in the trip. "Yes," he said, "I can go if it's necessary." This wasn't the first time he'd been sent trip on short notice.

"Good." Stafford said, reading the script, "Prepare to leave and I'll call and tell them to expect you."

"Ok. Anything you want me to take along? Any special instructions?"

"Your procedure manuals, that's all. Make all your own travel arrangements. I'll be out most of the day." He began to panic in fear of his life as the call came to a close. "Goodbye...it's Noska...," he blurted loudly. Rashidii's finger had snapped the button down just after the "goodbye". Noska was smiling.

They also forced Stafford to leave a message on his home answering machine. The message said that he had to make an unexpected trip to the New York office and would return the following evening. This would buy them an extra day, in case none of the drivers stopped at the diner today.

They gagged and blindfolded Stafford and Rashidii went to work in the kitchen. The tissue box was upside down on the counter, the bottom cut on three sides and flapped open. Wearing latex gloves, Rashidii put an inch of tissues in the box. He had brought the box containing the C-4 that morning. He took out the rectangular six pound slab and began to carefully cut it down with a kitchen knife. He cut small slabs from the end and two sides. He placed the remaining piece on plastic wrap on the table behind him. About three pounds, he judged from the percentage he had cut away. Enough to blow a good-sized hole in any plane, he surmised. He took two small timer detonators from his pocket. The plane was scheduled to leave at 2:40 P.M.; 1440 hours. Mid-flight would be about 1830 hours over the Atlantic. Allowing for the fact that States Airlines international flights had been twenty minutes late in recently published statistics, he set the timers at 1850 hours; 6:50 P.M. He pushed both of the detonators into the soft explosive. Then he removed the gloves and washed his hands thoroughly in the sink. After donning new gloves, he covered the explosive in several layers of plastic wrap, careful to touch only the plastic. He hoped his precautions would defeat the purpose of any bomb-sniffing dogs or chemical detectors that might be in use.

As Rashidii busied himself in the small kitchen. Noska, still wearing the wig and mustache, was carrying a box of trash from the kitchen down to the dumpster in the alley. Stafford stirred a few times, then remained quiet at a

warning from Rashidii. Noska had sold his motorcycle and
reduced his worldly belongings to his old car and a small
carry-on bag he would take on the flight to California. The
bag sat next to the door. As Noska bustled about in the living
room, Rashidii placed the package into the tissue box. He
packed tissues around it and on the bottom. Then he glued the
bottom back in place.

He heard Noska leave, shutting the door behind him.
Now Rashidii moved quickly. He laid out another piece of
plastic and picked up the remaining pieces of C-4. He shaved
off a few slivers and tossed them on the floor, out of sight
against the counter kickplate. A gift for the police, he was
thinking. He then washed his hands again and wrapped the
remaining pieces. He opened another box on the table and
quickly took out handfuls of polystyrene packing material. He
removed a couple layers of books and then a package
containing one hundred and seventeen thousand dollars in
small bills. He removed another layer of books and put the
explosive inside above the bottom layer. He took a small .38
caliber automatic from his pocket and put it in above the
explosive. He repacked the box, putting the packing material
on top just as he heard Noska at the door.

The box had a large address label on it. It was
addressed to Fred Hamm at the Crescent Moon Motel in Los
Angeles. Another large label read "BOOKS". At first, Noska
had been reluctant to mail the money, but Rashidii had
convinced him it was the only safe way. Noska should carry
only a couple of thousand dollars with him, Rashidii told him.
If he were caught with more than ten thousand in cash,
especially one hundred thousand or more he would surely be
detained as a suspected drug dealer or launderer of drug
money. Questions would be asked, his disguise discovered.
Noska became convinced it was a good idea, but insisted on

packing and mailing the box himself. Actually, the mailing had been the Baron's idea. It would serve the purpose of keeping Noska where Rashidii could find him, waiting for the package. Then Rashidii would kill him and retrieve the money. Now it would serve another purpose for Rashidii. Unknown to the Baron, he was working on a second deal with El Alamien. A deal that would require the more than three pounds of C-4 he had hidden in the box.

Noska came into the kitchen. Rashidii nodded toward the tissue box on the counter as he slipped on the thin leather gloves he usually wore. Noska opened the flaps on the box on the table, removed the top layers of books and checked the money. Convinced everything was okay, he sealed it with tape. He put the box next to his case in the living room, where he could watch it. He sat in the easy chair and lit a cigarette. Rashidii checked his watch, it was 9:10 A.M. Noska chain-smoked as they waited in silence. On the couch Stafford struggled and moaned through the gag. When he became too loud, a "shut up" from either of the men would quiet him.

At 10:00 A.M. Rashidii nodded to Noska. Noska stubbed out a cigarette and stood up. Abruptly he turned to the couch and unzipped his pants. "You wanta know what the fuck I think of States Airlines?" Noska asked as he began to urinate on Stafford's face and head. The terrorized, blinded man struggled around on the couch to avoid the spray. "That's what the fuck I think, you bastard," Noska said, giggling.

Rashidii had seen people abused, tortured and mutilated in ways unimaginable to most people, but this act both surprised and deeply disgusted him. Another manifestation of Noska's insanity, he thought. Noska zipped his pants and went into the kitchen. He put on a shoulder holster and shoved the Taurus nine millimeter automatic into it. Rashidii helped him into the harness they had fashioned. It had shoulder straps and a wide belt around the belly. Attached to the belt were an insulated jar of ice water and the battery, wiring and electrode clips and several tools. Noska put on a loose, navy blue nylon windbreaker over it. He picked up the tissue box, now in a slightly larger box for protection.

Rashidii leaned over and whispered in Noska's ear, "Now that he's recognized you, we can't take any chances. I'll take him where he can't ever be found and put a bullet behind his ear." Noska stared at Rashidii for a moment, realizing there was no other way now. Feelings of both fear and relief came over him at once. Then Rashidii tapped the pistol under Noska's left armpit, "If you are caught, I suggest you use this on yourself."

Back in the living room, Noska picked up his case and the package and left. Rashidii shut the door behind him, then went behind the couch and peered out on Pulaski Road. A few minutes later, Noska drove around the corner, headed south as planned. Again Rashidii acted quickly. In the kitchen he wrapped his left arm and hand with the plastic wrap. Opening a drawer, he selected a large butcher knife. He thought for a moment, then pulled a latex glove over the leather glove on his right hand. He planted his right foot in the easy chair and leaned over the groaning Stafford. Stafford was half-sitting on the couch leaning toward the easy chair. Rashidii gathered the man's hair, which was wet with urine, in his right hand. With his left he stabbed the knife down into the right side of the man's throat. Stafford went rigid for a moment. Then, his body began to buck and shake as Rashidii cut through the throat with a downward motion of the knife. Blood spurted from the wound as Stafford's body continued to shake in involuntary movements. As Rashidii backed away, first the knife, then the body fell to the floor between the couch and the coffee table. The kill looked messy as intended.

Rashidii unwrapped the blood-spattered plastic from his arm, slipped off the glove and tossed them in a trash can in the kitchen. He unhooked the answering machine and put it in his case. No one was in the hall when he checked. He was out in a second, locking the door behind. To discourage easy entry, he shoved a piece of wire in the keyhole and broke it off. Carrying his case, he walked through the halls and out the back door. He rushed to the nearby post office in time to see Noska mail the package. It did not look as though it had been tampered with. He then followed Noska to Des Plaines Road. He pulled into a shopping center parking lot there and waited, keeping Noska under surveillance.

From the States Airlines database he had the numbers of three scissor box aircraft loading trucks that would be carrying tissues for the flight: 789, 344 and 322. The trucks were white with dark blue trim and lettering. The number was visible on the front door and in the center of the header, just above roll up door in the back. Also, the trucks used for loading the massive Boeing 747 aircraft were larger than the others. It would be easy for Noska to spot them at a distance. Truck 789 had left promptly at 11:30 A.M. and Noska followed it. The truck passed Peter's Kitchen and Noska turned around and went north past the caterers. He turned into the pharmacy parking lot and waited. At 11:50, truck 344 rolled out and Noska pulled out and followed it. This vehicle also passed the diner without stopping. Noska turned around and went north, again.

Noska now realized that it was unlikely the third truck would stop either. He was distressed at not getting Richards and now he might not get the rest of his money. On his way back north he noticed truck number 322 going south. He made a quick turn but the truck was out of sight. As he approached Peter's Kitchen he saw the truck backed into a parking place near the northeast corner of the lot! He followed a large, dark van into the lot. The van selected a place next to truck 322 toward the road and backed in. It struck Noska that this would provide cover. He backed in on the opposite side of the truck, it blocked the view of his car from the diner windows.

Noska slipped on a pair of thin leather gloves. He put the bulky tissue box inside the windbreaker and got out of his car. He walked to the back of the truck. The plastic seal hung from the padlock brackets on the roll up door. He took a look around. Behind him was a seven-foot high fence of weathered wood, which surrounded the storage area of the gas station next door. To his right beyond his own car was a small white house. There was a high, white picket fence along the side of the house. Only the roof peak and the top of one window was visible. He was out of sight. He took a battery powered screwdriver from his pocket. On the end he had installed a small, thin aluminum oxide cutting wheel. He held the seal in his left hand and pushed the button on the screwdriver. The heavy wire loop on the seal sliced through easily at the top center. Replacing the screwdriver, he took two pairs of pliers from the belt. He had taped the jaws to prevent scratching the metal. Gripping one side of the loop with both pairs, he bent the metal to open the loop without damaging the plastic case. He replaced the pliers and put the seal in his pocket.

Arun Rashidii was driving through the parking lot of Peter's Kitchen. He saw Noska's car parked next to the caterer's truck. He backed into a parking place on the other side of the lot, where he could see Noska's car and the truck.

Noska peered around one corner of the truck, then the other. No one was about. Carefully, he rolled up the large rear door a few inches and looked in. The ends of seven roll cabinets were there. Each had a blue, roll up door on either side. The doors were face to face and tight together. He would have to pull a cabinet out to look at the contents. He pushed the truck's door up several feet, until it was just above the top of the cabinets. There were plastic shrouded trays of utensils on top of the cabinets and papers secured to their top edges with cords. The paper and plastic rustled a bit in the breeze. The sound sent a cold shiver down Noska's spine. He released the foot brake on the caster on the first one and pulled it out a few inches. He rolled up the side door. The shelves were full of canned soda. He slid the door down, pushed the cabinet back in place and set the brake. He checked the second cabinet and the third. Nothing but canned soda in those also.

Noska was sweating now, his hands were shaking. He thought of checking around again, but decided to keep at it. Could he kill someone if he was caught in the act? Or kill himself? He had a queasy feeling in the pit of his stomach and his legs began to feel rubbery as he reached for the fourth cabinet. He pulled it out and slid the door up. The bottom shelf held two rows of light blue boxes of facial tissue! He regained composure as he concentrated on the task at hand. Pulling out the top box at the end of the row, he lifted the bottom one and replaced it with the box from his jacket. He crushed the box he had removed as flat as possible on the step plate of the truck and shoved it down the front of his pants. Quickly, he put the cabinet in place, locked the caster brake and rolled the truck door down.

Noska deburred and cleaned the ends of the wire on the seal with abrasive paper. He replaced it on the padlock brackets and bent the wire back into place with the pliers. Working rapidly, his hands trembling again, he slid a small, snug ceramic collar over the joint to keep the ends aligned and prevent oxidation of the weld. He clipped on the electrodes, one on each side of the joint. He opened the jar of ice water and brought it under the seal. He submersed the plastic and as much of the two protruding wires as he could. Pressing the wire ends of the seal tight together with his fingers he pushed the circuit button on his belt. Current flowed in the wire and in less than a second the weld was complete. A minuscule wisp of smoke escaped from under the ceramic sleeve. He broke the sleeve off with the pliers and put the pieces in his pocket. Immediately, he went to work with the abrasive paper, sanding off the tiny amount of slag. There was no visible line, a perfect weld. Looking both ways he brushed on acid paste. He blew the remaining water droplets out of the plastic case with a compressed air can and wiped off the acid paste quickly. The seal looked as though it hadn't been touched. In seconds he was back in his car starting the engine.

Less than a half-hour later, Noska pulled into the long term parking ramp at O'Hare International Airport. When he had left the lot Sunday night he had told the attendant he had lost his ticket. It cost eighty dollars to get the car out of the lot, but now he had the ticket dated Saturday in the glove compartment. When his car was found, he reasoned, this would be proof he had not been in Chicago since Saturday. He deposited the makeshift belt and his gun in a trash barrel in the parking lot.

In a dark suit, wearing a tie and his blonde wig and mustache, he was now David Kowalski. He stopped in a bar at the airport and had several boilermakers. He sat there for some time and finally he began to calm down. He began to have delusions of grandeur as the alcohol took effect. He thought of the beautiful women and shining, new cars and motorcycles he would have as a wealthy man. He left the bar, walking with a swagger.

The feeling of possessing great power swept over him as he walked the large corridors of the airport. He held the fate of John Richards and many others in his hands now. States Airlines and Richards would pay for the way he had been treated, he chuckled to himself. He remembered the smug Richards, telling him he was being terminated. Telling him he was under suspicion for theft. That son-of-a-bitch. The day had come for the bastards to pick up the tab they owed George Noska. Nobody, no matter how goddamn big, fucks with George Noska he thought. He took the escalator up to the next level, then the pedestrian walk above the rails and down the stairs to the train boarding platform. He took the train to the new international terminal. He disembarked and took the escalator up to the boarding level. He went into the main corridor. The front section of the terminal was a long, structural steel arch. The steel sections and girders were painted a gleaming white. Noska could look up in either direction and see the sloping arch. Everywhere above, it seemed, the bright blue sky could be seen in rectangular panels set in the framework. A gigantic ribbon of red, yellow, blue and green stripes, each several feet wide, was looped through the white crossbeams. It ran the length of the arc adding a huge streak of color to the otherwise pristine structure. At the floor level there was a long row of ticket counters either way and the din of people moving about. To Noska, in his inebriated state, the whole scene seemed spectacular and surreal.

In front of him was the wide corridor that led to the international boarding area. He walked forward with a confident swagger. Above him on either side, hung the colorful flags of many nations. To his left were restaurants and to his right, shops. Straight ahead was the security station.

A large sign above it read "TICKETED PASSENGERS ONLY" in large, white letters on a blue background.

At the security station he approached an officer dressed in gray pants and wearing a white shirt with a gold badge above the left breast. The officer asked to see his international ticket. Noska explained that his business partner was on flight 283 and had forgotten his credit cards. Could he go through to deliver them and a message? He would be back in a few minutes. The security guard wanted to see identification and Noska produced the David Kowalski driver's license. The officer was looking at Noska suspiciously. Then he took the license and looked at it. He nodded and said, "Ok, but we'll keep your case until you return."

Relieved, Noska nodded and entered the gate area. He walked down the corridor and found the boarding gate for flight 283 to London. It was full of people. He looked at his watch, it was after 2:00 P.M. The plane would be taking off in less than an hour. Noska selected a seat across the aisle from the gate. He studied the people in the waiting area. He didn't see John Richards. Over the heads of the people he could see the massive nose of the Boeing 747 through the windows. The feeling of power came over him again.

Rashidii had shadowed Noska all the way to the security area. He had sidled up to the barrier rope close enough to hear the conversation between Noska and the security guard, then moved away. What was the crazy American doing now? Was he smarter than they thought, taking an international flight? But what would he do for money? Part of the reason for allowing him only a couple thousand dollars was to insure his appearance in Los Angeles. Rashidii hoped Noska was only checking to see if Richards boarded. But what if Richards didn't board? He didn't want to take a chance on trying to talk his way through the security as Noska had. He had nothing technically illegal in his carry-on case but the security people would certainly be suspicious of him if they searched it. He waited.

The boarding gate doors opened and Noska watched the passengers shuffle into line and enter the gate. When the majority passed through he noticed John Richards coming down the corridor. He was a tall, thin man of thirty-five with dark, curly hair and the handsome face of a Grecian statue. He wore wire-rimmed aviator style glasses and his shirt sleeves were rolled up to the elbow. His suitcoat was over one arm and he carried an attache' case in his other hand. He glanced in Noska's direction and their eyes met. Noska looked away thinking he saw a flicker of recognition in the man's eyes. When Noska looked again Richards was in the waiting area talking to the employee there, his back to Noska. Finally, after the last of the passengers filed through Richards walked toward the gate. As he did so he turned and shot a quick glance back at Noska. Briefly their eyes met again and then Richards turned back and passed through the gate. "You son-of-a-bitch, I hope you fly first class," Noska whispered.

Rashidii was relieved to see Noska retrieve his case and walk down the main corridor under the brightly colored flags. When they were out of sight of the security station he approached Noska. "What are you doing in the international terminal?" he asked under his breath.

"To see if that fucker Richards got on the flight."

"And?"

"He did."

"I presume all else went as planned."

"Fuckin' perfect."

"You had better get to your flight," Rashidii said. They went down the stairs to the boarding platform and took the train back to the domestic terminals. Rashidii walked with Noska and watched him go through security, then head for the correct boarding gate area.

Quickly, Rashidii went to a pay phone and called Von Kloussen. He verified the flight number, 283.

Then Rashidii walked across the main corridor and located a women's restroom. The door was in an alcove off the main corridor. He watched it. A woman came out. Two went in. Another he had not seen before came out. He checked his watch and waited a couple of minutes. One of the two came out. After a couple more minutes, the second came out, but another entered immediately after. "Damn," he said under his breath. He couldn't wait any longer. He looked at his watch and counted ten seconds then slipped quickly into the restroom. It was empty except for a pair of feet he could see under the door of one of the stalls. He entered the end stall and opened his case. Swiftly, he took off his pants, socks and shoes and set them on the back of the toilet. He slipped on a pair of opaque, brown panty hose from his case. He then sat on the toilet and slipped his feet into a pair of women's black wingtip shoes. He stood and removed his jacket and shirt and donned a padded bra from his case. Then he put an ankle-length dress down over his head. It had a flower print in shades of dull brown. Over that, he put on a white, button-up, long-sleeved sweater. Moving as quickly as possible, he fastened a string of white beads around his neck. He put on a woman's hairpiece that was more blue than gray. He straightened it and anchored it with bobby pins. He quickly powdered his face and put on a pair of rimless women's glasses.

Rashidii took an open-topped bag with loop handles out of the case he carried in and unfolded it. It was decorated in flower print. He put the men's clothing in the case and crushed it flat. He looked out, the bathroom was empty except for one other stall. He stuffed the case and the remainder of his clothes into the trash container. The stall door opened behind him and a woman stepped out. Rashidii turned slowly. "Hello," the woman said. He returned the greeting in a voice as high and weak as he could muster. He looked in the mirror. He was, himself, surprised at how much he looked like a little old lady. He straightened his hairpiece and added a little powder. That morning he had shaved the black hair from his knuckles and hands. He adjusted the sweater sleeves to cover the hair on his wrists. He walked out into the main corridor. Now he was Lillie Reed. An elderly lady on her way to visit her sister in California.

Rashidii got to the gate just in time to board. Von Kloussen had asked for assigned seating, so that Noska's seat was near the rear of the Boeing 767 and Rashidii's near the front. This way Rashidii could check on Noska without ever having to pass him. He was doing this now, as people bustled about in the aisle stowing their belongings in the overhead compartments. He caught a glimpse of Noska in his seat staring out the window. Satisfied, he took his own seat.

The Baron had left the hotel and found a pay phone. He left a coded message at a London answering service to confirm that the plan had been executed.

TWELVE

Due to some mechanical checks, flight number 283 bound for London was well over three hours late. John Richards sat in a left window seat in row fifty of the Boeing 747. Frustrated at having to sit on the ground for well over two hours he was relieved that they were finally moving. He knew well that when aircraft maintenance ordered a delay, it was done. The pilot might be God in the sky, but on the ground it was the mechanic. Finally, at five forty-eight P.M. they were rolling along the taxiway.

Captain Richard "Rich" Diener was at the controls of the three-hundred and fifty ton engineering marvel that was the Boeing 747. At age forty-eight he had more than thirty years of flying experience, including fighter pilot service during the Viet Nam war. He was considered one of the best pilots in the employ of States Airlines. Al Guise was the co-pilot and Janice Mullenix was the flight engineer. There were twelve cabin attendants and 418 passengers aboard.

Diener queued the plane up at the end of the taxiway. As the planes in front of him moved out onto the runway for take off, he made the turn until he was facing the runway. He was cleared for takeoff. With a set of nose wheels larger than truck tires, he steered the craft onto the runway. Without hesitation, he pushed the throttles forward even as he straightened the craft on the runway center line. Lumbering and bobbing in response to the uneven surface at first, the runway ride became smoother as the plane quickly accelerated. At 6:05 P.M. flight 283 left the ground at O'Hare Field under the humid, dusky Illinois sky. At three thousand feet Diener began a slow, climbing bank to the right. On an east, northeast heading over Lake Michigan the giant plane continued its slow ascent.

* * *

Minutes later, the Boeing 767 touched down at Los Angeles International Airport with Noska and Rashidii aboard. Noska caught a cab to the Crescent Moon Motel. Rashidii was confident about Noska's destination. He rented a car at the airport and drove to the International Inn, not far away. He walked to the counter in the lobby and asked for a room.

* * *

At that moment an air traffic controller at Ottawa, Ontario had flight 283 on radar at 34,440 feet passing north of the city. The cart containing the tissue box was stowed under a counter in the back service area near the rear pressure bulkhead. Ten rows of seats ahead, John Richards had loosened his seat belt and relaxed. The seat belt warning light was out and several passengers were up and about in the aisle. He lifted the his coffee cup.

Suddenly, there was a deafening, roaring blast behind him. First the noise and then the increased pressure caused excruciating pain in Richards' ears. Then, his eardrums burst and he heard only a faint ringing. Instinctively, he bent over in his seat. As he so did the back of the seat came with him. Debris was blasted forward from the service area in a gust of smoke. The bomb had destroyed the front wall around the service area and the rear bathrooms. The ceilings and back walls of the bathrooms were ripped open. The aluminum-alloy pressure bulkhead behind the bathrooms and the access hole cover to the vertical stabilizer were blasted open. The shock waves of the bomb, amplified by the cabin pressure, exploded into the unpressurized tail section area. This caused aluminum skin panels on the thirty-five foot vertical stabilizer to rip loose. The panels blew away into space. All that remained of the huge vertical fin was the skeleton framework, useless for control of the plane as the icy wind sailed through it. The floor directly below the blast was torn open. Parts of the floor and its structural support became shrapnel that was blasted downward as though out of a giant cannon. This shrapnel shattered the heavy, fiberglass duct below the floor. It carried the hydraulic lines and electrical wires to the tail section. These provided control of the rudder and trim, so the pilot could control horizontal direction and most importantly, flight stability.

The control of an airplane involves nothing more than presenting solid surfaces at various angles to a mass of fast moving air. The process of maintaining stability is one of frequent small adjustment by moving the various surfaces of the wings and tail slightly. Direction of the airplane is changed by moving them a bit more. The loss of control or the loss of the surfaces themselves puts the plane in danger of going hopelessly out of control.

Both the cabin level loading door and the cargo door below popped from the starboard side of the plane like corks from an over-agitated champagne bottle. Aluminum panels at the narrow section of the fuselage bowed out, but the structural ribs held.

In seconds, shockwaves of the bomb subsided and a great hollow whoosh signaled the drop in cabin pressure. The pressurized cabin air was escaping rapidly to the atmosphere through the tail section and door openings. Oxygen masks fell from the compartments above the passengers. The cabin filled with a white mist. This resulted from the rapid cooling and condensation of the cabin air caused by the sudden pressure drop. In the first moment after the blast, there were many people dead. The occupant in each of the five rear bathrooms, the dozen people waiting at the bathrooms and the three flight attendants in the rear service area were killed instantly. The shock of the blast hurled their bodies or crushed them in the wreckage amid flying shrapnel. Nearly all of the people in the last six rows of seats suffered a similar fate. Seconds after the blast, those bodies and parts of bodies that had not been twisted into the wreckage or otherwise secured were forced out the loading door. The raging, powerful torrent of air rushing from the plane spewed debris and bodies of the dead and the near dead out into open space. In the fiftieth row, John Richards bent over and tried to secure his oxygen mask.

He had barely escaped sudden death. He felt the plane begin to shake violently.

The plane lurched suddenly down to the right and dipped into a dive.

In the cockpit the crew had secured their oxygen masks. Captain Diener was frenzied, as he surveyed the flashing, warning lights and accompanying readouts. He spoke loudly and frantically into the small microphone under his oxygen mask. "Cabin pressure gone...rudder inoperative...tail auxiliary power unit out.....going out of control and into a downspin!!!" He pushed the throttle forward quickly and dropped the flaps slightly. The giant plane slowed and leveled.

"Have you at twenty-eight thousand feet," the controller said. "Should we prepare for emergency landing at Ottawa?"

There was no response. The plane rolled down to the left. Diener dropped the left flap to correct and then there was a roll to the right and the plane went into a wide, downward spiral again.

In the cabin, human beings both alive and lifeless, were thrown about like rag dolls. Carry-ons, books, pillows, clothes, cups and other items flew about as the plane dropped through the skies. John Richards, bent forward in his seat, felt the sudden, heavy impact of a body crash onto the back of his seat, then lift off as quickly.

"Have you at eleven thousand feet!" The controller said loudly, "Can you stabilize?"

Diener saw the green forest far below as the nose of the plane dipped. He again pushed the throttles forward and leveled the plane with the flaps. It went out of the spiral at a tangent in a slow roll, first dipping one wing then the other. Diener's face was covered with sweat now. The co-pilot and flight engineer watched in terror as he worked the individual engine throttles with his right hand and the flap lever controls with his left. He was attempting to find some coordination of them that would keep the plane level and stabilized. This was nearly impossible with the vertical stabilizer gone and without control of the rudder and tailplane. The plane leveled and actually gained altitude momentarily, then lurched into a downward spiral again.

The controller at Ottawa watched in horror as the image on his radar screen dropped below ten thousand feet, then disappeared from view.

The plane spiraled down over the small city of Wakefield, Quebec, just northwest of Ottawa on the Gatineau River. In a last desperate effort, Diener dropped the flaps and pushed the throttles forward. The residents of Wakefield saw the huge plane suddenly appear out of the west, wavering with engines screaming, on a path directed at the center of the city. Suddenly, as if by the hand of God, the plane leveled and lifted a bit, clearing the city. The thunderous roar of the engines shook the ground as the plane passed over just above treetop level. Four streams of black exhaust rolled down on the city like the wrath of hell. The giant aircraft went over the river to the east, rolling from side to side again like a staggering drunk. Still traveling at more than two-hundred miles per hour, it crashed down into the forest flattening giant pine, oak and maple trees in its path as though they were so many dry, dead weeds. The trees tore the aluminum skin from the underbelly of the fuselage and then from the wings. The plane broke up as it crashed to the ground, some sections bursting into flames. Amid the trees, clouds of black smoke belched up and the debris stretched for more than a mile.

* * *

George Noska kicked open the door of his room at the Crescent Moon. He had visited the liquor store down the street. He carried a case of beer in one hand and a bag containing two liters of Southern Comfort whiskey in the other. In his room, he searched in the phone book for a few moments. Then he called and ordered a pizza to be delivered. He sat on the bed and popped open a beer. By now, he thought, the bomb should have gone off. He was afraid to turn on the television. Outside, parked across the street Rashidii had watched him enter the room. Satisfied, he went to find some men's clothes to return to his usual disguise. After an hour and a half, Noska had eaten most of the pizza and washed it down with several beers. He walked to the liquor store again for cigarettes. When he returned he poured himself a generous glass of whiskey and switched on the television. He lay back on the bed and watched lazily for twenty minutes. Then a newsbreak came on. An international flight originating in Chicago had gone down near Ottawa. The cause of the crash was unknown. Reports indicated it was unlikely that there were any survivors. The flight number was being withheld pending notification of nearest of kin. Noska, feeling the effects of the alcohol, leaned forward. "Richards, you fucker, welcome to hell," he said angrily to the television screen.

Denmark, Wednesday, June 29

Nick had returned to Odense by noon. After studying the information at the Froslevlejren Camp, he had decided to continue on south to Hamburg, Germany, for further research. There at the National Museum, he spent Monday and Tuesday researching the activities and whereabouts of SS personnel assigned to the Danish-German border area fifty years earlier.

A picture had begun to emerge as he researched names and dates. He rode to Kiel early and took the morning ferry to Bagenkrop on Langeland, a large Danish island connected by a bridge to the southeast coast of Fyn. In his room at the Tre Roser he waited until after 2:00 P.M. then called Langley through the scrambler. It was just past 8:00 A.M. in Langley and Joe Ronzoni had just arrived in his office. He took the call.

"Bradshaw here," Nick said, "Mystery solved, I think."

Joe paused for a moment, thinking. "Oh, yeah. That plane is almost certainly Halvorsen's. It was assigned to the squadron that he was part of at Steeple Morden in early nineteen forty-four."

"Not only that. SS guards took twenty-five prisoners from the Froslevlejren Camp on Jutland early February of forty-four. Enough men to build the road and dig out the hill on the Von Kloussen estate by April. Supplies and equipment were requisitioned for them during that time. The location of their work was secret. They were never returned and never turned up after the war. People at the camp thought they might have been sent on to the death camps, but there's no record of that. My guess is that Himmler had his guards execute them when the work was done."

"All in a day's work for that son-of-a-bitch. He's on record as having murdered Hitler's enemies over the years."

"Then I checked German historical records. Eighteen SS officers and guards were assigned to Denmark in early February. They also disappeared without a trace. I think the bastard executed his own men. This would explain why the location was unknown. Everyone who knew about it was murdered."

"The only way to insure no one talks in a conspiracy," Joe commented.

"So, I guess I'll get ready to head home. Somebody will have to negotiate with Von Kloussen for permission to dig, probably."

"Yeah and that's going to be a real problem. The FBI gave me an update on him today. They traced some of that equipment on the Cabal back to a factory in Philadelphia. The FBI got together with Interpol and Scotland yard and they figured out that Von Kloussen owns controlling interest in the factory. Technically his 'estate' owns stock and records show that it was purchased through a broker in London. There are a couple of layers of holding companies too, all set up to look like Von Kloussen didn't even know he owned the stock. The expert bean counters say it's obvious he was trying to cover up his ownership. The agencies are all convinced he's guilty of managing illegal arms shipments. They tell me he's partners with that goddamn Cha-Turgi, whoever he is. They've cost us the lives of a lot of good men. They want him, but there's no way to prove anything at this stage. Hell, I doubt that a guy like this would ever talk to investigators under ordinary circumstances."

"So?"

"So, we act unofficially. I know you're supposed to be retired from this kind of work. But, you're right there and you have a safe cover. I want you to interrogate Baron Von Kloussen, no holds barred."

Nick thought for a moment and then said, "Yes, sir." Then he paused and added, "Some vacation junket."

"By the way, we'll be assisting the Bureau on the investigation of the flight 283 bombing."

In her room, Eva had been listening to both the bug in Nick's room and the phone tap, simultaneously on the receiver. She had barely been able to make out Nick's words since there was a ringing buzz, apparently from the tap. Her phone rang, it was Kurt Kohfer. He had returned from his trip to France.

"Anything new?" he asked.

"I just tried to listen to a call. Still, I can only hear him, not the other party. There must be something wrong with your tap."

"Damn. What did he say?"

"Things about war research on Germans and their prisoners. Something about digging on the Von Kloussen estate. Getting permission from the Baron to dig. I am not certain. I could not hear very well."

"Hmmm," Kohfer said, "it doesn't sound very important." He was wondering why a man like Barber would be talking about digging up war artifacts at all. Perhaps he suspected he was being spied upon and was playing his role to the hilt. "The Baron is due to return late tonight."

"And the Baroness?"

"In Copenhagen with her cousin for a few days."

"Then I'm sure Soren will want to see me tonight."

"I'm sure," Kohfer said sarcastically. He rang off.

A minute later there was a knock at Eva's door. It was Nick. "Hello, Professor she said cheerfully, but with a nervous edge in her voice, "I take it your research trip was enjoyable."

"Very much so. I'm going to pay a call on the Baron Von Kloussen at his estate near the southwest coast. Would you like to join me?"

Eva was incredulous. She stared at him for a moment, thinking. Then asked, "Why would you want to see this man?"

"When I first came here, I inadvertently trespassed on his estate. I'd like to offer a proper apology."

"Actually," Eva began carefully, thinking fast, "Von Kloussen's estate manager is my cousin."

"Ah, the one who lent you the car?" This explained everything, he thought.

"Yes. Recently, I spoke with him and the Baron is not there. I believe he'll be in tomorrow."

"Well then, perhaps we could pay a call on him tomorrow morning."

"Yes, of course."

"Dinner this evening?"

"Sorry, I have a prior engagement."

An hour later Eva walked into the Baron's office at the castle. Kurt Kohfer was at the desk. She shut the door. "Kurt, Bradshaw is planning to pay a visit to the Baron. Says he wants to make a formal apology for trespassing. I told him you and I were cousins."

Kohfer stared at her. So, he thought, Barber is making his move. "Those damned Englishmen are so proper," he said. "Uh, fine. I'm sure it'll be a harmless visit." Kohfer's well-trimmed black beard framed an evil, toothy smile. If Barber were here to assassinate the Baron, Kurt hoped he could accommodate the man in some way. And then, with a well-aimed shot, he could look like an avenging hero and collect the price on Barber's head at the same time.

Langley, Virginia, 9:00 A.M.

Major Tommy Garcia entered Joe Ronzoni's office. He was still limping slightly from the bullet wound in the calf he had received in the takeover of the Cabal. He wore a dark suit and glasses with dark, smoke lenses. Joe took a seat at the head of the small, conference table next to his desk. He motioned Tommy to sit.

"How's Eli doing?" Joe asked referring to the Mossad agent who had been with Tommy on the Cabal.

"Better. They think he'll regain the use of his arms. Whether he'll be one hundred percent," Tommy shrugged and shook his head, "they don't know."

"You heard about the crash of flight 283 near Ottawa?"

"Just the news reports on TV and in the papers."

"What I am about to tell you comes from me and no one else." Tommy nodded. "There is a red top secret 'finding' that any and all conspirators responsible for deaths by air piracy or sabotage will be neutralized as quickly as possible."

"Psychology 101, swift and sure punishment. What about evidence, due process?"

Ronzoni ignored the question. "It's only necessary that the authorized agencies involved be reasonably certain of guilt. We will have the responsibility for following through." Joe then explained about the request by Mac McGinnis to have the heads of the Votilinni family assassinated. "At the time we had no interest. But the Votilinni's were approached by someone shopping for sabotage services. Right now, it's all we have to go on. Stein, Vanlandingham and McGinnis are on their way here now. As far as they're concerned, we're involved only because this is an international incident and we're helping with the investigation. You feel up to taking out a couple of crime bosses, if it comes to that?"

"Jesus!" Was all Tommy could say. Then he looked at Joe and nodded.

Leslie came on the speaker phone, "Your guests have arrived."

Mac, Sally and Jack Vanlandingham entered and took seats across the table from Tommy. Jack spoke first, "We just picked up Mr. McGinnis from the airport, so we haven't had a chance to talk. Actually, we had to lose a tail he was carrying as well." He laid a couple of file folders on the table.

Joe introduced Tommy as Agent Phil Smith. He leaned over and shook hands with them. Sally had a slight smirk on her lips and a knowing look in her eyes. They had worked together on an assignment before.

"There any reason you guys hire so goddamn many Smiths over here?" Jack said in a weak attempt at humor. Joe ignored the question.

"Well," Jack began, "Reports from the scene indicate a bomb was detonated near the rear of the plane. There have been calls to the press with claims that the Liberation Army of the Holy War is responsible. A call I received this morning confirmed that and plastic explosive is likely. C-4 or Semtex placed in the rear service area. Possibly in a supply cabinet. Not in the luggage or cargo area. It looks like someone who knew his way around airports was involved. By the way, there were four survivors, damned miracle. A States Airlines employee named John Richards and a woman and her two small children. They're all in the hospital at Ottawa now. Severe injuries, but we think they'll make it. The pilot managed to get some control of the plane using only the engines, flaps and ailerons. A heroic effort that may have saved the whole goddamn town of Wakefield at the last minute. Our Chicago office has been busy all night. They've compiled a list of individuals who have been terminated from employment at States Airlines during the last two years. They faxed it over this morning." He looked at Mac. "Did James Votilinni have access to the same information you did regarding the offer made to his grandfather?"

"Uh, sure. I knew he was generally aware of the offer. Vito discussed everything with Jimmy, although Jimmy didn't always listen well."

"Is it possible that James Votilinni may have contacted these people after the death of his grandfather and taken the offer?"

"It's possible. He's cut me out of the loop lately so if he had contacted them I wouldn't necessarily know about it. But, this isn't his style." Mac chose his words carefully now. "Jimmy only does things he's motivated to do in some way. Vito left him enormously wealthy, so it wouldn't have been the money."

Sally broke in, "This El Alamien did leave a phone number with Vito. We checked it out. An answering service in London. He paid them for a year's service in advance. They don't know what he looks like, only that people occasionally call with messages and he occasionally calls to get them. Probably uses pay phones. We don't have any leads on him right now." She looked at Mac. "You're the only lead we have right now on the brutal murders of four hundred and twenty-nine innocent people."

"We understand Votilinni enjoys the thrill of the chase, the near miss, getting away with things by the skin of his teeth," Jack said.

Mac knew painfully well this was true, but he didn't agree or disagree visibly. "Last year, I took a course in computer science to upgrade my knowledge. On the final exam one of the questions was: A computer criminal is often a person who is: a. a disgruntled employee; b. has personal or family problems; c. attracted to the challenge of the crime; d. all of the answers. The answer was d. I found answer c. about the challenge, uh, interesting."

"So, possibly Votilinni was attracted by the challenge?"

"Like I said, I doubt it. But hypothetically speaking, if there was a reason that would be it."

Vanlandingham opened one of the folders in front of him. He put a stack of faxed photos in front of Mac. "These are all former airline employees living in the Chicago area. Please look through them and tell us if you recognize anyone."

Mac shrugged and leaned back in the chair with the stack in his lap. Slowly, he went through the entire pile, often shaking his head. When he had finished, Jack reached for the papers, but Mac said, "Wait!" Slowly, he examined each cloudy gray face again. This time he stopped in the middle and laid a sheet on the conference table. "This man, I've seen him before. Met him somewhere," he said, thinking out loud. He bent over the paper. "Sure. This guy worked for the-uh-the organization. Doing some computer work for Veldon. I met him once. Saw him around a coupla' times."

"Christ, he works for Votilinni?" Jack asked.

"Did, I think the job is finished now."

Jack looked down at the fax. He read the fuzzy text at the bottom: "George Noska. Terminated from States Airlines for cause (suspected theft) on January 28, 1994. Was employed as a supplies loading specialist and baggage handler. Criminal record on file." He looked up at Mac. "Just exactly what kind of work did this guy do for you people?"

Mac stared back at him, "I'm not going to tell you, except that it involved computers and had nothing to do with any airline flights or bombings. Actually, it is my opinion as an attorney, that in a technical sense, the work wasn't illegal."

A frustrated look on his face, Vanlandingham turned to Sally. "I'm putting you in charge of this case. Put everything else on hold and track this goddamn Noska down. Call the Chicago office and get our people and the police working on it. Then fly out there. I want you to pull out all the goddamn stops on this."

"And I want Smith here to work with her," Joe said. "This is an international terrorist incident and we have certain directives."

Jack glared at Joe, "And if I refuse?"

"Then I'll call the Director of Central Intelligence and he'll persuade you to change your mind."

Jack sighed, "Ok, but as far as I'm concerned this is an FBI matter and Stein here is in charge."

Joe nodded. "Now we'd like to have a private discussion with Mr. McGinnis."

"And I'm sure I don't want to hear it," Jack said, standing.

After Jack and Sally left, Joe looked at Mac. "What exactly was this Noska doing for Votilinni?"

Mac was silent.

"You can tell me. Our discussions won't leave this office. Our agency is not interested in local mob shit."

"He put the gambling data on computers. Allowed them to run a book store with less people.

Joe laughed, "So even the mob is saving labor, automating, getting efficient?"

"Not exactly. It's not fewer mouths to feed that's important in this case, it's fewer that can talk. Also, this guy wrote some software to scramble the databases in case of a raid. They could be unscrambled later with a keyword."

"I thought you said what Noska did wasn't illegal."

"He wrote and tested the software. Strictly speaking that isn't illegal by itself. The potential use of the software might be," Mac said cautiously.

"I see. And what do people spend their money betting on in Chicago that's so damned important?" Joe asked with a grin.

"Anything you can name, horses, sports, whether the next goddamn guy to walk down the street will step off the curb with his left foot or his right."

"Your former request, about-ah-chopping off heads. It's possible under the present circumstances that something could be done. A partial compliance, perhaps, if you cooperate with us. Phil here will be your contact with us. Take a good look at him, he may be disguised when you see him again."

Tommy removed his glasses so Mac could study his face.

"And, this meeting never took place." Mac nodded and Joe pointed a finger at him, "You'd better remember that. I don't care how many tough, goombah buddies you've got; nobody in this world fucks with us."

THIRTEEN

By 1:00 P.M. FBI agents and Chicago police were breaking down the door of Noska's apartment on Pulaski Road. Detective Sergeants Fritz Grinke and Tanya Williams were on the scene. They found Stafford's body. After a thorough combing of the apartment, they put the slivers of C-4 and other items in evidence bags. Tommy Garcia had arranged for a CIA Falcon Jet to fly he and Sally to Chicago. They rented a car at Midway airport and drove to the apartment. It was hot. Sally had her jacket over her arm as she entered the apartment. Tommy was behind her still wearing his jacket and the dark glasses. The smells of urine and rotting food were strong. The smell of death and dried blood was weaker, but detectable. She greeted the agents on the scene and showed her ID to Grinke.

He nodded, "So you're the one in charge, huh?"

"What have you learned so far?"

Investigators and officers were hustling about. "Let's step out inna' hall," he said.

Sally motioned FBI inspector Tadd Nippy of the Chicago office to join them. He was a tall, thin young man with blond, curly hair and a pale face. He wore a blue pin-striped suit and a red tie.

Out in the hall the odors were much weaker. Tommy stood next to Sally. Grinke looked at the smaller man with the dark glasses and perpetual smile. "Whatta' you feds on drugs now? Light hurt yer eyes?"

"Oh, this is Agent Phil Smith, CIA," Sally said, "This is an international incident and they're participating in the investigation."

"A goddamn spook, huh?" He reached out to shake Tommy's hand and squeezed hard. Tommy squeezed back and Grinke was surprised at the strength of the shorter man's grip. He turned to Sally. "My partner an' me got here first. The place is a fuckin' pigsty. This goddamn Noska musta' used his livin' room for a pisser." Then Grinke chuckled, "This guy musta' whacked off inta' the clothes, furniture everything. Yer people'll have plenty of DNA to work up." He guffawed and looked around at them. If his comment was intended to shock Sally it hadn't worked. She only made another note and looked at him blandly. He resumed serious composure and continued, "The dead man is Don Stafford. Throat cut with a goddamn butcher knife. Messy one. His wallet was on him. He's a manager at States Airlines, we verified that with a call. Noska musta' kidnapped him or lured him here somehow, then used him somehow in the sabotage.

We checked on the whereabouts of the victim's wife and son. Apparently they're ok. They ain't been notified of the death yet."

Sally nodded, making notes, "And Noska?"

"Oh yeah. Ain't found a trace of him. Looks like he skipped. He's got a record, though. Headquarters is puttin' all that together now. We got a local APB out on'em an' I got somma our people out canvassin' the neighborhood askin' questions. See if anybody's seen 'um lately."

"What else?"

"Plenty. We found some slivers onna kitchen floor. Looks like plastic explosive." He turned toward the apartment door, "Hey Williams, could'ja bring that plastic here?"

In a moment, Tanya Williams walked into the hall and held up a clear, plastic evidence bag. Sally took the bag and handed it to Tommy. He removed a sliver, lifted his glasses and examined it closely. He pinched off a small piece, squeezed it between his forefinger and thumb and smelled it, then tasted it with the tip of his tongue. He looked at them, "It's C-4, manufactured in the U.S. during the second quarter of 1993."

Grinke looked at him, an amazed look on his face, "Now how the hell do you know that?"

"That's classified information," Tommy responded.

It was humid and stuffy in the hall. Beads of sweat were forming among the few remaining strands of hair on Grinke's head. He took out a handkerchief and mopped his brow. "Uh, let's see, we got the butcher knife. There's a lot of junk and crap all over in there. We're gettin' it all in tagged evidence bags. This is a rubber-glove job if I ever seen one." He looked at Tanya and nodded.

"Actually," Tanya began, "when we got the FBI's call this morning Sergeant Grinke and I were just getting ready to come over here and talk to George Noska anyway. He's wanted for questioning in a murder investigation we've been working on since Monday morning. Last Thursday night a man was stabbed outside a tavern about two blocks from here. We haven't ID'd the victim. Looks like a homeless drifter. The bartender was out of town for a couple of days. We finally located her this morning. Seems Noska was in the bar that night flashing a lot of cash around. The stabbing victim was there and saw this. She thinks the man left just before Noska. Might have been laying for him to rob him. The victim was found in the alley with a knife in his hand. The body was covered with trash."

"You think Noska might have killed him?" Sally asked.

"Probably not," Tanya responded. The bartender said that Noska was so drunk he could barely walk when he left. And, the wound. Very thin blade, top of the throat. Didn't look like it was inflicted during a struggle. The med examiner says no trauma to the head or other parts of the body. Strange one. I don't know if this has anything to do with the bombing, but I don't believe in coincidences."

"Neither do I," Sally said.

Tommy said, "Where's the body now?"

"Still at the temporary morgue in the basement of the precinct."

Tommy nodded to Sally. "We'll need to see that body," she said, "and round up everyone who knows Noska. We'll have to interview them. Everybody's around the clock on this one until it's solved."

"I'll have to talk to my Captain," Grinke said. "We got a lot of other goddamn cases, murders, you name it."

"I'll talk to your Captain," Sally said. "This damned plane sabotage is four hundred and twenty-nine murders."

Fritz looked at Tanya, "Well I guess we drive out to the 'burbs and see the widow. You feelin' up to it?"

She sighed, "It's part of the job."

"Forget it," Sally said, "we need you on the mainstream investigation. Call the local police out there. Have them take care of it."

"Whatta we takin' *all* of our fuckin' orders from the feds now?" Grinke said sneeringly.

Sally frowned up at him. "Listen, we can't fuck around on this. It's a national security top priority. I told you I'll clear it with your Captain."

Within the hour, Tommy and Sally entered the precinct basement escorted by Captain Duane Trochinski. He was a tall, slim man in his early fifties. He opened a metal door and waved them through. A dark man wearing a white lab coat stood there. Trochinski announced Sally's and Tommy's names and titles. "This is Doctor Walt Winfrey, Assistant Chief Medical Examiner for the city."

"I'm afraid I've got some bad news for you folks," Winfrey said. "Our cooling system has been broken down for twenty-four hours."

Sally sniffed the air and nodded her head, "My keen investigator's nose suspected something like that."

"You think it's bad out here? Wait'll we get in the so-called cool room. We just ordered some dry ice, but, well the people here should have used their heads and ordered it yesterday."

"It's all right, Doctor. Just show us the body." She said.

He took a tube of Camphor creme from his jacket pocket and smeared some on his upper lip. He handed it to Sally and she did the same. He then handed her a breathing filter and put one on himself. He held the items out to Tommy. He said, "No thanks."

"Are you sure?"

Tommy nodded.

The Doctor shook his head and said, "Suit yourself." He led them through two sets of doors into the autopsy lab. "He's laid out on the slab." The body was there on a stainless steel table. It was wet, tiny streams of water were still running in the gutter around the perimeter. "I just washed him down with cold water, but..."

The stench was overpowering. Sally pushed her upper lip up so the camphor would cover the smell. Her eyes began to water. Tommy was bending over the body looking at the throat wound. It had been cut back on each side to the tendons, apparently with a scalpel. He looked at Winfrey, "I need to see where the point of the murder weapon stopped. My bet is the spinal cord is severed at the cervical vertebrae."

Winfrey shrugged his shoulders and slipped on a pair of latex gloves, snapping the wristband on each. He picked up a scalpel and, grasping the forehead, sliced through the tendons and strap muscles on each side of the neck. He pulled the head back as he carefully cut through tissue on each side, following the path of the wound. He pushed upward under the back of the neck. The wound opened like a gaping meaty mouth. A few maggots were visible, at work on the flesh. He sliced through more tissue and then only the vertebrae connected the head and body. He scraped tissue from the bone and examined it closely. "Yes, yes, you're absolutely right, Mr. Smith. The tip of the knife entered between the third vertebra body and the fourth vertebra body. The spinal cord is completely severed. Very sharp knife."

A few minutes later Sally, Tommy, Captain Trochinski, Doctor Winfrey, and Tanya Williams were seated upstairs at a table in the conference room. Fritz Grinke came in with a coffee tray and set it in the middle of the table. "Help yourselves, I'm the fuckin' parlor maid today."

"Sergeant Grinke," Trochinski said, "would you please watch your language? There are ladies present."

He looked around the room, "What? Where, sir? I don't see any. Oh, uh, you couldn't mean Agent Stein here, sir. She curses like a goddamn stable boy standing knee deep in horseshit." He sat down at the table, grinning.

"Never mind, Sergeant," the Captain said, an exasperated look on his face. "Did you bring those people in?"

"Just Wanda Black, the bartender an' a Ed Boelter, owns a restaurant across from Noska's place. So far, they're the only ones we could find who actually knew who the guy is. He's got a couple ex-wives in town, but they claim they ain't seen'em in years. Don't wanna see 'em neither. We'll talk to'em some more anyway." Grinke suddenly turned to Sally. "Say, how did you people connect Noska to this in the first place?"

"An informant," Sally responded.

"And who was that?"

"That's classified."

Grinke sat back in his chair. "How are we supposed ta' help with this investigation if every time I ask a goddamn question I get told it's classified?"

"We have our orders. That's all I can say." She said.

"And the body downstairs?" Trochinski looked at Winfrey then at Sally.

Sally Stein took a sip of her coffee. "Agent Smith and I have been discussing the evidence gathered so far. With the kidnapping of Stafford, procuring the C-4 and all of the other things that had to be done to plant that bomb, we don't think it's possible that Noska could have acted alone. The information I am about to provide is to stay in this room." Everyone nodded. "We know that Middle Eastern terrorists have been shopping for someone to sabotage a plane. It's unlikely that they would have approached a man like Noska directly. But, someone else who agreed to do the job for them might have enlisted his help." She didn't mention the offer made to Votilinni. There were to be no leaks that Diamond Jimmy or his people were suspects. It was believed that the Votilinni mob employed informants in the Chicago Police Department. "We need to find Noska. Short of that, we need to know everyone he has communicated with in recent weeks. Use your street contacts. Run down every lead. The full resources of the FBI are at your disposal, day and night. As for the body downstairs, Phil?"

"This kill was done by an expert," Tommy began. "Someone who has probably done it many times before and practiced often. The weapon was a German type stiletto. It was done in European style, known to us as the 'European standard'. It's a technique used by highly trained people on both sides of what we call 'sovereign sanctioned law' in the trade. Allow me." He reached below the table momentarily and stood. In his hand, seemingly appearing out of nowhere, was a double-edged killing knife. The metal of the seven-inch blade was flat black except for the narrow, silver razor-sharp edge. Eyes around the table widened at the sight of it.

"You gotta permit for that toad-stabber?" Grinke asked. The Captain shot him a wary glance.

"As a matter of fact I do, Sergeant." He took out his wallet and pulled out a laminated card. He slid it across to Grinke. It was a federal concealed weapons permit.

Tommy continued, "This is the Fairbairn-Sykes commando knife that we use. It's heavier and stronger than the stiletto, gives a bit more margin for error. I like to think we Americans are more interested in results than style and finesse. Anyway, we teach a similar technique. You approach the target silently from behind. The target may be carrying a weapon as in the case in question. That will usually be in the right hand, so you must use your own weapon with your left." His words were practiced, he had taught the technique many times. He held the knife in his left hand and pointed it toward his throat. "You quickly reach over the target's left shoulder and pull the knife in near the top of the throat. Simultaneously, you grasp their weapon hand to keep it around the weapon and force your head or chin against the back of the target's neck as a backstop. Often, it's necessary to keep the subject's weapon from falling to the ground or floor and making noise. First, the blade of the knife slices through the windpipe and blocks it. Then the point severs the spinal cord through the body of a cervical vertebra or between two of the cervical vertebrae. The entry angle is very important to accomplish this. In this case it was perfect. No arteries are severed. There's little or no blood, yet the target is rendered immobile and quiet almost instantly. The stiletto blade is narrow. To completely sever the spinal cord it's necessary to move the tip horizontally using the entry wound as a pivot point. This was also done perfectly in this case." He looked at Winfrey. "Would you concur, Doctor?"

"Oh, yes, definitely. The spinal cord was completely severed," Winfrey said. He had been totally absorbed in Tommy's comments, as were the others at the table.

"Executed correctly," Tommy continued, "this is probably the most effective killing technique known that is both silent and tidy." He smiled broadly at the group. "There is one caution though. If you drive the knife in too hard or enter at the wrong angle, the point can exit the back of the target's neck. You can stab yourself then, too. Like this." He pointed to a small horizontal scar on his chin.

Grinke, his elbows on the table and his chin in his palms muttered, "I'll be a son-of-a-bitch."

"As you suspect, your victim may have indeed been attempting to mug Noska," Tommy said. "But, perhaps Noska was watched over by a guardian angel. One with special skills who may have been part of the bombing plot. I've told you all this, so that during the investigation you can recognize the technique and the circumstances, under which it is used. Have any of you ever seen evidence of this technique before?"

Trochinski, Williams and Winfrey shook their heads slowly. Grinke looked around the table. "Not in twenty-one years," he said. "Usually, if there's a knife involved it's a big goddamn mess like Stafford's murder. Or maybe, I should say the target's neutralization, now that we're workin' with you people." He looked around the table with a smirk on his face.

Trochinski then asked, "Any clues to Noska's whereabouts?" No one responded.

"My guess is that he's dead by now," Tommy said. "If he was used in this plot, as we suspect, the people who hired him wouldn't have let him live a second longer than necessary."

Sally nodded and said, "Let's have a talk with these two people you brought in."

Tanya led Sally and Tommy out. Walt Winfrey was staring at the door they shut behind them. "Jesus," he said.

"What's on your mind, Doc?" Grinke asked.

"That guy didn't apply any camphor, didn't wear a mask, nothing when we examined the corpse. I've been doing this for eighteen years and I almost retched up my lunch with the camphor and mask on. He had his nose right down in the wound with the maggots and he didn't even hold his breath. What kind of godawful training do you suppose those people go through?"

Los Angeles, 3:00 P.M.

Arun Rashidii relaxed in an easy chair in his hotel room reading the paper. He sipped from a glass of cognac. He had called the Crescent Moon, and posing as a roomer checked the mail delivery time. It usually came about 2:00 P.M., he was told. He had plenty of time. The box would arrive in the next day or two and he would be waiting, watching for Noska to retrieve it. When he was sure that someone else, such as a postal inspector who may have opened it was not also watching, he would move in. The phone rang. He reached over and picked up the handset.

"This is your good friend."

It was El Alamien. "And this is your very good friend," Rashidii answered.

"It will be at six. No other possibilities. Number is 749219. You may check. Call with the confirm."

"Did you know there were four survivors?"

"Yes and this is very good news. The purpose of terrorism is to terrorize and you cannot terrorize the dead." He hung up.

Six million! He had hoped for more, but it would do. With this and his five million share from the Baron, he would be able to retire a very rich man. The number was a special escrow account at Rashidii's bank in Switzerland. The six million was already there. An ok from the holder of the numbered depositing account would make it available for Rashidii to transfer it to his own account. He looked at his watch. It was after 2:00 A.M. in Switzerland. He would call in the morning to verify the escrow account. He had been trying to formulate a plan. Perhaps he could use Noska again in some way. The Baron was so much better at planning at the strategic level. Rashidii had always been the junior partner, carrying out the plans, making last minute tactical decisions. But, he would develop something workable if he thought about it enough, he mused. He returned to the paper. Scanning the pages, he flipped to the classified advertisements. Always a motorcycle enthusiast he scanned the ads in that section. An ad caught his eye. He read it twice:

> Honda NR 750. Special order limited production ER model of world's fastest street bike. Purchased six months ago special order from Japan for $79,000. Like new. Will sacrifice for $60,000 firm. Red w/black trim, must see! Once in a lifetime opportunity. (213)555-9462

Only in California would one see such an ad, he thought. He had dreamed of owning that model of motorcycle ever since he had read about it a couple of years earlier. If the words "limited production ER" meant what he thought they meant, this was a special order model with the one-hundred and sixty horsepower endurance racing version of the engine. This was at least thirty-five horsepower more than the standard version. The machine would be capable of speeds in excess of 220 miles per hour. Even the standard version had been made in only very limited numbers and was difficult to obtain. This might be his only chance, he thought. He could have it crated and shipped to Europe. He dialed the number.

Forty five minutes later, he was driving his rented car though the quiet, sloping roads of Beverly Hills. He saw the address on the high, wrought iron fence. A huge, sprawling ranch style house could be seen beyond the tree-studded, rolling hills of the grounds. The gates were open. Rashidii steered up a winding, blacktop drive and stopped in front of a four-car garage. The residence and grounds were plush and spacious even for Beverly Hills. He got out and rang the bell on the service door. A couple of minutes later the door opened. A tall, gangly youth stood there. Half his skull was shaved bald. From the other half grew a long shock of hair, dyed bright green, some of it in braids. His ears were studded with rings and a small diamond sparkled on the left side of his nose. At first Rashidii thought he was looking at someone dressed for a costume ball or some kind of lunatic. Then he realized this was the style among many young people.

"Mr. Berry?" The young man asked.

"Yes, I'd like to see the motorcycle."

The youth pressed a button behind the doorjamb and the furthest garage door opened. Rashidii followed him to it. The motorcycle was there next to the wall. The red and black machine was polished to a glossy shine. The bright-red, carbon fiber reinforced cowl was aerodynamically designed. It enclosed the engine at the sides and culminated in a bullet-nosed headlight housing at the top front. On the cowl was a small windshield, swept back at a low angle. The lower cowl and windshield formed an arrowhead shape with the headlight at the apex and the seat and exhaust as the arrow shaft. This made the machine look as though it were flying forward at breakneck speed even as it stood still. On either side of the windshield was a red rear view mirror housing, designed to allow onrushing air to slip by with minimum resistance. Small, matching hard plastic saddlebags were installed on the upswept rear fender. The fender jutted, seemingly unsupported, over the black, swing arm rear suspension and rear wheel. The side plates of the chain links were gold in color. Rashidii recognized the tires. They were racing grade rated at two-hundred and fifty miles per hour.

"Computer controlled electronic ignition, electronic multipoint fuel injection and sensor-based load leveling. Digital readouts on everything. Heads Up Display for the tach and speedometer, right in the windshield," the bejeweled young man began. "And, of course, the oval piston V-4 engine. The one-hundred and sixty plus horsepower endurance racer version. Technically illegal in this country. Eight valves per cylinder, gear driven twin overhead camshafts. High compression at eleven-point-seven to one. Means it requires premium fuel, of course. Took six months to get it from the factory in Japan. And, my father had to make some special arrangements for the shipment."

Rashidii was squatted, examining the machine. He looked up at the young man, "Why are you selling it?"

"Shit, I'm afraid of it. We were riding and a friend of mine went off a bridge at about a hundred and fifty miles an hour on his crotch rocket. His neck was caught in some tree branches." The youth sighed looking down at the garage floor. He shook his head, "His head was ripped off. It was awful. That happened five months ago. I only had this a month then. Haven't touched it since."

The youth started the machine and Rashidii listened to the engine. "You have anyone else interested," he asked?

"A few calls. Everybody wants it for less, but I know I can get the sixty thousand."

"I have no problem with the price, but I will not have it all for one or two days. Will four hold it?"

"Well, if someone comes with the sixty in cash..."

"I understand, please call me before you sell it. Would four-thousand now guarantee me right of first refusal?" The young man nodded. Rashidii gave him four thousand in cash and his number at the hotel. The youth wrote him a receipt.

Chicago FBI Office, 4:15 P.M.

Sally Stein sat in a guest chair in Chicago Bureau Chief Dan Barnes' office. Barnes nervously tapped a pen on the desk. At fifty-three he was a medium sized man. His hair was powder white and he wore a set of dark, horn-rimmed glasses from an earlier era. The thick lenses were perched on his large nose in front of pale blue, expressionless eyes. His white shirtsleeves were rolled nearly to the elbow and his striped tie was loose at the collar. She noticed that his shirt was wrinkled and bloused out of his pants above his beltline. He appeared a bit disheveled, a very unusual appearance for this man. Sally had known him a long time and he had always been neat and meticulous about his appearance. He was rarely seen without a suitcoat, even in sweltering heat. Perhaps he had been busy on some important case and had missed sleep, she thought.

Ed and Wanda from Noska's neighborhood had been questioned but authorities learned nothing concerning the Noska's whereabouts. Agents and police were at O'Hare Airport and Chicago train and bus stations with photos of the suspect, but there had been no results yet. Noska's ex-wives had contributed nothing, except to say that they wanted nothing to do with the man. Sally sipped her coffee and looked at the preliminary report from the lab that had just been handed to her. "Pieces of what might be a seal used on airline supply trucks," she read. "Strands of hair from cheap wigs, black and blonde. Probably men's. He's apparently using some kind of disguise." She looked at Barnes, "Dan, I think I'll give Jack Newman a call. His program airs tomorrow night." She pulled an electronic databank unit from her purse. She opened the cover and keyed in Newman, Jack. His phone number and address appeared on the small screen.

FOURTEEN

Jack Newman was producer and host of a nationally syndicated television program called "Fugitive Intercept". Each week he profiled wanted criminals, asking the viewing audience to report any sightings or information.

Sally waited, while the phone rang in Newman's Burbank, California, office. Someone answered and Sally said, "I'd like to speak to Mr. Newman, please. This is FBI Chief Inspector Sally Stein and I am calling concerning a matter of national emergency."

"Yes Ma'am," the voice said, "I'll see if he's available."

A few minutes passed, then Newman answered, "Hello Sally, haven't seen you in a while. What can I do for you?"

Sally had worked on a couple of cases with "Fugitive Intercept" over the years. But, she was surprised that Newman even remembered her. If he actually did remember her, she then thought. A former FBI agent himself, he was now a major television personality. Guys like Newman were big schmoozers, she mused.

"Glad I caught you in. I'm working on the bombing of flight 283."

"Jesus! What have you got?" he asked.

"A major suspect we can't find. Probably still in the country, somewhere. So far, we have only a local APB in the Chicago area. We haven't gone public or national yet. You'll have an exclusive. We have mug shots, description. Can you get it on your program tomorrow night?"

"The show is taped and ready to go, but for this, sure. We'll cut something and squeeze it in. Everybody's talking about the bombing. I could probably even get the network to do some promo spots, starting a couple hours before we air, pump up the size of audience. Damn! This'll be great."

He sounds too happy about this, she thought. "I'll send the info by courier tonight, so you have good copies. A couple of things. Our man's almost bald, but he may be wearing a medium length wig, black or blonde. And he's known to wear a mustache at times, although he's clean-shaven in the mugs."

"We'll scan the mugs into the computer first thing in the morning. With the police artist software we'll have all the facial possibilities generated for a spot on the show tomorrow night. Let's see, black and blond wigs. Know the hairstyles?"

"No, you'll have to use something typical."

She hung up the phone. Dan Barnes looked across at her, "You might as well know, and this is not to go beyond this office. We're picking up James Votilinni. His Capos Tosco and Veldon too. The U.S. Attorney gave us the tentative go-ahead a couple of weeks ago. Now it's finalized."

Sally looked up, surprised. "Where? When?"

"His place, you know, the Black Olive. Sometime after dark tonight, we haven't set a specific time yet. Our surveillance and our informant tells us the three of them meet every Wednesday evening in Votilinni's office. Usually lasts late."

That would explain why Barnes had been so nervous and excited, since she had arrived at his office a half-hour earlier. "You know he's a suspect in planning the bombing of flight 283," she said. "I suppose there's no hope of holding off, until we gather some evidence against him on that?"

"We've been planning this for weeks. You can talk to him all you want, after he's in jail."

"If you can keep him there. Evidence connecting him to bombing an airliner would go a long way toward ensuring that."

Then he frowned and looked at her, "Gather evidence? What are you talking about? The police aren't supposed to know Votilinni's a suspect and none of my people are working on this angle." His voice was rising anxiously, a worried look on his face, "Just how in the hell could you be collecting evidence?"

"The police don't know. And it's true none of your people are in on it. A CIA agent, a ah-Phil Smith was assigned to work with me on the case. The powers that be in Washington set it up. He's undercover right now at the Black Olive trying to set up a meeting with Jimm-uh-Votilinni right now."

242   Take It To The Limit

Barnes was livid. "Well, that's just fuckin' great," he said. "A CIA agent! I can't believe you would do this, Sally."

"I didn't do it. I told you the powers that be set it up. Going undercover was basically Smith's idea. I wasn't totally sold on this, but I'll admit I concurred with it. You have to understand my influence over him would have been very limited anyway."

He squinted at her, "And just exactly what is this Smith going to try to do?"

"You know Votilinni owns a trucking company among his quasi-legal enterprises. Smith is going to ask to purchase their services to ship military ammunition to the East Coast for overseas shipment. He's going to tell Votilinni that he's cut a deal, under the table, with the owners of a factory in northern Illinois, near Rockford. They produce the ammunition there. A lot of money will be talked about for the services, of course. The whole point is to get inside and engage Votilinni in conversation about international dealings. Smith will see if he can pick up any clues that might tie them to the bombing."

"And he's there now?" Barnes asked.

"Yes, I believe so."

"This territory is my responsibility. You people from Washington think you can come out here and do any goddamn thing you want. Why the hell didn't you tell me about this plan before he went in?"

She was a bit embarrassed now, realizing she should have called Barnes and discussed the plan with him. She blew out a breath, "Sorry Dan, my mistake. I am responsible. But I didn't think you'd be moving on Votilinni this soon."

"You know goddamn well this is the biggest arrest of the decade. We can't very well broadcast it."

"Diamond Jimmy might decide to shoot his way out, you know."

"We'll be ready for him. Meanwhile, you better get your man out of the goddamn way and do it without screwing up our operation."

"It might arouse more suspicion if we try to contact him. He'll come out on his own within a few hours."

* * *

On the west side of town Tommy Garcia got out of a cab in front of the Black Olive Restaurant. The four-story gray brick building was on a corner in an old industrial section in Chicago near the Cicero city limits. The main local thoroughfare ran in front and a side street ran along the side and up a hill to the north. Jimmy Votilinni owned the three buildings to the north. The first was a two-story brick with a coffee house on the first floor and a couple of apartments upstairs. Votilinni leased the building to the coffee shop proprietor. Beyond were two four-story apartment buildings that Votilinni owned through a holding company, set up by his grandfather. Vito Votilinni had them built in the 1930's. They were of dark, red brick and each had twenty-four one or two bedroom apartments. Beyond the second of those was another, similar apartment building. It was at the top of the hill nearly a block from the Black Olive. They did not own that one. Underground tunnels connected all of the buildings.

Tommy was wearing a brown suit and a beige shirt, open at the collar. He wore gold, wire-rimmed glasses with dark lenses and his hair was dyed a light brown, almost blonde. Under his left arm was a .38 caliber automatic pistol; it was intended to be obvious. The restaurant and bar were on the first floor of the gray brick structure. Tommy knew that

Diamond Jimmy Votilinni owned the entire building. He also knew that on the second and third floors were offices and apartments that Votilinni and his people used. Tommy went in the front door and then, through a second set of doors. On the other side of the inner doors, he stepped onto a thick carpet. The interior was of dark varnished wood. The air-conditioned environment was cool and dry, in contrast to the heavy, humid air outside. He felt a sudden chill from the abrupt change. To his left was a hostess' station and to his right, a coat check room. Ahead was a wide entrance to the restaurant area. The bar area was along the left wall, separated from the dining area by a series of posts and a waist high wall. There were small tables along the bar side of the wall. There were a few people at the tables in the dining area and several men at the bar.

Suddenly, a woman stepped through the wide doorway into the lobby. She came from the direction of the bar. Tommy was mesmerized for a second. The woman was beautiful, strikingly so. She was probably about his age, late twenties. Her face looked as though it had been carved by a Roman sculptor. It was an ideal oval with high cheekbones. She had deep green eyes. Her nose was small with a slight upturn, just the right size. On her lightly tanned skin was a smattering of freckles. She wore a long, white gown that was slit on both sides from her waist to the floor. Her beautiful long leg and bare hip were revealed on each side. On top there was only a swath of loose, narrow pleated material around her neck that plunged over her breasts. Rounded, tanned flesh peeked out on either side of each ribbon of material. Tommy didn't know whether to look up or down. When she smiled at him, her sensuous lips parted over a row of perfect teeth. It was a wary smile, probably because she didn't recognize him, he thought.

"May I help you?" She said in a voice that was a bit harsh. Certainly less sensual than he expected.

"I'd just like to get a drink."

She shot a glance in the direction of a dark, heavyset man who now stood in the center of the restaurant behind a table. Tommy's eyes followed hers. He recognized the man from photos Sally had shown him. It was Tough Tony Tosco. If there had been some sort of signal from Tosco, Tommy didn't see it. But then, he surmised, the very fact that there was no signal may have been the signal.

The beauty held out her left hand and thumbed back to her left, "The bar's in there."

Tommy walked through the large door and turned into the bar area. He was sure the heavyset man's eyes were on him. The bar was long and rectangular with customer access all around. One long side faced the street windows and the other the dining area. He walked around the far side and took a seat by himself. All eyes were on him. This was definitely not the kind of place where strangers went unnoticed. He had expected this. The bartender, a tall, blond middle-aged man with a bullish-looking head and shoulders approached. Tommy ordered a Sharp's non-alcoholic beer. In a minute, the bartender returned and set a tall, chilled beer glass in front of Tommy. As the man tipped the glass and poured the beer expertly down the inside, Tommy slipped out a ten-dollar bill and put it on the bar. There was a perfect half inch head on the beer. The man set the bottle down and looked at the ten.

"People here usually put it on the tab," he said.

I've never been here before," Tommy replied. "Say, I understand Mr. James Votilinni has an office here. Any chance I could see him for a few minutes?"

Ignoring the ten on the bar, the bartender turned and walked to the other side of the bar. He waved Tosco over and they talked for a few minutes. The heavy man sauntered around the bar and approached Tommy. Tommy glanced at him thinking the man was about five-eight, five-nine and probably weighed more than three hundred pounds. All the time he approached he was staring at Tommy with bulging eyes. Those eyes were cold, dark, discs set in yellowish globes. The man wore a dark blue suit, obviously tailored so that it could be buttoned over his great, protruding belly. He wore a black dress shirt and wide tie splashed with bright, surrealistic flowers in reds and yellows. Tough Tony Tosco was "wearin' it", looking his part. He pulled out the barstool next to Tommy and with some difficulty, pushed himself up and onto it. His body fit snugly between the wide expanse of the armrests. Flab bulged slightly above and below them. He perched there, his thighs at a downward angle since his huge belly would not permit raising his knees further. There was a fat, unlit cigar in his left hand and he pulled out a lighter and puffed it lit. He kept Tommy covered with the bulging eyes as the end of the cigar turned to a red coal. Then, he blew out a massive blast of smoke.

Finally he spoke, "Ah hear you wanna talk wit Mr. Vot-il-inni," he said, dragging out the name with an Italian bounce in his voice.

"Yes, I have a business proposition." Tommy was working in a trace of foreign accent.

"First you gotta tell me."

"I'd rather speak with him directly."

"I do'n give a flyin' fuck what you'd radder do. Who da' fuck are ya anyway?"

"My name is Alfor Jaddahr. I want to transport some goods from here out east. And you?"

"Tony Tosco." He held out a meaty hand and they shook briefly. The bulging eyes rolled around in their sockets taking in the bar. A television above the bar blared with sports news. If they spoke low, no one was close enough to hear, "Wha' kinda shit ya' talkin' about?"

"How do I know I can talk to you about this in confidence? You work for Votilinni?"

Tosco turned to the bartender, "Hey, Willie, gimmie dat fuckin' newspaper, would ya? Ya know, dat one wit' me an' Jimmy." Within a minute, the bartender slid a yellowed, folded newspaper in front of them.

Tommy looked at it. The paper was a couple of years old. There was a photo of Votilinni and Tosco being escorted by federal agents after their arrest. Tommy read the caption. He looked at Tosco. "Says you're his right hand man."

"An' doan you ever fuckin' forget it."

"Well," Tommy began, his voice low, "I have been able to make a deal with people here in Illinois who produce military ammunition. They will sell us a percentage of their production at a fair price, secretly, of course. We buy in truckload quantities..."

"Net margin," Tosco interrupted. Tommy looked at him. "A legit' business is coverin' dere fixed costs. But dey ain't puttin' nuttin' on da' bottom line. De're willin' ta do anna-ting, sell a little extra ta anybody, ta have some fuckin' profit, ya know. Somptin' ta say grace over at da enda da goddamn day." He waved his fat hands over the bar, "I know da score on dat."

Tommy was surprised at the man's sagacity. But then he supposed he shouldn't be surprised. Tosco wouldn't be a Capo in the Votilinni organization if he was as stupid as he looked and acted. "You have the situation correctly, Mr. Tosco. We need to transport the goods to New York, New Jersey, places on the East Coast for further shipment. We can pay well for this service."

"Why not jus' fuckin' ship otta Chacaga? Dat can be set up, too."

Tommy thought for a moment. "I cannot answer this. I am not running the whole operation. I have only my instructions. I can listen to any ideas you may have and suggest them to my superiors." He emphasized the accent.

"Where da' fuck a' ya from?"

"Eastern Europe," Tommy said. "Far Eastern Europe," he added with a mystical hint to his voice.

"Da big man ain't here now. I tink mebbe he'll be back inna coupla' hours. You gotta stick aroun' here 'til den. Have a coupla' fuckin' drinks, dinner." He waved toward the restaurant. "I'll talk to 'em. See if mebbe you can talk to 'em too." Tosco tapped Tommy's jacket lightly where it covered the shoulder holster. "I see yer carryin'. Ya afraid'a somebody?"

"You can't be too careful."

"Dis is a class joint. If ya gonna stay here ya gotta gimmie da' rod. I give it back ta' ya when ya go." Tommy had expected this. He removed the pistol and handed it to Tosco below the bar. He was surprised Tosco didn't frisk him. The heavy man slid down from his perch and walked along the bar toward the rear of the building. Tommy watched him. The rocking gait was unusual. Tosco rolled his barrel-shaped body to the left, as he lifted his right foot and to the right, as he lifted his left foot. He disappeared into a door beyond the bar area.

Tosco went upstairs and entered Votilinni's office and closed the door behind him. He sat down at the desk and switched on the closed circuit television system. There were several cameras mounted above the bar and dining area. They were hidden above dark, hemi-spherical, one-way surveillance tiles in the ceiling. Their lenses of the cameras could be rotated in various directions and at various angles automatically. There was a microcomputer workstation on the desk that controlled the system. It converted the analog signal from the cameras to digital and displayed the camera images on the monitor. Digital snapshots of the images could be taken and stored at any time. Motion images could also be stored, although this took considerable disk space. Tosco switched back and forth between two cameras over the bar. To adjust them he rolled a track ball that was attached to the computer. He stopped when he had a good frontal view of Tommy in one camera and a profile in the other. Tommy was nursing his beer. Tough Tony Tosco didn't care much for computers. They were confusing to him. When he tried to learn anything, he became frustrated quickly. But he liked the surveillance system and had learned the basics of using it.

Vito and Jimmy had the first version of the system installed several years earlier, to provide security both inside and outside the building. It had been upgraded to the latest digital technology the previous year. About that time, they were having the heating, ventilating and air-conditioning systems in the two apartment buildings to the north upgraded. As this work was begun, an idea had occurred to Diamond Jimmy. He had technicians install camera mounts above the ventilator grilles in the ceiling of the bedroom and bathroom of each of the forty-eight apartments. He had wiring installed for the system also. The wiring was run down through the underground tunnels to the Black Olive building. He had paid off the technicians well to keep them quiet about the system. They knew who they were dealing with and would have been afraid to say anything, anyway. Then, while the tenants were out, Diamond Jimmy had some of his people mount the cameras or remove them. At any point in time, there were eight or ten cameras installed in each building. Diamond

Jimmy Votilinni got his jollies watching the people in their most private moments. His grandfather, Vito, wouldn't have approved, of course, but Jimmy had kept knowledge of the system from him.

Tosco remembered the first time that Jimmy had shown them the system. They had been on the third floor in Jimmy's private apartment. It was late on a Friday evening; Mac, Veldon, and a couple of the other boys and their girlfriends and Jimmy's girl Molly, were there. They had been having a party. They had been drinking. Tosco thought he had polished off nearly a liter of bourbon by the time Jimmy switched on the system and announced he had something to show them. On the screen had appeared some couples having sex, people masturbating, bathing, urinating and defecating. All live. All tenants in the apartment buildings to the north. They had all roared with laughter. But the funniest thing, Tosco now recalled with a smile, was the transvestite. A single man, apparently living alone, had stripped naked in his bedroom. Then he selected his evening attire from a closet full of women's clothes. They had guffawed wildly as the somewhat overweight man put on a bra and panties. When the man began to shimmy into a girdle, Tough Tony Tosco had rolled from the couch onto the floor in uncontrollable laughter. He rolled around like a big medicine ball and then suddenly was unable to catch his breath. He had gone clammy and pale for a few moments and broken out in a cold sweat. The next day he went to the doctor for a checkup and was told he had suffered a mild heart attack.

Only one tenant had discovered the surveillance system and complained to the manager, one of Votilinni's people. Votilinni had dispatched maintenance people to remove the equipment. They told the tenant a vague story about the authorities accidently having forgotten to remove the camera after an investigation. The tenant had moved out at the end of the month.

After seeing the live show a few more times, most of the people grew tired of it, but not Diamond Jimmy. He was obsessed with the images. He tuned in nearly every night. He's nuts as hell and gettin' crazier every day, Tosco thought. His mind returned to the serious matters of the present. He knew that Votilinni was making a list of people who had crossed him or who he thought had. And, Votilinni was out right now killing one of those people.

He made the first of a series of phone calls.

At that moment, Diamond Jimmy Votilinni waited in an abandoned warehouse a mile west of the Chicago loop. His bodyguards, Johnny Grimm and a short, stocky blonde man named Gary waited with him. They wore dark suits and dark shirts. They all wore thin leather gloves. The front windows of the warehouse overlooked West Randolph Street, a main thoroughfare. They were on the fifth floor in a closed back room. A dirty skylight above provided the only illumination. They sat in mismatched wooden chairs around a large old beat-up table. Votilinni had made a list and burned it into his mind; a list of people who had ratted. A list of people he wanted to kill. For a couple of weeks now, he had gotten the word that the feds were closing in. This had come not only from his consigliori, Mac McGinnis, who himself was on the list, but from several of his grandfather's old contacts as well. People placed at high-levels in the police department and local District Attorney's office. He had begun to make plans to leave and hide out; but first he wanted to get revenge. He had hired three men from New York to do the jobs. It was standard practice to hire out-of-town hit men, usually from New York, Los Angeles or some other large city. When the job was done they left quickly, leaving a broken trail for the police. The Votilinni crime family had both hired and supplied many such men over the years.

He was frustrated now, they had been waiting more than an hour longer than expected. Johnny Grimm watched anxiously as Votilinni took a small packet from his pocket. He opened it and shook an orange pill into his mouth. The pill contained fifty milligrams of amphetamine, a powerful dose.

There were noises near the rear stairs. The heavy green metal-clad fire door at the rear of the room swung open with a loud squeak. A middle-aged man was shoved through. His hands were cuffed behind him and he slapped his feet out in front of him to stay upright after he was pushed. It was Harley Bowman, a Chicago police lieutenant. He was a dirty cop who had been on Vito's payroll for many years. Behind him was a dark, wiry man nearly six-feet in height. He had wavy, black hair, a thin face and pointed nose. His eyes were dark and evil and carried the glassy cast of insanity. He grinned a lot, a nervous habit, he called himself Ferro. Behind him came a woman and two men. One of the men was white with blonde hair. The other was black with a scarred face and flattened nose. They were large and muscular and ominous-looking. All three men wore dark glasses and a dark, nondescript shirt and pants. The white man held the woman roughly by the upper arm, his huge hand wrapped around it as though it were a stick. The woman was moderately attractive with short, brown hair. She was of medium build and wore a floral print blouse and white slacks. Her mouth was open and she had a terrified look on her face. When they were in the room Ferro turned, motioned toward the door and said, "Bones." The black man closed the fire door behind them. The room was soundproof for practical purposes.

Diamond Jimmy stood and faced them, "Who da' fuck's the broad?"

"His wife," Ferro said in a thick foreign accent.

Gary and Johnny Grimm looked unhappy at this news. Diamond Jimmy smiled broadly displaying a row of perfect white teeth. Then he frowned at Ferro momentarily, "What took ya' so goddamn long?"

Ferro grinned, "We had to follow him all over town looking for a good spot to take him. Then he met her and we followed them into a parking ramp. We pulled up right behind when they got out of their car. Shoved them both in the van there. No one saw a thing."

Votilinni pointed to Bowman and one of the heavy, wooden chairs near the table. Gary and Bones sat Bowman in the chair and Johnny Grimm drew his small .38 automatic and pointed it at the man. "Look Jimmy," Bowman protested frantically, "I haven't said anything..."

"That's not what I hear, you motherfucker," Votilinni said viciously. "You been talkin' to the goddamn fuckin' feds. You ratted our asses out. I got the fuckin' word."

"No, man, no. L-look man, please let my wife go. She's not involved in anything."

"You fuckin' goddamn squealed, you prick." Votilinni's eyes were bloodshot, the pupils dilated. He was obviously jumpy. "She can pay the fuckin' price right along with you." Votilinni turned to the woman. She opened her mouth as though to scream. Nothing came out. Votilinni kicked her savagely in the abdomen. She bent over with a groan and the white man let go of her arm. She dropped to the floor.

"Bowman tried to rise, "No, nooo-ooo," he screamed, his voice becoming hysterical. He was slammed back into the chair.

Votilinni kicked her brutally and repeatedly in the stomach, ribs and breasts. Bowman struggled and screamed.

With horror his eyes followed Votilinni's large, leather wingtipped shoe as it pummeled his wife like a jackhammer. The woman brought her knees up to her chest and Votilinni went behind her and drove the hard, leather toe of the heavy shoe into her back several times. Johnny Grimm wanted to say something, but then Votilinni stopped for a moment. The woman lay on the concrete floor groaning, her body wrenched with pain and muscle spasms. Bowman was howling as though in agony himself now. Tears were streaming down his face. Votilinni walked over, a smile of grim, sadistic satisfaction on his face. His dark eyes were glassy and wild. He lashed out with his foot, kicking the man in the stomach also. Then he jumped back laughing as Bowman caught his breath, leaned back on the chair and lashed out with his feet. Powerful hands held the handcuffed man in the chair. Votilinni walked over to the woman. As he walked he skipped and picked up his foot and drove it toward her stomach again. This time the momentum of his body went into the kick. The force of the blow doubled her up again. He stood over her. She retched involuntarily and blood spattered from her mouth onto the concrete. Her eyes rolled back in their sockets, the whites showing eerily. He brought his foot back again.

Johnny Grimm could no longer hold his tongue, "Jimmy, you can't kill her now." Grimm was afraid she would die any second as it was. "The alibi, man. We gotta get outta here."

Votilinni stopped and turned. His expression changing, as though he was coming out of a trance. Then he nodded. He pulled a packet of bills from his coat and handed it to Ferro. "You know what to do and when." He held out his watch and tapped it. Ferro nodded. Votilinni, Johnny Grimm and Gary left through the back fire-door. They put on dark glasses on the way down the stairs. At the ground floor, they emerged into a deserted alley. Gary peered out to check. Satisfied that no one was about, he waved them along. There was an old, four-door Chevrolet there parked next to the rusted, dark red van that Ferro was using. They got in the car with Gary at the wheel. He wound the car through a preplanned route in the alleyways to West Lake Street. There they turned right toward the city.

FIFTEEN

Tommy had nursed through two beers for over an hour and then decided to order a meal. He had walked up to the beautiful, green eyed hostess and asked her to seat him. She had done so. He couldn't keep his eyes off her as she sauntered back to her station. The waitress came over and he ordered a ribeye steak. Upstairs, Tosco had focused the dining room cameras on Tommy. He had made a number of calls. So far, four people from the area had stopped by. These were people who got around a lot and were on the Votilinni payroll in one way or another. Each of them had studied the screen and shook their heads. None had seen Tommy before. Tosco had been trying to call Andy Berlowski, but each time he tried Andy's home phone, no one answered. He hit the redial button again. Berlowski was the desk sergeant at the local precinct. He had provided information to the Votilinni people for years. For this service, he received a nice second income that would eventually allow him to retire early. He had just arrived at his apartment now. As he put the key in the door he heard the phone begin to ring. Within a minute he was inside in the kitchen picking up the wall phone, "Hello," he said.

"Hullo," Tosco said into the phone. Berlowski recognized the voice immediately. "I needja ta git ova' here right away."

Berlowski was surprised at the request. Almost all of his communication with these people was by phone. Usually a randomly selected pay phone. "Where are you?"

"At home."

Berlowski knew he meant the Black Olive. "Jesus, you know I can't do that. You shouldn't even call." They both knew that if Berlowski was seen there by certain people he would fall under suspicion.

"This is kinda a fuckin' emergency, ya know. Anyhow, doan' worry. Dere ain't no tap on dis line. I need ya ta look at somebody. See if ya reckanize 'um."

Berlowski didn't even want to have this conversation on his own phone, "Can't you sen' a picture over or somethin'?"

Tosco thought for a minute. "Mebbe. Ya' gotta modem on yer goddamn computer, right?"

"Yeah."

"Well, gimme da goddamn number and I'll see if I can sen it ta ya dat way."

What, was the tough fat man a computer junkie now?" Berlowski wondered. He read Tosco the dial up number for his computer. "I'll switch it on and be waiting," He said, relieved to be able to hang up the phone. He went into the den, switched on his system and waited.

Tosco hung up the phone and dialed the bar downstairs. "Willie, tell Molly to get her tits up to Jimmy's office. Right away!"

Tommy heard the bartender yell, "Molly". The beautiful hostess bustled through the dining room. With quick stride, she exposed first one long, gorgeous leg up to the bare hip, then the other as the split white dress opened up on either side. She conversed briefly with the bartender, then she disappeared through the door Tosco had gone through earlier.

Upstairs, she came into the office. Tosco explained he wanted her to send the images of Tommy to another computer. He knew it could be done, but he wasn't sure how. He gave her the number and stood, offering her the chair behind the desk. On the screen Tommy was chewing his salad. She sat down and put her hand over the mouse. She clicked it to point to an icon and selected a communications program. She keyed in the phone number. The machine had a built-in modem with automatic dialing.

A minute later the phone in Berlowski's den rang and then his personal computer automatically answered it. A message asking if he was ready to receive printed at the bottom of the screen. He typed, "Yes". Suddenly, his screen filled with the image of a man eating in a restaurant. He leaned forward and studied the screen. Then his other phone rang. He picked it up. As he expected, it was Tosco.

"Ya see 'im?" Tosco asked.

"Yeah. He looks familiar all right." The view on his screen switched from frontal to profile. "Yeah, yeah. Saw him the first time today. I think he's an FBI agent. Came in this afternoon with a lady agent named Stein. I can't remember his name though."

"Wit Stein, ya say? Sally?"

"Yeah. They're here investigatin' that airline bombing. They met with the Captain." Berlowski was thinking out loud now as he stared at the screen. He had forgotten to be careful about his wording. He chuckled a bit, "Say, ya know who's workin' on the case with'em?"

"Who?"

"Fritz Grinke."

Tosco hated the man and Berlowski knew it. "Stinky" Grinke, as Tosco referred to him, had never missed a chance to give Tosco a hard time when he was picked up for questioning or on some charge. Tosco thought of the times Grinke had roughed him around, "That cocksuckin' son-of-a-bitch." Tosco's voice was cold, "Fucker allus tinks he's tough when he got his cop buddies around." He'd be dead if he wasn't a cop, Tosco thought to himself. Then he turned to the business at hand, "What else?"

"Grinke's been assigned a new partner. A short little woman name a' Tanya Williams. She's a nigger, too."

"Haw, haw," Tosco guffawed into the phone, "serves da' fucker right." Tosco did not know Grinke well personally, but he suspected the man would not be happy about working with an African American woman. Then he became serious, "Say, what da hell are dey lookin' at aroun' here dat has ta do wit dat goddamn bombin'?"

"Guy name a' Noska's a suspect. Lives over on Pulaski. They can't find him though. Probably skipped town."

There was silence at the other end of the phone. Then Tosco spoke, "Dis Noska. Name a' George?"

"Yeah," Berlowski said, then suddenly, he was gripped with fear as he went over their conversation in his mind. "This line, you sure?"

"Yeah. Dey'ed have ta tap every phone in da whole fuckin' 'hood ta get dese lines." It was true. The lines on which they had been communicating with Berlowski were hooked into the phone system in the second apartment building to the north. Like the camera system, the lines ran through conduit in the underground tunnels. Vito and Jimmy Votilinni had been careful about such things. As soon as Tosco put the phone down, it rang. He put it to his ear as he waved Molly out. "Hullo," he said.

It was Jimmy Votilinni calling from a pay phone a couple of miles away, "What the fuck's goin' on?"

Tosco recognized his boss's voice immediately, "Plenny. No police 'er nuttin' but we gotta unnacova' FBI man down in da restaurant. Says he wans ta meet witcha' about shippin' some illegal ammo, but what he says don't hol' watta, I checked 'im out."

Votilinni laughed, "A goddamn fed? Sittin' right in the fuckin' restaurant? You goddamn fuckin' sure?"

"I checked 'im widda good tipster. I'deed 'um sure."

Diamond Jimmy looked at his watch. It was 7:45 P.M. "This is just exac'ly what I need at this fuckin' minute. You tell that son-of-a-bitch I'll meet 'em in the bar in ten goddamn minutes. Nah, make it five fuckin' minutes." He hung up.

Tosco sat down and looked at the screen. Tommy was not at the table. Tosco clicked to the cameras over the bar and Tommy was there in his old seat nursing another Sharps. Tosco rolled the track ball and scanned the bar. He saw Mac McGinnis coming from the dining room to the bar area. The man was wearing a heavy suit. Unusual for the hot weather, Tosco thought. Then he sat forward and studied Mac's face. He was at the bar now staring across in Tommy's direction. There was obvious recognition on Mac's face. Quickly, Tosco switched back to the camera on Tommy. Tommy was looking at Mac, expressionless, then he turned his attention back to his drink. "Well, ain't dis fuckin' interestin'." Tosco said aloud to himself. He shut the computer system off and went down to the bar.

By the time Tosco had again perched himself on the chair next to Tommy, Diamond Jimmy Votilinni was stepping into the bar. He was flanked by Gary and Johnny Grimm. Votilinni immediately came around the bar and stood next to Tommy. He held out a thin, bony hand and Tommy shook it. Tosco offered the introduction, "Dis is Jimmy Votilinni".

"Alfor Jaddahr," Tommy said.

"Tosco here tells me you're interested in talkin' about some fuckin' shippin' service." Tommy nodded. "Let's have a goddamn drink first," Votilinni waved the bartender over.

Tommy went into a long explanation about shipping the ammunition. Votilinni listened, as he puffed on a cigarette, asking an occasional question. He seemed only pretending to be interested. Tommy noticed he was checking his watch periodically. At one point Votilinni asked Tommy, "What the fuck time ya got?"

Tommy looked at his watch. "8:10," he said. He noticed that Tosco motioned to Votilinni a couple of times trying to get his attention. After another ten minutes Votilinni said, "Let's go up to the goddamn office and finish this. Look's like we could make some goddamn fuckin' scratch on this deal."

A shiver of fear shot up Tommy's spine. The man hadn't seemed interested at all and now, he wanted to discuss it more? These people seemed to have an agenda. Had they made him? It was possible. They had him waiting a long time. They had a lot of contacts in the area and they were probably very careful about who they dealt with. But they wouldn't kill a federal agent when he was on a job in their own place. Or would they?

Before he could think further, Votilinni spoke to him again. "You fuckin' go on up with my boys, Johnny and Gary here. We'll be there inna coupla' goddamn minutes."

Gary led the way and Tommy followed him toward the door in the back. Johnny Grimm followed behind.

When they had gone, Votilinni turned to Tosco, "Send Molly up, I gotta git my fuckin' rocks off, now."

Tosco sighed, murder always sexually excited Votilinni. "Yeah, but I gotta talk ta' ya, quick." Votilinni listened as Tosco whispered about Noska and then, Mac's recognition of the Federal Agent. Mac was still sitting across the bar. Tosco then came around and said to Mac, "See ya upstairs inna office inna few minutes." He then went to tell Molly to join Votilinni.

Votilinni had gone up to his third floor apartment. There he switched on a police scanner radio and began to remove his clothes. He was already aroused.

In the office below, a large conference table ran most of the length of the room. At the south wall was the huge oak desk. Gary motioned Tommy to sit at the end of table opposite the desk, "We wait for Jimmy. Getcha somethin' ta drink?"

Tommy shook his head. He looked around at the potted ferns and palm tree. He studied the ceramic tiled fireplace and ornate woodwork around the old windows. He was pondering an escape route. The windows were single-pane, but the wood frame and latticework was heavy. It was also old. There was a door behind to his right along the wall. A closet? What a fool he had been! They hadn't even frisked him as Sally had assured him they would. He could have carried his .22 supermagnum hidden pistol. He did have a stiletto rod pencil in his inside jacket pocket. It looked like an ordinary mechanical pencil, but had a spring-out ice pick-like blade. He also had a cigarette pistol in a pack in his upper left shirt pocket. He could fire one .22 caliber bullet with what looked like an ordinary filtered cigarette. The weapons were standard CIA issue and might be useful against one, maybe two, men. They would be of little use against a roomful of armed gangsters.

Gary sat at the table near the entrance on the east wall. Johnny Grimm came around the table and leaned next to the window, just a few feet to Tommy's right. Grimm folded his arms in front of him. The big expressionless pock-marked face stared down at Tommy. Gary and Grimm started talking about baseball. They waited a half hour. It was nearing 9:00 and darkness was descending rapidly over the city. Mac and Ellie Winks Veldon came in and took seats next to Gary.

In a minute, there were steps in the hall outside. Tosco had been waiting in the room across the hall. Finally, Votilinni and Molly came down from the floor above. Votilinni looked at Tosco, "Ya know that fuckin' downtown cop Lieutenant Bowman?" Tosco nodded, he knew what was coming. "Well you ain't gonna believe this but the son-of-a-bitch an' his wife jumped outta the fifth floor windows of an old warehouse over on Randolph. Heard it on the goddamn scanner."

"No shit?"

"Yea, took a header right into the fuckin' traffic. Musta been one hell of a goddamn mess. Right at fuckin' 8:10 tonight."

"I'll be goddamned. Suicide pact, huh?"

Votilinni was already opening the door to the office. Tommy eyed him as he came in. He looked flushed and disheveled. His suitcoat was crooked and his shirt bloused out at the waist. Molly came in behind him, straightening her dress. Her hair was a mess. They looked like they had just had sex. This was getting weird, Tommy thought. Votilinni sat in a leather executive chair at the head of the table opposite Tommy. He waved Molly over, then snapped his fingers and pointed his thumb back at his desk. Molly picked up a pack of cigarettes and a lighter from the desk. She put one of the brown-filtered cigarettes in Votilinni's mouth and held out the flame. He leaned back laughing, the cigarette dangling from his lips. She had to push the flame at him. Finally, he puffed it lit. Tosco came in and walked around behind Votilinni. He sat at the man's left; Veldon was already at the right. There was a ritual here; Tommy thought, some kind of posturing going on as far as who sits on which side of the kingpin.

Votilinni hiked Molly onto his lap and they leaned back in the plush executive chair. He ran his hand from her knee up her lightly tanned thigh and then squeezed it. Votilinni's eyes were wide and dilated. Tosco and the others in the room, with the exception of Tommy, knew for certain he was amped up on the pills. Even Tommy suspected it. Votilinni had been a speed addict for many years. Amphetamines to get up and alcohol to bring him down. He had used both with some moderation for a long time. His use had become heavier in recent months, as the pressure of his grandfather's approaching death came to bear. He looked at Tommy, "So what the fuck do you want?"

Tommy explained again about shipping the ammunition from the Midwest. Then a comment Tosco had made struck him. "Mr. Tosco here said you might have some connection to ship it overseas right from Chicago. If you have any connection with the shipping-lines or airlines, perhaps you could tell me about it."

Votilinni glared across the length of the table at the man. He squeezed Molly's thigh, and she squealed and jumped in his lap. He turned to Tosco and said, "We know any fuckin' thing about ships or goddamn airplanes?"

"Notta goddamn fuckin' ting," Tosco's large head turned until he was looking at Tommy. "We jus runna goddamn restaurant here. Dat's all. You mus' have da wrong fuckin' Votilinni or sumpin'."

Tommy looked at Mac. The big man was expressionless, but his eyes told of fright. Tommy shot a glance at the impassive, redheaded Veldon, then Molly let out a loud squeal and Tommy looked at her. Votilinni's hand was well up under her skirt now and she was wriggling around in his lap. Votilinni squinted at Tommy, "What the fuck are you lookin' at, you horse's ass?"

"If you don't want to do the deal," Tommy said, "perhaps I should leave."

Votilinni ignored the comment as he turned to Tosco, "Hey, Tony, I fuckin' feel like killin' somebody tonight. I ain't killed nobody in a week or so. Mebbe we oughta kill this bastard." He nodded toward Tommy.

Tosco giggled, "Yeah, let's kill da fucker." Tommy looked from one face to another, not sure if these people were serious or not, but knowing it was possible.

Just then there was a loud knock at the door, before anyone could say anything, the door burst open. Gary and Johnny Grimm drew pistols quickly from under their jackets. The bartender, Willie, leaned in and looked at Votilinni. He was frantic, "The boys say there's a lotta cars linin' up all around the place, up the street, everywhere! Looks like a raid!"

Votilinni stared at him for a minute. His mood went to obvious wide eyed anger. "You don't let the cocksuckers in," he roared. "Tell every fuckin' body down there to start shootin' at the sonsabitches! The fuckers ain't taken us alive!"

Willie ducked out and slammed the door. Votilinni reached under the table as he shoved Molly from his lap. She hit the floor hard and rolled toward the fireplace. Votilinni's hand came up, his bony fingers wrapped around the grip of a huge, black .45 automatic pistol. He waved it around momentarily, his hand quaking, and then aimed it at Mac. "You motherfucker," he screamed as he stood. "You fuckin' double-crossed my ass for the last goddamn time," he raged. He waved the pistol in the general direction of Mac's head and shoulders. Votilinni's hand shook and wavered in his drug-amplified fury. Mac, white with horror, was getting up quickly out of the chair and starting to back away. Votilinni squeezed the trigger once, then again. The two massive explosions rocked the room and the barrel spit smoke and sparks in Mac's direction. A bullet slammed into Mac's right breast and then another bullet slammed into his left. He fell back against the wall and then slid to the floor against the baseboard, face down. His body quivered in convulsion.

When Tommy had seen the pistol aimed at Mac, he knew he would be next. He had slid the chair out from under him and crouched. When the first shot erupted, Tommy sprang for the window next to the open-mouthed Johnny Grimm. He hit the wooden center crossbar with his right shoulder as the second blast came. He broke it, but the strength of the heavy wood stopped his momentum for a split second. He pushed hard again and jumped out in a hail of splinters of glass and wood. Now he was airborne, over fifteen feet from the pavement below. Instinctively, he brought his knees up and spread his hands out in front of him, elbows bent slightly. The street came up quick and hard. His hands slapped the pavement with a painful snap. The balls of his feet hit hard behind, driving his knees up on either side of his chest. Head down, he absorbed the impact as best he could with his arms and legs. He rolled to his right shoulder on the hard pavement. When he looked up, there were red, blue and white lights everywhere, vehicles pulled to screeching stops all around. Tommy squinted in the bright headlights and searchlights. Several people in riot gear were approaching him. They carried rifles. "Hands on your head. This is the FBI," someone yelled at him. Tommy complied.

Upstairs, Johnny Grimm and Tough Tony Tosco were scrambling around the table. Molly was on her feet behind them. Veldon opened the door into the hall. Votilinni was backed against the desk, the .45 hung limply at his side. He nodded at Gary and down at Mac's body. Gary put his shoe on the body and rolled it away from the wall. Mac's right hand fell away from his chest and hit the floor with a limp thud. There was a splotch of fresh red blood on his white shirt, between the lapels of his dark suitcoat. He lay there still. His lifeless eyes were open, staring at the ceiling. A trickle of blood ran down his cheek from the right side of his partly-open mouth. "He's dead," Gary said quickly.

Votilinni aimed the automatic down toward Mac. "Mo-ther-fuck-er," he screamed. Tosco bumped him and the gun went off. The bullet creased Mac's jacket below the left armpit and smashed into the carpeted hardwood floor below.

"Let's getta fuck outta here," Tosco yelled. He pushed Votilinni through the door behind Veldon. Gary, Molly and Grimm followed. With the exception of Molly they all knew where they were going. They followed Veldon north along the center hall of the building. When he reached the last door on the right Veldon opened it and went in. It was a small room, piled with junk. Veldon wove through piles of boxes until he came to a metal fire door on a rectangular structure in the corner. They heard crunching and crashing sounds from below, then shots. Veldon pulled open the door and let the others enter. It was an old wooden staircase with a pipe railing. As Veldon pulled the door shut they all quickly made their way down the dark stairs. Votilinni was in the lead now. He bounded down the stairs, his heart pounding from the thrill of the chase as well as the amphetamine. They went down three levels, one below the basement. They opened a rusty, metal door on the north wall and went through. They walked along a musty, concrete walled passageway. Tosco was striking a cigarette lighter occasionally to show the way. Above them was the galvanized conduit for the surveillance system and phone lines. They passed a door that led up to the basement of the coffee shop and continued on. After another hundred feet, they passed a metal door that led to the basement of the first apartment building. Tosco continued to strike the lighter. Votilinni loped along in front, partially feeling his way along the wall. There were cracks in the ceiling and walls where the shifting earth had damaged the tunnel over the years. Rats scurried about ahead of them, squeaking and making way. Molly was afraid, but she kept silent assuming this was a safe way out. They passed more doors leading up to the second apartment building and continued on. Another fifty feet along, they heard a smack and Votilinni cursed. Tosco flicked on the lighter and they were facing a concrete wall that appeared to be the end of the tunnel. Diamond Jimmy had walked right into it and bumped his head. He and Tosco pushed on the concrete and it opened, exposing more tunnel. They went in and pulled the concrete door shut behind. They continued along, leaving the Votilinni property now. In another thirty feet or so, they came to another apparent end of the tunnel. There was a rusty metal door. Votilinni and Tosco opened it and they all climbed one level up a staircase. The others could hear both men's labored, heavy breathing. They opened another door into a dusty, cob-webbed storage room. Votilinni made his way around some junk as Tosco struck the lighter. Votilinni opened a door a crack. A sliver of light appeared in the storage room. He was looking out at the underground parking garage of the large apartment building at the top of the hill. Cars were lined up against the walls and there were a couple of rows in the center, broken by large, square concrete pillars. Votilinni could see or hear no one in the garage so he waved them along out into the open area. They cautiously walked along a row of cars to the first large pillar, then followed Votilinni around it. They continued along the next row of cars.

Suddenly, a car door slammed to their right. An older, white-haired woman stood next to her car. She stared at them. Five tough-looking men disheveled and covered with cobwebs and filth from the tunnel turned to her. She looked at the young woman in white, also covered in dark, stringy grime. The old woman's eyes widened in fear. Votilinni approached her between the cars and grabbed her arm in his left hand. As she tried to scream, he brought his right hand down under her chin and jerked it up exposing the pale flesh of her neck. Votilinni motioned to Veldon, who was there in an instant the silver glint of a knife blade in his hand. He plunged the knife in under her jaw and ripped her throat open with a slash. She went limp as blood gushed forth, soaking the front of her blouse in red. Veldon pried open the fingers of her spasmodic hand and took her keys. He opened the trunk of her car. They stuffed the body in, threw the keys in and slammed the trunk. Molly had watched this in horror, her hand over her mouth. Gary had to help her walk as they moved quickly across the aisle. There Votilinni had stashed a getaway car for such an emergency. It was a large burgundy Chevrolet Caprice. Gary popped the trunk, Tosco rolled his heavy body inside and scrunched up behind the back seat. Veldon followed, then Votilinni beckoned Molly in. There was a look of protest in her bright green eyes, but she crawled in. Gary was already in the driver's seat with the doors unlocked. Votilinni shut the trunk then he and Johnny Grimm got down on the floor of the back seat. Gary backed the car out and drove to the door on the north side. He touched a button on the visor and the door opened. They were on the far side of the hill from the Black Olive.

Vito Votilinni had the tunnel built in the mid thirties some sixty years earlier. This was the first time it had been used for an escape since the forties. The FBI knew that Votilinni owned the three buildings to the north; they even knew there were tunnels under those. They had posted people all the way up the hill to cover the those three buildings. What they didn't know was that the tunnel continued to the third apartment house; the one that Diamond Jimmy didn't own. Gary drove the car slowly around the curved driveway and turned right into the street. He drove away down the hill into the black night.

The Castle, Fyn, Denmark, June 30, 9:00 A.M.

Von Kloussen sat at his desk. He had spoken to El Alamien and the deposits had been made in his Swiss bank accounts. Strangely, the man had alluded to another bombing planned by Rashidii. Was the goddamned raghead planning something else on his own? The Baron had let the remark go without comment. Anxiously, he called Switzerland and verified the deposits. He hung up the phone and rubbed his hands together and cackled. He called up his spreadsheet software and entered the passwords. He had decided to kill Rashidii and close off the only possibility of tieing him to the awful crime. He would keep the entire fifteen million and the Von Kloussen estate would again be solvent, would be well ahead, in fact. He entered the fifteen million as income from a "construction project" in France. He scrolled down to the bottom line. It looked good, very good! He could put a bullet in Rashidii's head himself when the man returned for his share in a couple of days. Then, he thought about it again. Rashidii was a dangerous man, always on guard. Perhaps he would need Kohfer's help. And, in some way, he would have to dispose of the body. He would ponder these decisions.

He summoned Kurt Kohfer. A minute later the man came through the french doors and sat down in a guest chair. "Welcome back, Baron. I visited Marseilles as you requested," Kohfer began, "Here is the report." He took a folded page from his pocket and handed it across the desk. Von Kloussen opened it and read:

The man identified is Cecil Bradshaw, Professor of History at Chatham College in Northumbria, England. Has occasionally done research work for the British government. No known security clearance.

Kohfer had typed it himself.

Von Kloussen looked up from the paper, "But why would the people in Marseilles have such a man on file?"

Kohfer thought of a lie, "They mentioned that they had new access to computerized fingerprint files." Changing the subject quickly, Kohfer said, "He's returning to England soon. He's planning to visit you this morning to make a proper apology for trespassing."

"Oh, really? Well, I suppose we can show him our best Scandinavian hospitality."

SIXTEEN

At the Tre Roser Motel Nick had loaded his bags and clipped them to the sides of the motorcycle. He checked the G11 pistol and put it in the holster under his left arm. He pulled on a tan blazer and buttoned the front. Eva had called and said she would be at the Baron's estate to greet him.

At 9:40 A.M. he parked the motorcycle under the large portico. He looked up at the huge three-dimensional black claw in the center of the arms above the front door. He read the motto "FORSVARE UDEN NADE" and mused that "Defend Without Mercy" might be a good motto for the CIA, as well.

Eva opened the door and led Nick into the gold-trimmed foyer. His pipe clamped in his teeth, the Baron stepped up and stood next to her. He shook Nick's hand. Kurt Kohfer joined them and Eva introduced him as her cousin.

"Baron," Nick began, "I must apologize once again for trespassing. How foolish of me."

"On the contrary, it is I who should apologize for my rudeness," the Baron replied. "You are a guest in our country. As a peer it is part of my sacred responsibility to be sure that visitors are comfortable and feel welcome. Noblesse oblige, of course. Now, won't you please join us for brunch? It's ready in the sunroom."

"Of course," Nick said concentrating on his British accent, "I'd be delighted."

The Baron led them along a wide corridor to the east end of the house. They entered a large room. The ceiling and three outer walls were of latticed glass. The sunlight sparkled down through the panes and danced off the edges of the large, silver tray in the center of the table. The tray was on a pedestal and was lined with rows of marinated herring in groups, each group differently spiced. The table was set with Danish porcelain plates in traditional white trimmed with blue. The silverware sparkled like the platter. There was orchestra music in the background.

On an invitation from the Baron, Nick sat first at the side of the table. Eva and Kohfer sat across from him and the Baron took his place at the head of the table. The cook, an older woman in a black uniform with a white apron, appeared and poured white wine for Nick, as he was the guest. He swirled it around in his glass and tasted it. "Light and dry," Nick said, "with a touch of sweetness. An excellent wine for the morning." He smiled and she poured wine for the others and left the room. Nick sampled several of the herring with sauces and bread and butter, telling the Baron to compliment the cook.

A new music piece began with a light, strumming start from the string section, fading to gently wavering violins. The violins built to a crescendo, then quieted and rose again with seeming hesitation.

Nick looked at the Baron and said. "Valse Triste by Jean Sibelius, isn't it? Originally from Kuolema...Death."
The Baron smiled warily, "You have a good ear, Professor. Not many people are so familiar with our great Scandinavian composers."

"Good music is an interest of mine."

"So, you have completed your work here?" The Baron said, hoping to lay some verbal groundwork for Nick's departure.

"Yes, as Gertrude may have told you, I located a fighter plane off Ander's farm in the sea. The pilot is buried in the churchyard. I'll use the information in an historical book I'm writing. Speaking of planes, isn't it terrible? Another airliner lost."

The Baron shot a glance at the man. Nick seemed nonchalant. Of course, everyone in the world was talking about the incident, Von Kloussen mused.

"How awful," Eva said, "They think it may have been another bomb."

"Yes, yes, terrible," the Baron muttered, shaking his head. He was anxious to return to the subject of his guest's departure.

The music of Valse Triste rose to an jarring, robust cacophony then faded to a quiet finale. A light violin piece began.

Suddenly, Kohfer had an idea, "Do you hunt birds, Professor?"

"Why yes, of course. I especially enjoy hunting grouse," Nick said, trying to portray himself as a typical professor with leisure time and manly pursuits.

"They're plentiful on the estate. Perhaps, if you have a little time, you could try your skill."

The Baron shot Kohfer an irritated glance. It was damned presumptuous of his estate manager to offer such an invitation.

Nick quickly saw the potential in this. He also sensed that the Baron was trying to hurry him along on his way. Nick studied his watch carefully, "I'm taking the ferry from Esbjerg to Harwich. Let's see, I could spare two hours, absolutely no more."

The Baron's sigh was almost audible, "Very well. Kurt, if you would select three of the shotguns. Of course you will join us." He was still wary of the stranger; he wanted Kurt there for protection. As Kurt left the table, the Baron turned to Nick. "I always use a small bore gun. It requires more skill. Makes more of a sport of it. Don't you agree?" He added, his pale blue eyes studying the man next to him.

"Oh, quite", Nick said thinking more of his small caliber G11 than of small bore shotguns. "The sport is the important thing, Baron."

The three men, shotguns over their shoulders, walked the gravel path toward the woods. Eva watched them from the Baron's office window. As they walked, Kohfer babbled incessantly on about grouse hunting on the estate. He was saying it was best near the wooded shore and was more or less steering them in that direction. The Baron was becoming irritated with the man's chatter as well as his unusual impetuousness. Kohfer rarely hunted and now he was talking as though he were an expert. After some twenty-five minutes they were nearly a mile from the castle. The sea was visible now in the distance through the trees. Suddenly, Kohfer said, "Oh, my God!" He looked down at his watch. "I nearly forgot. The butcher. He's closing for his summer holiday at noon today and I have to pick up our monthly meat supply!" As he ran back toward the castle, he yelled, "Sorry!"

The Baron looked after him, exasperated. He turned to Nick, "I apologize for my estate manager. He is behaving quite strangely today. Ah, perhaps we should return."

Nick watched Kohfer disappear among the trees. This is an unbelievable stroke of luck, he thought. The man is likely to be gone for some time. "Yes, perhaps we should return," Nick replied.

The Baron turned toward the castle, his shotgun held loosely over his shoulder. Nick grabbed it by the barrel and jerked it away, stepping back several paces. His G11 pistol was out, aimed at the Baron. "Hands behind you," he ordered.

The Baron was incredulous, "Who are you?" He hissed, fright overtaking his surprise.

"Do exactly as I say and I won't harm you. I'm only after a little information."

"In the name of the Queen, I protest."

"Turn around and be quiet or I'll shoot you in the stomach."

Von Kloussen looked into the cold, green eyes. He believed this. He complied. Nick tossed the shotguns on the ground. He took a flattened roll of duct tape from his jacket pocket and secured the man's wrists and hands. He picked up the shotguns and told the Baron to walk toward the sea. After several minutes, they rounded the hill that Nick had explored and walked down near the shore. Nick unloaded the chambers and the magazines of the two shotguns and tossed them and the shells out into the water among the reeds. He marched Von Kloussen toward the small castle-like ruins. Inside the first room, Nick closed the outer door. He pulled open the inner door to the small, round tower and shoved Von Kloussen inside. The Baron slammed into the far wall and fell to the floor. Nick pulled the huge door shut and crouched, holding his pistol on the Baron. Only the small, vertical rectangular slits at the top of the chamber provided light. The men could barely see the details in each other's faces.

Nick decided to start by keeping it open-ended. See if the man was willing to talk without clues. "People tell me you have recently been involved in some very serious criminal activity. Of course, I would like to hear about it directly from you."

"Von Kloussen stared at him, his eyes those of a cornered animal. He thought of the bomb and the plane. "Kurt will return soon. And, others will come as well. If I were you, I would leave while I still could."

"You must understand, sir," Nick said, still maintaining the British accent, "that we are here to talk about your criminal activities and nothing else. Talk to me now!"

"I-I know of no criminal activity," the Baron said nervously. He uprighted himself and sat against the wall, raising his knees so that his feet were flat on the floor.

"I'll give you one minute to start talking." Nick pointed the pistol at the Baron's left foot.

"You won't shoot me."

The seconds ticked by. "Talk." Von Kloussen remained silent. Nick squeezed the trigger. The weapon made a sound like a loud, sharp cough. It echoed in the round chamber. The small bullet passed through the Baron's instep and cracked against the stone floor.

Von Kloussen looked down in horror, his foot felt numb. He sucked breath then froze, waiting for the inevitable pain. Blood began to drip from the hole in the bottom of his boot. He let out the breath loudly, "Ahhhh...you bastard. You'll pay for this."

Nick raised the barrel, aiming at the left knee. "So far this is just a hunting accident but if you don't start talking soon...well, in Ireland, so I'm told, they like to shoot the kneecap off. I think we'll try that next."

The Baron was sweating and in terror now, "I h-have nothing to say to you."

Nick squeezed the trigger again and the Baron's left leg jerked outward as blood and bone splattered from his left kneecap. He rolled to the floor and screamed. Nick walked over and grabbed the man's jacket, pulling him back to a sitting position. Blood was pooling on the floor below the wounded knee. "You act like a man who wants to die. You could bleed to death right here and you will, if you don't talk."

Von Kloussen's entire body was quaking, racked with fear and pain. "All right, God, l-let me live!" He was still in Denmark, the Baron thought frantically. It would be almost impossible to extradite a Danish Baron. He could say anything now and deny it later. He would have plenty of time to build a plausible defense, he rationalized to himself. He could blame it all on Rashidii. "It was Rashidii. It was h-his idea. He made the deal with El Alamein."

"What deal? Tell me about it and I'll tape up that knee of yours. Stop the bleeding and then get a doctor."

"The bomb. God...help me now. It was Rashidii. He arranged to have a man named Noska put it in the supplies. Jesus Christ, ohhh...I'm bleeding all over." He was staring in horror at the wound. The knee had been numb, but the numbness was wearing off and a burning pain was shooting up his thigh.

Nick pulled his Fairbairn-Sykes knife from it's sheath. He sliced the man's pantleg off and wrapped duct tape tightly about the knee. As he worked, he continued the interrogation, still unaware of the subject of the Baron's confession. He fished for further information, "Where exactly was this bomb put?"

"At the back of the plane. Flight 283, ahhh..." The man winced as Nick pulled the tape tight, stanching the bleeding.

Nick stared at the man, this was incredible. He was confessing to sabotaging the airliner that had gone down only the night before. The Baron's body continued to shiver, he was going into shock. Nick laid him on the stone floor. Then composed himself and asked, "El Alamein paid you and this Rashidii for this?"

"Yes."

"How much?"

"Fifteen Million U.S.," he answered breathlessly. "I'll pay you well to let me go."

"This Noska was hired to plant the bomb? Who is he?"

The man nodded. "Eva and I went to the U.S. to place a newspaper ad to find him."

"Eva? Who is that?"

With difficulty the Baron raised his head and looked at Nick. "Gertrude, you goddamn fool," he said, a hint of triumph in his wavering voice.

So, Nick thought, the beautiful woman is a conspirator in this. "And who is this Rashidii?" The name had a slight familiarity to Nick. The man was silent. Nick aimed the pistol at his right knee.

The Baron looked at the pistol. He was shivering and cold sweat ran down his face, "Arun Rashidii, ahhh...damn it, known as Cha-Turgi."

"And, where is he now?"

"In Los Angeles, the bastard is with that goddamned Noska." He was breathing irregularly now. Nick motioned him to go on. The man spoke between gasps, Crescent Moon Hotel. That is all I know."

Nick recognized the name Cha-Turgi as the elusive and long-sought deal maker in illegal arms. "And, you and Rashidii shipped arms on the Cabal and other ships?"

"Yes, now get me a doctor, goddamn it." He lay there breathing heavily.

Nick checked outside for a moment. He saw no one. But, he realized time was running short. He returned and stood over the Baron. "Baron Von Kloussen, I'm going to execute you for the death of hundreds of innocents. Do you have any last words?"

The Baron stared up at Nick. He made an effort to compose himself. "Ahhh, Jesus, my knee. W-who are you?" The Baron decided to buy time with questions in hope of Kohfer's return.

"An American agent. That is all you need to know."

Von Kloussen's mind raced. Was this man's cover so good that even the people in Marseilles couldn't identify him? Then a terrifying thought came to him. Was that goddamn Kraut bastard Kohfer double crossing him in some way? The man was supposed to be his bodyguard for Christ sakes. "H-how did you know about the plane?" Von Kloussen asked in a wavering voice.

"I didn't. You offered that information yourself, if you recall. My orders were only to question you about the arms' shipments."

Von Kloussen screamed in terror and frustration at his own fatal mistake. The scream echoed about in the small tower. Then, he calmed down, tried to compose himself a bit. "Please don't take my life," he pleaded, tears coming to his eyes.

"I have no choice. There exists what we call a 'finding' about people like you. Someone has finally realized that if you are allowed to live others will also sabotage planes."

"Then I must die with dignity in defense of my property...please help me up."

Nick helped the man sit upright against the wall again, then leaned close to the man. "There is one other thing you can know before you die," Nick said almost in a whisper. "We think Heinrich Himmler buried loot here during the war. Millions, tens of millions may be buried right outside of here in that hill. Right under your nose."

The Baron's eyes were glassy now. He was having trouble thinking clearly. "I-I used to play here every day as a child, I can't believe...MY LEG, it's on fire." He was moaning loudly.

Nick aimed the pistol between the man's eyes and slid the selector to three-round-burst.

"WAIT," the Baron screamed, "Rashidii is planning another bombing".

"Where and when?"

"Let me live."

Nick dropped the pistol to his side, "Where and when?"

"Another p-plane? I don't know where. I don't know when. From L.A., perhaps? That's all I know."

"Are you sure?"

"Yes...yes...that is all I know." The Baron's voice trailed off. His eyes rolled and his body shook harder. He was becoming delirious. He tried to look at Nick, "When I was here many years ago I was the knight defending the castle with my sword," he said weakly, his breath coming in gasps. "My weapon was the claw...I...the....knight."

"If it's any consolation, you're being executed by a knight of the most powerful Round Table to ever exist in the history of the world. I am a Knight of the Order of the Floating Silk," Nick said under his breath.

Nick raised the pistol and aimed between Von Kloussen's eyes and as the man screamed a final cry of "Nooo," he squeezed the trigger. The man's forehead opened up like a split melon. Blood, bone and tissue splattered against the stone wall behind his head. This was followed by the back of the head slamming against the wall, then bouncing forward in reaction. The head and shoulders slumped forward, then rolled to the side and hit the floor. The body lay still.

Outside, Kurt Kohfer was crouched behind a tree at the top of the hill behind the ruins. At a distance through the trees he had seen the man disarm the Baron. Satisfied, he had then run to the castle and dismissed the maid for the day. The groundskeeper and his wife, the cook, lived on the estate. Kohfer, managing to keep himself composed, sent them quickly on a shopping errand to Odense that would take several hours. In the Baron's office, Eva looked up from her work at the computer. She saw the servants' cars leave. She left the office and walked through the foyer and down the long corridor to the sun room at the east end. She saw Kohfer enter the door to his apartment above the garage. Within a minute the door opened and she stepped back into the sunroom doorway to avoid being seen. She saw Kohfer come out and look around suspiciously. He held what looked like an automatic pistol in his hand. Quickly, he ran for the woods behind the castle. She decided to follow him.

She had followed him very cautiously through the woods toward the sea keeping a good distance behind. As he neared the sea, she could see him hiding behind trees, searching about quickly, then running on. Finally, near the top of the hill behind the old ruins, he had stopped behind a tree. Kohfer heard muffled moans and a barely audible scream escape from the rectangular openings in the small stone tower. Then a sharp, echoing sound that could have been a shot. He then heard the squeaking sounds of the old doors in the ruins being opened and closed. Nick Barber emerged on the exposed stone floor of the ruins. He looked around briefly, then broke into a dead run around the far side of the hill, apparently toward the castle. Eva also saw Nick running, pistol in hand.

When Barber was out of sight Kohfer moved quickly down the hill, a Walther automatic pistol was in his hand. He pulled open the outer door of the ruins and looked around. He went to the tower door and pushed it open. He saw the Baron's body on the floor. He was not surprised to see the body, but he turned abruptly at a sound behind, swinging the pistol toward the door. Someone was approaching on the stone floor. In relief, he saw that it was Eva. She looked at Kohfer and walked slowly toward him. Then she saw the body. Her mouth opened in a silent scream.

"He has assassinated the Baron," Kohfer said quickly. "Now I will go and seek revenge in the name of Von Kloussen." As he left, Eva dropped to her knees next to the body and screamed audibly.

Nick ran along the gravel path and came around the west end of the castle. He leaned against the building for a moment, winded, his chest heaving. He had run a mile. His motorcycle was still there under the portico. He had to get to a phone! He decided not to bother with the scrambling unit. Every second counted now. He went in the front door and looked around. West of the foyer was a set of large french doors, one wide open. It looked like an office. He approached carefully, his pistol held out. He looked around the office and behind the door. There was no one there. He went behind the desk and picked up the phone. He quickly punched in the international direct dial code and the New York CIA station number. There was a series of clicks. Then a pause and more clicking. "Com'on, com'on," he said keeping an eye on the open office door. He waited as seconds ticked by. Finally, he heard the ring. It rang three times. Someone picked up. "Code red," he said quickly. Password... Suddenly, three gunshots exploded into the office. The first bullet smashed into Nick's pistol splintering the black plastic housing and ripping it from his hand. The second two hit the phone, sending it skittering off the desk, pieces of white plastic flying everywhere. Kurt Kohfer stepped into the room holding the Walther out, leveled at Nick. He was panting heavily from the run back to the castle.

Instinctively, Nick began to crouch, reaching back for the .22 automatic at the back of his pants.

Another loud explosion, Kohfer had fired again. The bullet whizzed by Nick's right ear and smacked into the wall behind. A cloud of plaster dust erupted out of the wall. "Hands up! Now! On your head!" Kohfer shouted as he moved closer.

Nick slowly stood straight and put his hands on top of his head. His right hand was numb and bleeding a bit from the shot that had hit his pistol. He judged that this man would not hesitate to kill him. Eva, also winded, appeared behind

Kohfer. Her face was tear-streaked, a mask of rage. "You bastard," she screamed at Nick.

Without taking his eyes off Nick, Kohfer fished a pair of handcuffs out of his pocket. He handed them to Eva, "Put these on him, now!" She snatched them out of his hand and walked around behind Nick. Kohfer walked to the edge of the desk, the barrel of the Walther in his wavering hand pointed between Nick's eyes. Eva clicked a cuff on Nick's right wrist and pulled his arm down behind him. "Get that other arm down behind you," Kohfer raged, shaking the pistol at Nick nervously.

Nick complied and Eva clicked the other cuff on. This was ok Nick thought. If he couldn't talk his way out of this, he had ready access to his .22 automatic. Kohfer looked a bit relieved. He handed the pistol to Eva. "Keep it in his face. If he tries anything, blow his goddamned head off." With the practiced movements of the police officer he had been for many years, he began to pat Nick down. He located the killing knife in Nick's ankle sheath and pulled it out. "Unusual toy for a professor," he said. "These goddamn assassins always carry hidden weapons." He continued to feel around Nick's jacket and pants. Earlier, he had missed the lump at the back of the pants, but now he patted it again. He squeezed it. He quickly unhooked the belt and zipper.

"Look, I can explain," Nick protested, concerned now that he was truly being disarmed. "Baron Von Kloussen was an international criminal. Responsible for the loss of hundreds, perhaps thousands of innocent lives."

"Liar, liar, liar," Eva screamed at him even as she realized there may be some truth in his statement.

Kohfer pulled the pants to the floor. He stood and viciously shoved Nick to the floor. He pulled the pants from Nick's feet and sliced them with the knife. He pulled out the

.22, holding it between his forefinger and thumb, "Another interesting toy. I think a very thorough check of this murdering swine is warranted." He bent over and removed Nick's shoes and socks and examined his feet. "Stand up, goddamnit," the nervous Kohfer shouted. Nick struggled to his feet, using his elbows on the desk to steady himself. With the confiscated killing knife, Kohfer sliced up Nick's jacket and shirt, removing them and casting them aside.

Nick stood handcuffed in his briefs, "The Baron is responsible for the bombing of flight 283. His partner is planning another bombing. He gave me information that may prevent it. I must call the proper authorities, Now! If you prevent me, you too will be responsib..."

Kohfer backhanded him across the face brutally, "Lies." He turned to Eva, "The lying murderer will say anything to save himself, to get free. Pay no attention."

But Eva was thinking about the Baron's activities in recent weeks. And the sudden cash inflow since the Baron had returned. Nick looked at her, his eyes pleading. "Eva, that's your real name I understand, didn't you help place an ad in the newspapers? You could be an accomplice but if you help me now..."

Eva had a horrified look on her face. The pistol quivered in her hands. "I-I know of no involvement in that bombing," she stammered.

"Shut up, both of you," Kohfer said. He cut through Nick's briefs on one side, the tip of the razor sharp knife creased the skin, drawing blood. He then sliced the other side and dropped them to the floor. He told Nick to bend over the desk. As he began to do so, Kohfer grabbed the back of his hair and slammed his face into the desk. Nick could see and taste the blood from his nose and upper lip as Kohfer ordered him to spread his legs. Kohfer spread the man's buttocks and examined his anus. He picked up a pencil from the desk and pushed the blunt end inside. Nick winced as he twisted it around, checking for hidden objects. He then jerked Nick upright and examined his penis and testicles, lifting and pushing them from side to side with the pencil. "The dungeon," Kohfer said. "We'll keep him there until we decide what to do."

"Shouldn't we just call the police?" Eva said.

Kohfer looked at her, thinking. "And suppose you were an accomplice to some major crime, even if you didn't know. They'll lock you up forever, you goddamned little fool. I have another idea. For now, let's get this bastard downstairs."

The dungeon wasn't really a dungeon, but a series of storage rooms next to the wine cellar two levels below the ground floor. They walked Nick to the kitchen area at the east end and then down a flight of stairs to a well-kept pantry. Kohfer pulled open a heavy door and they went down a circular staircase of stone to the next level. There were long rows of wine bottles in racks, covered with dust and cobwebs. Kohfer opened a thick wooden door and pushed Nick through. A bare hanging lightbulb came on and illuminated a long, wide hall framed with timbers and huge stones. The stone floor chilled Nick's bare feet as he was pushed along. The cobwebs were so large that he could not pass without tearing them down with his body. They stopped at a door at the end of the hall. Kohfer lifted a heavy, timber crossbar from the door and set it aside. He shined a flashlight in. More cobwebs. The floor and walls were of solid stone, the ceiling of massive timbers. Satisfied, Kohfer shoved Nick inside. Eva held the flashlight as Kohfer secured Nick's elbows behind him with rope. This was to prevent him from getting his cuffed hands in front of him. In Nick's mouth Kohfer placed a gag hastily made from a cloth rag and tied it tightly behind his head. Then Kohfer shoved him to the floor and tied his ankles with the rope. They left, slamming the door. Nick heard the heavy crossbar being slammed back into place. He saw the faint light around the edge of the door go out a moment later. He lay bound and naked in total darkness on the rough stone floor.

Back in the office upstairs, Kohfer plugged in another phone. He pulled a paper from his pocket and dialed the Marseilles number. Eva tried to speak, but Kohfer shook his head and frowned, "This is the man from Denmark," he said into the phone. "I have the man identified last week in custody. I want the bounty." The voice at the other end said the message would be noted and they would call back. Kohfer read him the number. "And call today, as soon as possible, this is urgent." He rang off.

"Who is he?" Eva asked.

"I don't know, an enemy of the Baron's, a British agent perhaps," he lied. "When I had his fingerprints and photos checked last week, I learned only that he is an assassin with a price of one million dollars or more on his head. I'll give you a quarter of it if you'll go back to Germany and keep your mouth shut about this." He was already pondering ways to kill her.

"Why did you come back from hunting, instead of staying to protect the Baron?" She cried at him, her face wet with tears.

Kohfer racked his brain for an explanation. "I-I had forgotten to send the servants on errands as I was supposed to. And...and, I had forgotten my pistol to better protect him. I was gone only a few minutes."

SEVENTEEN

Los Angeles, Thursday, June 30, 2:15 P.M.

Arun Rashidii was parked down the street from the Crescent Moon Motel. He had seen the mail delivered before 2:00 P.M. and had then watched the roomers begin to come to the motel office to pick it up. Noska had apparently picked something up, but not the box. Rashidii waited for a half hour, then a taxi pulled into the motel parking lot. Noska came out of his room wearing the black wig and mustache and got into the back of the cab. Rashidii ducked as the cab drove by his car and then he pulled out following at a distance. After driving a few miles, the cab stopped in front of the local post office. Noska went in while the cab waited. Rashidii stayed back a half block. In a few minutes, Noska emerged carrying the box that had been mailed in Chicago. He had gotten a post office pickup slip in the mail, Rashidii realized. He hoped the box hadn't been opened. He followed the cab, staying back, keeping a sharp eye out for any others who might be following. He saw no one. The cab stopped at a liquor store and Noska went in, carrying the box with him. A few minutes later, he came out balancing a case of beer and a bag on top of the box. The cab dropped Noska at his room and he went inside. Rashidii parked down the street and got out. He surveyed the area carefully until he was sure there was no one watching. If anyone had found all that money, the gun and especially the C-4, the place ought to be surrounded by federal agents by now, he thought. He walked over to Noska's door and knocked.

"Who is it?" Noska yelled.

Rashidii could see the man peeking at him from behind the curtain on the picture window at the front of the room. "Grant Hopper here. I want to talk to you about the rest of the money," he said the last words in a lower tone as he looked around suspiciously. Noska opened the door and let him in. Rashidii's eyes went immediately to the box, still unopened and sitting on the bed. "Well, we've been successful," he began. "We should have a celebration toast. Would you have a drink for me?" Noska had been there only a day and already the reek of stale sweat and cigarette smoke permeated the air.

Noska went to the bathroom and retrieved a cup. He took a recently opened bottle of Southern Comfort from next to a full one on the dresser. He poured in a couple of ounces and handed it to Rashidii. "How do I get my four hundred grand?" he asked directly.

Rashidii looked at the even shorter man. He looked sick. Rashidii suspected he had been drinking heavily ever since he had arrived at the motel. And now, he was apparently starting another binge. "Three hundred and eighty thousand to be precise. You've already received one hundred and twenty. Five hundred thousand was the deal." Rashidii made this statement in hopes that the reference to the precise amount would allay any fears on Noska's part.

"Yeah, yeah, so how and when do I get the fuckin' money?" Noska picked up his cup and gulped down the remaining whiskey in it. He chased it with a long pull from a can of beer.

"As you can see," Rashidii said motioning to the box on the bed, "the U.S. mail is quite reliable. I've mailed the rest of the money to my hotel here. Just sit tight and I'll bring it over in a couple of days." Rashidii set down his drink and walked over to the bed. The box did not appear to have been tampered with. He stripped off the tape and tore open the top flaps.

"Hey goddamnit, that's mine," Noska protested.

"Only the money. The books belong to me." As Rashidii said this, he brushed aside the packing material and removed the top layers of books. He handed Noska the package of money. The man looked relieved. Rashidii replaced the books, resealed the box, and set it down by the door. "Maybe you better count that to be sure," he said, hoping to get Noska to open the package.

Noska looked down at the package, "I counted it before I packed it." Then, he frowned suspiciously at Rashidii and tore the package open. Packets of bills spilled onto the bed.

Rashidii poured more of the whiskey into his cup and then filled Noska's nearly to the brim. He handed the cup to

Noska and said, "Look at that money. Let's celebrate. Hell," he said, trying to sound American, "maybe we can collaborate again someday, get even richer."

Noska took a couple of gulps of the whiskey and said, "Yeah, sure, maybe." He put the cup on the nightstand table, then sat down and tore open a packet of money and began to count it. He looked over at Rashidii, "Did you know that goddamn fuckin' Richards survived the crash? I heard it on TV. And after all that fuckin' trouble we went to get him on that fuckin' plane, the bastard."

Rashidii swirled the dark liquor around in his cup, "Perhaps you should be pleased about this. I have it on very good counsel that you cannot terrorize the dead, only the living. This man will live with his terror for the rest of his days."

"Yeah? That's a fuckin' load of bullshit. I'd rather see the son-of-a-bitch dead."

Two hours later, Rashidii sat in a guest chair with his feet up on the bed. He was nursing the whiskey from his cup. According to the Baron's plan, he was supposed to have killed Noska by now and left with the money. Rashidii was laboring hard mentally on his own strategic plan. He looked at Noska, the first phase of his plan was working. The filthy little man lay with his head against the headboard of the bed. The cup next to him on the nightstand was nearly empty again. Rashidii had kept it filled regularly as he talked on and on to Noska about future riches and the things that could be bought with them. Noska had never quite completed the money counting. As he had gotten more intoxicated, he had lost count and started over several times. Finally, he gave up and lay back on the bed. The packets of money and loose bills were scattered around the bed. Some had fallen to the floor. The first bottle of whiskey was empty. Rashidii got up and stepped to the dresser. He opened the second bottle and once again filled Noska's cup. He opened a fresh can of beer and put it on the nightstand within easy reach. He put another splash of whiskey in his own cup and sat down again.

Noska picked up the cup and took a gulp of the whiskey with a robot-like action. He then reached for the beer and took a long drink. When he attempted to set it down again, it slipped from his hand and fell to the floor. The beer splashed and foamed over the worn carpet and the money. Noska paid no attention to this. He looked at Rashidii. "I'm goddamnnn fuckkkin' rich, man. I'm a goddamnnn richhh shonnn-ovva-bitschhh," he said, slurring and garbling the words. He took one more drink of the whiskey then closed his eyes. Within a few minutes he began to snore loudly.

Rashidii took sixty thousand dollars of the money and put it in his pocket. He scattered the remaining fifty-seven thousand around a little more. It will be a long time before he's in any shape to count it again, Rashidii thought. He picked up the box and left.

* * *

In the room of the castle subcellar, it was completely dark. There had been no discernible sounds of any kind. Nick shivered now from the cold that had permeated his naked body. At first, he had managed to stand and feel his way around the room using his cuffed hands behind him. The walls, like the floor, were of rough stone. Unfortunately, the stone was not rough enough. The rope held his elbows tied behind him about a foot apart. He had searched for a place sharp enough to cut the rope. He tried several places without success. Kohfer had been smart, Nick thought. He had known that the elbows would need to be secured to prevent bringing the cuffs around front and using the hands.

Nick wished he had inserted a CIA escape and evasion suppository. This was a capsule that contained an assortment of small saws, lockpicks and files that could be carried in the anus. Nick had used it before, but he had no expectation of being captured this time. Anyway, he thought, Kohfer's search had been thorough, he probably would have found it.

Nick noted that the mortar was crumbling and chipped away between many of the stones. None seemed loose, though. He could feel the heavy, smooth wood of the door as he moved about. The hinges were inaccessible, hidden between the jam and the edge of the door. With his feet he felt a hole about five inches in diameter at the base of the back wall. Probably drainage to the lower, forested land toward the sea, he thought. After hours of exploring and attempting to cut the rope on whatever sharp edges he could find, Nick lay on the floor again exhausted, cold and covered with grime. The rope was only frayed slightly after all his efforts. Worst of all, his movements had served to tighten the rope around his arms. His forearms, wrists and hands had become so numb from lack of circulation he could barely feel them. Suddenly, he saw the light around the edge of the door then heard footsteps outside. The bar was lifted and the heavy door creaked open. A flashlight shined in on him briefly and then the door slammed shut. The bar fell in place and then the faint crack of light around the door went out. Someone was checking on him. He judged he had been there twelve to fifteen hours. Actually it had been less than ten.

As he rested, he tried to memorize and organize in his mind all of the information the Baron had provided. Cha-Turgi was Arun Rashidii. He and the Baron were paid fifteen million to sabotage flight 283. Eva had been a conspirator.

They had also arranged for the Cabal and other ships to transport illegal arms. Cha-Turgi was planning another bombing, perhaps another plane. Perhaps from Los Angeles. Nick then wondered again what Kohfer's plans could be. Did he know who Nick was, maybe looking into collecting some old bounty or was he simply trying to be a hero by killing the Baron's killer? If so, why was he keeping Nick alive? Whatever the man's plans, Eva didn't seem to be a part of them.

Upstairs, Kurt Kohfer was snoring on the couch in the Baron's office. Eva sat outside the office in the parlor on a couch. She was unable to sleep. The groundskeeper and his wife, the cook, had returned and retired to their cottage behind the castle. The phone in the office rang. Kohfer came awake and answered it. Eva came into the office and closed the door. Kohfer checked his watch, it was nearly midnight. "Office of the Baron Von Kloussen," he said.

"This is Marseilles. You have the man identified in custody?"

"Yes."

"Exactly *where* is he and how do you have him secured?" The voice said in a disbelieving tone.

"Handcuffed, tied with ropes, locked in a cellar room he can't get out of."

"Are you sure? This man is reported to have made difficult escapes before." The tone still disbelieving.

"I checked on him only recently."

"Do you happen to have a bank account in Switzerland?"

"Yes." Kohfer, like many Europeans had a savings account there, although his was small.

"A man will arrive within eight hours. He will take your prisoner with him. We will place one million dollars in an escrow account at your bank to be transferred to your account upon verification that this has been accomplished. You have your bank and account number?"

"Yes, yes," Kohfer said excitedly. He took out his wallet and searched for a card. He read the bank and account number into the phone.

"Now give me specific directions to your location from Odense." Kohfer provided this information. "Now, I suggest you get a gun and keep watch on this man all the time. Keep him disabled. If he dies, we will pay two hundred thousand for his head and right hand." He rang off.

This was good, Kohfer thought. He looked at Eva, "One million dollars and they'll even pick him up. A man will be here within eight hours. Have you thought about my offer to take a quarter of the money and disappear?"

She was tired and upset, "I don't have much choice, do I? What do you plan to do about the Baron, uh...his body?"

"We'll tell the goddamned police that Bradshaw killed the Baron and escaped, of course. For now, we sit tight and wait." Kohfer was mulling some way to make it look as though Barber had killed Eva as well. He had put the unusual pistol that Barber carried in a drawer of the Baron's desk. He opened the drawer and looked down at the weapon. The plastic case was smashed on one side, but if he could get it working and kill Eva with it that would be enough evidence for the police. He pondered the words of the man on the phone. He went down and checked on Barber once again. Back in the office a few minutes later, he laid down on the couch. He was satisfied that Barber was secure.

* * *

Rashidii had taken a taxi to Beverly Hills and purchased the motorcycle. He rode away on it, relieved that the young seller had forgotten to remove the license plate. The bike was responsive and powerful as he cruised the smooth, sloping blacktop roads. He came out of Beverly Hills and leisurely rode the Sunset Strip back to Los Angeles. He parked the bike at his hotel and returned his rental car, taking a taxi back to the hotel. He checked his watch, it was getting late. He decided to call on Noska.

At the Crescent Moon, Noska was just waking up. It was nearly 7:00 P.M. He was still intoxicated, although the effects of the alcohol had begun to wear off a bit. Slowly, he rose from the bed. As he did so, packets of money and loose bills fell to the floor. He stepped on the beer can he had dropped and fell to one knee, then pulled himself up by grabbing the nightstand. He went into the bathroom and sloshed his face with water. Back in the main room a few minutes later, he switched on the television. He opened a fresh beer and lay down on the bed. He rested his head against the headboard again. He sipped the beer and squinted at the television. "This is Fugitive Intercept," Jack Newman's voice was saying. Video tapes of captured, handcuffed criminals being escorted by police flashed across the screen. "And tonight," his resonant voice continued, "we have our biggest, most exclusive story ever. We are tracking a fugitive sought in connection with the bombing of States Airlines flight 283. Stay tuned for details."

The words didn't register with Noska. He stared at the television, not really listening. The narration was just garbled sound to his alcohol soaked brain. A few commercial announcements and ads played through and then the television screen caught Noska's full attention. What looked like his own face suddenly appeared in full on the screen. He thought he was hallucinating. He rubbed his eyes. The voice began again, "This man's name is George Noska. He is sought in connection with the bombing this week of States Airlines flight 283 over Canada." The side view of Noska's Chicago mug shot flashed on the screen. He sat forward on the bed, eyes wide now, staring at the screen. "He may be disguised in a black or blonde wig and is known to wear a mustache. Our computer enhanced images show how he might look." Noska's face appeared on the screen again, a dark hairpiece on his head. After a moment a neatly trimmed mustache appeared on his lip. It looked exactly like him in his disguise.

He stood up, sobering now, "Jesus fucking Christ, how in the hell?" He said aloud. Staggering a bit, he threw the nearly full beer can at the television screen. His aim was high and the can skittered across the top of the set. It hit the wall behind and fell to the floor. Beer had splashed and foamed on the wall and the hot back side of the television set, creating steam. He watched the wisps of steam rise from behind his own face on the screen. Then suddenly, the thought struck him that he had better be quiet, not call attention to himself by making noise.

The hairpiece and mustache on the screen had turned to blonde now, "...and this is how he might look in a light colored wig and mustache." This image looked exactly like him in the other disguise. The hairpiece and mustache disappeared and the image returned to the original, frontal Chicago police mug shot. "This man was last seen in the Chicago area, but he may be hiding out anywhere in the country now. He has worked with computers and is known to smoke cigarettes, drink heavily and frequent taverns."

"Fuck you, cocksucker," Noska said to the screen.

"Consider him to be armed and dangerous," Newman's voice continued in an ominous tone. "If you see him or have information on his whereabouts, do not approach him. Call the Chicago FBI office or dial our toll free, eight hundred number." The numbers flashed on the screen. Finally, the face faded from the screen.

Noska began to panic. He didn't know what to do, but he decided he couldn't stay in the motel. Hopper would know what to do. But Noska didn't have his hotel phone number. He didn't even have the name of the hotel. He got a plastic bag from the bathroom and began to gather up the money. With shaking hands, he stuffed the bag of money and his clothes into his case and shut it. He picked up the whiskey bottle from the dresser and swigged the amber liquid. With the bottle in his hands, he sat on the bed to think. He sat there several minutes. He had money, he could buy a disguise. Someone could be calling in to the goddamned television station right now, he thought. The airlines people and others who had seen him on the way to Los Angeles, the motel owner, the fucking cab driver who had taken him to the post office, the jackoff at the counter in the liquor store where he'd been three times. He tried to think clearly, to come up with a plan as the television buzzed on about wanted criminals. He couldn't leave without a disguise. One that hadn't been shown on that goddamn television, he thought. A hat! If he only had a hat. Suddenly, there was a loud knock at the door. Noska looked at it in terror. The police, he thought. He felt a sharp, wrenching pain in the pit of his stomach. The whiskey bottle slipped from his trembling hands and fell to the floor. The golden-brown liquid dribbled out onto the carpet. There were three more loud knocks. I'm surprised the bastards are bothering to knock, he mused.

"Noska, are you in there? It's Hopper."

Noska felt a sudden wave of relief come over him. Still trembling, he got up and opened the door. Rashidii, wearing a plain black leather jacket and carrying a red, full coverage helmet under his left arm, came in and closed the door. He looked at Noska. The man was ashen faced, sweating and trembling. "What's wrong, too much drink?" Rashidii asked.

"I-I thought you were the goddamn police," Noska stammered.

A look of concern came over Rashidii's face, "Police? Why would you think that?"

Noska pointed at the television screen, "They...the sonsabitches got me on TV. Jesus Christ, look."

The spot on Noska was running again, just before the station break. Rashidii stared at Noska's face on the screen. How did they track down Noska so soon? What else did they know? It was probably a result of a search for Stafford or a routine check of former employees, he reasoned to himself. At least they didn't know where Noska was yet or they would be here. If they knew where he was, they wouldn't have him on this program in the first place, Rashidii reasoned to himself. He looked at Noska's case, "The money and your things are packed?"

"Yeah, when you came, I was sittin' here tryin' ta' figger out where in the fuck ta' go."

He handed Noska the helmet and said, "Put this on and flip down the shield. I came on a motorcycle. I'll pull up to the door. Grab your case and get on the back and we'll get out of here."

"Where the hell to?"

"My hotel for now. I'll get you in the back entrance where you can't be seen."

Rashidii pulled up on the bike and Noska came out with his case, slamming the door behind him. He got on, sandwiching the case between them and they cruised out of the parking lot. Inside the office of the Crescent Moon, the owner was dialing the Fugitive Intercept 800 number. Several blocks down the street the liquor store clerk had called the number several minutes earlier.

Rashidii's room at the International Inn was at the end of a wing on the second floor. He parked close to the entrance door and opened it with his room key. Noska stayed near the motorcycle still wearing the helmet. Rashidii checked around the hallway and stairs, then motioned Noska in. Noska entered Rashidii's room without being seen. Rashidii closed the door and said, "Stay here and don't answer the phone. Don't answer the door for anyone but me. I have to go run some errands. I'll bring back some food and liquid refreshment in a couple of hours." Noska nodded and lay down on one of the double beds. Rashidii had formulated a plan now. He checked several addresses in the yellow pages, making notes as he did so and then left.

He located a leather specialty shop in a mall not far from the hotel. He went to the counter and asked if they could sell him a leather thickness gauge. The clerk said they had a few, but did not ordinarily sell them to customers. Rashidii offered fifty dollars and the clerk sold him a gauge. He then found a discount department store with a hardware section and purchased a cheap micrometer, a riveting tool and a spool of light, insulated wire. In housewares, he bought an aluminum rolling pin, a roll of waxed paper and plastic wrap and some glue. Then, he drove to the airport and bought a ticket for flight number 327 on States Airlines to New York at 1:35 P.M. the next day. On the way back to the hotel, he picked up two submarine sandwiches, a twelve-pack of beer

and two liters of Southern Comfort whiskey. When he entered
the hotel room Noska was snoring loudly.

Rashidii unlocked his attache case and took out the C-
4. He took Noska's large attache case and the other items he
had bought and went into the bathroom and locked the door.
He laid the waxed paper out on the floor and placed half of
the C-4 in the center. He flattened the material and placed
waxed paper on top of it. With the rolling pin, he began to roll
the explosive plastic out between the paper. He worked it
carefully, adjusting the material to reshape it, until he had a
thin, rectangular piece. He measured along one edge at several
places with the micrometer. Then he rolled that edge and
measured several times again, until it was one hundred and
twenty thousandths, or just under one-eighth of an inch thick.
It had to be that thin or the TNA machines could detect it. He
checked along the edge with the leather gauge and then made
a mark on the gauge where the small needle on it indicated.
The leather gauge had a deep throat and could reach more
than halfway across the piece. He rolled the entire piece down
to the right thickness, checking it often in the center area with
the leather gauge. He trimmed the edges and set the piece
aside. He repeated the process with the other half of the C-4.
With two pieces complete, he washed his hands and opened
Noska's case. With the riveting tool, he removed the rivets
that held the metal lips on around the edges of the case.
Carefully, he pulled out the liner from the top and bottom of
the case. Then he glued one piece of explosive into the top of
the case and one into the bottom. He then took two small
detonator timers and wired them together using the insulated
wire. He set each one for 15:35 hours the next day and pushed
one into each slab of C-4. This way, he had a backup
detonator and when the first slab went off, the other would go
too. He taped the wires down across one of the case hinges.

The liner covered the hinges as well as the rest of the case interior. The wires wouldn't be seen on a routine inspection. He glued the liner back in and riveted the metal lips of the case back in place.

        After replacing the money and the rest of Noska's things, he shaved the top of his head. Then he dyed the fringe hair and his eyebrows white again to renew his disguise. He opened the bathroom door, Noska was still snoring, louder than ever now. Rashidii set the case back in its spot near Noska's bed. He gathered all the paraphernalia from the bathroom in a bag and took it to a trash can in another section of the hotel. When he returned, he laid on the other double bed and tried to get some sleep.

Take It To The Limit

EIGHTEEN

In Denmark, it was after 5:00 A.M. In the subcellar, Nick lay on the cold floor shivering. Several more hours had passed. Periodically, he got up and moved about to warm himself. He massaged his arms against the walls to restore the circulation as best he could. Now he heard a faint scratching and squeaking. It seemed to be coming from the drain hole. A mouse or rat? He listened carefully. The sound came closer. Nick formulated a plan.

He sat against the wall and bent his knees up. He bit a piece of skin from his knee, causing some blood to flow. He leaned over and quietly spat it into the hole, then repeated the process several times. First spitting the small pieces of his own bloody skin closer to the edge of the hole then onto the floor of the room near the hole. He sucked the wounds and with his lips dribbled bloody saliva onto the floor next to him. He silently reached back and swept it up with his fingers and coated his palms with it. He waited. The sounds of scratching from the hole became slightly louder. Quietly, Nick positioned his feet near the opening. The animal, devouring the pieces of flesh, came closer to the edge. Nick sat still, trying to breathe as quietly as possible. The scratching on the stone echoed faintly in the room. Nick heard the animal move further, licking and scratching at the bloody bait on the stone floor. Nick moved his feet over the hole. He could see nothing in the darkness, but the creature was trapped in the room. He lay on the floor and crawled along the base of the wall, until his stomach covered the opening. The animal was still. Nick opened his hands and waited, still trying to keep his breathing quiet. He heard scratching again on the stone and a squeak. Then he felt a tiny cold nose sniffing his buttocks. He felt the rough tongue of the animal on his skin. He lay perfectly still. The rat explored his lower back and began to sniff his hands. It recoiled and was silent for a moment and then he felt the tongue licking at the bloody saliva on his fingers. Suddenly, sharp teeth bit into the end of the third finger on his right hand. Even as numb as his hands were, the pain was sharp and his entire being cried out for a reaction. But, he lay still and quiet. The rat tore a small piece of flesh from the finger, then chewed briefly and swallowed it. Nick felt a raw, painful tickling sensation as the animal licked blood from the wound. The sensation continued on his palm as the tongue moved quickly around. Then, he felt the chewing action of the front teeth and the gathering of a small bit of skin in his palm. The needle sharp teeth sunk in again. As the animal began to tear out the chunk of flesh, Nick closed his hand quickly over the head. He was surprised at the large size of the skull. He swept his other hand under the animal in an attempt to grab its body, but it wrenched around violently and he was able to grab only the right front leg. He held it tightly. As the huge rat struggled wildly to free it's head and leg, Nick sat up and backed into the corner. A large Norway rat, Nick thought. The rat continued to struggle, its claws tearing into Nick's back. Nick got his left hand around the animal's abdomen and lower back. He released the head and the animal bit savagely at his right hand. The man got his thumb and forefinger around the neck. The numbness of his hand had masked the pain like a local anesthetic as bits of flesh were torn away. Nick felt blood flow around his wrist from the wounds.

Using great effort he guided the animal's head up to the rope. His half-numb arms shook as he made the effort to hold it there. The slashing teeth found the fiber and began to tear at it. Sporadically, the rat chewed the rope then stopped and struggled wildly with the rest of its body. Then it would chew on the rope again. It took all of Nick's concentration and effort to hold the small, writhing beast behind him in the proper orientation. Finally, Nick felt the rope begin to stretch, so he pulled his elbows apart and the remaining strands snapped. He let the rat go. It darted about the room for several moments, then found the hole and scurried away.

Nick stretched his arms down behind him and felt sharp pain as he flexed his spine. He successfully brought his cuffed hands around his buttocks and then brought his legs through. The maneuver had been much easier when he was younger. He worked quickly on the ropes knotted above his elbows. He was losing the sensation in his hands. After digging at the knots for some time, he got them loose. He massaged life back into his arms as best he could with the handcuffs on. As he got the gag removed and as he closed his mouth, he realized how sore his jaw was. He dug apart the knot on the rope at his ankles. He stood and began to feel around the walls. A couple of the stones had felt as though there was no mortar holding them when he searched before. There were deep crevices between some of the stones where mortar had fallen away or perhaps been chewed away. The ancient walls were old enough to have been built in medieval times, when the blood of oxen was mixed with shredded straw for mortar, Nick thought. The protein-based mix made a chew for rats and other vermin for many years. He felt around a stone nearly the size of a basketball. The mortar crumbled around it as he clawed at it with his raw, bloody fingertips. He wrenched the stone as hard as he could. It loosened, then came out of the wall. He held the heavy stone in his hands and tightened the handcuff chain over a rough protruding ridge on it. Using the stone as a combination hammer and chisel, he slammed it against the floor pinching the chain. Again and again, he drove it against the floor. He stopped to check the chain several times and went back to his work. He slammed the stone against the floor so quickly and persistently it was as though he were killing snakes. Finally the hardened metal gave way under the relentless hammering. His wrists free, Nick fell to the floor, sweating and exhausted.

Upstairs, Eva came into the Baron's office. Kohfer was on the couch, staring at the ceiling. "Kurt, do you hear a tapping or pounding somewhere. Maybe the cellar."

He sat up and checked his watch, it was nearly 5:30 A.M. "I didn't hear anything, but I suppose I'd better check on the bastard." He stood and pulled the Walther out of his pants pocket and checked it. Eva watched him go down the east hall. She sat at the Baron's desk and lit a cigarette.

In the subcellar, Kohfer entered the wide hall and switched on the light. He lifted the bar from the door and set it aside. A flashlight in his left hand and the Walther in his right, he nudged the door open with his foot. The flashlight beam began to scan the room as the heavy door creaked open. Nick was crouched against the opposite wall. Squinting in the light, he saw the hands holding the pistol and flashlight. Then he saw Kohfer's head emerging from behind the edge of the door. Nick sprang at the door, using all the strength he could muster in his legs. His shoulder hit the door. Kohfer sensed something wrong and started to pull back, but not soon enough. His right wrist was crushed between the jam and the door. He screamed in agony. The pistol went off as a result of reflex action in his now disabled hand. The bullet ricocheted from the stone in the small room with a ping and whine. As Kohfer continued to scream, Nick pried the gun from the hand. He fumbled with it momentarily to orient it in his own hand, then grabbed the edge of the door and jerked it open. Kohfer, his eyes wide with terror, pulled his right arm away, the limp hand hanging loosely from the smashed wrist. He backed away against the wall on the other side of the hallway. He looked into the barrel of his own pistol. Nick squinted in the light, the image of Kohfer was a bit blurry as his eyes painfully adjusted to the light. In a rage, Kohfer came at him raising the flashlight in his left hand. Nick squeezed the trigger and shot him between the eyes. Kohfer's head snapped back, then his body crumpled to the stone floor.

Nick reached down and quickly checked the dead man's pockets. The paper which described Nick's CIA identity and history was there. It explained a lot. He took it and went quickly for the door at the end of the ancient stone hall.

Upstairs, Eva heard a muffled sound. She was afraid it might be a shot. A few moments later, she heard another, louder similar sound. She froze in the Baron's desk chair and listened, it was quiet. She waited a couple of minutes thinking Kurt should have returned by now. She began to panic, thinking she had better get out of there. Then the side of the french doors that had been closed swung open. Nick stood there naked, covered with blood and dirt, a silver cuff on each wrist. He pointed the Walther at her. She screamed loudly at the sight of him.

"Shut up." Nick said as he checked the room and then walked over to her. He grabbed her arm and pulled her up out of the chair. "Put your hands on your head and stand over there," he said, pointing to the middle of the room. She complied, her legs weak with fright. Nick frisked her briefly and then walked to the window and tore down the drape pull cord. He checked outside. The sun was low, but bright in the southeastern sky. Above, there were rain clouds gathering. He secured Eva's hands behind her and pushed her down on the couch. He sat in the Baron's desk chair and picked up the phone. He punched in a number, then looked at Eva. "I'm going to ask you some questions and if you don't give me straight answers, I'm going to shoot you starting with your feet, just like Von Kloussen." She shivered with fear and nodded. There were tears in her eyes. "Who else is on the grounds?" he demanded.

"O-only the groundskeeper and his wife. In the cottage in back. And Kurt Kohfer," she added hastily, raising her voice as though it were a question."

The CIA operator in New York answered. Nick said, "This is a code red. Password BJPL needs to speak immediately with AJAR or whoever's on watch!" He said, using Joe Ronzoni's code name.

Moments later, the phone rang on Joe Ronzoni's bedside table. He awoke and fumbled for the handset. "Joe here," he said sleepily.

"Bradshaw, code red. Tape this." Joe hit a button on his phone. "Baron Von Kloussen is responsible for the bombing of flight 283. He has been neutralized. He and Arun Rashidii, also known as Cha-Turgi were paid fifteen million dollars to plan and accomplish this. They enlisted the help of a man named Noska." He looked at Eva and waved the barrel of the gun at her, "Your last name is Van Damme. Correct?"

"Y-yes." She said nervously.

"A German woman named Eva Van Damme and a German man named Kurt Kohfer may have been accomplices." Eva was shaking her head. "Kohfer has also been neutralized." Eva winced at this. "I have the woman in custody here with me. Important. Rashidii and Noska are in Los Angeles. Possibly planning another bombing. A plane from L.A. or something else, I don't know." He paused.

"Jesus." Joe muttered, coming fully awake now. "Where are you calling from? You all right?"

"The Baron's estate. Ok for now."

"We know about Noska. Sally Stein's in charge of the case. Let me see if I can get her on the other line. We'll conference."

Chicago, 10:58 P.M.

The phone on the table at the FBI office rang. Sally picked it up. It was Jack Newman. "Hello Jack," she said.

"You get any calls?"

"Yeah, several hundred now," Sally said, "still coming in. Everybody in the whole damned country has seen Noska, except for us. They're all taped and we're going through them now. Categorizing them for patterns, similar locales...but a couple of airline employees, who didn't recognize the mug photos earlier, called in after the program. From what they're saying, we think it's possible that Noska boarded a plane for L.A. yesterday wearing a blonde hairpiece and mustache. We're running down the details now."

"Fantastic," Jack said, "that ties in with what I have. We've gotten a ton of calls too. My staff and your people out here are working overtime going over the tapes. Two calls sound like they are genuine sightings. In fact I may have him for you."

"Shoot."

"Guy working in a liquor store over on Pico Boulevard called. Said Noska came in twice yesterday and once today, wearing the black getup. Said he looked just like the image we generated. Then, a few minutes later the owner of a roomer motel called the Crescent Moon called. The place is just a few blocks away from the liquor store. He said Noska checked in on Saturday night, paid for a few weeks in advance. Then, he hadn't seen him around again until yesterday. Black getup also. He might be there now, but the owner's afraid to go anywhere near the room. I listened to these tapes myself, several times. I've been doing this for a long time now and I'm telling you they're genuine sightings. We decided we'd better check with you since you're in charge."

"Who's our agent in charge there?"

"Morry Jackson."

"Put him on."

"Jackson here, Ms. Stein."

"You'd better get some people over to that motel and see if you can pick him up. Plan it carefully and keep us posted. Oh, and tell Jack thanks."

"Yes, Ma'am. 'Bye."

Sally hung up the phone, it rang as soon as it hit the cradle. She lifted it, "Sally Stein here."

"Joe Ronzoni. I've got Nick Barber on the other line calling from Europe. He has information pertinent to your case. Hang on, I'm going to get us on conference."

She heard Nick's voice, he repeated the information he had given Ronzoni. Sally sat there listening, dumbfounded. Then she said, "Then the Votilinni's weren't involved?"

"Possibly not." Joe said.

"Then, Agent Smith's efforts were for nothing," she said.

"Smith?" Nick asked.

"Tommy Garcia," Joe said, "We suspected the Votilinni crime family might have engineered the bombing. They have a tie-in with Noska. But then, I suppose they have a tie-in with every goddamn criminal in Chicago. Anyway, Tommy went undercover to try to establish a contact with them as part of the investigation."

"Dangerous job," Nick said, "where is uh-Smith?"

"In a hospital here in Chicago," Sally said. "The Bureau raided Votilinni's office while he was there. He did a superman out of a second floor window when the shooting started. A few sprains and a bump on the head. He'll be ok."

Nick looked at Eva, "You know of anyone named Votilinni or any Chicago criminals being involved in the bombing? Or did the Baron ever mention the name?"

"No," she said, tears streaming down her face. "And I wasn't involved either. I didn't know why we were placing those damned ads."

"No knowledge of the Votilinni's at this end," he said into the phone.

"What you said ties in with what we have, Nick," Sally said. "We got a couple of good leads on Noska in L.A.

We think he's checked into the Crescent Moon Motel there. In fact, our agents should be picking him up soon, if he's still there."

"Oh, yeah," Nick said, "Von Kloussen mentioned the Crescent Moon."

"This Rashidii. Any pictures?" she asked.

"Nothing," Joe said, "We've been aware of this man's activities for a long time but no pictures. Didn't even know him by Rashidii until now."

Nick had been holding the phone to his ear with his shoulder. He wrapped his wounded hand and fingers with cellophane tape from the desk. He said, "Hold on." He cupped the phone. "You have any photos of Rashidii?" He asked Eva.

"Uh, the Baron had me take some with a telephoto lens once. For insurance, I suppose." She looked over at the fireplace and nodded. "Lift the mantel on this end about two centimeters and remove the tan stone. There is a secret compartment. I think they might be..."

Nick was up in an instant. He pushed the heavy mantle up and tugged on the stone. It came loose. He pulled out several envelopes and sat at the desk. He opened three, spilling their contents onto the desk. The fourth one contained photographs. He held them up to Eva and she nodded forlornly. "I've got some pictures of the guy talking to Von Kloussen on a park bench. They were taken with a telephoto lens. I can fax'em but they're not going to be very clear." As Sally read him her fax number, he put the photos on the machine. He keyed in the international code and then the number. They waited until transmission was complete. "Get'em?" Nick asked.

"Yes," Sally said, "but they're not good at all. We'll do our best with them."

"Don't worry, I'll deliver the originals in person as soon as I can, Dean," Nick said, using Joe's code name for the mission. "You're going to have to get me out of here. If the Danish authorities get ahold of me we're going to have problems. There's a twenty-six hundred foot private grass airstrip near the coast a mile east of here. Should be on the charts. Get somebody to pick me up there as soon as you can." He looked out the window between the drapes. "Cloud cover looks like it's about five thousand feet and falling. It's starting to rain."

"A grass strip?" Joe asked. "What condition is it in?"

"Looks good when it's dry. I'll be there within the hour. I'll...," He looked at Eva, "My motorcycle?"

"Kurt put it in the garage."

"I'll send a digital SATCOM signal from the bike, uh-my password. By the way, try to send something big enough to get that damned motorcycle on board. You-know-who will kill me if I don't get it back."

"So will I," Joe said. "It's got technology that's top secret. We'll get you out. If we don't have anything close, maybe the Brits do. Call for the 'bird' on your radio, frequency 280."

Sally said, "Nick, I'm catching an overnight flight to L.A. I'll leave word for you at the FBI desk at LAX."

"Ok, FBI desk at LAX." Nick repeated, then he looked at Eva, realizing he shouldn't have repeated the words. "You should see me now, dear. I'll tell you about it. 'Bye." Sally said goodbye and hung up. "By the way, Dean, Von Kloussen confessed to conspiring with Rashidii on the Cabal and other shipments."

"You invoked the 'finding' after the interrogation?"

"Yes," Nick said and hung up the phone. He looked at Eva and motioned with the pistol, "Downstairs, you know where to go."

She got up and walked nervously, crossing the foyer and entering the hallway to the sun room. "Y-you're not going to leave me down there?" She said sobbing.

"That depends," he said, "on how convincing you can be about not knowing about the bombing of the flight ahead of time."

"I swear I didn't know a-anything about it," She protested repeatedly as they went down the stairs. She described the Baron's request for her to go to the U.S. and place newspaper ads and rent a post office box. "When I asked what it was about he would tell me nothing."

They passed the wine cellar and Nick opened the door to the hallway and switched on the light. Eva sucked air as she saw Kohfer's body there, below a bloody streak on the dingy stone wall. She stared down at the red hole between his eyes. She shivered as the unseeing eyes stared back. Nick grabbed her arm and spun her around to face him, "And the arms' shipments? I believe you knew about them." She nodded dejectedly. He checked her wrists. They were still secure. He turned her to face him again, "I'll think about this. If I decide you're telling the truth about the plane, I'll tell the Danish and international authorities you're here. They'll arrest you and put you in jail. It'll almost certainly be an improvement over these accommodations, though. Then you'll probably go to prison for a very long time, perhaps for life." Her eyes were wide with terror. "If I decide I didn't believe you, well, maybe someone will find you and maybe they won't." He pushed her inside the storage room, pulled the door shut and put the crossbar in place. He had every intention of informing the Danish authorities where she was as soon as he was out of the country. He believed her about the bombing.

If he had not believed her, she would be dead.

Upstairs, he checked the office and found his G11 pistol. He fired it into the desk drawer and was surprised it still worked. He ran in the light rain to the garages, past the east end of the house. The motorcycle was in the third bay. His helmet was still on the machine. He opened a suitcase and got dressed in his kevlar lined leathers and pulled on his kevlar lined leather boots. He put on the helmet and started the machine. When he arrived at the grass airstrip, it was raining harder and cloud cover was nearly down to five hundred feet. He parked at the windward end of the runway. He pulled back the tank flap and activated the sending unit. On the small keyboard, he typed the "send" code and his password "BJPL". He picked up the phone handset and switched it to "radio" and keyed in a frequency of two-eighty. "Is the bird approaching", he asked into the mouthpiece? There was no response. He waited, repeating the message at three-minute intervals.

As Nick left the castle drive, the cook was entering the kitchen area through the back door. Her husband was still in the cottage. The house was quiet. As yet, she had no instructions for preparing breakfast, so she began to check around the house. She had seen no one on the first floor as she knocked, then opened the french doors to the office. Her hand went to her mouth as she looked at the splotches of grimy blood on the desk and on the floor next to it. A mess from hunting? she wondered. Then, she looked down at the shattered phone on the floor. Through the parted curtains, she saw a small van arrive in the drive and stop outside the portico. She went over to the window quickly and peeked through the curtains. A short man wearing a dark blue trench coat and medium blue fedora came around the van. She heard the door knocker. Cautiously she went to the front door and opened it. The man stood there, a few drops of rain dripping from the brim of the fedora. He was white with a narrow face and black hair at the sides. He was wearing black horn-rim glasses with dark lenses."

"J-ja," she said nervously?

"Mr. Kurt Kohfer, Please," he said in German.

"I'm not sure if he's here," she said in the best German she could muster. "Come into the foyer and I'll see."

He stepped in and she closed the door behind him. She went upstairs to check the bedrooms. Then she checked Kohfer's apartment above the garage. A few minutes later she came back down and walked into the foyer, "I'm sorry. No one is here." She was relieved that she had found nothing unusual.

The man stared at her for a moment, then reached inside his coat and pulled out a Luger nine millimeter pistol and aimed it at her. She looked in terror at the black barrel, seemingly a part of his black gloved hand. She suppressed a scream. "The wine cellar," he said. "Take me there and you won't get hurt."

She led him out of the foyer and down the hall toward the sun room. He followed her to the right and they entered the kitchen area. Across the kitchen the back door opened. It was her husband. "Frederick!" She said in what was nearly a scream.

The man stepped from behind her, pointed the pistol at Frederick and ordered, "Hands on your head." Nervously, Frederick obeyed. "Is there anyone else here?" the stranger asked. She shook her head. "Then, to the wine cellar, both of you. You first," he nodded to the woman.

She went to the cellar door, followed by Frederick. They walked to the first level of basement and then through the door to the subcellar and down the curved, stone staircase. "A storage area?" the man asked as he looked about the area, "Locked rooms?" Frederick pointed to the door to the hallway. "Open it," he was told. Taking the lead now Frederick opened the door and turned on the light. The man followed the couple down the hall.

Suddenly the cook screamed shrilly at the sight of Kohfer's body. She fell against the wall and her husband cradled her in his arms. "Who is it?" The intruder asked.

"Kurt Kohfer," Frederick replied, "please let us go. We'll tell no one."

There was pounding on the door across the hall from the body. "Who is in there?" The man loudly demanded.

"It's Eva, get me out!"

"And the man who was captured?"

"He escaped. He left only minutes ago. Let me out. Please, I'll explain."

The man waved the gun at Frederick and motioned to the door. He unbarred it and opened it and helped Eva out. Dirty and exhausted, she leaned against the hallway wall. The man motioned to Frederick and his wife. "Inside," he said. Frederick helped his wife into the storage room and pushed the door shut. The man put the bar in place. He motioned Eva down the hall and followed her back to the first floor. She walked with difficulty, her hands tied and her eyes adjusting to the light. In the foyer he checked outside then turned to her and said, "Tell me everything, and quickly, or I will kill you right here and now."

She spoke frantically, terror in her eyes, "When Kurt went to check on Bradshaw the bastard killed him and escaped. Bradshaw made a phone call to someone. I-it sounded like someone is going to pick him up at the grass airstrip near here. Then, he mentioned meeting someone at Los Angeles International Airport, at the FBI desk. I'm just the Baron's secretary, please let me go."

"You know this airstrip?"

"I know where it is."

"Then come now!" He swung open the front door and motioned her out with the Luger. As they walked under the portico toward the van, they heard jet engines roaring in reverse thrust in the distance.

Nick had waited nearly forty-five minutes, then he heard in a British accent, "bird approaching". Nick switched on the headlight of the motorcycle. He could hear the jet engines. "I have my light on at the windward end of the runway," Nick said. Suddenly, the small jet appeared, shrouded in the low clouds like a ghost. The plane's image became clear as it dropped below cloud level, landing gear and flaps down. It touched down on the grass runway, the engines then going into loud, reverse thrust. Nick recognized the plane as a Dassult Myste're-Falcon 10MER, a military version of the Fan Jet Falcon 10 executive jet. The plane had British markings. As it rolled to a stop, Nick rode the motorcycle down the runway to meet it. As he approached the plane the door opened and the stairs flopped out. A man in a dark suit was at the doorway holding an HK-G11 assault rifle pointed at Nick.

"Password?" He asked.

"BJPL," Nick said loudly as he shut off the cycle.

"Welcome aboard then, mate. Flight Lieutenant in Command Henry Jones and Flight Lieutenant Nigel Cook, RAF, at your service."

"We have to get this motorcycle on board."

"Yes, I understood you had some special cargo." He came down and the co-pilot appeared at the door. Nick and Jones hoisted the heavy motorcycle up on the stairs and the co-pilot pulled on the handlebars. With some maneuvering, it barely fit through the door. They wedged it in between the cockpit bulkhead and the front passenger seats. Jones climbed over it into the cockpit and Nick followed, pulling in the steps and door behind. As Nick crawled over the motorcycle into the passenger area, the engines were already revving. The plane began to move forward, then turn toward the other end of the runway for takeoff.

"LAX?" Jones yelled back to Nick.

Nick leaned over the motorcycle, "Yes, as soon as possible! This is a national emergency."

"We'll have to make one refueling stop on the way."

"Fine. I can get on the radio and get you clearance wherever you like."

"Are you CIA, mate?"

"Can't say."

"Then you must be," Jones said laughing. He turned the nose wheel as he approached the windward end of the runway. He was already pushing the throttles forward as he completed the turn. "Is that forest beyond the runway, mate?"

"Yes. This has the high-lift wing devices?"

"Aye."

You're going to need them," Nick said. He sat in a second row passenger's seat and secured the lap belt as the plane roared down the runway and lifted off. As the powerful jet engines pushed it into the sky, the landing gear began to retract, just clearing the treetops.

Below on the ground, the van had just pulled up to the runway. Eva and the man in the driver's seat watched the jet disappear into the low cloud cover. He slammed on the brakes.

"He's gone. Let me go now," Eva said.

"You would like to see this man dead?"

"Bradshaw?"

"His name is Barber, not Bradshaw. He is an American agent."

"God, an American agent. Just as the Baron suspected. And Kohfer knew this?" The man shrugged and nodded. "Then that bastard Kohfer *was* double crossing the Baron."

"Would you like to see him dead? Answer me!"

"Yes. He murdered the Baron Von Kloussen in cold blood and Kohfer, too. And he locked me up in that cellar. I could have died a horrible death in there."

"The man has a price on his head and I intend to collect it. I have a leased jet plane waiting in Odense. We can leave within an hour for Los Angeles. If you agree to help me find and identify the man, I'll pay you two hundred thousand in U.S. dollars and guarantee your safe return to Germany...."

"And if not?"

"If not, I will drive over to that forest, put a bullet through your head and throw your body in among the trees."

Eva sighed and slumped against the seat. The United States, she thought. Maybe a good place to hide. They would be hunting for her all over Europe. And, if she were caught she could truthfully say she was kidnapped. "I'll cooperate, but I want to know who you are. I can tell from your speech that you are German, from Saxony."

"You may call me Karls."

NINETEEN

Los Angeles, 11:19 A.M.

Rashidii paced the floor in his hotel room. Noska had arisen a half hour earlier looking sicker than ever. Rashidii had tried to get the man to eat, but he wasn't interested. Rashidii then had to practically march him to the bathroom at gunpoint to make him take a shower. Noska had been in the bathroom twenty minutes, sloshing around. From his bag, Rashidii had taken the disguise that he used on the trip to California and laid it out on the bed. Noska was only a little shorter. It should fit the man, Rashidii thought. He went to the bathroom door and knocked, "Come on," he said loudly under his breath through the door. "I've got a disguise for you. No one will know you."

Finally, Noska emerged in his filthy, stained undershorts sopping his head with a towel. He still looked ill. "I wouldn't be in this goddamn mess if it wasn't for you and your fuckin' ideas." He looked down at the dress and other items on the bed, "Jesus, now you want me to dress like a goddamn woman?"

"That's right. No one will know you in this. You'll take a flight to New York this afternoon. Get a room there, then call me right here. I will bring or send you the rest of the money there. Believe me, it is part of my job to protect you and make sure you get what was promised to you."

"Yeah? Well, maybe you can go to hell. Maybe I'll just take what I have and go on my own. I'll be better off if I fuckin' stop listenin' ta' you."

"If you are caught you will surely face the death penalty," Rashidii said, a touch of sympathy in his voice.

Noska pondered this. He picked up one of the bottles of whiskey from the dresser and opened it. He took a long pull and then suddenly bent over, retching. He picked up a cigarette and lit it. After a long drag, he went into a coughing spasm. He sat on the bed as Rashidii slapped him on the back, trying to help dislodge whatever was causing the fit. Finally, it subsided. Red faced, eyes and nose watering, Noska looked up, "Ok, I'll go to New York, but I'm taken' this goddamn money with me this time. I don't give a fuck what you say."

Rashidii looked relieved, "Of course. No one is going to stop a little old lady. But you'll have to check your case through. That way, it won't be searched at the boarding security check." This was Rashidii's plan anyway. "You can carry this on," he held up the bag with loop handles. "Now get dressed."

* * *

The Myste're Falcon 10MER touched down at LAX at 12:10 P.M. During the trip, Nick had cleaned and taped up his wounds as best he could with the first aid kit on board and managed to get a few hours sleep. They had made a refueling stop at Teterboro Airport in New Jersey. Nick had spoken to Joe and he had arranged an emergency clearance for the stop. He had also arranged for entry to the government facility at LAX. Jones steered the plane into a special U.S. government paddock. Nick's first concern was to get Rashidii's photos to the FBI desk quickly. They wrestled the motorcycle out of the small plane and Nick parked it on the blacktop.

A uniformed Air Force officer wearing a field cap approached. Frowning, he asked, "What are you doing with the motorcycle?"

Nick turned to him, "I'm Barber, sir, and these two fellows are RAF. Gave me a lift in. I have to find the FBI desk immediately."

"I know who you are. You can't leave that motorcycle here. You can take it to the parking ramp that way." He pointed under a viaduct, toward the parking ramp area. The FBI desk is at the other end in the customs office. Information at the front entrance across from the parking ramp will direct you."

At that moment, a Hawker Siddley executive jet touched down on a runway not far away. Eva Van Damme and Karls were aboard.

Nick saluted the British Flight Lieutenants goodbye and started the bike. He found a parking place at level three. Then, he took the elevator down to the ground level and walked across World Way Street into the main entrance. There, information directed him to the customs office in the international terminal wing. He took an escalator up and walked quickly along a wide corridor, among bustling throngs of people. He found the door marked U.S. Customs. The receptionist looked up and was startled at Nick's appearance. He wore the black leather motorcycle jacket, pants and boots. On his face were several pieces of adhesive tape covering wounds. His hands and fingers were taped up with gauze and adhesive tape which was dark with dried blood. "FBI desk please?" he asked.

"Uh-one moment."

She stepped away from the desk behind a wall and returned a moment later with a uniformed customs officer. He looked at Nick suspiciously, "Who are you?"

"Nick Barber, "I have some important information for the FBI."

"You got an ID?"

"I lost my wallet."

The man looked Nick over carefully, "Are you armed?"

"Most definitely. I have an automatic pistol in my jacket pocket. I rarely go anywhere without it."

The man drew his pistol and aimed it at Nick. "Get some help," he said to the receptionist. She disappeared behind the wall. "Put your hands on top of your head, please," he said to Nick, "you're not allowed to carry weapons in here."

Nick complied and the door opened. Sally Stein walked in. "Nick!" she exclaimed, "Am I glad to see you!" Three other officers appeared from behind the wall. She looked at the customs officer, "It's all right, officer. He's with me."

"Her, I'm with her," Nick said, pointing his finger at Sally from the top of his head.

The officer looked at the FBI badge and ID pinned to the waistband of her slacks. He knew she was the agent in charge of the terrorism investigation. He holstered his pistol.

Sally said to Nick, "Follow me." They walked toward a door along the inside wall. "You have the photographs?"

"Right here," Nick said. He pulled the photos from his pocket and handed them over as they entered an office area with a number of desks in cubicles.

Sally examined them for a moment and handed them to an agent standing there, "Rick, take these to the downtown office and get fifty copies made immediately and bring them back. Leave the originals and have the photo shop start working on blow-ups. Tell them to call me as soon as they're ready." The man took the photos and left. She turned to Nick and looked up at him, "Jesus, what happened to you?"

Nick smiled, "Well, it's a long story but I ran a door into a guy..."

"You mean you ran into a door?"

"No, I ran a door into a guy and a big, fat Norway rat helped me by chewing through my ropes. He chewed up my hands a bit too. And, at that, he was my only ally."

She held his hands for a moment looking at them, then said, "I'm so glad you made it back safe."

He put his arms around her and kissed her full on the mouth. Her hands went instinctively to the back of his neck, massaging it as they kissed. At a desk a few feet away, a secretary watched in surprise then looked away. Sally pulled her mouth away. "We have business now, Nick. We'll finish this later, ok?" Her voice had a dreamy quality as she said this.

"Absolutely," he said. "So you haven't found any evidence of another bombing?"

"Nothing. We must have just missed Noska at that motel. The TV was still on when the agents got there. We're watching the place, but I doubt if he'll return. He probably saw himself on 'Fugitive Intercept' and split. We've got agents and police all over the airport, up at Union Station, the bus depots with those faxed pictures of Rashidii. Nothing yet."

"Maybe the TV program spooked them out of whatever plans they might have had."

"I hope so. Coffee?" she asked.

"Yes dear. I haven't slept well recently."

"Neither have I. I think I've been up for over forty-eight hours now." A minute later she set two mugs of steaming coffee on the desk and sat down. She switched on the computer in front of her. When it had booted, she clicked the word processing icon. She typed a few words on the machine and turned to Nick, her eyes were bloodshot from lack of sleep, "Now, how did you get the confession from this Baron Von Kloussen?"

"He was uh, motivated, yeah, strongly motivated to speak to me." He related what the Baron had told him as she typed.

"And where is he now?"

"No longer among us. Uh-hunting accident."

"I'm sure," she said sarcastically. She typed "deceased", and Mr. Kurt Kohfer?"

"The same."

"You know, we'd be a hell of a lot further ahead if you people would leave us someone to question," she said in a frustrated tone.

As she typed, Nick took one of the small transmitter buttons from his jacket pocket. He activated it by sliding a tiny switch with the point of a pencil. He dropped a pencil on the floor and bent down under the desk to pick it up. Sally was wearing pumps with a small, decorative leather bow over the toes. He slipped the transmitter button into the bow on the right shoe and said, "excuse me", as he came up with the pencil. This would be fun later, he thought, the tracking system on the bike would always tell him where she was, at least for a few days.

"Actually, Eva Van Damme is still alive," he said, smiling. "In fact, the Danish authorities should have picked her up by now." Nick related as much about the other events in Denmark and at the castle as he could. "That's about all I know," he said. "Hell, they did it for the money, what else do you need to know? Eva told me she thought the Baron was in financial trouble after losing the Cabal shipment."

"This Eva, you said she spied on you at the motel?" Sally looked at him, "She good looking?"

"I can't lie to you. Beautiful. A blonde, blue-eyed German goddess."

"And, no doubt she enticed you into the sack to get information."

"That's classified information. Anyway, a gentleman never tells."

Sally finished the report, hitting the keys hard now. Nick picked up a photo of Noska from the desk and studied it. "A seedy bastard," he commented, "looks like a troll. It's said they devour humans."

"You don't know the half of it," she said, snapping the mouse button to save the report on disk.

At that moment, on the level below, Rashidii and Noska stood in line at the States Airlines ticket counter near the front entrance of the Airport. When Noska had put on the disguise, Rashidii had been very pleased at the result. The man looked like an aged, sickly woman. He hoped they hadn't attracted any undue attention when he had ridden him the short distance to the airport on the motorcycle. But then, Rashidii had mused, it would probably take more than an old lady on the back of a motorcycle to attract attention in California. When their turn came, Rashidii presented the ticket packet to the man at the counter, "One bag to check through for my aunt." He set Noska's large attache' case on the scale. The man checked the ticket and affixed a tag to the handle of the bag. Rashidii was relieved as the man hoisted the case onto a conveyor belt behind him. He watched, through the corner of his eye, as the case disappeared through some plastic air barrier flaps. He then guided Noska away from the counter. The airport was crowded. They moved slowly through the stream of people, Rashidii's hand on Noska's elbow.

At the entrance to the boarding gates, they went through security uneventfully. Rashidii was unaware that a fuzzy copy of his own image was taped on the x-ray machine for the employees to check. In his disguise, he was almost impossible to spot without a better likeness. In the crowded boarding gate area, they took seats and waited. After a few minutes, the boarding doors opened. The man at the counter took a microphone and announced that flight number 327 was boarding and that handicapped persons and those with children were to board now. Noska stood at Rashidii's nudge and he helped the man over to the attendant near the boarding doors. He was pleased that Noska actually doddered like an elderly person. He realized it was no act. Holding Noska by the elbow he said, "My aunt, Lillie Reed. She's going to stay with her sister in New York. I'm afraid she's ill. A bit of an upset stomach is all."

As the attendant reached out to take Noska's other arm, he belched. She could smell the whiskey. She brought her hand up to cover her mouth and nose to fend off the fumes and conceal a slight smile. "Now don't worry Ms. Reed," she said, "you'll be fine on the flight." She led Noska through the boarding doors as Rashidii smiled and waved. When they were out of sight he walked briskly from the area.

Karls and Eva walked down the hallway, past the customs office entrance, then stood against the wall. They had returned to the castle long enough for Eva to get her Gertrude Reinhard credentials, including a passport and a change of clothes. Now she wore a scarf and dark sunglasses, a hasty disguise. Karls held his dark glasses in his hand with his suitcoat over his arm. The fedora was cocked low on his forehead, his dark eyes barely visible under the brim. They were whisked through customs as business people from Germany. Karls' 9mm Luger pistol was buried in his suitcase and it hadn't been opened for a check. Now it was under the seat of a dark blue Pontiac Bonneville he had rented and parked in the parking ramp. He had rented a second car from another agency and parked it in a hotel parking lot near the airport for a backup escape, if necessary.

Nick finished his coffee and set the cup down. He was tired. "I don't think I can be of much more help," he said to Sally. "Think I'll get a room and catch some sleep."

"You ought to get to a doctor and get those wounds looked at," she said, "you might have an infection."

Nick shrugged, "What number can I reach you at? I'll call as soon as I get a room. By the way, could you lend me a few bucks? I couldn't find my wallet at the castle."

Shaking her head, Sally opened her purse and counted out one hundred and fifty dollars in tens and twenties. She sighed, "That's almost all I have." From the desk, she took a sheet of stationary with the FBI letterhead at the top. She wrote:

To whom it may concern:
This man is working with the FBI in Los Angeles.
Please call 555-9000 to verify this.
Sally Stein, Chief Inspector

She handed it to him, "In case you get stopped with that weapon."

He looked at the note, then folded it and put it, with the cash, inside his jacket breast pocket. "Gee," he said, "my allowance and a note from mom." He stood and leaned over and kissed her on the cheek, "Thanks mom, I'll call as soon as I can." Smiling, he walked out of the office area and along the wall, toward the door. Sally looked after him with an exasperated look on her face. The FBI secretary was struggling to keep from laughing out loud now.

Karls nudged Eva as Nick emerged from the door into the wide, crowded corridor. "That him?"

"Yes," she said under her breath. Then she turned quickly toward the wall, pretending to search in her purse.

Nick walked to the end of the corridor in the direction of the main entrance. He stepped onto an escalator that conveyed people down into the main entrance area. Glancing down, he scanned faces by force of habit. He took a second glance at a bald man, a white fringe around his head, a black leather jacket slung over his shoulder. A thought flashed through his mind: The man's face look's like Arun Rashidii in the photos! Nick hurried down the escalator, stepping around people. By the time he got to the bottom, the bald man, walking quickly, had gone out through the main doors. Nick, almost running, went for the doors. As he went through, he saw the man disappear into the parking ramp entrance far across the busy street. Nick broke into a run now, dodging traffic as he crossed the street. Several cars had to screech to a halt.

He reached the first level of the ramp and checked around. He didn't see the man. He darted up the stairs to the second level and came out checking the area quickly. The third and fourth levels were busy with people and cars moving about. Still, he could not see the man. He decided to try one more level. Then, he would go to the exit at the lower level and wait. He ran up the stairs to the fifth level and came through the door, panting. His chest heaving, he leaned against the outer wall of the stairway. There, across the rows of cars, he caught a glimpse of the bald head and white fringe. The head disappeared into a red, full coverage motorcycle helmet. Nick saw that he was astride a red and black motorcycle, the engine idling, exhaust popping from the pipes. Nick began to run toward the man. Rashidii secured the helmet and pushed the shift lever into first gear. He darted away quickly in the exit lane. In moments, he was cruising down the ramp to the next level, some distance away. Nick could see the red helmet disappear below the rows of cars. Nick stopped and ran back to the stairs.

He vaulted the railings down to the third level and ran to his motorcycle. He unclipped the helmet and put it on and switched on the interior headset. He opened the tank bag and clicked on the power to the communications gear. Just as he was going to call Sally, he saw the red and black motorcycle across the building. It came down quickly from the fourth level, then disappeared down the exit ramp. Nick started the bike and pulled on his gloves. He snapped the machine into gear and headed toward the down ramp. He didn't see the motorcycle again until he reached the first floor. Rashidii had apparently paid his parking fee at the booth and as the gate in front of him rose, he zipped out into the street turning left toward the city. There were two cars in line behind Rashidii. Nick sped around the rows of parked cars, until he was coming up to the line. The first car was pulling out now. Nick could see no way to get through, so he waited. As the car in front of him pulled out, he stayed on its bumper and followed it into the street. He ducked to clear the descending gate. He could barely hear the booth attendant yelling for him to stop. As he quickly passed the car, he could see Rashidii more than a block ahead, just making a yellow light as he turned left on Lincoln Boulevard. Nick pulled up to the light, between the lanes of vehicles, but traffic was too heavy to make a turn through it. "Telephone," he said loudly and clearly into the microphone in the helmet chin guard.

"Yes," responded the sweet but mechanical synthesized female voice in his ear.

"Dial five-five-five-nii-on-," he dragged out the "nine" like an old time telephone operator to be sure the audio sensor picked up the right number, "zero-zero-zero-zero". He heard some clicks as his traffic light turned green. Far ahead in the traffic, he saw the red helmet. Then he heard a busy signal. "Goddamnit," he muttered.

"Excuse me," the voice responded sweetly, "I do not comprehend."

"Fuck you computer," Nick said, frustrated as he zipped through the lanes between vehicles, barely clearing rear view mirrors on either side.

"Excuse me, I do not...."

"Redial," Nick said loudly and clearly. The voice stopped at a valid command. Nick cruised along Lincoln Boulevard, passing cars, barely keeping the red helmet in sight far ahead. Rashidii stopped in the traffic at a stoplight well ahead. There were clicks again and then the phone was ringing at the other end.

"Federal Bureau of Investigation, Los Angeles International Office, Lorrie Cervantes speaking."

"This is Nick Barber." He said loudly into the helmet microphone. "This is an emergency. I must speak to Sally Stein immediately. I was just there with her a few minutes ago."

"Oh yes, Mr. Barber. She just stepped out. I'll page her on the other phone."

"Get her on quick. Tell her I've got her man Rashidii in sight."

"Just a moment," she said excitedly.

The traffic was moving again. Rashidii stayed on the boulevard headed northwest. He, too, was dodging in and out of lanes passing cars. Nick was having trouble gaining on him in the heavy traffic. He lost sight of the red helmet a couple of times. After several more minutes, they had passed through two miles of the crowded city. Nick was catching up. He was only about six vehicles behind Rashidii now. Then, Rashidii made a quick left onto Olympic Boulevard in heavy traffic. Nick kept him in sight, following as he merged onto the Pacific Coast Highway.

* * *

The Boeing 767 that was flight 327 to New York was pulled by a towmotor-tractor away from the boarding gate area. The engines of the plane then revved and roared. Under its own power, it began to lumber across the tarmac toward the taxiway. Noska looked out the cabin window into the bright sunlight. Every joint in the plane seemed to squeak as the plane moved across the uneven, paved surface. Relaxed in his seat, he felt better, his mind clearing. Then he was struck by a terrible thought! What if that goddamn Grant Hopper had put a bomb in his case? It was possible, Noska thought, gripping the armrests of the seat tightly. But no, where would he have got explosives out here? Noska relaxed a bit, thinking. Hopper was resourceful. He always seemed to come up with anything he needed. But...then another horrifying thought...The box I mailed. Why did he want it back right away? He could have put explosives...anything in there. If you can mail a lot of money you can mail anything, Noska thought with horror. He sat forward suddenly in the seat, gripping the armrests even harder. In the next seat, a young man wearing a white shirt, his red and silver paisley tie loose at the collar, also sat forward. Noska turned to him.

The man looked into Noska's rheumy, wide eyes. A rivulet of sweat ran down the center of his forehead. "Are you all right ma'am?" the young man queried. Having forgotten about his own disguise, Noska just stared at him in surprise at the question.

* * *

Nick followed Rashidii down toward the ocean. He was gaining slightly as they rode between Palisades Park and The Promenade. Trucks and vans blocked his line of vision and he had to weave in and out of the crowded lanes to keep the red helmet in sight. "Damn it," Nick said under his breath, "com'on, Sally. Christ, I should have just called 911." Finally he heard her voice.

"Nick! What is it?"

"Followed a man I think is Rashidii out of the airport ramp. We're going north on the Pacific Coast Highway, approaching Palisades Beach. He's wearing a red helmet and a black jacket. Riding a red and black crotch rocket. Honda, looks like. California tag, I think. Couldn't get the number. I'm on a black motorcycle with a British tag 'DU-412'."

She was frantically writing on a pad, "Are you sure it's him?"

"Pretty sure. I got a good look at his face from the escalator. Couldn't catch him at the airport."

"Oh God, I hate to think what he might have been doing here. I'll get out an APB right away. Stay on the line." He heard Sally put the phone down.

He could see the coast now. The ocean was bright blue and calm as they sped along. There was only barely visible white foam as puny waves played themselves out along the sandy beach to his left. The sun was beating hot from above and Nick was sweating in the heavy leather and kevlar outfit. He could see Rashidii now on the lower ground ahead as he rode along between the beach and brown cliffs.

Rashidii's HUD read sixty-six miles an hour. He wanted to avoid any chance of being stopped for speeding. He planned to ride to San Francisco and take a plane from there.

Nick speeded up a bit and passed a couple of cars. He was close to Rashidii now. The Honda was in the next lane to his right, just in front of the car next to him. He held his speed.

Rashidii was observant. He had noticed the black helmeted rider on the chrome-trimmed motorcycle weaving in and out of traffic behind, coming up on him. Now it stayed in the left lane, pacing him. He slowed a bit. Still, the other cycle did not pass. Was he being followed? He thought. No, not on a motorcycle, it wasn't a police motorcycle. Probably just a kid playing cat and mouse. The way looked clear ahead now as they sailed along by the long stretch of beach that framed a only tiny section of the Pacific Ocean. Rashidii varied his speed and still the cycle hung back there, seemingly following. A black and white California Highway Patrol cruiser pulled out from some trees below the high cliffs at the right side of the highway. The huge Chevrolet Caprice accelerated quickly and pulled up on Rashidii's tail. In a moment, the flashing red and blue lights came on. Rashidii saw this in the mirrors. He heard the siren begin to scream in bursts. He cracked open the throttle on the Honda. The bike accelerated quickly, pulling rapidly away from the squad car, even as the officer at the wheel slammed the gas pedal to the floor. The officers in the car watched the cycle pull away quickly, weaving in and out of the traffic some distance ahead. Suddenly, another motorcycle screamed by to their left. It was black with chrome-trim and the rider was crouched down. It also disappeared into the traffic ahead, leaving four widening streams of swirling black jet exhaust smoke behind.

TWENTY

It was 1:40 P.M. Flight 327 left the ground five minutes late. On board, Noska was becoming increasingly agitated. His mind was racing with thoughts of pure terror now. They were in the air! He heard the grind, squeaks and clump of the landing gear being folded below the wings. Jesus, he could face the fucking electric chair if he revealed himself. Or would it be the lethal injection now? He imagined himself tied down to a gurney, the IV in his arm. Maybe he could get off with life imprisonment if he cooperated with the authorities. Would it be worse than being blown to pieces in the air? He stirred in his seat, unhooking his seat belt. As he nervously stood, the man next to him pushed the call button for the stewardess. Noska was sweating profusely now, beads of sweat rolling down his face. As the plane leveled slightly, a stewardess approached their row. "I think this lady's sick," the young passenger said, "she's babbling and sweating."

The woman leaned over the seats, "Can't you please sit down ma'am? We're still in our takeoff pattern. Please sit and put your seat belt on."

Noska collapsed back into the seat.

* * *

In his rear view mirror, Rashidii saw the motorcycle approach out of the traffic once more. He pulled into the left lane, accelerating to over one hundred miles an hour. The black motorcycle stayed with him. He decided he'd better leave the highway soon, find some way to ditch the tail and hide from the police. He continued to accelerate as he wove back through the traffic to the right lane. His HUD readout was at one thirty-five. Thoughts of his racing days returned. Again the cycle was there in the rear view mirror as he sped along in the right lane. He moved onto the narrow concrete shoulder at the right to pass cars. The other motorcycle followed.

Sally picked up the phone on the desk. She could hear the roaring of the motorcycle engine in the receiver, "Nick, what's happening?"

He heard her words faintly as he concentrated on the rapidly moving pavement and Rashidii's helmet. "In high speed pursuit of suspect," Nick yelled into the mike, trying to sound police-like. Passed Will Rogers Beach a few seconds ago. Last sign I could read."

"I just got the airport director to halt all outbound flights and have the passengers disembark. I'm going to get in

a van and head out there, I'll have this call patched through."
Sally was concerned about Nick. She also wanted to be there
to question Rashidii. There could be hundreds of innocent
lives at stake.

Ahead Rashidii slowed. He took a curving exit off the
highway to the right onto Torrenca Canyon Boulevard. He
checked his mirror and the other cycle was rounding the exit
curve behind. There were wide curves in the road now,
sloping upward into the foothills of the coastal mountain
range. He opened the throttle. He accelerated past eighty, past
one hundred then to over one-fifty. Still the pursuer stayed
behind, even gaining on him. They flew by other vehicles on
the right and left. There was a straight stretch with no traffic
ahead now, Rashidii cracked the throttle. His HUD readout
was climbing quickly to two hundred. He checked the mirror
and the cycle was still there. Rashidii couldn't believe it, no
other motorcycle was as fast as the Honda NR 750. He kept
the throttle open.

Nick hit the button on the right handlebar and the
spoilers came out as the bright orange heads up readout
passed one eighty. The cycle hugged the road in response to
the updirected mass of the airflow over the small wings. He
kept the throttle wide open now. The gas turbine engine was
screaming loudly. Power was being assisted by the liquid
oxygen burning the fuel more rapidly in the combustion
chambers. The readout passed two hundred and still the
rocket-assisted gas turbine engine accelerated the bike
rapidly. Nick's hands felt numb as he tightened his grip and
hunched down behind the small windshield. Then he
remembered, from his study of handling motorcycles, that this
was an undesirable survival reaction. He relaxed his grip to
restore circulation to his hands. Rashidii shot by a car, then
another and pulled back into the right lane. Nick pulled out

and flew by the next car, then he was gripped by sudden fear as a semi-tractor approached head on. He moved slightly to the right and raced past the car, between it and the massive vehicle.

Ahead, Rashidii saw a road to the right. He rolled off the throttle dropping his RPMs to ten thousand. Applying the front brake judiciously, he slowed for the ninety degree turn. He leaned into the turn, coasting momentarily, then opening the throttle to transfer weight to the rear wheel for traction and balance and to accelerate out of the turn. Nick, slowing as rapidly as he could, overshot the turn. He had to slow drastically and turn off the highway, riding across the gravel terrain. Rashidii was climbing the mountains, nearly out of sight, as Nick sped onto the side road in pursuit. Nick opened the throttle trying to keep Rashidii in sight. As they climbed into the mountains, Rashidii took each winding turn with a riding expertise that Nick couldn't begin to match. They wound along the mountain road, past residences. Nick cautiously slowed on the curves, while Rashidii moved out of sight. The road came back down onto the same highway with no other outlet. As Nick came out of the high hills, he could see Rashidii far below. The man was leaning into another expertly executed turn back onto the highway. Nick followed, with Rashidii out of sight again, as he turned back onto the highway headed north again. Nick realized he couldn't hope to outride this man in rough country. The superior speed of the turbine powered machine on a straight highway would be his only hope to catch the man. He opened the throttle all the way and the bike surged forward.

In the mirrors, Rashidii, unbelieving, saw the chrome and black image of his pursuer grow larger once again. His readout was now two hundred and ten, near the theoretical maximum for the bike. He kept the throttle wide open to take it to the limit. The speed continued to increase slowly, finally hovering between two-eighteen and two-twenty. On the right, buildings were whizzing by. They were coming into a more populated area. They passed above U.S. Highway 101 on the viaduct and down into a populated area with a straight stretch ahead.

Nick was gaining now, his readout at two hundred and thirty-nine. Rashidii's speed seemed to have leveled off. Far ahead there was a stoplight. The intersection was one half mile ahead. At the speed they were going they would be there in little more than eight seconds. Rashidii did not slow. Nick backed off the throttle. The light was red and there was a group of small schoolchildren crossing the street. The crossing guard, holding a red stop sign, looked up and saw Rashidii coming. The guard yelled at the children and they scattered. The light was just turning yellow on the intersecting road. The Honda switched to the left lane to get by cars at the stop sign and then back to the right lane as it whizzed through the intersection. It went through a narrow opening in the group of children. Nick held his horn button down as he took the same zig-zag through the intersection, still traveling at over one hundred and fifty miles per hour. Rashidii had taken a chance in hope of losing his pursuer. It hadn't worked.

Buildings whizzed by as Nick speeded up again, keeping his eyes on the road far ahead. He swerved out to avoid a car in his lane. Such maneuvers had to be planned far ahead at these speeds. He could see the red helmet again. A large discount store was coming up fast on the right. Beyond it, Nick could see what appeared to be open country again. Rashidii, seeing Nick in the mirrors, held the throttle wide open again. Ahead, past the discount store yard was a fork in the road. The right branch led to a one lane viaduct that passed over a highway they were approaching. The left branch led to a frontage road. Rashidii leaned slightly to the right, guiding the cycle into the right branch. He checked his speedometer readout, as he accelerated up the incline leading to the viaduct, two hundred and eight.

Nick opened the throttle again and the powerful acceleration kicked in. As he leaned into the long, wide curve toward the viaduct he was going over two hundred and twenty.

In the rearview mirror, Rashidii could see Nick approaching again, gaining on him quickly. In disbelief, he turned his head quickly and looked back. In that split second, the front wheel of his motorcycle had left the pavement. It was on the gravel, then on the paved sidewalk between the guard rail and the road. He had lost control! The left side of his cycle slammed the formed ribs of the metal guard rail at over two hundred miles per hour. The force of the impact crushed his left leg between the motorcycle and the rail. As he slid along, the friction of the motorcycle sliding along the rail tore away first the skin and then the muscle of his left thigh. His upper body leaned hard to the left from the force of the blow. A black and yellow striped rectangular warning sign flashed in a blur, only a few feet ahead. It was at the end of the guard rail, where the concrete rail of the viaduct started. It seemed he would slam right into the sign. Instinctively, he raised his left hand to ward off the blow, keeping his right on the handlegrip. The handlebar shimmied in his hand. As he reached the end of the metal rail it flattened out, the top edge now a sharp, square corner. That corner severed his thigh nearly all the way through, like a giant knife, as he slid along helplessly. His outstretched left hand hit the sign and the impact straightened his body momentarily. His left arm, instantaneously broken in several places from smashing into the sign, snapped behind his back as it recoiled from the impact. The front wheel of the bike now hit the four inch curb at the beginning of the concrete viaduct itself. Rashidii and the bike went airborne.

Nick saw Rashidii hit the guard rail and he began to slow immediately. He clicked the gearshift down into second and popped the clutch as he worked the front brake. He was careful not to apply too much pressure or the cycle could go over. In an instant, he saw Rashidii and his motorcycle pop into the air. As they seemingly floated, tumbling twenty feet above the viaduct road surface, Rashidii's body separated from the machine. His right hand, his last contact with the bike, let go in midair. The motorcycle continued on in flight, making a great arc off toward the other end of the viaduct. Rashidii's body tumbled faster, spinning in the air. The centrifugal force of Rashidii's involuntary, airborne pirouette tore the remaining strands of flesh connecting his left leg. It ripped away in midair. Rashidii slammed to the pavement and bounced up several feet at the far end of the viaduct. The motorcycle hit the road well beyond, bouncing and springing about. Finally it slid to a halt on the gravel shoulder. Nick swerved slightly to the right to miss the skittering left leg as he rode up onto the viaduct pavement. He swerved again to the left to avoid the rest of Rashidii, now on his back on the pavement. Nick finally was able to stop well past where the Honda had come to rest.

Nick rode back near Rashidii and climbed off the motorcycle. He flipped the kickstand down and let the machine idle. Rashidii was struggling, trying to raise his right shoulder. His right arm was flailing about on the pavement. His back had been broken when he hit the pavement. The back of his helmet was crushed in like a dented egg, but it had protected his head. Nick looked down at the bloody stump, where the man's left leg had been. The end looked like a mass of red, raw hamburger. The raw meat was interlaced with gray, fatty tissue. The jagged, shattered white thigh bone protruded from the wound. Next to the bone, blood pumped from the femoral artery. Nick hunched down and flipped open the Rashidii's face shield. The man's eyes were wide, the dark pupils dilated.

"Lookin' back is a bad habit, Mr. Rashidii. That is your name isn't it?"

"Who are you?" He asked in a strained, breathless voice, staring up at the dark shield on Nick's helmet.

"I'm your worst nightmare. The one you'll wake up screaming from after you're dead and in hell. Arun Rashidii, that is your name?"

The helmet moved slightly as the man nodded, his eyes darting about. "Help me up," he asked weakly. He was completely unaware of the extent of his injuries.

"Only if you talk. Did you take a bomb to the airport?"

Rashidii frowned now, thinking he was a dead man anyway. A slight smile formed on his lips, "Fuck you, as you Americans say."

Nick looked around quickly, then back at Rashidii. "You will talk."

"No." The man coughed and a trickle of blood appeared at the corner of his mouth.

Nick thought for a moment. He didn't think a gun or knife would scare this man. He stood and ran along the viaduct pavement toward the crashed motorcycle. On the way, he stopped and picked up a cup-shaped piece of broken red plastic that had been the front directional light housing. Gasoline was bubbling out of the crushed gas tank on the twisted wreck. Nick held the plastic housing under the tank and tilted the machine. When the cup was full of gas he ran back to Rashidii. Nick stepped into the bloody stump. He pressed the sole of his right boot into the spongy, muscle tissue stopping the surges of blood with the pressure. He crouched down over the man. Holding the cup down where Rashidii couldn't see it, he splashed the gasoline up over the side of the helmet and into the man's face. Rashidii coughed and sputtered. More blood appeared at his mouth. "Do you smell that?" Nick asked. "There is gasoline everywhere. You will talk or," Nick held a cigarette lighter up where Rashidii could see it, "you will die screaming in the flames of hell." A flame appeared on the lighter.

Rashidii's wide eyes fixed on the flame, "No, no."

"The bomb. Where? Talk and you will live."

Rashidii's entire body felt numb, his vision and thoughts were foggy. The thought that he could live another day, escape from these people, came to him. "States Airlines flight number 327...New York." Rashidii said panting as he rasped out the words. "In Noska's case." His body began to shiver with shock.

"His carry on?"

"No. Luggage. Large tan attache' case."

"What kind of explosive?"

"Plastic. The liner. Two detonators set...for mid-flight." Blood began to well up into Rashidii's throat from his internal injuries now. He gagged and then retched. The blood filled his mouth and spilled over his lips. It bubbled and foamed as he gasped for breath.

Nick reached down under the chin guard of the man's helmet and applied pressure just above his adam's apple. He pressed, cutting off the man's windpipe to hasten the impending death. He shook back his left sleeve and exposed his watch. As he counted off the seconds, he said, "Sally," into the mike. He heard a car pull up behind him from the direction of the discount store. He looked back. It was a plain, beige Chevrolet. The bumper stopped two feet away. A woman in a starched, white uniform dress got out.

"Oh, my God," she exclaimed, "Can I help?"

Nick's helmeted head turned to look up at her, "Go call 9-1-1," he said.

She looked down at the dark face shield, then at Nick's right hand under the man's helmet chin guard. "What are you doing," she asked?

Nick shot a glance at the plastic card above her left breast. It read "Julie Summers R.N." "Takin' his pulse," he said.

"With gloves on?" she asked in an incredulous tone.

Rashidii's right arm and leg moved around on the pavement.

"It's thin material," Nick said loudly in a frustrated tone. "Now go get in your car and drive down there and call an ambulance. Now!" he yelled. The woman backed away and opened her car door. With his left hand, Nick pulled the Fairbairn-Sykes double-edged killing knife from the sheath in his boot. As she slammed the car door, he scooted over to the car and leaned his back against the front bumper. He jabbed the knife into the left front tire. The razor sharp blade of the Fairbairn-Sykes knife went through the steel belted radial as though it were tissue paper. As the car began to roll backward, he jerked the knife out slashing it down. Air began to rush out of the three inch gash in the sidewall. As Nick turned his attention again to Rashidii, he heard sirens in the distance. He realized his attempt to delay the woman was wasted time. Blood still bubbled on Rashidii's lips. The bastard is still alive, Nick realized, as he pressed the windpipe closed again. The body shuddered as he checked his watch once again.

The woman backed around, turned and started down the incline. As she began to roll forward, the flat began to flop and bump on the pavement. She stopped halfway down the incline and got out. The sirens grew louder as they approached. "I've got a flat," she yelled nervously at Nick.

"Then walk down and call for chrissakes," came Nick's loud, exasperated voice from under the helmet. She began to trot down the hill. Nick watched as three police cars, two black and white state and one county squad car following appeared around the bend, near the discount store.

He didn't notice the blue Pontiac behind the police cars, as it turned left onto the frontage road below. Karls and Eva had followed Nick from the airport, then lost him in the traffic. Later, traveling on the Pacific Coast Highway in the direction Karls suspected Nick had gone he saw the police. He found it easy enough to follow the police to Nick. Karls drove around behind the police now and along the frontage road.

In the Pontiac, Eva was frantic. She looked over at Karls, "How do you plan to escape with all these police coming?"

"I have several plans," he answered. He didn't verbalize the fact that most of the plans called for quickly killing anyone who got in the way, including Eva. "We'll get away. I'm not going to let this much money slip through my fingers."

"Sally, answer," Nick said loudly into the mike. Still there was no answer. He checked his watch. Below at the base of the hill, the nurse had flagged the first state squad car to a stop. She ran to the driver's side window.

Rashidii's right arm flew up in an involuntary jerk, then fell back to the pavement.

A minute later, Nick looked up and saw the dark blue nose of a Pontiac Bonneville pull up quickly and stop next to his motorcycle. Karls had driven down the frontage road and crossed the highway. Then, going against the "One Way" sign, he drove up the single lane ramp to the viaduct. Another Good Samaritan, Nick thought. He looked down at Rashidii. The man's eyes were open, staring into the bright sun. Nick was satisfied that he was dead. Behind Nick, a California state Highway Patrol car screeched to a stop, less than fifteen feet away. Then a second pulled up and stopped some distance behind it. On the opposite side of the viaduct, a man wearing a fedora and dark glasses had stepped out of the Pontiac driver's side door. Nick felt the impact on his helmet and the awful jerk on his head and neck. A split second later heard the crack of the shot. He looked up. Karls fired a second time and again Nick felt the nasty jerk on the helmet and saw the shield crack in a spider-web pattern directly in front of his right eye. He stood, his G11 pistol already out of his pocket. He aimed quickly at Karls, who, startled momentarily at Nick's resilience had squeezed off another shot. Nick felt a sudden numbness under his left breast as the nine millimeter bullet slammed into his jacket. A tiny, red spot from the laser sight on the G11 pistol appeared between Karls' eyes even as he fired the luger a fourth time. Nick squeezed off a three-round-burst just as the fourth bullet slammed into his jacket above his right breast. Karls' head snapped back and his hands jerked instinctively toward his face as the three high-velocity bullets entered his skull less than a quarter of a millisecond apart. He fell back behind the open car door.

Nick felt a sharp, heavy impact at the rear of his thigh. It nearly knocked his leg out from under him. Then he heard the explosion of the shot. He stumbled forward, nearly losing his balance, then swung around holding the pistol out and planted his feet firmly. "Drop your weapon and put your hands on your head!" Came a voice from a bullhorn. A female officer was behind the open door on the passenger's side of the squad. She held the bullhorn in her left hand and a smoking .357 magnum revolver in her right. Behind the open driver's door was a male officer, his short pump shotgun trained on Nick. He fired and the birdshot pattern caught Nick full in the chest.

They watched in amazement as Nick began to walk toward them, his pistol held out. "Stop firing," he yelled from under the helmet, "I'm a federal officer." Holding the .357 in both hands now, the woman squeezed the trigger again. The bullet slammed into the jacket at the center of Nick's chest, knocking the wind out of his lungs. This was followed by a shotgun blast that sent BBs pinging off of his helmet. Nick flipped the selector lever on the G11 to full auto and fired at the front of the car. The headlights and the grill began to burst apart in pieces. Then, continuing to walk forward, he blasted at the light rack on top. Pieces of glass and plastic flew everywhere. The two astounded officers had taken cover, crouching behind the doors. Running on adrenalin now, Nick limped to the driver's door and went around it. His pistol was aimed at the officer's head. With his left hand, he reached down and grabbed the shoulder of the man's uniform shirt. "Get up and drop that weapon," Nick said, his voice gravelly from the dry heat. The police officer stood and let the shotgun fall from his hands. "You too, missy," Nick yelled over the front seat of the car as he waved his pistol at the female officer on the other side. She dropped the revolver to the ground and raised her trembling hands.

Well behind, in the other two squad cars, officers crouched behind open doors with their guns drawn.

Nick held the driver's door open. "My name is Nick Barber. I'm a federal officer. Get back in your car. Now!" They scrambled in, somewhat relieved looks on their faces. "Listen carefully. There's a bomb in the luggage cargo compartment on States Airlines flight 327 to New York. Do you understand...?" They nodded. "Radio that in. I have to get back to the airport safely or hundreds of lives may be lost. You tell every other car in the area to give me the open road or...or they'll think they were at high speed and hit some goddamn thing that doesn't move. Like he did!" Nick pointed to Rashidii's body. "You follow?" They both nodded again.

Nick was gone in an instant, jogging in a limping fashion back to his motorcycle. He swung his leg over and rode toward the Pontiac. He steered around the front end of the car. He glanced down into the front seat and there, saw Eva, huddled under the dashboard. Nick climbed off the cycle and jerked the car door open. Eva looked up. "You," Nick said, "How?"

"I was kidnapped. It's the truth."

"Get on the back." She stared at him for a moment. "The motorcycle. Get on or I'll blow your brains out...right now!" he screamed at her in German. He got off the motorcycle, grabbed her arm, and pulled her out of the car. He swung his leg over the motorcycle and she climbed on the back. As he cruised down the incline, he called "Sally" into the microphone again. Still no answer. He rode the short distance north to highway 118 and turned west. He said, "Navigator".

"Yes."

"Locate number two." He was referring to the transmitter button he had slipped into the bow on Sally's shoe."

"Going northwest on Pacific Coast Highway, north of Los Angeles, California. Sixty-seven miles per hour. Passing highway ten," the synthesized voice responded.

"Telephone."

"Yes."

"Redial."

There were a few clicks, a pause, and then a voice came on. "Federal Bureau of Investigation, Los Angeles International office, Lorrie Cervantes speaking."

"This is Nick Barber again. You've got to get me through to Sally Stein. We must have lost contact. She's traveling north on the coast highway. This is an emergency. If you can't get her, then get another agent on the phone!"

"I'll try her, sir."

In a few moments, Nick heard, "Sally Stein," in the speaker at his ear.

"This is Nick Barber. Rashidii talked. There is a bomb in the luggage cargo compartment on States Airlines flight 327 to New York. Noska's on the flight, it's in the liner of his case. Large tan attache' case. Two detonators set for mid-flight."

"Hold on," Sally said, "I'll call it in right away."

Nick continued to cruise along at seventy miles an hour. He noticed a state police cruiser fall in behind him, following, keeping its distance. Sally's voice came on again, "Nick, 327 is in the air. Left five minutes late at 1:40. They're going to have it return to LAX. It's 2:28 now..."

Nick had already done the calculation, "That means it's set for about 3:35."

"They should be on the runway at 3:15, or sooner."

"It better be sooner. I'm now going west on Highway 118. Just about to turn south on U.S. 405. Turn around and get on U.S. 10. Meet me on 405 just south of ten. I've got a prisoner for you." Eva gripped Nick's leather jacket as they sped along, slicing through wisps of smog under the warm California sun. There were now three police cruisers behind them.

"How do you know where I am," Sally asked?

"That's classified."

"And Rashidii?"

"He, uh, died after he had a serious motorcycle accident. He's a reckless rider if I've ever seen one."

TWENTY-ONE

The pilot of the Boeing 767 banked to the right, under orders from the tower at LAX. His voice was cool and calm as he announced to the passengers that there was a minor mechanical difficulty and they would have to return to Los Angeles. Inside he was terrified. In the passengers' compartment, Noska was slumped in his seat. When the pilot made the announcement, he wasn't listening. Then all the passengers groaned in a din of voices. Noska felt the plane banking in a sharp turn. He sat forward as the pilot repeated the announcement. Minor mechanical difficulty, this was perfect, he thought. They would probably have everyone get off the plane and reclaim their luggage. He would go on his own. To Mexico, he mused. It wasn't that far and he had heard you could live well for lifetime there on one hundred thousand dollars.

* * *

Nick whipped in and out of the increasingly heavy traffic as he moved toward the heart of the metropolis. He was trying to keep his speed at eighty or more and at that, he wasn't much faster than the traffic. In his ear, the synthesized voice spoke, "Fuel low. One liter remaining." Nick was already aware of this from the digital readout in front of him. Behind, the police cars followed, their sirens screaming and lights flashing. Ahead he could see the intersection of 405 and 10. He slowed. Beyond the intersection, a dark blue van was pulled off on the shoulder. He saw Sally get out and step around the nose of the van. She was wearing a navy blue vest with "FBI" emblazoned in large, yellow letters on the front and back. He rode up and stopped at the rear of the van. He flipped the kickstand down, slid his right leg over the gas tank and dismounted. He grabbed the stunned, angry Eva by the arm and helped her from the cycle. Tadd Nippy climbed out of the driver's door of the van. He was wearing a dark blue, pin-striped suit and a red tie. He wore the FBI vest over his jacket.

Nick walked toward Sally, Eva in tow, "I got a prisoner for you. Sally Stein, meet Eva Van Damme."

Sally looked at her, then at Nick, "But, I thought you said she was in Europe."

"Apparently she flew over right behind me with some guy who was out to kill me. To collect a bounty, I suppose."

"And, where is he," Sally asked?

"He's dead." She frowned up at him. "Well, he was shootin' at me for chrissakes. It was self defense." He pushed

Eva toward Sally, "Now this lady... you can arrest her for conspiracy to transport and sell illegal armaments for openers."

The police cars pulled up behind, several officers got out and walked toward them. Sally already had a set of handcuffs out of her purse. She pushed Eva up against the side of the van and ordered her to put her hands on the van and spread her legs. Sally repeated the illegal arms charge as she frisked Eva and cuffed her. Nick repeated Sally's words in German to be sure.

"She was involved in the bomb plot, too," Nick then said to Sally, "although it may have been unwitting on her part. And, on top of everything else, she's a Nazi, a genuine master race enthusiast. So, don't say I never gave you a good collar."

Sally looked over at Nick and shook her head slowly. "A Nazi?," she repeated, shaking her head, an incredulous tone in her voice. She recited the Miranda Rights as she marched the woman around the van. Nippy slid open the side door. Sally helped Eva inside the rear of the van and belted her into a side jump-seat behind the driver.

Nick checked his watch. It was 2:51. They were about fifteen minutes from LAX. "We're going to have to leave to meet the plane," he said to Sally and her partner. "But, first we'll have to load my motorcycle in your van. I'm nearly out of fuel and they'll have my ass in Washington if I don't return this baby."

Sally introduced her partner to Nick, "This is Agent Tadd Nippy of our Chicago office."

The taller man looked down at the bandaged hand as Nick held it out. Nick shook his hand, "Barber, Nick Barber, CIA." Nippy's handshake was tight and aggressive. Nick felt pain from the sores on his hand. "Easy on the hand. Pleased to meet you."

"Forget the damned amenities and let's get going," Sally said as she opened the back doors of the van. Nick was already rolling the motorcycle toward it. Nick grabbed one side, Tadd the other; they hoisted it up and in, one wheel at a time. The heavy motorcycle seemed light to Nick as Tadd did most of the lifting. This thin young man was much stronger than he looked, Nick realized.

Nick climbed in the back of the van and began to secure the motorcycle with nylon straps. Outside, Sally was asking the officers for an escort to LAX. Tadd got into the driver's seat and as soon as Sally climbed in next to him, he headed back onto the highway. The motorcycle secure, Nick sat in the jump seat across from Eva and behind Sally. The front wheel of the motorcycle was between them.

Sally leaned around from the front, "They told me on the radio you had some kind of shoot out with the state police."

Nick's face was strained as he looked at her, "I didn't hurt any of 'um".

"Small wonder," she said.

"They started shootin' at me from behind, what was I supposed to do?" He sucked breath, his face showing obvious pain now.

"What's the matter?" She reached back and put her hand on his shoulder.

"Damn it," he said, his voice strained. "I've just been shot several times and the pain is really coming on now. The kevlar keeps you alive, stops the penetration, but it doesn't stop the force of impact. And, this outfit has leather and padding too." He unzipped his jacket and pulled up his shirt. There was a large, oblong purple bruise below his left breast.

It ran to the center of his chest and the entire area was swollen. There were two lumps nearly the size of golf balls, one rising from each side of the swelling. Above his right nipple was another purple bruise and swelling.

"Oh my God," Sally exclaimed. She reached back and put her hand on the back of his neck. "Is there anything I can do?"

"Ice would help," he said.

Sally leaned forward in the front seat. She turned back holding out a can of Coca Cola. "No ice, but this is cold."

Nick took the can. He opened it and drank from it, then rolled the smooth surface of it over the wounds. He stretched out his left leg and felt the painful swelling at the back of his left thigh. The muscle was tight and he massaged it. "I think the lady cop was using a .357 magnum," he said, she wanted to kill me, all right."

Eva looked at him sullenly from her captive position on the other side of the van. She had been carefully watching the interplay between Nick and Sally. She was thinking they seemed pretty chummy. "It's unfortunate that she wasn't successful, "Eva said in German, her voice raspy and guttural.

"Be quiet," Nick replied in German, "I don't want to hear from you."

"Oh? That's not what you said," she was now speaking in heavily accented broken English, "when you were fucking me on the beach in Denmark." She shot Sally a triumphant glance.

Nick grimaced and shot a sidelong glance at Sally, the tendons of his neck standing out. "I was under orders," he said sheepishly.

Sally shook her head sadly, "Don't try to be funny!" She sighed, looking down at the floor. "We should get you to a hospital. You've probably got a couple of cracked ribs or worse." This was said clinically and there was an edge to her voice.

"Not until the job is done," he said.

Tadd Nippy, listening to this exchange with interest, was wheeling the van into the LAX security entrance. It was four minutes after three. They passed clearance and crossed the tarmac, near the runway where flight 327 was scheduled to land at any moment. There were emergency vehicles lined up along both sides of the runway. Sally was on the radio with airport security, "They're going to stop the plane out at the end of the runway and unload the passengers in emergency fashion. The Los Angeles Police Department bomb squad is on the way."

"Then we'd better head out there," Nick said.

Tadd looked around and Sally nodded to him. Just then, the plane appeared low in the smoggy sky to their right. The landing gear was down and the flaps were visible, angled down at the back of the wings. As the wheels of the plane touched the runway, Tadd was already driving along the taxiway.

"Make sure they have some equipment there, so I can get into that baggage compartment," Nick said, "but first we better get Noska so he can identify his case."

Sally was on the phone with the tower as they sped along. The huge plane came to a stop out in the open, at the end of the runway. The pilot set the brakes and shut down the two massive jet engines. The engines' impellers were still spinning when the van pulled up and stopped behind the left tailplane. The emergency exit doors on both sides of the aircraft popped open. Sally, Tadd and Nick emerged from the van. From each aircraft door an expanding inflatable slide snaked out into the air and dropped to the ground. Almost immediately, a uniformed crew member slid down each one and stood at the bottom. From there, they waved the passengers to slide down. Tadd went to the right side of the plane while Sally and Nick stayed on the left.

One by one the passengers came down, assisted by the crew at the bottom to stand and move quickly out of the way on the runway. Sally moved close to the front door and Nick was at the rear. Airport security people and other FBI agents were arriving on the scene. Sally waved them over and gave them instructions. Passenger after passenger slid down. Some were screaming with fright and some acted as though they were at an amusement park. Nick watched every face carefully as they were helped from the ground and sent on their way. FBI agents further from the plane scrutinized them as they walked away.

An elderly lady appeared up at the door. Her hair was bluish in color. Nick shot a glance at the face. Astonishingly, she jumped out well down on the slide and bounced in the middle. Nick kept his eye on her face as she came down. That face! Could this be Noska? Nick thought, quickly. Foolishly, he had neglected to ask Rashidii if the man was in disguise. Of course, he would be, and it would have to be a good one! The man's face had been on national television. She slid to a stop at the bottom. The dress flew up to the waist and Nick got a quick glance at the men's briefs. The legs were hairy and the knee-high nylons were taped at the top of the calves. The steward bent down and grabbed Noska under the arms. The short man sprang to his feet surprisingly quickly, brushing the dress down awkwardly. Following the others, he walked toward Nick. As he walked by, Nick reached out, gathered the blue/gray hairpiece in his hand and jerked it off of Noska's balding head.

Noska's hands went instinctively to the top of his head. Then, as he turned to look up at Nick he instead focused on the G11 pistol barrel he was facing. "You're under arrest, Mr. Noska. Keep those hands on top of your head or I'll shoot it right off of your shoulders." Then Nick yelled, "Sally, I've got him." He looked at Noska again. "You alone on this flight?"

Sally was running over. Noska gripped the top of his head. His rheumy, bloodshot eyes were wide, he was petrified. He managed to nod slightly. Sally took one look at the man's face and immediately announced that he was under arrest for the bombing of flight two eighty-three. She frisked him quickly. Tadd came over and they were joined by several other agents. He snapped a handcuff on Noska's right wrist and then jerked it down behind him. He pulled the other wrist down and snapped on the other cuff in one swift, practiced motion.

"Now, let's get over to those cargo bays," Nick said in a commanding voice. He broke into a limping jog under the belly of the plane. The others followed. Airline security people had pulled a large luggage wagon under each of the bays. They had climbed up and opened the cargo doors.

Nick turned around and Sally and Tadd were leading Noska toward him, surrounded by the other agents. Nick spoke loudly to the them, "I want three volunteers now! Single men! We're going to unload that luggage. There's a bomb in there that could go off at any time!"

Noska swooned and Sally and Tadd had to hold him up.

One of the airport security officers pulled off his communications headset. "Who the hell are you?" He yelled at Nick, "We're supposed to wait for the bomb squad!"

"I *am* the bomb squad," Nick replied.

Sally put a bullhorn to her mouth, "My name is Sally Stein and I'm in charge here. You're to do as he says. Three volunteers and everybody else clear the area!"

Tadd Nippy and a couple of other young agents stepped forward. Nick ordered the two to the front cargo bay. He and Tadd took the larger one in the rear between the wing and the tailplane. The four men climbed up on the luggage wagons and into the bays. There was barely room to stand. They unfastened the cargo straps and began to loosen the suitcases. Below, Sally walked the rubbery-legged Noska over in between the two wagons, her Beretta nine millimeter pistol was out and aimed at him. She told him to identify his case when he saw it. He nodded groggily.

One by one, each man would hold out a suitcase or attache' case. When Noska shook his head, the man would throw it to the ground and turn quickly to pull out another. They all went at it as though they were killing snakes. It was physically hard work and Nick's hands were sore. He pulled out his leather gloves and slipped them on. After a few minutes, the wagons and the ground were littered with luggage. Tadd pulled out a large brown suitcase and held it out. Noska shook his head and Tadd let it fall to the ground. It bounced and opened, spilling clothes on the runway. Nick, holding out two suitcases, said, "You should consider a job with the airlines. You've got the touch they seem to look for." Tadd paid no attention to this remark as he turned back and reached for more luggage, sweat pouring down his pale face. Sally had turned Noska's attention back to the other two agents in the front bay. He shook his head and more suitcases hit the ground. Then, he looked at the two Nick was holding out and shook his head once again.

Up in the passenger cabin there was a panic as the last of the passengers crowded toward the emergency exits.

368   Take It To The Limit

Rumors of a bomb had spread. There were screams as people stumbled and fallen over one another in a rush to get out. People were lying on top of one another in the aisle, while others climbed over the seats toward the exit doors. The pilot and co-pilot were there helping the cabin attendants straighten out the mess and get people moving in an orderly fashion again.

Tadd reached back into the expanding hole of the cargo bay and jerked hard on two handles. He pulled the cases from the top of the pile and swung around with them. He took a step toward the bay opening once again and held them out. Nick had just thrown a couple of suitcases down and as he turned back, he looked at the case in Tadd's right hand. It was a thick, tan plastic attache' case the size of a small suitcase! He waited for Noska's reaction. Down in front of the luggage wagons, the small man squinted up. The bright sunlight reflected into his eyes from the surface of the plane. He focused on the case for a moment, then he nodded.

Nick reached out, "I'll take that," he said to Tadd. The young man handed it over without hesitation. The case in hand, Nick jumped to the top of the luggage wagon quickly. A couple of suitcases slipped under his feet, he skidded off the edge and fell to the ground. Out at the edge of the runway, some two hundred feet away, the bomb squad had pulled to a stop. There was a dark L.A.P.D. van pulling a small two-wheeled trailer. On the trailer was a round bomb canister, a bit larger than an oil drum. Behind that, on the trailer, was the squad's field robot which also looked like an oil drum. It had a small, bulldozer style track on each side for mobility over rough terrain. There was an arm on the front end with shoulder, elbow, wrist and hand. The arm was similar to a small, industrial robot. As though an invasion from space were taking place, helmeted beings in protective suits and heavy gloves emerged from the van. They ran to the trailer and in a moment, the robot was rolling down a small ramp.

Nick picked himself up and limped around the luggage wagon. He held the case out to Noska and yelled at him, "Are you sure?"

Noska looked at the case. His eyes fixed on the broken corner, exposing the white inner liner. Noska was nodding, "The-the broken corner. Fuck, it's mine," he said nervously. Then he turned away in fear.

Nick abruptly turned toward the bomb squad van and began to walk briskly but with a limp. "Take cover," he said loudly. Sally repeated this into the bull horn, then walked Noska quickly around the other side of the luggage wagon. The two men climbed down from the cargo bays and joined them. The other agents and passengers were far away, on the other side of the plane.

Nick tried the clasps on the case as he walked. It was locked. The robot was rolling toward him now, the cover on its canister open. On the machine's robot hand was a small gun barrel which could be fired directly at a suspected bomb to detonate it. The hand also had a clasping mechanism which could pick up a suspected bomb and place it in the canister. Two people from the bomb squad began to walk some distance behind it. One held a small control box and was operating the robot.

Nick pulled out his pistol and flipped the selector to three-round-burst. As he walked, he held the case away from him and aimed into the keyhole of the right lock. He fired a couple of three round bursts. The small bullets gutted the lock and snapped through the back rib of the case. They smacked into the concrete below near Nick's feet, with small dusty eruptions. He repeated this with the left lock and put the pistol back in his pocket. He cradled the case in his left arm and flipped the latches out. With his right hand, he opened the case. With his teeth, he gathered the fingers of his right glove and pulled it off. Still walking, he pushed his elbow against the lid and grabbed the file holder in the top of the case. Pulling on it, he ripped the liner away from the cover. The small, gray detonator cap was there. It was about the size of a dime. Two wires protruded from it down into the case. The digital clock on it read 15:34. He had to get both detonators out quickly. There was less than a minute! The robot was rolling toward him, one hundred feet away now, arm out in front, its gaping mouth ready to accept a bomb. Nick had to get the bomb further from the plane. There wasn't time for him to get it into the robot's canister! Nick held the case top by the edge in his right hand and ripped out the detonator with his left, breaking the wires. He closed his gloved hand around it and suddenly there was a crack and a terrible sting in his clenched hand. He looked at it. His hand had been forced open by the blast as the small detonator went off. The other detonator could go off any second! The palm of his glove was smoking. The thick, leather palm pad of the glove was burned away, exposing the kevlar liner. The hand was numb and useless. Nick looked at it in surprise for a moment. "Get back, get away," he yelled at the approaching bomb squad personnel. He let the case slide down his body for a second, while he got a grip on the lower metal lip with his right hand. He swung the case back and threw it around forward with all the force he could muster. He hurled the case up at a forty-five degree angle, for maximum distance, in a path centered between the plane and the bomb squad van. It spun horizontally as it made a lazy arc through the air. Nick turned back toward the luggage wagon in a run. He thought only about gaining ground as he pumped his legs to push him forward. The robot stopped on the runway. The helmeted bomb squad people were running in a direction opposite the airborne case. The case landed on the runway and skidded further away, still spinning on the concrete. Nick was only a few feet from the wagon now. He dived for the concrete and his head slid under the heavy diamond tread step plate. His hands instinctively went to the back of his head to cover it as he slid to a stop.

There was a blinding flash at ground level and then two deafening explosions. They came in such rapid succession, one could scarcely tell there were two. The remaining cap detonated the C-4 in the bottom of the case. That blast in turn caused the thin sheet of explosive in the top to go off also. The powerful shock wave of the bomb depressed the thick concrete below in a crushing implosion for a split second. In reaction, the material sprang back with tons of force. A cloud of concrete dust rose instantly. Pieces of concrete the size of baseballs and dinner plates spewed from the cloud. These were followed by a shotgun blast of smaller fragments, as though a giant sized claymore land mine had been detonated. Pieces rained down about the area and skidded along the runway, pushed by their own momentum. Several hit the bomb squad van and a few glanced off the plane. Nick felt a few shards hit his back. When the rain of debris and the noise stopped, he stood and looked around. There was screaming from the other side of the plane, but apparently, no one had been hurt. More than two hundred feet away near the edge of the runway was a crater in the concrete. It was four feet across and two feet deep. Dust continued to rise from the crater and was dispersed in wisps and puffs by the moderate California wind.

PART THREE
THE NEW HEROES

TWENTY-TWO

Tuesday, July 5, 1994, 5:00 P.M.

Saint Agnes Hospital was on the northwest side of Chicago. It was an older, six story plain rectangular building of brown brick. Nick Barber walked past the front desk and found the stairway beyond. He was dressed in a blue suit, white shirt and bright red tie. There were still a few small bandages on his hands. He had applied some makeup on his face to cover a couple of scabbed-over gashes. He wanted to look his best for a night on the town, for later. He went up to the second floor and strode down a long corridor, checking the numbers on the doors. He came to two-thirty-six. A plain clothes FBI Agent stood outside the door. Nick showed the man his CIA identification and the man told him to wait. A minute later he was back, ushering Nick in. Nick passed through a room with two other agents who were obviously not in plain clothes. They were wearing vests and carrying M-16 assault rifles. One of them nodded toward an inner door. Nick went in. Major Tommy Garcia was sitting on the bed in khakis and a white T-shirt reading a magazine. He wore a shoulder holster that housed a G11 automatic pistol. He looked up and hopped off the bed.

"Nick, good to see you. Heard you had a little action in California."

Nick laughed, "Yeah. And in Denmark, too. All of it unexpected. I was told I was on a damned vacation junket assignment. You look fit. How is it you're still in the hospital? And why all the guards?"

Tommy pointed his thumb at the varnished door near the head of his bed. I'm actually helpin' the FBI guard someone. Joe offered my services, since I was here as a patient, anyway. It's all top secret. The name's Phil Smith by the way."

"So I heard."

He knocked on the door. A man's voice said, "Phil?"

"Yeah," Tommy said as he opened the door; he and Nick entered. The big man lay on the bed wearing only print pajama bottoms. A wide, heavy bandage circled his body at the chest. He had big shoulders and huge biceps both adorned with slightly fading tattoos. On the side of the upper arm was a skull wearing a top hat, a cigarette dangling from it's teeth. Just below, a flowing ribbon read, "Love, Honor, Death". A fire-breathing dragon done in blues, greens and reds, wound its body around the forearm.

"Nick Barber, meet ex-heavyweight contender, Mac McGinnis," Tommy said.

"We've met briefly once before," Nick said, studying the man's face. "But, I certainly didn't expect to meet you again. You're dead. I heard it on the news."

Mac laughed with difficulty, "To quote Mark Twain, 'News of my death was exaggerated.' You can't believe everything you hear. Actually, I had taken to wearing a bullet-proof vest under my suit. For safety around Diamond Jimmy and his boys. The son-of-a-bitch shot me twice with a .45. Fortunately, it was in the chest, but he almost killed me anyway. I can't tell you how much it hurt."

"You don't have to tell me," Nick said. His chest and left thigh muscle were still quite sore.

"I know how to take a dive though."

"I know that for a fact. I saw you fight on television, what, twenty-five, twenty-six years ago?"

Tommy laughed, "I was three years old".

"This was the dive of my life," Mac continued. "I fell back on my face after he shot me. Jesus, I couldn't breathe. I was barely conscious. When I hit the floor I bit my inner cheek, at first, by accident. Then I bit it hard on purpose, to draw more blood. I wiped it down onto my shirt before they turned me over. I was convincing, I guess, although Jimmy fired another shot at me. It missed and then they all got away. They believe I'm dead though."

"So, you'll talk to the FBI now?"

Mac nodded, "I guess I don't have much choice."

Nick said goodbye to Mac, then they returned to Tommy's room and shut the door. Tommy looked up at him, "So where you goin' all dressed up?"

"I managed to get a date with Sally Stein. She's still in town working on the bombing case. We're going out to dinner, a little place I know not far from here, the Filet Mignon. Best steaks in town. She got me into a hospital in

L.A., then never came back to visit. She's pissed at me, because I, well, there was this woman in Europe. It was all in the line of duty, of course."

Tommy was laughing, "Sure, of course."

"She came back to Chicago on Monday. I spoke to her several times on the phone, had to beg her to go out with me for chrissakes. I sent her a dozen roses. She's afraid I'm going to give her AIDS or something."

"Well, you never know," Tommy said mischievously, but with a serious undertone.

"The woman was the mistress of a Danish Baron, you think she's going to have some disease? It isn't like I'm screwing every woman I meet...contrary to what some people seem to think," Nick said in an exasperated tone.

"Ah, Sally's just jealous," Tommy said, "you know how women are."

"No, I sure as hell don't," Nick replied. "Votilinni, he's still on the loose?"

"Yeah, the FBI's working on it. They figure he must have skipped the country."

"By the way, Joe Ronzoni put out a message to people who might be considering planting bombs on airplanes."

"The whole idea of the 'finding' about saboteurs was to send a message, right?" Tommy drew his forefinger across his throat.

"I mean a literal message. An internet page and a one-page FAX that went all over the world. It talked about the swift and sure punishment of Rashidii and Von Kloussen and the quick apprehension of Noska and Van Damme. Then, a severe warning to others. Of course it's not signed by anyone, just an anonymous statement. He even put a skull and crossbones at the bottom. Joe has quite a flair for the dramatic."

Tommy laughed, shaking his head, "Well, it might drive the point home. Save some lives."

A half an hour later, Nick pulled in to the parking lot of the Day and Night Inn on Pulaski. It was not far from Noska's apartment. Sally had taken a room there the week before to be close to the scene of the investigation. She hadn't used the room until she returned to Chicago on Monday, since she had to make the unexpected trip to California the prior Thursday. There were two Chicago police cars under the portico, emergency lights flashing. Following the directions Sally had given him, Nick turned left and pulled up to the first hallway entrance. He could see more flashing lights around the corner of the building. He opened the glass door and went in. He took the stairs to his left and went up to the second floor. He turned right into the hall and stood face to face with a tall uniformed Chicago police officer. Next to him was a burly plainclothes detective, his badge hanging from the pocket of his blazer. Behind them, the door to the first room on the left was open. Another uniformed officer stood in front of the door. The detective turned to Nick and stared at him for a moment. Nick was looking beyond them at the open door, there were voices in the room. Sally had told him first door on the left! Panic shot through Nick. Then, he composed himself. He looked at the detective and asked, "What's going on here?"

"Who are you?" the burly man asked.

Nick looked around the man's balding head at the door, "I'm here to see Sally Stein. We're going out to dinner..."

"Oh, uh-you better come in, sir." He motioned toward the open door, "I'm Detective Sergeant Grinke, Chicago P.D. And, your name...?" he said as he turned toward the room.

With an effort, Nick retained his self-control, "Barber, Nick Barber. What's going on here?" He said again, impatience building in his voice.

"Now, jus' calm down and come with me," Grinke said. Nick followed him into the room.

Chicago FBI Bureau Chief Dan Barnes was there, standing at the foot of the first twin bed. FBI Agent Tadd Nippy and Chicago Police Detective Sergeant Tanya Williams were at the back of the room examining the open window. A man wearing a blue toweling robe, tied at the waist, sat on the foot of the closest bed. Barnes looked at Nick, "Barber, isn't it?" They had met before.

"Yes. I'm here to see Sally..."

"Sally Stein has been kidnapped," Barnes said gravely.

"What?" Nick said incredulously. "Impossible, nobody kidnaps an FBI Chief Inspector. There must be some mistake."

"I'm afraid it's true," Barnes said, his voice a bit shaky. "She was forcibly taken from this room a little over an hour ago. In broad daylight."

"It can't be," Nick said, shaking his head.

"There were witnesses. This man," he motioned down toward the man on the bed, "says he got some of it on video tape from the room below. We're waiting for the manager to bring up a VCR and the correct wires, so we can have a look at it. I'm sorry, I..." He stepped aside and exposed a dozen roses in a vase on the dresser. "You send the roses?"

Nick nodded slowly, looking at the roses and their reflection in the mirror, "But how?"

Barnes sighed. He was under a lot of pressure. First, Votilinni's escape, and now an important Washington colleague snatched from under his nose. He rubbed his forehead, "They must have gotten into the room, somehow.

Tied her hands and gagged her. A man pulls up in an rusty old blue van. There's a ledge outside the motel room window. A second man jumps down from the ledge and a third man hands her down. The two men get in the back of the van with her and they drive off." Barnes motioned to the man in the robe, sitting on the bed. "This man heard the commotion, picked up his camcorder and stuck the lens between the drapes downstairs." He sighed again, "We've got an APB out on the van. Hopefully, the evidence we need to apprehend these people immediately will be on the tape."

Just then the manager came in with the VCR under his arm. He hooked up the machine to the television. The man in the robe plugged his camcorder into the VCR. They switched everything on and rewound the tape. Within a minute, a blue van, covered with rust spots appeared on the screen. It was some twenty feet from the motel window. A large black man jumped down from the ledge above, his back to the camera. They got a brief glimpse of his profile, his nose was nearly flat against his face. He straightened up and caught the struggling Sally in his arms a moment later, his knees buckling slightly. Barnes stood back at the night table, between the beds. He was on the phone. "Old Ford Econoline van," he dictated the Illinois plate number to someone at the other end. The black man carried Sally to the rear of the van. A large blond white man now jumped down from the ledge, blocking the view of the others for a moment. He swung around quickly, looking everywhere but at the camera lens. As he ran to the van, the driver stuck his head out of the window for a moment and looked back. His face could just be seen at the edge of the screen. He was dark with black, wavy hair and a pointed nose. In seconds, they were putting Sally in the back. Her feet could be seen flailing, then they disappeared behind the open van door as she was pulled in.

The blond man got in, pulled the doors shut behind him and the van rolled away out of sight. "Play it again," Barnes ordered between giving descriptions of the kidnappers over the phone.

"The driver," Nick said, "he looks familiar." Nippy and Williams had stepped over near the set. All eyes were on the set, as Tanya Williams rewound the tape and played it again. Williams rewound a second time and Nick said, "Pause it at the driver." She did and Nick squinted at the screen. "Jesus!" Nick said.

Barnes cupped the phone, "You know this guy, Barber?"

"I can't be absolutely sure. He looks like somebody I've dealt with before, overseas. We heard rumblings he was in New York the last few years."

"Who the hell is he?"

"Dushad Goatzba," Nick replied, gritting his teeth, "known as the Hand of the Devil."

"And the others?"

Nick turned back to Barnes and shook his head, "Never seen either of them before." Nick was doing his best to contain his rage.

* * *

At that moment Dushad Goatzba, who had been calling himself Ferro, was now driving through River Forest, Illinois, just west of Chicago. He was traveling west on Washington Boulevard. He had left the Chicago city limits only minutes earlier. They had dropped the old van in a warehouse and picked up two different vehicles, as planned. Bones, and Ax, his blond partner had driven on in a white minivan. Sally Stein was tied securely and gagged, under a panel in the back of that vehicle. Goatzba was in an old pickup truck, its red paint faded almost white in spots. The truck had a white camper cap on the back. They had gotten behind schedule and he was moving as quickly as he could. He had a precise rendezvous. He crossed into River Forest and drove several blocks. He turned right on Thatcher. He drove through the business district and then past the green park to his left. The college buildings were just a few blocks ahead on his right. It was dusk now and growing dark fast. He hoped he would be in time. The college buildings were just in sight now. The boys were there. Nearly every weekday after school, they played street hockey in a large parking lot there. They always played on Wednesday. They were in a group talking, it looked as though they were getting ready to go home. Goatzba was just in time. He swung around the buildings and backed into a service alley between two buildings. There were no windows in the these walls of the buildings and the immediate area was usually deserted at this time of the evening. The boy he was after always came through the alley on his way home from the game, usually alone.

Goatzba stopped the pickup and put the gearshift in neutral. He got out and crawled in the back. He opened the small rear aluminum door and peered out. The windows in the door and sides of the cap were painted over. He waited. It was quiet in the alleyways, the mild wind sending papers scratching along the paved surface. No one was about. Then, Goatzba heard the sound of the inline skates on the pavement. The boys whipped quickly around the corner of the building and began to come down the alley, toward the back of the truck. They were carrying hockey sticks and helmets. Damn, there are two of them, Goatzba thought as he watched the boys slow at the sight of the truck in the alley. Goatzba studied the faces. His quarry was the boy on the left. He pulled out his silenced .22 caliber automatic pistol. As the boys approached, Goatzba swung open the small door and jumped out. He aimed quickly at the boy on the right and pulled the trigger. There was a pop and hiss, not much louder than an air rifle. The bullet entered the middle of the forehead and the boy's head snapped back. His arms flailed about, for a moment, as if he had only lost his balance. Then, his skates came out from under him and his body flopped to the ground, arms and legs flailing about and quivering. The other boy stopped quickly next to the brick building wall. He looked down in surprise at his fallen friend. Then he looked up and the dark man was almost upon him. There was sudden terror on the boy's face and he swung the hockey stick clumsily at the man. Goatzba ducked the blow and came up close to the boy. Goatzba backhanded him hard, on the right side of the neck, with the butt of the pistol. Stunned, the boy bent over and Goatzba slammed the butt of the pistol down on the base of his skull. The boy fell to the ground unconscious.

Goatzba dragged him toward the truck. The boy was much larger and heavier than he had looked at a distance. With difficulty, Goatzba dragged him into the truck. Sweating and nervous now, Goatzba poked his head out the door and looked around. Still there was no one to be seen. If he had a van, he would have driven away from a murder scene as quickly as possible. Then, after having gone some distance, he would have tied up the still unconscious captive. In this case, he had a pickup truck that required him to get out and come around back to reach the victim. He decided to take a minute and do it now. He secured the boy's wrists behind him with a pair of handcuffs and put a piece of duct tape over his mouth. He wrapped duct tape around the boy's ankles. He thought of securing him in the truck bed, but decided the delay wasn't worth it. He had a half hour's drive, at most. Goatzba got out and secured the rear door. He returned to the cab and drove off. Within fifteen minutes, he was on Washington Boulevard, just entering the Chicago city limits. As he pulled up to a stop sign, he heard some banging in the back. He looked through the rear window into the cap. The boy was kicking the side window with the inline skates. The louvered glass window crashed out onto the curb next to them. Then, the still dazed boy pivoted on his back and kicked at the back door. Goatzba swung around the corner quickly to the right. He pulled over next to a gas-station drive entrance and got out. He went back around the left side of the vehicle. He approached the back door and suddenly, it flew open, the inline skates came out at him like pumping battering rams. He tried to grab the right one and the wheels of the left one caught him in the jaw. Stunned, he backed away for a moment.

"Hey, what's goin' on there?" A uniformed Chicago police officer was yelling as he ran toward Goatzba. The dark man squinted and came to on his feet. There was a squad car parked up near the gas station building. Goatzba pulled out his automatic then aimed and fired in one quick motion. The bullet entered at the officer's nose. His head snapped back, then forward, as the momentum of his body carried it down to the pavement, his face slapping the hard surface. Goatzba was back in the truck and slamming it into first gear. A plainclothes officer, his pistol out, had taken cover behind a customer's car near the gas pumps. The boy hooked the back wheels of the skates on the step plate of the truck. He pulled himself out and slid onto the road as the pickup truck roared away.

* * *

The FBI forensics crew had arrived at the motel and were dusting everywhere for prints and searching for other bits of evidence. Nick and the others were in the adjoining room, which was not occupied by guests. They had watched the tape many times now. All pertinent information had been called in to the FBI and police as it became available. Barnes motioned Nick and Tadd Nippy back into Sally's room, out of hearing distance of the police and closed the door. He looked up at Nick. "What's your take, you think anybody involved in the bombing might have come back for revenge?"

"Not likely. All the people that were involved are dead or in custody, as far as we know. What about Votilinni?"

"It's possible," Barnes said, "although I would think he would be seeking revenge against me, not her."

Suddenly, there was a knock on the adjoining room door. Barnes opened it. Tanya Williams was there, an excited look on her face. "We just got a call from precinct headquarters. Come in, quick."

Fritz Grinke was standing between the beds with the phone handset jammed to the side of his face. His bugged-out eyes stared at them as he listened. Then he cupped the mouthpiece. "Mr. Barnes, your grandson was kidnapped just a few minutes ago. He's OK, he escaped unharmed. The perp matches the description of this Goatzba bastard. The son-of-a-bitch murdered one of our people at the escape scene just now."

Barnes' face turned nearly as white as his hair, "I-is it Eric?" He asked.

"Yeah, the boy's name is Eric. He's down at precinct headquarters. Don't worry, he's fine." Grinke looked at Williams, "It's Foley. The bastard gunned him down, in cold blood, at that Sun Station on the west side of the precinct."

"Oh, Jesus," Tanya said under her breath.

"Where is the suspect now?" Tadd asked.

"They got'em surrounded up on the north side of the precinct. Shots have been fired."

Barnes was livid. He pointed his right index finger at Grinke. "You make goddamn sure he's taken alive, so he can be questioned."

"That's the orders the men have," Grinke responded, "they'll take him to the precinct station."

Nick looked at Barnes, "I'll meet you there, I have to stop at my hotel on the way." He left the room quickly.

Grinke looked at Barnes, "Who in the hell is that guy anyway?"

"CIA man. Was working on that bombing case with Sally."

Grinke looked at the door Nick had just closed behind him, "He the guy that threw the bomb outta the plane in L.A.?"

Barnes nodded.

* * *

Christi Stordock was tall and attractive with chestnut hair and pale, green eyes. At nineteen, she was a sophomore at Northern Illinois University in De Kalb, fifty miles west of Chicago. She was majoring in accounting and had taken a summer school course in Management Information Systems that met on Tuesday and Thursday afternoons. She had stayed late in the computer laboratory and it was 6:30 P.M. now, as she walked between the buildings. She took care to avoid the rubble the campus construction. She walked toward the apartment buildings clustered on the south side of the campus. A few minutes later, she walked through the alley at the rear of her building. It was a brown brick, two-story structure.

There were brown wooden stairways and walkways outside along the driveway. There were six apartments in the building. It was warm and humid. A white minivan parked in the driveway, close to her side entrance door. She paid no attention to it as she walked past it. She tried her key in the door of her apartment and strangely, it was unlocked.

She swung the door open and went into the living room. Suddenly, the door slammed shut behind her. A muscular, male arm went quickly around her just below breast level. Her arms were pinned to her sides. She struggled and began to scream, then a huge hand clamped an ether-soaked pad over her face. She fought, but was nauseated and then overcome by the fumes of the chemical.

TWENTY-THREE

Nick Barber had not rented a car. His plan had been to do the night on the town with Sally by cab, since parking was difficult to find in the city. He had grabbed a cab and returned to his hotel. There, he strapped on his ankle sheath with the Fairbairn-Sykes knife and put on his shoulder holster with the G11 automatic pistol. The only weapon he had carried before was the hidden .22 supermagnum. He then took a cab to the precinct station. At the station he asked for Bureau Chief Barnes and was led upstairs and through a maze of crowded work cubicles. On a chair in the last cubicle was Barnes, his arm around his grandson. They looked up at Nick.

Barnes looked much relieved. "This is my grandson, Eric. Eric, this is Mr. Barber."

Nick reached out to shake the boy's hand, "Nick to you." Eric was holding an icebag on the back of his neck. He was still wearing the inline skates. There was some dried blood on the left side of his neck. "How are you feeling?" Nick asked.

"Ok," the boy said, obvious pain in his eyes.

"He refused to go in the ambulance at the scene, but I think we'd better get him to a hospital just to check it out. He kicked the man off with the skates and managed to get out of the vehicle. He's ID'd the suspect."

Eric put his head down, "H-he killed Andy." The boy began to sob.

"You acted bravely, Eric. Your actions may save innocent lives. I represent the President of the United States and I am thanking you personally, on his behalf." Nick shook the boy's hand again, "We appreciate what you've done." Nick stood straight and looked at Dan Barnes.

"They haven't captured him yet. The last word I got is he's apparently out of ammunition and quiet. Holed up in a garage. They're going to do everything they can to take him alive. Williams and Grinke are at the scene."

"Maybe I ought to go over there," Nick said.

"Forget it," Barnes said, "there's nothing you can do. Either they've got him alive now...or not."

Nick got a cup of coffee. They waited nearly three hours. Tadd Nippy came in a couple of times with reports that the situation had not changed, but the police were moving closer. Several other FBI agents arrived. Barnes' son and daughter-in-law came in. After a tearful reunion, they left with their son. Barnes sent two agents with them to guard the family.

Finally, word came that Goatzba had been taken alive, and was being brought in.

After nearly a half an hour, Tanya Williams appeared around one of the partitions, "Down the hall, second door on the right," she said.

Nick, Tadd Nippy, Barnes and two other agents followed her down the hall and went in, closing the door behind. Williams motioned them to a window across the small room. It was a one-way observation glass looking into a brick walled interrogation room. They looked in. Goatzba was seated at the left end of a small table. Grinke stood at the other end in a short-sleeved white shirt, arms akimbo, his right hand above the holstered revolver on his belt. There were beads of sweat on his head.

Williams looked up at Nick, "That your man?" she asked in a quiet voice. Nick studied Goatzba. His face was puffy with lumps and bruises. He wore bright orange jail coveralls. His hands were cuffed at the sides of a leather and chain waist belt. He glared at Grinke, the sergeant glared back.

"I think it's him," Nick said, "Christ, it's harder to tell now, than on the tape. Your people must have done a job on him."

"He's lucky," Tanya said in a somber tone, "we've got no sympathy for cop killers. The bastard seriously wounded another officer, before they got control of him."

Suddenly, Grinke slammed his fist on the table with a bang and said, "You're going to talk now! Where were you taking the boy?" Goatzba sat silent, his dark eyes continuing to glare at Grinke. "You fuckin' stay right there!" Grinke ordered. He came out of the interrogation room and slammed the door behind him. He looked at Nick, "The sonofabitch won't say a goddamn word. Nothin', not even a gesture." He mopped his brow with a handkerchief. "Didn't make a sound even when they kicked the shit out of 'im." Then he looked around at the FBI agents, a chagrined look on his face at having made the last comment. He looked back at Nick. "You know 'im or not?"

"You strip search him?" Nick asked.

"You goddamn right we did. Jesus, he looked..."

Nick interrupted, "Left nipple burned off?"

Grinke's eyes widened, "Yeah. Christ, he's burned and scarred all over. I ain't seen anything like it since Vietnam. Can't the bastard speak English?" Grinke asked as an afterthought.

"He can speak English," Nick said.

"Our people will take over now and interrogate him," Barnes said.

"That won't do any good," Nick said. "You can talk to him all night or all week and he won't say a word. And we haven't got any time. All he wants is for you to throw him in jail, so he can start figuring out a way to escape. And he's very good at escaping."

"Then I'll beat it out of 'im," Grinke offered.

"You ought to know by now that won't work either," Nick said. "I'll talk to him. Com'on." He motioned to Grinke and they went in. Barnes told Nippy to stay and called the other agents out, so he could meet with them. Grinke slammed the door behind him, leaving Nippy and Williams looking through the glass.

Nick walked to the end of the table opposite Goatzba. The brown steel folding-chair there banged on the floor as he pulled it out. The noise echoed hollowly in the small, brick walled room. The chair squeaked as he sat in it, facing the swarthy faced man. Grinke walked around the other side of the table and stood, arms akimbo again. He looked back and forth at the two seated men, as though watching a ping-pong match. Nick folded his hands in front of him and stared at Goatzba. As the room fell silent, he could hear the prisoner's raspy, labored breathing. Goatzba was taking in Nick's face also; his dark eyes darted about studying the features. Then Goatzba's eyes widened. He let out a loud cry in terror, "GOTT-A-ALLAH." He rose quickly, then fell back over his chair. The front of the chair seat came up and it folded and crashed to the floor. Goatzba was laying on top of it, grappling in his chains. He sat up and continued to move, pushing himself back into the corner with his heels, the chain between his ankles clanking loudly on the metal chair. He was moaning and the light of fear was in his eyes. In the corner, he pushed with his heels and struggled with his shoulders to rise.

"Jesus!" Grinke exclaimed.

"I have interrogated this man before," Nick said calmly by way of explanation. "Sergeant, would you please put him back in his chair at the table, so we can talk?"

"Gladly," Grinke said. He picked up the fallen chair, opened it with a squeak and set it down with a bang. He grabbed Goatzba's left arm and dragged him out from the corner. Then, he gathered a shoulder of the man's coverall in each hand and hoisted him from the floor. He slammed the man down into the chair and jockeyed the chair back to its position at the end of the table. Goatzba sat there, glaring nervously at Nick.

From below the table, Nick brought up the double-edged killing knife. Goatzba's eyes widened at the sight of it. Nick rested the end of the handle on the table and spun it between his hands. The silver, razor sharp edges caught the light from the bulb above and reflected flashing glints around the room. "Mr. Goatzba," he began, "you are going to tell us the location of the woman you kidnapped from the motel.

You are also going to tell us where you were taking the boy, and, who hired you."

Goatzba grinned in a way that was at once pained, evil and fearful, "I know your laws. I have rights. I will say nothing."

"You have no rights. You will talk," Nick said. Goatzba shook his head. "Sergeant Grinke, do you have any rats in this building?"

Grinke looked at Nick with a puzzled look, then playing along said, "Yeah, we do. All kinds." He looked at Goatzba.

"Are they hungry?"

"They are," Grinke said in a certain tone.

"Mr. Goatzba, if you don't talk now, I'm going to cut you up and feed you to the rats, piece by piece."

"You will not do this," Goatzba said, shakily, uncertain.

"Where to start?" Nick said, as though to himself, as he rose and walked around the table. He flipped the lock on the door in place. "Sergeant, would you please hold this man's head steady?"

Grinke, enjoying what he thought was a threat, walked to the man, grabbed a handful of his hair and gripped the man's scarred left ear. Goatzba moved his head in struggle, fear bright in his eyes. Grinke held him fast. His back to the observation window, Nick grabbed the top of the man's right ear tightly between his thumb and forefinger. He sliced through the auricle, close to the head, making one quick drawing motion with the razor sharp edge. Grinke stared in disbelief and his mouth dropped open as Nick held up the bleeding piece of flesh. Goatzba screamed. Nick threw it down onto the table in front of the man. He screamed again. Grinke had released the hair and backed away staring at Nick in disbelief. Blood gushed from the wound and ran cold down Goatzba's hot, sweat-lathered neck. Nick gathered the black, wavy hair, damp with sweat, in his left hand. He brought the tip of the knife to Goatzba's nose.

In the next room, Williams, incredulous, stared through the glass at the bloody piece of ear on the table. Nippy had gone to get Barnes.

"The nose next?," Nick was saying to Goatzba, "the lips? Perhaps an eye now and the other later." He brought the tip of the knife so close to the man's left eyeball, it nearly touched. Goatzba squeezed the eye shut and Nick pressed the knifepoint into the eyelid.

Goatzba groaned. He realized he could never escape as a blind man. He blurted out, "Wisconsin," in his thick accent. "I was to take the boy to Wisconsin..ahhh.."

"Where in Wisconsin?" Nick asked, still holding the knife near the man's eye.

"I-I have memorized the way...," he coughed and gasped for breath,"...in the north." Nick gripped the hair more tightly. "Highway ninety to..."

Nippy had returned with Barnes and they were pounding on the door. Nick frowned at Grinke and motioned back toward the door. Grinke went to the window and waved them away from the door. He quickly unlocked the door and exited, pulling it closed behind him, then fended off Barnes and Nippy using his forearm. "Goddamnit he's startin' ta talk. Be quiet out here!"

Frowning, Barnes backed away from the heavy-set man. Nippy, also backing away, looked at Barnes for guidance. "I will not have people in my charge mutilated," Barnes spat out angrily.

"This is my precinct," Grinke said in a low, rough voice, "he's in my charge until I release him to you. And, you better fuckin' be quiet out here, if you ever want to see your lady alive again."

Suddenly, they heard steps outside in the hall. A uniformed officer poked his head in the door behind them, "Mr. Barnes, we have an emergency call for you."

Inside, Nick repeated, "Highway 90 to...," to resume the interrupted interrogation.

"To s-seventy-eight then fifty-one to Pine lake," the man's body was quivering. "T-the river, ah, follow the road along the Montreal River to the place...t-that's all."

Nick repeated the words and memorized them, "Where is the woman?"

"With the others."

"Who are the others, the white man and black man?"

"I know them only as Bones and Ax. Hired them on the street in New York. Used them before..." His voice trailed off.

"Where are they now?"

"They went to take the girl at the University. Northern Illinois."

"Who is she?"

"I Do not know. They h-have a picture and address."

"What vehicle?"

"White van."

"License plate?"

Goatzba shook his head slightly, "Don't know."

"Are they to take anyone else?"

"No."

"Where will they take the woman and the girl?"

"S-same place in Wisconsin."

"Are they waiting for you?"

"No. They were to go on to the destination."

"Who hired you? El Alamien?"

Goatzba's breathing was very labored now. There was a bubbling sound in his chest. "No, no," he rasped.

"Votilinni from Chicago hired you then?"

The man coughed and choked. He tried to nod. "He did not tell me his name but I know that is the man, yes." Goatzba's eyes glazed over, now. His dark skin had taken on an ashen pallor. Nick released him and the man slumped in the chair, then fell forward, his head lolling on the table. The right shoulder of the coveralls was soaked with blood.

Nick picked up the ear and put it in his jacket pocket. He opened the door. Grinke was there. "Get somebody in here right away with some oxygen and bandages," Nick said.

"Why oxygen?" Grinke asked.

"Apparently, this man was hit or kicked in the chest. He has fluid in the lungs, maybe one collapsed. Get him to a hospital as soon as you can or he'll never be able to talk again. And keep him under heavy guard. You don't know what he's capable of."

"I've got a pretty goddamn good idea," Grinke said as he left the room.

Fritz Grinke got a paramedic and some uniformed officers up to the room right away. Within a few minutes, they were carrying Goatzba out on a stretcher, his head bandaged and an oxygen mask over his mouth and nose. Nick was feeling drained. He leaned against the wall. Williams and Nippy just stared at him, saying nothing. Finally, Nick said to Williams, "Could you get me a Wisconsin map, please?" She left and Nick went back to the interrogation room and sat down in his former chair. Tadd Nippy followed him. Within a few minutes, Grinke, Barnes and Williams returned. She handed Nick the map.

"Well, what did you learn, Barber?" Barnes said in a frustrated voice, his eyes on the smears of blood at the other end of the table.

Nick opened the map and studied it for a few moments. Then, he pointed to a spot in the far reaches of the northern Wisconsin forest, near the Michigan border. "Here," he said, "They were to take their captives here. Sally, your grandson, and some girl from Northern Illinois University."

"I just got a call on that," Barnes said. "Several hours ago a student named Christi Stordock was kidnapped from her apartment, near NIU in De Kalb. Her roommate was knocked unconscious. The local police report that a white minivan was seen in the driveway."

Nick looked up at him, "That ties with what he told me. The other two are driving the van. They're supposed to have Sally with them. Who's the girl?"

"Her mother is Pat Stordock. She's the U.S. Attorney in charge of prosecuting the case against Votilinni. Barnes looked at the spot on the map near Nick's finger. "There's nothing there but woods, no roads. You think he was telling the truth?"

"Probably," Nick said, "but you can never be sure." He turned over the map and studied the mileage chart. "They were supposed to go right there. Looks like a five hour drive or better. When was she taken?"

"About six, six-thirty."

Nick looked at his watch. It was after 11:30 P.M. If they drove straight through they could be close by now."

"I'll go make some calls, get some roadblocks set up around the area," Barnes said. "And all along the route."

Then, suddenly, a thought struck Nick, he slammed his fist on the table loudly. "DAMN," he roared. He was trying to recall the image in the video, as they put Sally in the van. Did she have shoes on? He thought she did. Were they black pumps? Perhaps. If they were the same ones with the bow, would the transmitter battery still be good, after all these days?

"What is it?" Barnes asked.

"Just wait," Nick said. He pulled a cellular phone out of his pocket and opened it. He switched a small button on it, so the conversation would be encrypted. "Damn, why didn't I think of this before?" He said loudly to himself, as he punched in a number. The others heard him say, "Y-Z-8-O, this is a code red, get me department four-C," into the receiver. On the other end, the CIA operator transferred his call to the satellite surveillance office at Langley. In a minute, the night duty officer came on. Nick repeated his password, the "code red" and gave his name. "I need you to track a button number two, from a navigation system I was using," Nick said.

The others in the interrogation room looked at each other. Barnes shrugged.

At Langley, the officer went into the next room and picked up the phone. He sat at a computer terminal and keyed in Nick's password and accessed a file of equipment issued to Nick. As he did so, Nick said, "I have the approximate route." He gave the directions Goatzba had described.

At Langley, a map of the United States appeared on the large video screen in front of the officer. He moved the computer mouse and zeroed in on northern Wisconsin. He keyed some information on the keyboard in front of him. A faint red blip began to appear intermittently on the screen. "I've got it," he said to Nick. "It's your number two transmitter, all right. The battery power is fading."

"Where?" Nick said.

The officer zoomed in closer on the blip and then, entered the command to bring up the overlays that showed the road and highway system. He studied the screen for a moment. Then he said, it's in a small town named Mercer...wait, it's moving. Apparently northwest on highway 51.

Nick looked down at the map in front of him. He sighed, "Please continue to monitor. Hang on," he cupped the phone. "They're less than ten miles from the turnoff. I know Sally's with them."

Barnes looked at him, "But how?"

"That's classified," Nick said. Grinke let out a snort and shook his head.

"We'll radio the police up there, maybe there's a patrol on the highway nearby." Barnes said.

"In seven or eight minutes, they'll be at the turnoff. One squad car isn't likely to be able to handle these guys. But I suppose it's worth a try."

Barnes went to the other room to make the call. The minutes ticked by. Nick spoke to the officer at Langley. He explained that the transmitter had left the highway near Pine Lake. Barnes came back in, "There's no squad car close," he said.

"We need information," Nick said. "I think I'll go talk to a special informant."

Barnes looked at Nick, frowning. Then he nodded. "Nippy, you go with Barber. Check in with me as soon as you can. My primary responsibility now, is to arrange for protection for others involved in the case. We can't have anyone else kidnapped." Barnes walked out.

"I don't know where you guys are goin'," Grinke said, "but we're still on this investigation, too."

Nick looked at Grinke then at Williams, "Then come along. And, what you're going to see is highly confidential. You're never to say anything. You follow?"

They both nodded.

TWENTY-FOUR

Within a half hour, Tadd Nippy was pulling into the parking lot of the hospital with Nick, Williams and Grinke. Nick had called Tommy from the car with his cellphone. When the four of them came down the hall in the hospital, Tommy was out in the hall in a bathrobe. Nippy greeted the agents there as Tommy led them into his room. After being briefed by Nick, Tommy opened the door and waved them into Mac's room.

Mac was lounging on the bed. Grinke's backed up in surprise at the sight of the man. "Hey, you're supposed ta' be dead, you goddamn Irish goombah."

"That's what I keep reading in the papers," the big man replied.

Nick began to explain the situation to Mac. When he mentioned Sally's kidnapping, Mac interrupted, "Damn, Jimmy practically told me he was going to kidnap her. Shit, I didn't believe him."

Nick continued and when he got to the part about the northern Wisconsin site, Mac broke in again. "I know where they're going. It's Ken Rudolph's place. Of course, that's where Jimmy went. I should have thought of it."

"Who is Rudolph?"

"Big time swindler, stocks and other scams. Hell, he's been interviewed on a couple of national newsmagazine shows. They could never get enough on him to convict him. He's a retired multi-millionaire now. Got a place in the Bahamas and this place up in Wisconsin. Over the years, he needed some strongarm help to make collections a few times. Vito and Jimmy supplied it. I don't think the authorities ever knew of his connection to the Votilinni's, though. Anyway, he built this big place up there. Big fancy house, horse barns, paved airstrip. Way back in the woods on the river, miles from the nearest paved road. Jimmy went up to party with him a few times. I was along a couple of times. Rudolph didn't exactly relish having Jimmy and his people around, but he couldn't refuse either."

"So what do you think Votilinni's plans are?"

Mac rubbed his chin, "To abuse these kidnapped people, torture them, kill them."

"No ransom?"

Mac shook his head. "Probably not. Jimmy's insane and getting worse every day now. I don't know how to describe it. Multiple-personality complex, maybe. You'd have to know him. One part of him actually believes that he can lay low at Rudolph's place for a while, and everything will be OK. Another part insists on revenge against people he believes have wronged him. Still another part realizes the world is closing in on him. Not just the authorities, either."

"What do you mean?"

"Jimmy has serious health problems. About a year ago he began to have chest pains. Angina, the doc told him, the beginning of serious heart disease. He refuses to do anything about it. His lifestyle, well, he's been a heavy smoker for years, drinks booze every day. Never gets any exercise, eats greasy food. Worst of all he's a speed freak. He's been taking amphetamines for years. Gettin' so he eats them like candy now and hallucinates. It's all catching up with him."

Nick and Tommy both remembered Votilinni's cold, bony handshake as Mac spoke.

"Jesus, the guy's a speed freak, too? How much amphetamine is he taking?" Nick asked.

"I don't know, exactly. Uh-he's got yellow fifteen milligram pills and orange fifty milligram ones. Two, three hundred milligrams a day the past few months as a wild guess, maybe more."

Nick sighed, "That's a lot. An ordinary person could be capable of anything on that dosage. But a guy like this?"

Mac continued, "He's not going to change his lifestyle, though. His solution is suicide. He's told me that. When the time comes, it's my opinion he'll take some people with him."

"So what if we surround the place?"

"I think you'll force his hand. He'll kill Sally and the girl. Then, probably kill himself if there's no escape route."

Tommy broke in, "What about the others, Tosco, Veldon and the two bodyguards?"

"Veldon, Gary and Johnny Grimm are fiercely loyal to Jimmy. Especially Veldon. He'll do anything at Jimmy's command, and I mean anything. Ellie Winks has probably done more killing over the years than any of them. But, he's somehow managed to keep a low profile. It's my bet it was his hand that slashed that woman in the parking garage during their escape."

"I always figgered that sly son-of-a-bitch was the worst," Grinke said. He looked at Williams and she nodded.

"He's smart, too," Mac said. "Tosco, he's probably sorry he got caught up in the escape. He knew the end was coming and I think he was tryin' to figure out a way to get out. If he's with them now I'm sure he'll try to get away at the first opportunity."

"So," Nick said looking at Mac, "you think we'd have to go in covertly? Get in before they know we're there and then, get the hostages out that way?"

"If you want the women alive," Mac responded, nodding.

"How long you think we've got before he kills them anyway?"

Mac shrugged, "I'm guessing you've got a couple of days, maybe longer. Jimmy likes to play with his victims. Like a cat playing with a ripped up, half dead mouse. That is, if Jimmy thinks he's safe."

Grinke spoke up, "How can you be so goddamn sure he won't kill'em right away?"

"Because I've known Jimmy Votilinni all my life. I know exactly how he thinks. If he just wanted them killed, he would have simply had them shot right here in Illinois. It would have been much simpler and less risky. He'll keep'em alive for at least a couple of days. I'd stake my own life on it. In fact, they both make good hostages, in case he has to deal with the authorities at some point. Their lives probably won't even be threatened for some time. Of course, they may be kicked around some, probably raped, if I know Jimmy. But, you close in on him...if he thinks he's cornered, he'll kill them and then himself. I guarantee it."

Nick looked at Tadd Nippy and motioned to the phone next to Mac's bedside table, "Get Barnes on right away." He looked at Mac again, "What's the terrain around this place?"

"Surrounded by at least several miles of thick woods. Nothing but a one lane gravel road and a couple of footpaths to get in. The river runs through his property, a hundred feet or so from the house. Rudolph wanted it to be secluded and it is. He's got a few employees there to take care of the house and grounds."

"Ever see anyone else around?"

Mac thought for a few moments, "Hunters, fishermen come into the area near the house, even though it's posted 'no trespassing'. I've heard Rudolph talk about it. He really doesn't care as long as they don't get too close. He'd get damned nervous if anyone who looked like the police came around. And, with Jimmy and his people there, I'm sure they're keeping watch for intruders."

"If Votilinni is there. You said Rudolph has an airstrip? Maybe they're just going to fly out of the country when the hostages get there."

"Doesn't make much sense, to risk driving them all the way up there, when they could pick them up at a closer airstrip. Jimmy likes Rudolph's place. I'm sure he has a sense of security there, false as it may be now." Mac replied.

Nick nodded. Nippy was motioning him to the phone. Nick took the phone and explained to Barnes what they had learned from Mac. "I've got an idea," Nick was saying into the phone.

"Jesus Christ," Barnes said, "U.S. Attorney Stordock is wild. She's on her way here now. She's going to want immediate action to get her daughter freed. What's your idea?"

"I'm formulating a plan to go in there covertly and get them out."

"Goddamnit, Barber, you haven't got any jurisdiction in this. The FBI will take over."

"Technically, Votilinni's still wanted in connection with the air terrorism and we're officially involved in that investigation. That's good enough for me. If you don't do as I say, her daughter and Sally will never get out alive. According to McGinnis, we've got some time to get them out. By the way, to make things worse, our boy Diamond Jimmy's a heavy amphetamine user of late."

Barnes sighed knowingly, "We've picked up rumors to that effect."

"Now listen. Put out a press release. Goatzba was killed in a shootout with the police. Squelch anything about the murdered boy or your grandson's kidnapping. We have to make Votilinni believe that Goatzba was killed before he kidnapped anyone and before he could talk. If he finds out what happened, he may flee with the hostages, or worse. And I don't want any police activity up in that area. You follow?"

"I hear you."

"I'll be working through our people and your people in Washington. We'll keep you advised, 'Bye." He hung up the phone.

He walked around the bed. Tommy Garcia said, "You have a plan?"

Nick sat in the chair and looked up at Mac again, "I'm thinking. Anybody besides hunters and fisherman around there? What about delivery people, campers?"

"I suppose, I don't know. Say, I do remember some Harley bikers camping out in the woods, not far from the house one of the times I was there. Grubby bunch. They had a wild party out there all day and all night. Drinking and fucking, doing drugs. Jimmy and Rudolph watched 'em through a telescope and got a big yuk out of it."

"Bikers?" Nick said, looking at Tommy. "You think we could get in close, disguised as bikers and check the place out, Mac?"

"Possibly. That was just about one year ago that we saw them. Jimmy and Rudolph might think the same bunch is back again. They didn't see 'em up close."

"All right, we'll start with that plan. Tommy?"

"Ok with me."

He looked at Tadd Nippy, "You'll go with us, Nippy?"

"Of course," he said. Then he added, "I'll have to clear it with Barnes."

"Sure," Nick said. He checked his watch. It was twelve-thirty A.M. "We'll leave within the hour. Mac, I'd like you to ride along, so we can get all the details about the place on the way. You up to it?"

"Sure, I'm doing ok. I'll go all the way in with you. Where you going to get motorcycles and...?"

"I'll make a call and take care of it."

Grinke had been listening intently to all this. He and Williams were standing at the wall, near the door to Tommy's room. He looked at Williams, then at Nick, "Whatta we, chopped liver? Stein was kidnapped in our precinct. We got the legal right to cross a state line in hot pursuit. Ain't that right, Tanya?" The woman nodded.

Nick turned and looked up at Grinke, "This is a national security paramilitary mission now," he said. "We can't endanger your lives. This isn't going to be like poppin' winos for jaywalking in the Chicago streets."

Grinke's expression turned to anger. He stepped from the wall threateningly, "I've had just about enough of your shit, you G-man or spook or whatever the hell you are. I've hauled Votilinni's toughest people in and kicked their asses around plenty a' times. They know they don't fuck with me...I know these goddamn wiseguys. I know how the bastards act an' think. That's somethin' you goddamn people from Washington don't know jack shit about." He was pointing his right index finger in Nick's face. He caught his breath and continued, "Besides, I did two tours in 'Nam with the Marine Corps. I was in some 'a the bloodiest, goddamn fighting that ever happened in this world. Ain't took a hard shit since, neither."

"I was in Vietnam, too," Nick said calmly.

"As what?" Grinke demanded, still angry and frustrated. "A titless Wac, sittin' at a goddamn typewriter in the rear echelon, shinin' the ass of your pants on the seat of a chair?" He folded his arms and stood there with a smug expression on his face.

"I was a Marine Corps officer. I worked for the CIA then, too."

"Ho, ho yeah. I remember you goddamn spooks comin' into our camps, safe behind the lines, in yer pressed and tailored uniforms. Hookin' up electrodes to the nuts a' the Cong prisoners ta' make 'um talk after we risked our asses draggin' 'um in from the goddamn rice paddys. Yeah, yeah, real tough guys."

"Once, on a mission behind enemy lines, I helped rescue some of our officers from a makeshift prison camp," Nick said. "It got hot, but we were successful."

"Haw. Now, why would they send a goddamn spook on a mission like that?" he squinted and looked around at the others. Tommy's grin was broader than usual. He was enjoying the exchange. Grinke returned his gaze to Nick, "You think I don't know why? What if you got in there and you couldn't get'um out? Or you could get'um in the sights of your weapon? You were gonna kill your own people, right? Hell, I knew a sergeant that was on a mission with one of you people. They were watchin' from up in the trees, while some Viet Cong were draggin' one of our guys down a road with his arms tied out to a stick. The spook blew our own guy's head off with a' fuckin' M-14. After they got out that CIA bastard told the sergeant the same thing would happen ta' him if he didn't keep his goddamn mouth shut." Grinke frowned with knowing self-satisfaction.

"It didn't happen that way. We got them out."

"Maybe that time. But, ya had orders ta' kill'um if ya didn't, right?"

"It's true that orders like that were sometimes issued. But, you have to understand, sometimes people have information that puts the lives of many in grave danger."

Grinke snorted through his nose, "Sounds like a typical load of government bullshit to me. You ain't nuthin' but a paid hit man, just like those goddamn people you're talkin' about goin' after now."

Nick held up his hand and grinned, "All right, all right. Cool your jets, Sergeant. If you're willing to go along with us, I'd appreciate it. You know the targets and your combat experience would be useful...but you go at your own risk and you take your orders from me. Understood?" Grinke nodded. Nick looked at Williams, "And you?"

She nodded, "He's my partner. Where he goes, I go."

"Fine," Nick said. He stared at her for a moment. Years ago, a woman would never have even been considered for an operation like this. Not unless there was a specific reason, such as using sex to entice or distract the target.

Things had been different in recent years. It was all equal opportunity now. He looked back at Grinke, "You married?"

Grinke folded his arms again and sighed, "No. Not in ten years."

"Kids under eighteen?"

"No."

Nick looked at Williams, "You?"

"Never married, no kids," she said. "I've got a boyfriend but, it's not that heavy."

"All right. But it's your decision and your personal risk. It could be extremely dangerous."

Nick went into Tommy's room and called Joe Ronzoni. He got the Deputy Director for Operations out of bed. He briefed Joe on the situation. Joe said he would talk to the bureau and get the wheels in motion for backup. Then Nick made another call and woke up Thom McCormick at his Virginia farm. He read a list of equipment and supplies to Thom, giving him the time to make notes. They discussed the delivery. Nick knocked on Mac's door and asked him to come in. The big man, in the process of putting on his shirt, came through the door. A Wisconsin map was open on the bed. "We need an airport, somewhere up near the place, but not too close," Nick said, "three-thousand-foot runway minimum. Any suggestions?"

Mac leaned over and looked at the map. He winced slightly from the pain in his chest. "There's nothing real close anyway. Wausau or Central Wisconsin, maybe." Nick gave Thom the locations and asked him to call back to verify. He snapped the phone shut. They went back into Mac's room and closed the door.

Nick looked at Mac, "Now, we've got to get you out of here somehow."

Tommy pointed to a door on the other side of the room. "We can walk right out of here through that door. It leads to a stairway and down to the lobby. I checked it out," he said in a low voice.

"Good," Nick said, "we can't wait around for official OKs. Nippy, you can call your people here and let them know what's happening when we're on the road. Let's go."

The six of them left quietly and within a few minutes were in Tadd Nippy's navy blue Ford LTD rolling out of the parking lot. Williams and Grinke were in the front with Nippy at the wheel. Nick and Tommy were in the back on either side of Mac. They picked up Interstate Ninety and by the time they passed Rockford, Illinois, it was 2:00 A.M.

Nick had a pad of paper and was making a sketch of Rudolph's place as Mac described it. The others listened intently. The house, Mac explained, was an expansive two-level affair, built on the west bank of the Montreal River. He guessed the size of the place to be four or five thousand square feet. It was shaped like a huge arrowhead pointed north. It was set on a hill so the west wing had both levels exposed. That entire end of the wing was glassed-in on the west and south sides. There was a huge recreation room at the lower level. This was next to an enclosed gym, with a quarter-size basketball court, near the center of the house. At the end of the second level was the master bedroom. Next, a formal dining room overlooked the pool and grounds on the south side. There were other bedrooms and a large den on the north side of the west wing.

The hill sloped up from the river to the house at the east wing so that only the upper level was exposed. The end of the east wing was about one hundred feet from the river. There was an underground tunnel from the river bank to the basement. On a tour, Ken Rudolph had taken them through the square concrete tunnel. He explained that he had it built so he could have shelter going to the river in inclement weather. The underground lower level in the east wing was vast, with a huge well equipped workshop and a maze of storage rooms. The second level included a long, wide living room. Half of the room's glassed-in wall overlooked the pool. The other half looked out onto the terraced yard and golf course below. The kitchen was on the north side, near the center. There was a bar and guest room on the north side of the wing separated from the living room by a huge fireplace. The drive approached the house from the north and circled in front of the arrowhead. A five car garage jutted out in a northwest direction from the west end of the arrowhead. There were large, double oak doors under the point of the arrowhead. They opened into a large second level foyer. Halls led both ways around an open spiral staircase, with a massive corkscrew bannister, done in dark oak. The crown jewel of the place, Mac explained, was the huge, glassed-in swimming pool set into the underside of the arrowhead point. The pool itself was heart-shaped. It was between the first and second floor level. It was surrounded by a tower of glass panels, that went all the way to the second level roof. The pool could be seen through the staircase in the foyer. It was overlooked by the living room, dining room and most of the other rooms, on the south side, under the arrowhead.

The lawn to the southeast of the pool tower was terraced; concentric, circular stone walls led to successively lower levels. This opened to a nine hole putting and chipping course in the rolling lawn to the south and west. The course was bordered by the river on the east and thick woods on the south and west. To the north, below the hill that lead up to the front of the house, was a flat cleared area of ten acres. In the center was a paved runway, the main strip running north, away from the arrowhead point of the house, for three quarters of a mile. A connecting strip ran to the west for over one-half mile. South of that strip was a huge hangar. Between the river and the main strip, was an empty horse barn and arena, with fenced in areas around it.

"The place must have cost four, five million dollars," Mac commented. "And, that wouldn't include the airplanes."

"What kind of planes?" Nick asked as he worked on his sketch in the dim courtesy light.

"A twin engine jet. Must be eight or ten place. I don't know what kind. And a twin prop, Beech Baron six place. I've had a ride in that one. Nice plane."

"Now, tell me," Nick asked Mac, "why in the hell did you work for these people all these years?"

"Well, Vito treated me like a son when I was younger. The life, well, everything is first class, you know. Money, parties, booze, drugs, beautiful women, sleep with three or four a night if you like... Tanya cleared her throat loudly. Mac continued, "as much of anything you wanted, whenever you wanted. Several nights a week in the best night spots in Chicago, New York, anywhere. They put you in the front row for the shows, serve you the best food and wine. People kissing your ass constantly, serving your every whim. And the respect you get...or," he thought a moment, "probably, more likely fear. No real working hours. Most of the business is done in the evening. The rest of the time is your own. Anyway, you get caught up in it. You get spoiled. As long as strings are being pulled, you don't worry much about the risk. After a while, you begin to think you're invincible, like a Great White Shark in the ocean. No enemies. You can chew everybody else up and spit them out. Then, at some point reality sets in. You think about getting out and you realize they'll probably kill you if you try. You *know* they can shoot people down dead without remorse." He laughed hollowly, "Remorse hell, without a second thought, and for some of them it's fun. Then, the feds gather enough hard evidence to put everybody away, despite any connections and best legal efforts. This last year was awful as the goddamn FBI closed in."

In the front seat, Agent Tadd Nippy now cleared his throat loudly.

They passed Madison, Wisconsin, and continued north. Williams and Grinke rattled the road map in the front. They were checking the Highway 51 turnoff for Nippy. That highway would keep them on a due north course.

* * *

Ken Rudolph lay in bed staring at the ceiling. Next to him, Shelly, his bleached blonde girlfriend snored loudly. That wasn't the reason he couldn't sleep. He was thinking how hadn't been able to sleep since that goddamn Diamond Jimmy Votilinni and his wiseguy henchmen had arrived at dawn last Thursday. He now wished more than ever that he had not gone to the Votilinnis for help in collections years earlier. Votilinni and his people had come up to "party" a few times before. Rudolph had always breathed a sigh of relief when they were gone. Now, they were out and out fugitives for Chrissakes, he thought. Rudolph hadn't even found out they had escaped an FBI net until later on Thursday. They had arrived in a van, stowed it in the garage near the house and then made themselves at home. Votilinni had instructed Rudolph to be sure the gardener and his helper stayed away from the house. The two usually took their lunch in the hangar and left at the end of the day, anyway.

The woman who served as maid and cook was the first casualty. She lived in the house all the time, except for occasional visits to relatives. She had grown more and more nervous at the presence of the men the first day and Votilinni had decided to do her in. He had Veldon and Gary abduct the woman from her work in the kitchen. She had struggled as they dragged her down the spiral staircase to the basement. Rudolph surmised they had taken her to the basement workshop and there murdered her with a knife. There had been no sound. He believed they had taken her out the basement tunnel and buried her near the river somewhere. At any rate, Votilinni had informed him she was dead. Rudolph, along with his girlfriend Shelly, were prisoners in his own home. For days, they had been watched around the clock. They were told that they too would be killed, if they tried to escape or contact anyone. If the big, ugly Johnny Grimm or the blonde, muscular Gary were not watching them, then the evil Ellie Winks Veldon or the fatassed Tough Tony Tosco was. They had searched the house and garage and destroyed every telephone except one. That phone was in the master bedroom, which Votilinni and his girlfriend Molly had commandeered. They had disabled all the vehicles in the garage, except the van they had come in. And only they had the keys for that.

And, to make matters even worse, two men had arrived late the night before, actually only a few hours ago, with two female hostages.

They had all been in the living room, drinking, smoking and talking, as they did most of their waking hours when a call had come in. As usual, Votilinni had Molly go up to the bedroom and answer it, saying she was the maid. Votilinni sent Gary out with the van and he returned a half an hour later with the two men and the women. A rough looking white man and even rougher looking black man had half walked, half dragged the women into the living room. The men stood the two women in front of Jimmy. One was a small, middle-aged blonde, her glasses crooked on her nose. The other was a tall, lithe, beautiful young woman with chestnut hair and green eyes. They had obviously been drugged. Their clothes were wrinkled and disheveled and their eyes were glassy and half closed. Neither woman could stand alone. The men had held them up.

The living room in the second floor of the west wing was done in hues of white. The easy chairs, huge recliner and massive sofa were covered in imported Italian leather. The leather was pearl in color and soft as a cloud appeared. The deep, soft carpet had been as white as a new wedding dress until these men had arrived. Now, it was streaked with dirt and mottled with spilled drinks and crushed-out cigarette butts. The long north wall of the room was of eggshell lannonstone with a huge fireplace in the center. The south wall, like that of all the major rooms on the second floor, was of glass. It overlooked the terraced grounds and the pool. The centerpiece of the room was a coffee table eight feet long and five feet wide. The heavy glass top was set on an ornate gold-plated frame.

Rudolph reviewed the events in his mind. Diamond Jimmy Votilinni had sat in the massive, leather recliner gazing up at the two women. The mobster's eyes were glassy slits from drinking all day. He had taken a number of amphetamine capsules during the past several hours. Even this had failed to counteract the alcohol and make him alert. His pale, bony fingers were clutched around a drink in his right hand. The tumbler of bourbon and Coke was balanced on his right knee. His left forearm rested over the leather chair arm. A smoking cigarette dangled from his fingers above a patch of gray ashes on the white carpet. Molly, Veldon, Tosco and Grimm were all there, sprawled across the couch and chairs. Rudolph and Shelly sat on the long hearth as they were usually told to do. Gary had followed the men in from the foyer. With a weak toss, Votilinni heaved the tumbler toward the dark, open mouth of the fireplace. Rudolph ducked; the tumbler didn't even break this time. It rolled clinkingly to a stop next to him on the hearth, ice and brown liquid spilling out onto the white stone. Votilinni then tried to get up. He lurched forward and then fell back into the chair. He chuckled uneasily, then lurched forward again and managed to stand shakily. He dropped the burning cigarette onto the carpet and clamped one of his size 13 wingtipped shoes on it. He ground it into the deep pile carpet. Slowly, he made his way around the massive coffee table. Everyone sat frozen in anticipation, as he staggered toward the two women.

He stopped in front of Sally and looked down at her. Votilinni smiled slightly. His perfect white teeth were exposed. "Warbrasac," he announced groggily using Sally's birth name, "you are a fuckin' bitch and I got you where I fuckin' want you now. You gonna fuckin' wishhshh," he said slurring the words, "you was never fuckin' born." Votilinni weaved and wavered almost falling into her.

There was some recognition in Sally's eyes now, the glaze seemed to clear a bit. She began groggily, "I am an FBI..."

Votilinni swung his arm drunkenly and cut her off with a backhand across the cheek. It wasn't terribly hard, but Ax, who was holding her up, had to reposition his grip and bring her to her feet again.

Votilinni himself stumbled from the blow. Then, he straightened and turned to Christi Stordock. He pointed a wavering finger at her, "You...no...," he seemed to be thinking, "You goddamn fuckin' mother bitch". He shot a glance at Tosco for verification. The huge head nodded to indicate that this was indeed the federal attorney's daughter. "Your goddamn fuckin' bitch mother...," momentarily he forgot what he was saying, "...fucker...mother fucker." He tried to kick out at the young woman but fell back toward the glass coffee table. On the hearth, Rudolph covered his eyes. The custom-made table had cost twenty-two thousand dollars. Votilinni fell back on the glass, his arms and legs waggling like an overturned crab. To Rudolph's relief the table held. Then Votilinni grabbed the edges of the table and pushed himself up. "Fuckin' tomorrow," he said in a dazed voice looking at Gary. "Lock the goddamn fuckin' cunts up and we'll take care of 'em tomorrow."

God, Rudolph thought to himself as he lay in the bed. What if the woman really was with the FBI? They would search everywhere until they found her. Surely, they would come and surround the place. Votilinni had probably inadvertently left some clue as to where they were and if the FBI was involved they would find it. Rudolph had thought of escaping, but how? They were watched all the time. And now, there were two more of them, the white man and black man that had brought the women. They all possessed weapons. Each had an automatic pistol and some carried knives. They also had Uzi assault rifles and, at least two M-16's converted illegally to full automatic that they sometimes left laying around. Possibly this was just bait to see if he could be trusted. Rudolph imagined that if he touched one of the weapons, they would quickly cut his throat or blast him full of holes.

Even as these thoughts raced through Rudolph's mind he heard lumbering, heavy footsteps in the hall. That fatass Tosco, Rudolph thought, on his way to make another greasy breakfast of sliced potatoes and eggs fried in butter. The others didn't drink like Votilinni and Tosco. Gary and Ellie Winks Veldon, in fact, seemed to be teetotalers. But, they all ate the same meals several times a day. Always a greasy mess of food cooked up by the fat man. I may not have to wait long, he thought in sleep starved self amusement, until their arteries clog and they keel over. Then, I could just step over their bodies and leave. His mind returned to the serious question of why they had kept him alive. He believed they would force him to fly them out in his jet. Probably soon, now that these two women had been brought here. It seemed that Votilinni was going to kill them, or perhaps, take them along as hostages.

Rudolph and Shelly had been relegated to a bedroom in the center of the west wing on the south side. The drapes were drawn on the row of windows facing southeast. First, a hazy light had appeared on the drapes as dawn broke. Now, as Rudolph lay there pondering his plight, slivers of light played on the drapes as the sun rose high enough to peek through the narrow tops of the pines in the woods. The bedroom door opened and Johnny Grimm poked his pock-marked face in to check on them again. He slammed it, but not before the heavy, but pleasant smell of the food frying in fat wafted into the bedroom.

TWENTY-FIVE

The Central Wisconsin Airport is located on highway 51 halfway between the small cities of Stevens Point, several miles to the south, and Wausau, several miles north. It was 6:00 A.M. John Boede had worked there for several years as a night tower attendant. He had received a call that a military transport plane would be landing to make contact with an FBI agent. He was told not to tell anyone of the landing. It was a strange call. He had never received one like it before. Just as he was wondering if it was genuine, he noticed a dark blue Ford LTD sedan pull into the parking lot. A tall, thin young man got out of the driver's seat and walked into the office. The man showed his FBI identification, his name was agent

Tadd Nippy. They discussed the arrival of the plane and Nippy told him that this was secret business they were on and he was not to breath a word of it to anyone. He then asked if there was a place he and his people could rest. John pointed to a lounge off the main lobby. Nippy checked it out. There were four couches and some chairs. He went out to the car and returned with two men and a woman. They went in to rest on the couches. John could see that two other men stayed in the car.

An hour and a half later a plane radioed in an intention to make a landing approach. John cleared the plane and minutes later he heard a thunderous roar in the sky. The C-17 Globemaster III military transport plane was making its approach, dark gases rushing out of the four powerful jet engines. John studied the camouflage-painted plane as it settled onto the runway with a squawk of the tires. He had never seen this particular plane before. It looked like a baby brother to the giant C5A military transport. It must be a new model, he surmised. Actually, the plane had been put into service only a year earlier. It rolled along three-thousand feet of runway and stopped. John was about to run down and tell Agent Nippy, but he didn't have to. The dark blue sedan was already pulling away from the buildings.

By the time Nippy pulled up to the plane, the clamshell-style cargo door at the rear of the fuselage was open. Inside the plane, crew members were climbing down the ladder from the upper level cockpit. The six people got out of the car. A man in gray camouflage fatigues stepped up to the car. He wore a cap with the Marine Corps insignia. There was a flat black eagle on each collar tab. "General Barber?" the man asked loudly.

Nick stepped out around the car, limping. His left thigh was still swollen. The cramped, overnight trip and then sleeping in the car for a couple of hours had only made it worse. He stepped up to the Colonel and said, "Barber here." The man saluted and Nick returned the salute.

He handed Nick a clipboard, "The manifest," he said. Nick took it and began to study it.

Two marines were rolling a new Harley-Davidson Sportster motorcycle down the ramp on the lower half of the clamshell cargo door. They parked it on the runway and in a minute, were rolling another out.

"Everybody in the plane," Nick said loudly. He walked over to the aluminum steps that flopped out from one side of the cargo bay and climbed in. Tadd Nippy, Tanya Williams, Mac McGinnis, Fritz Grinke and Tommy Garcia followed. They all stood around in the front of the cargo bay. It was hot and stuffy. Nick was sorting through some packages and checking inside them. He handed a package to each of them. "These are kevlar lined leathers. Put them on. If anyone shoots at you they'll stop an ordinary bullet, save your life but it won't feel very damn good. Put the stuff on now. And we've got bullet-proof helmets, of a sort, and kevlar running shoes."

"Put it on right here?," Tanya Williams said holding the package in front of her.

Nick looked down at her. "If you're so damn modest then step behind the divider curtain behind you."

Tanya looked behind at the curtain then said, "Humph." And began to unzip her slacks right there.

All of them, including Tanya, stripped to their underwear and pulled on leather pants and jackets. There were hairpieces and mustaches. Nick put his hand inside a black hairpiece and full beard and held it up. The long, dark scraggly locks hung down around his forearm like the tentacles of a jellyfish. "These are very special hairpieces.

There is a hard skullcap of composite surrounded by a series of plates, also of composite. The plates cover the sides of the head, ears, sideburns and back of the neck. They all hinge on a kevlar skin to which the hair is attached. They provide an optimum combination of protection, flexibility and light weight." He continued in practiced fashion as though teaching a formal class in covert operations. Nick put the hairpiece on and Grinke and Tommy snickered. "Actually, the design is taken from the plated helmets the Huns wore when they invaded eastern Europe in the fourth and fifth centuries. They'll protect against a blow to the head, low caliber firearms and offer some protection in the event of a motorcycle accident. In addition, they are fitted with communications units. There's a transmitter at the right ear and a small microphone pickup in the mustache." He looked at Williams, "Except in your case, it will work if you just fasten it around your throat on a choker."

"Oh, I dunno," Grinke said, "she might look good in a mustache." All except Nick chuckled, albeit nervously, at this comment. "Say Barber, where the hell did you get all this stuff?"

"From our CIA bag of tricks. You remember the Boy Scout motto, we always try to 'be prepared'." He resumed his lecture. "Of course, these units don't offer much in the way of facial protection. We do have an assortment of sunglasses. The frames and lenses made of a new, tough composite. Select a pair and you'll have some measure of eye protection." Grinke picked up a pair and examined them with a smirk on his face. Nick bent down and opened a box of black running shoes. "These are kevlar, too," he said. "Disguise yourselves to look as scuzzy as possible," Nick said. "Try a few different things. As far as weapons just carry your own handguns. You're used to using them. There's no time for any special weapons training. We will be carrying assault rifles and explosive ordnance. I'll explain more details when we're on the road."

As the others continued dressing, Nick and Tommy climbed down to examine the motorcycles. Three pin-striped Harley Davidson Sportsters were parked on the runway. Next to them were two of Thom McCormick's gas turbine-powered motorcycles. Nick bade Tommy to follow as he wheeled one of the two machines some distance from the plane. "You and I will be riding these. The others will have the Harleys." Nick took a small manual from the tank bag and handed it to Tommy. "Read this when you get a chance. I'll give you a quick briefing." He explained the communications and navigation system to Tommy. Then he flipped open the large left rear plastic saddlebag. Tommy's eyes widened as he bent and looked in. Along the outer edge were five missiles with pointed red nose cones. They were nearly two inches in diameter and eighteen inches long. Tommy shook his head as Nick reached into the inside of the saddlebag and brought out a Heckler and Koch G11 automatic pistol and a pair of dark aviator style sunglasses. He held them out to Tommy.

"Great weapon," Tommy said, "I've been trying one out."

"This particular model has some very special features. Let me explain," Nick said.

Inside the plane Grinke had pulled on a brown wig. The stringy hair stuck out everywhere. "How's it look?" he asked the others.

"Look's like you stuck your finger in an electrical outlet," Tanya Williams said, laughing out loud.

Grinke busied himself putting on a heavy brown mustache and Van Dyke beard. Nippy had on a blonde wig and mustache and Mac was trying to get a black set adjusted.

Williams helped them all secure the hairpieces with pins and cosmetic adhesive.

The crewmen rolled a fourth Harley Davidson motorcycle from the plane. The four "bikers" climbed down from the plane. Nick and Tommy were walking toward them. Grinke was the last to come down. The aluminum access ladder sprung out to position as he stepped off. He turned and faced them. He wore a leather vest and pants. He held a leather jacket in his left hand. Tattooed on his upper left arm was the U.S. Army insignia. On his right was a pair of lovebirds that formed a heartshape. Their beaks touched forming the point at the bottom and a wing of each rolled in to form the top lobes. Their feathers had once been colored brightly in red and blue, the colors were now fading. He wore sunglasses and the bangs of the hairpiece sprawled to the top of their frame. The rest of the hairpiece covered around the back of his head from sideburn to sideburn down to his shoulders. He grimaced, trying to get his face used to the scraggly mustache and beard.

Tommy had approached and was looking the larger man over. He chuckled and said, "You even look like a Hun, Grinke. The tattoos are a nice touch."

All Grinke could say was, "Fuck you, man." Then he removed the sunglasses and squinted in the sunlight. He looked at Nick. "Jesus, it's gettin' hot. Gonna be a bitch in these getups."

"You'll have to get used to it. We can stow the leather jackets for now. You may need'em later if you don't want to risk getting shot to pieces." He waved them toward the motorcycles. Within a couple of minutes, the engines of the powerful Harleys began to come alive popping, rapping and roaring. Tommy climbed on his turbine-powered machine and it started with a whoosh that could scarcely be heard. Nick turned to the Colonel, "Make sure nobody gets wind of this."

"I better go up to the tower and talk to the people there, sir," he replied.

Nick waved a hand toward his motorcycle. "Hop on. I'll give you a lift." He walked toward the motorcycle. He stopped on the way and looked down at Tanya, who now sat astride a rumbling Harley. Her arms were outstretched and her hands were on the grips. She cranked the throttle of the Harley-Davidson with her right hand and the engine let out a deep-throated roar. She backed off and it popped back down to a rumbling idle. "Think you can handle that thing?" Nick yelled loudly.

She looked up at him. The sunglasses she wore had huge dark lenses and her round face was framed by a straight, black, Cleopatra style hairpiece. There was a black ribbon choker around her throat. "You won't have to look back for me, Barber. I'll be right behind you all the time."

"All right," Nick said loudly, pointing to his right ear, "Everybody switch on your communication sets and listen in."

It was nearly 8:00 A.M. now. John Boede stood in the tower looking out. He had finished his shift. He wasn't planning to leave until he could learn more about what was going on with the government transport plane out at the end of the runway. As the day employees came on they questioned him. He would tell them only that the FBI was there and the runway couldn't be used for a while. He had seen them unload several motorcycles. Now, those motorcycles were being ridden along the runway toward the tower. As they came closer, he could see that they were piloted by men and perhaps one woman, wearing leathers. On the rear of the lead machine was a man in military fatigues. The parade of machines stopped momentarily while he jumped off. They then continued out the airport drive, turning left toward highway 51.

* * *

Diamond Jimmy Votilinni lay on his back on the huge, round bed in the master bedroom he had commandeered from Ken Rudolph. Molly lay as far away as she could get, curled in the arc of the bed. She slept a fitful sleep. The drapes were pulled on the two glass walls, facing south and west and across the windows on the north wall. The room was dark except for slivers of light around the drapes. The sun was rising above the forest, beyond the terraced hill to the south. Diamond Jimmy Votilinni was uncovered and wore only his undershorts. He was not asleep. Quite to the contrary, he was about as awake as a human being can be. His pulse was hammering in his ears, but his eyes were shut tight and the sheet was gathered up tightly in each of his hands.

He lay still but the windows of his mind were filled with a rush of violent, colorful activity. It was activity he didn't enjoy. Sally Stein was a giant reptile. It was her head on the body of the...he tried desperately to get a grip on his conscious thought..the dragon? The snake? That was what she was. Yes! Her gaping mouth held giant sharp poisonous teeth that dripped venom and she breathed fire. Directly at him! His body shook slightly, jostling the bed. The snake continued to threaten him. Sometimes he could see only the greasy scales..were they red or green?. Sometimes he could smell the foul, rotting odor of the monster as the scales moved in front of his eyes. It brushed him. He could *feel* the slimy scales as it slithered by. Then the damned head again! It hissed at him, it lunged at him,...became giant in size...then retreated again.

There was another snake now and their huge bodies were intertwined. She had a younger face. She was beautiful. The scales around her head were chestnut brown and her eyes were green. But the pupils were vertical black slits..like a fucking snake he thought! Now this awful face lunged at him then shrank and lunged again! And there were other reptilian beasts all around..they were serpents and dragons all with vertical black pupil slits in bright yellow eyes! Why? He thought. Oh, yes, he tried to grasp at consciousness so he could think. If he could only think. He had been awake at two or three in the morning. Controlled thought slipped away again. The monsters were still everywhere slithering and flopping in yellow-green, putrid slime of floating excrement and urine. He was in it too. It was up to his mouth. A turd floated near his mouth. He batted it away and the rushing, swirling slime brought in several more! He wanted to cry out but there seemed to be no air in his lungs. He gasped.

He had to think! With great mental effort, he forced control of his thoughts again in spite of the beasts and the sewage. He had been afraid of going to sleep. The way he had felt at the time he was sure he would die if he fell asleep. He didn't want to die! So he took several more of the amphetamine capsules. He had taken nearly three-hundred milligrams in the past twenty-four hours. In the wee hours of the night, he gulped eight more of the yellow fifteen milligram tablets. He washed them down with bourbon. Now, several hours later, he was experiencing their full effect. Somehow he knew, as his thoughts fought with the swarming, swimming giant snakes for domination, that he was paying the price. But it was better than death, he reasoned, as the head of a giant black snake came at him, it's mouth blood red, its fangs silver and dripping flaming, yellow venom. It curled

in a circle and again he could feel its rough scales brush
against his skin again.

His body quivered almost violently now and Molly
awoke as the bed shook. She looked at the pale, bony man
lying on the bed. She was afraid. She knew he had taken too
many of the pills and was having hallucinations. This had
happened many times in recent months. For all the financial
benefit of being the man's girlfriend, she had decided this was
too much. She wanted a way out. She got up and pulled on a
white toweling robe, then walked to the door. Help might be
needed again, she thought. She looked back at him. His eyes
squinted even tighter than they had been.

Votilinni's mouth was moving, garbled sounds were
coming out. The reptilian monsters were hissing at him
loudly, telling him to open his eyes. No, the goddamn things
were insisting---*insisting*---that he open them. And their
voices were loud and real! "Open your eyes," they all hissed
shrilly. If he opened his eyes, he knew they would be
everywhere in the bedroom. He would be forced to physically
run from them; hide in a corner. He could go for the closet---
no!---it was full of the slimy, stinking bastards. If he tried to
open the closet door shit would flow out and fill the room!
Reptiles would swarm out on the tide and rip him apart!

Votilinni shook on the bed as Molly went around his
side and picked up his automatic pistol and shoulder holster
from the floor. She stood and walked quietly toward the door.

The demon monsters were reaching out for his eyelids
with a hundred clawed, scaly green hands. They would surely
rip them open. Votilinni let out an animal-like howl and
released the sheets. He slapped his hands to his face, driving
his palms into his eyes. His middle fingers dug into his ear
canals, but the dreadful *loud* hissing, screeching voices
wouldn't stop!

Votilinni's elbows were in the air. He rolled from side to side. He arched his back and made groaning noises. Molly ran out and slammed the door behind her.

She ran down the long west wing hall and through a small dining area to her left. Gary, Johnny Grimm, Ax and Bones were there, each shoveling in greasy fried potatoes and eggs and slurping coffee. She went through to the kitchen. Tony Tosco was at the stove spooning the dripping, fried potatoes from a hot, spitting pan onto a plate for himself. There were six fried eggs on the plate. A greasy apron hung in front of his pants, its waist strings stuffed into his size fifty-six belt. It barely served as a loincloth. A .38 automatic rested in a shoulder holster under his left arm.

Molly put the pistol and holster on the counter. "It's Jimmy. He must have taken a bunch of pills in the middle of the night. He's about ready to start climbin' the walls again."

Tosco looked out the kitchen window. The long airstrip stretched straight as an arrow to the north. There was a narrow, bright green strip of grass on either side, in turn, bordered by a forest of tall, dark green pine and bluish green spruce. A gentle morning breeze swayed their peaks. Far off to the northeast a bend in the river could be seen. There were a few deciduous trees along the river, mostly oak. Ellie Winks was on guard duty out by the incoming road. He would be coming in soon. The gardener and helper would be arriving, before long, to start work. Tosco looked down at the weapon. His yellowish frog eyes turned to her, "He ain't got no more fuckin' guns in dere, does he?"

"I don't think so."

"Good. Long as he doan try shootin' dem goddamn snakes again. He be ok inna coupla hours," Tosco said matter-of-factly.

"Do something," she pleaded, "he might jump out one of those windows and kill himself!"

That would be tough titty, Tosco thought. He picked up his heaping plate and a cup of steaming coffee and went into the dining area. He looked at Grimm who was nearly finished eating. "Johnny, ya betta check on da man, ya know?" he rolled his bulging eyes upward. Grimm nodded, got up and went to the hall. Molly followed him. Tosco shoved Grimm's plate back and set down his own.

Molly's legs were bare from mid-thigh below the robe. Ax's eyes were on them as she walked out. He nudged Bones and said, "I wouldn't mind gettin' a little a' dat shit."

Gary shifted nervously in his chair. Tosco had just shoveled an entire egg into his mouth. As he chewed, he spoke without looking up from his plate. "You fuckin' even looka' her again an' I'll cut your dick off an' stuff it up one side a' yer nose and pull it out da udder." He shoveled a load of fried potatoes into his mouth. The others ate in silence now. Tosco was close to making his move. Two nights ago while he was on guard duty, he had replaced the distributor rotor in the old Ford pickup truck by the hangar. He had started it for a moment and checked the gas. It was nearly full. He had a safe car stashed down near Grand Falls and money put away out of state under a false identity. Jimmy had talked of "having some fun with the broads" then killing them. Tosco imagined that Votilinni would orchestrate some sort of fuck fest. Tosco felt horny, he would stick around for that. He hungered at the thought of the young woman. Then he thought, hell either one or both. They'd all probably get a chance at them. Even the two dumb fuckers from New York, who sat across the table eating in silence now would get their turns, no doubt. After that, Jimmy would likely think of some imaginative way to torture and kill them. Winks Veldon would be given that job. Tosco, who had committed several cold blooded murders himself over the years, shuddered at the thought of how much Ellie Winks Veldon would enjoy making them scream. He swallowed a mouthful of the greasy food and washed it down with coffee.

The way it looked, Jimmy would then force Rudolph to fly them out in his jet. They had discussed two possible destinations: Rudolph's estate in the Bahamas and a remote fishing camp with an airstrip in Canada that Jimmy knew. In any case, Tosco wasn't planning on going.

Suddenly, he was struck by a shocking thought. He looked at Gary. "Dat fuckin' raghead bastard Ferro ain't got here widda kid yet. I betta get da Chacaga news on. Dat dumb bastard betta not'a got hisself caught."

Below in the gym, Sally Stein opened her eyes. Slowly, she became aware of her body. Her arms ached. Her wrists were cuffed behind her and her ankles were tied. She moved her fingers and toes. They were stiff and numb and seemed almost separated from her body. Above her was what looked like a blurry basketball hoop, the white net hanging directly above her. The room was dark and cold and smelled of concrete and mildew. There was a groan and cough that echoed hollowly around the place. She looked to her left. The young woman was there bound like herself. They were apparently laying on some sort of athletic mat in a gym. She raised her head from the mat to look around. Suddenly, a horrible pain shot through her skull. Ether! She remembered now, vaguely, that they had held an ether soaked pad to her mouth and nose. The hangover from the ether was terrible. She put her head slowly back down on the mat and closed her eyes. As the pain subsided in her head somewhat she realized how cold she was and that she had wet herself.

In the kitchen, Tosco fiddled with the small television set on the counter. Rudolph had a satellite hookup. Finally, Tosco got a Chicago station he was familiar with. Rudolph came into the kitchen behind him and said, "You wanted to see me Tony?"

Tosco turned. Rudolph stood there in a large blue toweling robe. He was blinking. His eyes were red from lack of sleep. "Yeah. We gonna be takin' a little trip. I wan ya ta sen' ya fuckin' gardener an his boy home for a week. Pay 'em off so he doan get suspicious. Get'em up ta da front door so I can hear what ya' sayin' ta 'em."

* * *

Pat Stordock sat in a guest chair in Dan Barnes' Chicago office. She was completely exhausted. She had been up all night, sick with worry for her daughter Christi's safety. Her husband Jack was in the chair next to her. Barnes came in, looking completely bedraggled. "They're approaching the site," he said. "Backup people are moving into place. We can fly up there but we can't go in too close. You know the assumption that's been made based on what McGinnis said. If we spook them they might..."

"Oh God," Pat blurted out, "I can't stand this any longer." Her husband put his arm around her to comfort her. "Are you sure these people can g-get them out safely?"

"To be straight, I'm taking my orders from Washington and they tell me these two CIA people going in are the best they have at this sort of thing. They tell me those men are under orders to risk their own lives to save your daughter, if necessary. Further they assure me that these men will carry out that order without question or hesitation. Our man Nippy is first-rate and McGinnis and the two Chicago P.D. people know Votilinni and his people."

"And what if they decide to fly out with-with Christi," her voice broke, "and Chief Inspector Stein on board as hostages?"

"We're formulating a contingency plan for that. The Air Force will track them. Try to bring them down safely."

Pat shook her head, "There was a time, when you could deal with these mobsters...they had family, they had roots, they had some semblance of conscience, at least in their own world. But not his generation." She went on through tears, her anger building. "James Votilinni, he's an animal..."

"You insult animals when you say that, dear," her husband said, hoping to help her vent the anger."

"He's a damned monster," she went on, her voice gravelly with hate. She looked at Barnes, "I just don't understand how can the others stay with him, follow him."

"You know as well as I do, it's like in any organization," Barnes said bitterly. "When one man owns it all or controls it all, holds the purse strings like Votilinni does. The ass-kissers, butt-boys and fawning lackeys who never question him, who do his bidding without hesitation, rise to the top. The mob is the worst. They get in so deep they can never get out." He wanted to add that they were all insane, but he stopped short of that for fear of upsetting her more. "But I can tell you one thing for sure," He added, thinking of Nick Barber, "Kidnapping Sally Stein was the biggest goddamned mistake Diamond Jimmy Votilinni ever made."

Tears flowed freely from Pat's eyes again.

TWENTY-SIX

The six motorcycles swooped downhill around a wide curve. They had ridden for miles along the smooth highway. Traffic was sparse and so were human-made structures. They had occasionally ridden along the edge of a lake or crossed a stream. But, for the most part, there were only the evergreen trees. Mile upon mile of them just beyond the ditch on either side of the road. The small town of Mercer was little more than a half-hour ahead now and the turnoff to Rudolph's property was only a few miles beyond that. There was a rest area in a clearing at the bottom of the hill. Nick, at the lead, signaled for them to turn in. They pulled up and parked on the blacktop drive along a fence of split rail. They were some distance from a large camper, the only other occupant of the rest area. Beyond the fence on a grassy, tree-studded hill were bathrooms, a water pump and picnic tables. There was a Wisconsin map in a glass case on wooden legs. They refreshed themselves and Nick called the group around a picnic table as far as he could get from the camper. The six of them sat at the table.

"I've formulated a rough plan," Nick said. "First, we have to get close enough to check the place out. Mac here says he thinks there's a back road, a path actually, we can take to get around back. We should be able to get into that camp the bikers used last year, before they know we're there. Then, we have to get into that house as quickly as we can."

"Why let them know we're there?" Tommy asked, "Why not just sneak up on them?"

"I've been thinking about that," Nick said. "Two reasons: one, if they are doing anything to the hostages, our presence, that is the bikers' presence, might get their attention and make them stop. We want that to happen as soon as possible. Two, we can probably get a closer look, then finalize the plan." Nick looked at Tanya Williams. "Williams, you and I will move out in the woods around the west side. We'll try to get up the hill, and go in the front door. I'm counting on the garage at the top of the hill in front of the house to provide a blind spot for them. Then he turned to Tommy, "Garcia, I want you and Grinke here to go around the east side along the river. Get in that tunnel to the basement. Check every room quickly for the hostages. Here, look at this again." He slid the basement layout he had sketched over to Grinke. Then get upstairs. Nick looked at Tadd Nippy, who was brushing the long yellow locks of his hairpiece out of his face. "Nippy, I want you and Mac to stay in the camp and make it appear that there's a lot of activity going on there.

Tramp around, light a fire, make a little noise. We need to divert their attention from our entry. Then, as soon as you hear shots, rush the house from the back and get in the door from the back patio. And be careful. The trees and terraces should provide you cover."

"What about me?" Mac asked looking across the table at Nick.

"That's up to you, McGinnis. If you feel up to it, come on in with Nippy. You aren't going to do us any good sittin' out in the goddamn woods." Nick squinted and looked around the table. "Now, folks," he began, "Getting those hostages out alive is our paramount objective. Recapture them and get them to safety at any cost. Beyond that, this isn't a police raid, it isn't an assault and it isn't a battle. It's an extermination. When you see Votilinni, Tosco, Veldon, Rudolph, those kidnappers called Ax and Bones or those two bodyguards, you shoot'um down dead right then and there if they don't immediately surrender. No asking questions, no announcing who we are, no warning shots. Shoot'em down dead. You all know they'll do the same to you if they get a chance. If anyone here isn't comfortable with that, speak now." He looked around the table.

"I'm all for it," Grinke said.

Nick thought about his words and his anger at Sally's kidnapping. "Now, I don't mean for you to go totally nuts with this, Grinke. Or any of the rest of you. If they surrender hands-up and it's obvious you can easily take them prisoner, then do that."

"You sure nobody can come back on us, legally, I mean?" Tanya asked.

"I have the authority to declare a national security emergency," Nick said. "I'm doing it in this case. Later, people in Washington might beat me over the head about it, but it's officially declared. You will be immune from prosecution, as long as you act in accord with my orders. There are CAR-15 assault rifles in the saddlebags. All you have to do is fold back the wire stock and they're ready to go. They're similar to the M-16, which I assume you've all used?" Everyone nodded. "Tommy and I will be carrying Heckler and Koch G11 assault rifles. Our pistols are similar. They're quiet, nearly like a silenced weapon. Let us do the initial shooting, if possible. We have to keep these people off-guard until the last possible moment. We have special burglar kits and grenades, just in case. Ok, we'll rest a few minutes, then hit the road."

All except Tommy walked down and through the gate at the split rail fence. Tommy looked off into the woods beyond the grassy hill. "What's the matter with you Nick? You seem unusually uptight. Are you that worried about Sally? We'll get her out," he said with as much confidence as he could muster.

Nick sat at the table and sighed loudly, "I'm sick about it man. I could have prevented them from being brought to Rudolph's place. If I had only thought! Goddamnit! That transmitter. I didn't think of it until the last minute. They could have been stopped."

"It was very unlikely that the battery would have lasted that long, anyway," Tommy offered.

"But it did last. At least until they got there. It's apparently burned out now, Langley hasn't been able to pick up any signal for hours. Because of my screwup, innocent people's lives are at risk now. Sally and the Stordock girl could be dead now for Christ's Sake. Those people with us..."

"What's done is done and we go forward from here," Tommy said firmly, "Isn't that what you always taught me?"

"I've also always taught, that you always think things through, consider every angle. I've acted unprofessionally. I was blinded by rage about Sally's kidnapping."

Below the hill on the drive, the others stood among the motorcycles. Grinke looked at the faces of Tadd, Tanya and Mac. He nodded his head toward Nick and Tommy on the hill and spoke under his breath, "Those bastards are nuts, man. I don't know about this."

Tadd Nippy looked down at the shorter man, "What do you mean?"

"Barber. He's wearin' that goddamn ear he cut off on a chain around his neck. I saw it. I mean, I seen guys do stuff like that in 'Nam, but now?"

Apparently none of the others had noticed this. A worried look crossed Nippy's face.

"Well, he said this is a paramilitary mission," Mac offered with a weak chuckle, "Hell, it's probably a good luck charm."

There was a loud rumble on the highway from the north. Their heads turned in that direction. Within a minute a dozen older Harley Davidsons, modifieds and choppers, were pulling into the drive. There were also a couple of older British Triumph 650's, also chopped and customized. The riders were scruffy men, their bare arms adorned with tattoos. A few of the bikes had women passengers on the back. Amidst much revving and popping, the motorcycle engines shut down one by one. They parked along the fence and in the circular drive and began to dismount. The apparent leader, a big, bearded man covered in greasy filth parked his bike in the drive behind Grinke's and swung his leg off. He walked toward them. His black leather vest was open, revealing a chest dark with hair, tattoos and grime. He looked over their motorcycles and then into their faces. "Yo," he said gregariously. Grinke and the others nodded and returned the greeting. The big man looked down at the bikes again. He motioned to Nick and Tommy's turbine-powered bikes. Assuming they were of Japanese manufacture, he said, "Who the fuck's ridin' them goddamn rice burners? Don'cha know them are made by a bunch of foreign, slant-eyed sons-of-a-bitches?"

Grinke looked over at the man, then at the group of bikers. "I see some of ya are ridin' British Triumphs," he said in a tone of friendly banter. "Lime burners, we call'em. They're foreign made, in England."

The man grinned in an unfriendly manner, showing darkly-mottled teeth surrounded by the bristly beard. "They ain't made by a bunch of fuckin' yellow, slope headed, slant-eyed monkeys," he said malevolently, as he walked toward them. Soon, he was standing near Grinke and Williams, looking down at both of them. "I seen this lil' nigger bitch from the road. You wanna sell 'er?" He reached down with his left hand and grabbed Williams' right buttock. She winced, one hand going out to slap him away, the other going instinctively for the pistol inside her jacket. The man turned to his people and grinned broadly. There were a few ripples of laughter from them. Still looking at them he said, "Or mebbe rent 'er fer a...."

Grinke kicked the man in the groin. He kicked so hard that the toe of his shoe drove one of the man's testicles into his prostate gland. Suddenly, the big man's mouth went wide-open. He sucked breath and turned back to Grinke. A look of surprise on the man's face quickly turned to rage then pain. As he bent forward in agony, Grinke smashed his knuckles into the man's nose with quick left-hook. He swung his considerable weight into the blow. Grinke's .38 automatic was already in his hand, the black pistol pointed into the man's face. As the big biker went down on his knees, Grinke grabbed the right shoulder of his vest and jerked up on it. He pushed the barrel between the man's eyes. Blood was running from the man's nose onto his beard as he stared cross-eyed at the menacing pistol.

"Com'on pissbucket," Grinke yelled down into the man's face, "Say somethin' else. Gimmie a reason to blow yer fuckin' brains out all over here, right now!"

Some of the other bikers had begun to move forward to help their disabled comrade, but stopped suddenly at a loud crack. Williams, McGinnis and Nippy had all drawn their pistols. Nippy had fired a warning shot into the air. Now, the three pistols were trained on the group of bikers. The big man groaned and gritted his teeth. He bounced slightly as he ratcheted one knee up to his chest, in hopes of easing the pain in his lower abdomen. His arms hung limp at his sides.

"Apologize to the lady, you goddamn scumsack!," Grinke growled into his face. The man was silent for a moment, "Now!"

The man choked out the words. "I-I'm sorry ma'am," he said squeakingly. He sucked breath again loudly.

"Apology reluctantly accepted," Tanya said crisply, keeping her eye and her pistol on the crowd of bikers.

Grinke went on, "Now, shit-for-brains, I want you to apologize to all the African-Americans and Asian-Americans in the world that you insulted in our presence today." He pushed the barrel of the gun hard against the man's forehead, tilting his face up into the bright sun.

Up on the hill, Nick and Tommy had also drawn their pistols. Tommy's perpetual grin had a wary cast. "This man obviously doesn't know he's dealing with the finest of the C.P.D.," he said under his breath to Nick.

"Christ, Grinke," Nick said, also under his breath, his teeth gritted, "let it go. We don't have time to screw around with these people." Next to him Tommy put the fingers of his left hand around a grenade clipped under his jacket.

Down on the blacktop the man squinted and said insincerely, "I apologize to a-all them African-Americans and Asian-Americans." His voice sounded as though someone had pushed a woodwind reed mouthpiece down his throat. Grinke pushed him away. The man rolled down onto the blacktop and lay there a moment, his knees drawn up to his chest. Then slowly he got to his knees facing his motorcycle, his back to them.

"Get on that bike and get the hell out of here!," Grinke yelled, pointing his pistol toward the back of the man's head with both hands.

From above on the hill Nick's voice boomed loudly, "All of you get on your bikes now! Get on that highway and ride south! And keep going!"

A gaggle of motorcycle engines popped to life, roaring and sputtering in the midday heat. The leader, obviously in pain, managed to hoist himself up using his own motorcycle as a brace. He carefully got on and started the machine. With a grimace he kicked it into gear and cruised down the drive toward the highway. He was bent over awkwardly with his head well down between the handlebars. He turned south. All of the others followed.

When the rumble subsided in the distance, there was silence except for the chirping of birds. Tanya Williams put a hand on Grinke's shoulder. "Thanks," she said.

"No thanks necessary," he said in a rough yet gracious way. "We're partners. Hey, nobody can say I ain't had no goddamn cultural diversity trainin', huh?"

"We could say it," Tanya said with a smile of relief as she holstered her pistol, "but it wouldn't be true."

Nick checked his watch. It was nearly 11:00 A.M. "Let's go," he said.

* * *

At that moment, Tough Tony Tosco bustled about the kitchen preparing lunch. He was stirring spaghetti sauce, deep red in color, in a pot. The radio was blaring a Tiajuana Brass number, the horns screaming with sharp precision. Ken Rudolph and his girlfriend Shelly sat silently in the dining nook sipping coffee. Bones leaned against the wall behind them, a beer in his hand. Tosco had sent Ax out to guard the main road. Gary was out somewhere also checking the grounds. Veldon came into the kitchen. He winked nervously and sniffed the humid kitchen air. "Spaghetti again?"

Tosco turned to look at him. Great wet circles of sweat were visible under the arms of his white shirt. The left one was just above his pistol. "Wattsa matta, you no lika da spagots?" he replied in mock Italian. Then, Johnny Grimm came into the kitchen followed by Diamond Jimmy Votilinni and Molly.

Votilinni was wearing a white bathrobe. He was hunched over and trembling slightly. His face was as white as a sheet in contrast to his eyes, which were as red as stoplights around pupils so dilated, they looked like black olives. He looked at Tosco, "Shut that Jesus fuckin' racket off! I can't even fuckin' goddamn think," he said angrily.

Before he had finished the sentence Tosco had reached over and turned off the radio.

Votilinni stared at him. "Where's that fuckin' raghead Ferro with the goddamned kid? That son-of-a-bitch shoulda been here a long time ago."

"He ain't comin'," Tosco said. "Fucker's deader dan da sole a my goddamn size elebens. I got dis onna Chacaga news dis mornin'. Cops stopped 'em just inside da Chacaga limits las' night. He shot it out widdem an' kilt' a fuckin' cop. Den dey shot 'em ta pieces. Ya know how dey are about cop killin'. News said his name was Goatzba or sumptin. Annaway dey showed a mug fum New York an' it was Ferro, awright. Nuttin' about da' kid. Da dumb somebitch mussa been onda way ta do da job."

"He didn't have a fuckin' chance to talk?"

"Hell no. Not from watta news said. If he'd a said annyting dis place'id be crawlin' wid fuckin' cops an FBI right now."

Votilinni nodded and blinked. "What about those two goddamn cunts?"

"Down in the gym tied up onna coupla' mats," Johnny Grimm offered.

With some effort, Votilinni grinned and looked at the pot of spaghetti sauce, "I'm so fuckin' hungry I could eat the asshole out of a rotten skunk. I'm gonna fuckin' get ready and we're gonna have a goddamn formal dinner. Everybody at the table the best fuckin' silverware and china that cocksuckin' Rudolph has got." He looked at Tosco then at Grimm. "An them two goddamn bitches are gonna join us too."

Grimm looked at him, "Jesus Jimmy, they pissed their goddamn pants. Shit'um too I think..."

"Then strip their goddamn fuckin' clothes off an' clean 'em up an' sit 'um up here at the table stark ass naked." He forced a raspy giggle. "The cunts can eat their last meal just like they were plannin' for us." He paused for a moment, then yelled toward the dining nook, "Hey Rudolph, you cocksucker, that goddamn fuckin' plane ready to go?"

"Yeah, yeah it's ready, Jimmy" he answered, staring down into his coffee.

Below, Sally rolled on the mat trying desperately to achieve some measure of comfort. Her body ached and her arms felt numb. She was filthy with her own sweat and urine and excrement. At least the headache from the Godawful ether hangover had passed. Christi lay next to her sobbing once again. Sally's heart went out to the young woman. She had probably never suffered more than a skinned knee in her short life. Now she was in the clutches of these people. Sally had tried for a couple of hours to comfort her with words of hope, trying at the same time to comfort herself. It hadn't worked well for either of them. There were two narrow, curtained basement type windows along the top of one long wall. During the last few hours the light from them had grown steadily brighter. She mused that it must be nearing midday. Johnny Grimm and a black man had been down to check on them several times. They had given the women water once. They begged to be released but the men had paid no attention to their pleas. Now the solid metal door in the corner of the gym opened again. Light spread into the room. It was Grimm and the black man again. This time Ellie Winks Veldon was with them. Grimm and Veldon pulled out knives. They squatted next to the women. Christi saw the blade of the knife flash in the light. She let out a blood-curdling scream.

Fearfully, Sally started to scream too. Then she composed herself and said, "Please leave her alone. Whatever you're going to do, do to me."

Grimm, kneeling next to her, said, "Shut up".

He and Veldon then reached down and cut the rope bonds from their ankles. They removed the handcuffs and stood the women up on the mats. They could barely stand alone. The men walked them out the door, into a wide hall. To their right several steps led up to a glass door that was an entrance to the pool area. Veldon and Grimm walked them around the bottom of the spiral staircase and pushed them into the first door on the right. Someone flipped the light on in the room. Sally and Christi found themselves standing in a large bathroom, done in shades of pink. There was a tub with a shower in one corner. Christi continued sobbing. She grabbed the wall for support. Sally had gotten her bearings and stood facing the three men, who stood just outside the door looking in.

"The two'a you get yer clothes off an take a shower now," Grimm said. He held a small .38 automatic pistol in his hand, pointed in their direction.

"With you watching?" Sally blurted out. Her mind was racing, trying to get a fix on their situation. She didn't know where they were, but her mind was putting together clues. She had noticed the smell of pine trees wafting through the halls. This was unmistakable to Sally, having been raised in a pine forested area. They were somewhere in the north woods. There was also the heavy smell of chlorine. It looked like a glassed-in pool area through the door they had passed. A fancy hunting lodge she was thinking. Probably secluded. Northern Wisconsin or Michigan? Canada perhaps, she thought since Votilinni would at least want to get out of the country. God, had they driven them that far? Her memories of the long, bumpy ride on the floor of a vehicle were sketchy, like a dream. "Can't you at least turn around or step aside?" she asked trying to buy a little more time to think. She shot a glance at Christi. The taller woman's face was pressed to the wall buried in her hands. Her sobs reverberated hollowly around the room.

"You do as yer goddamn told now and don't mind who's watchin'," Grimm ordered. "An be quick about it." He waved the pistol threateningly. "Or Veldon here will personally strip you down to yer bare asses and we'll all wash ya down." Veldon was still brandishing the knife. He smiled one of his evil, foxlike smiles amid a series of winks.

Sally stepped behind Christi between the tub and the wall, for a small amount of privacy, and slowly undressed. She was glad for an opportunity to clean up, but these were the worst possible circumstances. She had to buy time to think. Naked and holding a towel around her, she shoved her clothes into a pile in the corner. She tied the towel around the trunk of her body and put her hand on Christi's shoulder. "Com'on honey," she said gently, "We're going to get cleaned up." Christi pressed her face harder against the wall and wailed.

Veldon stepped into the bathroom, the knife in his left hand. He jerked the towel from Sally's body and threw it on the floor, "Shut that bitch up and get her goddamn clothes off or I'll cut 'em off. Now!"

Sally forgot her own embarrassment and quickly began to undress Christi. The young woman, in mental shock now, allowed Sally to manipulate her like a doll. Sally removed the blouse, slacks and panty hose. Then she faced Christi away from the door and unhooked her bra and removed her panties quickly, wiping away some of the filth as she did so. Ellie Winks Veldon leered from one side of the door, his eyelids flashing like a semaphore signal now. Johnny Grimm licked his lips as he eyed the two naked women from the other side. Bones, poking his head over the shoulders of the other two was also enjoying the view. Sally led Christi into the tub, helping her step over the edge. Then she got in and slid the shower curtain shut quickly. In a moment, the men heard the water come on.

When they had finished toweling off, Johnny Grimm waved the two naked women out of the bathroom with his pistol. Sally guided the dazed Christi out and stood next to her. Veldon walked up to Sally and stood in front of her, his evil eyes twitching. Suddenly, he slapped her across the face with his open hand as hard as he could. She fell against the wall of the hall and went down on her knees, her left ear ringing. Veldon grabbed her upper arm roughly. He dragged her to her feet, nearly as quickly as he had knocked her down. Veldon looked at Grimm, "We don't want Jimmy ta think we been molly-coddlin' the bitches," he explained.

Without a tear in either eye, Sally stood there. The side of her face stung terribly. She resolved, in her thoughts, she would be strong and maintain her dignity. She would deal with these criminal monsters as a professional.

Grimm, Veldon and Bones marched the two naked women up the spiral staircase. Tosco, a steaming bowl of pasta in his hands, stopped abruptly and whistled, as they crossed the hall into the formal dining area. Christi, still in a daze, walked in first. She was half successfully trying to cover her breasts and pubic area with her hands and arms. Sally walked behind her, guiding her.

Shelly had nearly finished setting the table according to Tosco's orders. She looked up and clasped her mouth in surprise as the women came in. "Oh, my God," she whispered.

Grimm ordered Sally to seat Christi on the long side of the table toward the pool. She did so. He then ordered Sally to sit on the opposite side. As soon as Sally's hands left Christi's shoulders, the young woman began to whimper. Sally tried to reassure Christi with words as she walked around the end of the table. As she walked, she looked down at the heart-shaped pool below, then out across the golf course to the woods. More like an elaborate house than a lodge, she thought. She took a seat as ordered. She felt the left side of her face. It was hot from the sting and swelling up around her cheekbone.

Tosco came in and set the steaming pasta on a ceramic plate near the center of the table. He turned and left the room. Shelly nervously left behind him.

Sally looked around the table. There was a formal place setting for eleven. Four along one side, five along the other and one at each end. The table looked as though it were set for a royal visit. In front of each place was a large plate with a cloth doily. On each doily was a salad plate heaped with a colorful Caesar salad. The polished silverware sparkled in the dazzling sunlight. There were several open bottles of wine on the table, each jacketed in a film of condensed moisture. Tosco burst in again with another huge steaming bowl and set it near the middle of the table. He went out into the hall and bellowed loudly, "Soup's on."

Within a minute, Diamond Jimmy Votilinni came in. He took a place at the head of the table on Sally's left. Sally looked at him through tired, fearful eyes. He was dressed like Saturday night in a goldtone sharkskin suit and starched white shirt. But, he looked ill. His hands trembled and he had an air of nervous agitation about him. His face was pasty. He managed a smirky smile as he looked at the two naked women. Molly came in and quickly sat down at his left. She was wearing a short blue silk evening dress that left her shoulders bare. She kept her eyes averted from Sally and the whimpering, fidgeting Christi. Rudolph and Shelly came in and took the two chairs to Sally's right. Sally's stomach turned in disgust as Veldon came in and took the chair between her and Votilinni. Within a minute, Johnny Grimm came in and occupied one of the empty chairs across the table. Bones came in and took the remaining chair next to Sally. Tosco came in and took the chair at the foot of the table. Votilinni announced, "Let's everybody fuckin' eat." Votilinni, Molly, Tosco, Veldon, and Bones dug into their salads with alacrity. Sally, Rudolph and Shelly picked at theirs. Christi only stared at her plate and shivered. The wiseguys shot hungry glances at the naked young woman as they ate. There was no conversation.

When Votilinni had nearly finished his salad he set it and the doily aside. He stuck a cigarette in his mouth, lit it, then leaned back in the chair. He looked at Tosco and pointed down at his empty plate with his right index finger. Tosco looked up from his half-finished salad. In a moment, he was up and grabbing the huge bowl of pasta. "Time fa da spagots," he announced. He forked a pile of the steaming pasta onto Votilinni's plate, then Molly's.

Sally had been thinking of escaping. She wasn't tied up now. She could dash out of the room she could make a run for the woods. She ran every day for exercise and she was certain she could outrun any of these people. But then, she couldn't outrun a bullet. And, she thought of Christi. Better to stay here and make whatever effort she could to protect the young woman, for now, at least. Sally looked around the table. The others were pushing their salad plates aside. It figures, she thought. When Jimmy finishes his salad, everybody finishes. When Jimmy eats the spaghetti, everyone has to eat it.

Tosco passed Christi and spooned some pasta onto Bones' plate. The big black man looked at the plate and then at Tosco, "There's no sauce," he said.

The heavy man stared at him, "Whatta ya mean dere ain't no sauce? Ain't ya eva' had spaghetti before?"

"From a can."

Tosco guffawed at this. "Man," he said, "you gotta be da dumbist fucker I eva' seen. Da sauce is dere," he said pointing to a covered bowl.

Tosco finished dishing out the pasta. Then, he took the cover off the steaming sauce and went around the table, dishing it out. The sauce was heavy with tomato chunks, sliced peppers and meatballs nearly the size of peaches. Again, Votilinni and his people ate with relish. The others only picked at their food. When Votilinni had finished about half of his heaping plate, he leaned over and whispered to Veldon. Veldon got up and motioned to Johnny Grimm. They walked over behind Christi and grabbed her by the arms. They jerked her out of the chair. She looked at Sally, her eyes begging for help.

"Jimmy," Sally pleaded, "please let her go. She has done nothing to you. Just let her go."

Votilinni looked at her, an evil grimace on his face, "The fuckin' bitch's mother was gonna kill me."

"Whatever you're going to do to her, let her go and do it to me," she begged.

Votilinni jerked his head at the men and they walked the young woman from the room. She began to fuss and struggle. He turned back to Sally. "We'll goddamn do plenty to you. If I can fuckin' get anybody to do anything to a goddamn dried-up old cunt like you." He laughed at this and so did Tosco and Bones, their mouths full of spaghetti."

"Please, Jimmy..."

"Shut up you fuckin' bitch," he said.

TWENTY-SEVEN

Mac McGinnis was in the lead now. They had left the highway and taken a dirt road. It was only two ruts with a grass hump in the middle. They went deep into the pine woods. It was shaded and cool. The sun starved ground below the great trees was bare except for a blanket of scattered brown pine needles. Mac took a couple of left forks and soon they rumbled along single-file on a narrow path. Mac was estimating this would take them to the biker camp in the woods behind Rudolph's place. He stopped several times to peer through the trees, then went on. They were circling far to the south and east of Rudolph's property. Then they came to the riverbank and Mac turned the motorcycle around in the trees and back-tracked. He went only about one hundred feet and located a little-used westward path through the trees. They followed him, the pine branches whipping around them. Mac held up his hand and they all pulled into a clearing and parked the motorcycles. Nick and Tommy parked theirs in the open part of the clearing and put them up on the stands, so they wouldn't fall over in the dirt. They looked up into the sky as they did so. There were the remains of a campfire surrounded by stones and a lean-to, about six feet high, constructed of rough-cut pine trunks. Half-crushed aluminum beer cans were scattered about the campsite. Mac pointed north through the trees. They could all see the sun glint off the walls of glass beyond the woods. About one hundred feet away at the edge of the trees, Rudolph's lawn started. The lawn was studded with golf pins set in exquisitely manicured greens. At the top of each pin a red and white triangular flag waved in the gentle summer breeze. The lawn sloped up to the terraced steps that ascended the east side of the large glass octagon that enclosed the pool. It leveled off to the glass doors of the lower level recreation room on the west side. Nick and Tommy had small telescopes out and were peering through the branches. To their right, up on the east wing of the house was the glass south wall of the living room. On the west wing, the master bedroom had a similar glass wall. Nick and Tommy handed the scopes to the others and let them study the place.

They could see no one about and most of the drapes were drawn on the south windows of the house. Nick and Tommy got the CAR-15 assault rifles and their own G11 rifles out of the saddlebags. Nick waved everyone inside the lean-to. They handed out the rifles and ammunition. Nick and Tommy had burglar kits and grenades under their jackets. "All right," Nick said under his breath as they all crouched around in the small structure, "we're going to execute our plan immediately."

In the house, Veldon and Grimm had returned to the dining room and continued to eat. Votilinni had left. Molly was fidgeting nervously in her chair and looking at the door. There was a scowl on her face. In the living room Votilinni had taken off his clothes. Christi was spread-eagled on the huge, white leather couch. Her right wrist and ankle were tied with ropes over the backrest. Her left wrist and ankle were tied with ropes down around the front of the couch. He stood looking down at her working up an erection with his hand. She looked at him, terror in her eyes. She shook her head and whispered, "No, please." This only turned him on more. He crawled on top of her and forced himself inside. His breath on her face was hot like fire and reeked of garlic, tobacco and bourbon. She turned her head aside and let out a low groan of pain. He bit her smooth cheekbone as he thrust into her.

In the dining room, low moans could be heard from the living room for several minutes, then muffled screams, then silence.

Fritz Grinke and Tommy Garcia crawled along the edge of the river under cover of the bank. The ground along the river's edge was soft and damp and mossy. Tommy felt a tug on his foot. He turned to look back. Grinke had grabbed his shoe. Grinke came up next to him and whispered, "Jesus, you smell that?"

Tommy nodded, "It's rotting human flesh," he whispered back.

"I know what it is," Grinke said, so low that Tommy had to read his lips.

Tommy nodded ahead to a torn up, mound of dirt on the bank. He crawled up to it and looked in. Grinke came up next to him and looked also, while he held his breath. The wet soil was dug up all around. There were claw marks and the prints of animals around the hole. At the bottom of the hole, the loose soil seemed to be moving. Tommy used his knife to scrape the soil away, exposing ashen-colored dead flesh. The surface of the flesh was undulating hideously. Tommy scraped the flesh. It tore away as easily as wet tissue paper, revealing a colony of gray-white maggots in motion. There were so many that nothing could be seen below them. "Watch the bank. I'll check this out," Tommy whispered. Grinke nodded and moved away, drawing his revolver. He checked over the edge of the bank. The house was not more than two hundred feet away now.

Tommy scraped the dirt away from the pelvis and pubis with his knife. Then he uncovered the head. He cleaned his knife in the soil and crawled back near Grinke. "Female," Tommy whispered. Probably middle-aged or older, I'd say from what's left of the skin. Face is chewed off. Buried shallow and dug up by dogs, coyotes, smaller animals, whatever's around here. Been there a few days I'd say. Com'on," he said, starting to crawl along the bank again.

Nick and Tanya moved silently and quickly through the forest, far southwest of the house. They carried their assault rifles. Nick watched every step, lest he step on a twig and he cautioned Tanya to do the same. A myriad of birds were chirping and the wind rustled through the branches, both covering the sounds, but Nick wanted to be careful. The main single lane gravel entrance road came into view through the trees. And then Nick saw him. The blond kidnapper Nick remembered from the video was sitting against a tree across the drive, apparently snoozing. He and Tanya stopped under cover of a tree and Nick put his finger to his lips. She nodded, indicating she had seen him too. The man was sitting so that he was hidden from incoming traffic. They must have sent this idiot out to guard the place, Nick thought. Nick turned to Tanya. A garrote had appeared in his hand. He pointed toward the man and held the black wire to his throat. He grimaced and stuck out his tongue. Then pointed to her and clasped his thumb and forefinger around each opposite wrist, then motioned his hands around the tree. Tanya nodded in understanding, her handcuffs already out. Nick pointed south and they crept off into the woods to circle around.

They came back, rifle barrels trained on the tree, walking on the worn, hard-packed rut of the road so as not to make any noise. The man's denims and black, running shoes became visible as they approached the tree. When they were just four feet away, Nick handed his rifle to Tanya. She slung it over her shoulder quietly. He took a wide step off the road letting the ball of his foot come down on solid ground between the dry, scattered pine needles. He grabbed the tree and pulled himself up to it without a sound. He peered around. He could see the blonde curly hair on top of the man's head. He reached around the tree with both hands and taking a metal T-handle of the garrote in each, looped it down over the man's face. Half-dozing with his eyes nearly closed, Ax saw something flit in front of his eyes. Nick jerked the handles snapping the wire up and back. It tightened under each side of the jawbone trapping Ax's head against the tree. The taut wire closed his windpipe and he couldn't breathe or make a sound. His eyes bulged in terror and his hands went instinctively to his throat. His legs flopped about in the pine needles. Tanya was there in an instant. With a quick snap she clamped a handcuff on his right wrist. Using the weight of her body for leverage she dragged the muscular arm down behind the tree in front of Nick's feet. Nick quickly clamped his foot on the wrist and Tanya went to the other side and forced the other arm back. She secured it with the cuff. Nick reached around the tree and clamped his hand on the man's throat, keeping the pressure on the windpipe. He put the barrel of his G11 rifle to the man's forehead above his left eye. Tanya had gone out to check the drive and returned quickly. She put the barrel of her M-16 to the right side of the man's forehead.

Ax's bulging, horror-filled eyes looked into the hard, frowning face of the white man with long, curly black hair. Then, they rolled to the face of the black woman with the straight hair and along the rifle she held. His lungs burned with need for air and he looked as though he were about to pass out.

"If you want to breath again," Nick said in a low, harsh voice, "then you'll be quiet." Ax managed a nod and Nick released the pressure. The man's lungs expanded and he sucked air. When he was breathing somewhat normally again Nick asked, "Where are the two women?" He nudged the man's forehead with the end of the rifle barrel.

"In the gym. The basement," he replied. The man's voice was squeaky and barely audible as though he had laryngitis.

"They all right?"

Ax's head nodded enthusiastically.

"You sure? They done anything to them?"

The man shook his head, "Mista Votilinni was gonna do somptin' to 'um last night but he was too fucked up. He slapped 'em around a little." Ax sucked a breath of air again.

"And how is he today?"

"Com'in aroun' this mornin' I guess."

"Votilinni's girlfriend, his bodyguard, Tosco, Veldon, Rudolph, your black buddy all in the house?"

Ax was nodding before Nick got the words out.

"Anybody else?"

"Um, uh, Rudolph's girlfriend," he squeaked.

"What are they doing?"

The man shrugged, as best he could, with his hands cuffed around a tree, "Gettin' lunch ready last I know."

Nick was thinking they had better get moving. Catching them at a meal would be perfect. He clamped the man's windpipe shut again as he withdrew a spring-loaded syringe from inside his jacket. He cocked it with his thumb. Ax struggled, his eyes bulging again. Nick held the end of the syringe in the crook of the man's elbow and jabbed it in. He then pushed the button on top. The anesthetic was pumped into the arm. Ax continued to struggle for a few moments, then his head drooped to his chest.

Nick nodded to Tanya and they moved quickly across the drive into the woods. "What was in that?" she whispered.

"Powerful anesthetic. He'll be out for a long time. Maybe forever."

"Dead?"

"Probably not. But it happens in a small percentage of cases at this dosage," Nick said under his breath. Personally, I don't give a damn if he's dead or not. If I didn't think I might have to answer to a lot of petty-fuckin' bureaucrats about our activities here today, I guarantee you he'd be dead now."

They crept through the woods in the direction of the house.

Diamond Jimmy Votilinni walked into the dining room, his shirt rumpled and his suitcoat over his arm. His shoulder holster was askew. He made a big production of zipping and buttoning his pants and clasping his belt. Molly stared down into her plate barely hiding the look of disgust on her face. Votilinni didn't even notice. Although it was becoming quite stuffy and hot in the house he put on his suit jacket. He sat down and lit a cigarette then snapped his fingers and pointed to his glass. Molly was up in an instant pouring bourbon into it. He took a gulp and leaned back.

Sally listened intently. There was no sound from the other room. She looked sadly at Votilinni, "Is she...?"

He looked at her, his mouth full of bourbon and shook his head. He swallowed and said, "You mean did I fuck the bitch to death?" He waited a few moments, staring at Sally. She sat in suspense. "No, but god damn near," he said and guffawed at his own joke. Tosco, Veldon and Grimm laughed. Bones chuckled nervously, Votilinni was eyeing him.

Tosco looked at Votilinni. He could almost read the man's mind. Jimmy was going to send the nigger out to do the girl next, Tosco thought. Tosco spoke, "How 'bout me goin' out onna couch nex, Jimmy? I ain't had my fuckin' nards off good inna while."

Votilinni looked at him, "Yeah, you ain't had a fuckin' boner, haw, haw, I mean bonus, for a long time. Go ahead and fuck her with that goddamn summer sausage of yours."

Suddenly, Sally said, "You can't, Jimmy. Please. Let her go."

Votilinni turned to her. His laughter stopped and his face turned to a mask of rage. He drew the big, black .45 automatic out of his shoulder holster and waggled it at her. "Don't fuckin' tell me what I can't do, you bitch! Or I'll shoot those goddamn fuckin' tits of yours off, right here." He stood and struck at her across the table with the barrel of the pistol, poking her in the left breast. She covered herself with her arms and jerked away, falling off the chair. Tosco stomped quickly from the room. Votilinni motioned to Veldon and Grimm. "Get that twat out of my goddamn sight! You know what the fuck to do." They reached down and dragged the struggling Sally from the room and down the hall. He turned the pistol on Bones, "Now you, nigger, you'd like a little goddamn poontang, wouldn't you?" Votilinni kept his eyes on Bones as he sipped his bourbon.

Bones was holding his wine glass, "Yessir, Mr. Votilinni. Anything you say."

"Then in about five goddamn minutes, I want you to go down that hall and screw the shit out a' that fuckin' FBI bitch. You got that?"

"Yessir," he said and sipped his wine. Muffled female moans drifted in from the hall.

Further down the table next to Bones, Ken Rudolph had been splitting his attention between the activity at the table and something out the south windows. His head was wrenched around now and he was looking across the pool area to the southeast. "What the fuck you lookin' at, Rudolph?" Votilinni asked.

He turned abruptly back to Votilinni, "Uh, I heard something and I think I saw something going on down at that biker camp. I think they're back."

"Fuck," Votilinni muttered, "You goddamn sure it's them?"

Rudolph shrugged, "I'll get the binoculars and check it out." He left the dining room and returned a couple of minutes later, carrying a pair of binoculars. "I checked through the bedroom window. There's some cycles and a couple of the scraggly bastards out there. I haven't seen'em since you guys were here last year."

Votilinni frowned, a warning shiver went up his spine. This was too much a coincidence, he thought, that they would arrive on this day. Votilinni laughed uneasily, "This could be the luckiest goddamn day of their lives. They can get their asses in here and get in fuckin' line." But his mind was racing, making other plans. Veldon and Grimm returned to the room. Votilinni waved the pistol at Bones, "Ok, nigger, go do your goddamn stuff." Bones nodded and left the room, a look of cautious anticipation on his face. Votilinni stood and said to Molly and Shelly, "You broads fuckin' wait here 'till I call for you. He motioned to Rudolph, Veldon and Grimm, "You fuckers come with me." They left, closing the door behind them. In the dining room, the two women sat in silence.

Out at the tunnel entrance near the river, Fritz Grinke and Tommy Garcia were feeling around the brown, metal double doors at the entrance. "Could be an alarm on these. Place like this," Grinke whispered.

Tommy took a small, hand-held oxygen-hydrogen torch from his burglar kit. "No problem," he whispered.

He lit the torch and a small flame appeared at the end. He held it to the door and hit the oxygen button. Immediately, it began to cut through the thin, steel jacket of the door. Grinke kept watch as Tommy quickly cut a round hole, eighteen inches in diameter, near the bottom of the door. The sandwiched foam insulation behind began to smoke and smolder. Tommy motioned to Grinke who then ran crouched, the few feet to the river and came back with his cupped hands full of water. Tommy had removed the steel circle. Grinke splashed the water on to quench the smoldering insulation. Tommy tore out the insulation and stuffed it behind the bushes on the hill next to them. He cut out the inner door panel. They crawled through the hole and found themselves in a long, musty-smelling concrete corridor. Tommy replaced the outer panel of the hole with duct tape, so the entry wouldn't be extremely obvious from the outside. Their pupils adjusted to the dark, in contrast to the bright sunlight outside. Tommy shined the flashlight on his G11 assault rifle around.

They could see seasonal outdoor clothing hung on wall pegs. Fishing poles, tackle boxes and other sports gear stood along the walls. There was a set of double wooden doors at the far end. As planned, Tommy switched on his communications unit and tried to raise Nick.

Nick and Tanya were near the edge of the trees. They could see the long garage at the top of the hill, across the expanse of lawn. To their right at the south, the long west wing of the house jutted onto the lawn. The hill sloped down along the north face exposing the glassed-in floors at the master bedroom end. Along the top of the hill near where the house joined the garage, were two, narrow basement windows at ground level. Nick heard Tommy's voice in his ear, "We're through and in," he said.

"Proceed to gym. Believe hostages are held there. We're going to try the windows on this side. Meet us there, we'll secure them first," Nick said hurriedly.

Back at the camp, Tadd Nippy listened to their words on his receiver.

Votilinni led Rudolph, Veldon and Grimm through the foyer and out the west front entrance doors into the long garage. They walked around two cars and a van. Votilinni stopped and turned around. He looked at Grimm, "Johnny, you go out along the fuckin' river and check out those bikers. Just have a goddamn look ta' see if there's anything unusual. Then, get the fuck back here. On the way, you tell that fuckin' Tosco ta cut that young cunt loose and bring her here. We're takin' her along." He looked around slyly, "I got a strong feelin' we're gonna need a goddamn fuckin' hostage." Grimm stood and looked at him for a minute. Votilinni said, "Now." He left, through the service door in the front corner of the garage, closing it behind him. Grimm walked in front of the garage doors toward the formal front entrance. He went through the foyer and to the left around the spiral staircase and into the living room. He saw Tosco's massive bare white buttocks in motion from across the room. Grimm walked around the back of the long, leather couch and looked down. Tosco's big face turned up to him. Sweat was pouring from his pudgy, whiskered chin down onto Christi's face below. Her eyes and mouth were clamped shut and her head turned to the backrest of the couch. She shuddered each time a huge, hot rivulet of sweat dripped to the smooth skin of her neck or cheek. Tosco propped himself up on his thick arms and his bulging eyes looked up into Grimm's pock-marked face. He frowned in disgust at having been disturbed.

"Jimmy's inna garage. You supposta' cut her loose and take her in dere," said the laconic Johnny Grimm, looking down at him.

"Yeah, get da fuck outta here now," Tosco grunted.

Grimm's face disappeared from Tosco's sight. He leaned over to pick up a weapon. Two M-16 assault rifles lay on the long, white hearth. He picked one up. He went back out the front door and around the east wing, down toward the riverbank.

In the garage, Votilinni turned to Veldon and then nodded to a red two and one-half gallon gas can on the floor. It was an old metal can shaped like a cylinder, painted in red with yellow lettering and trim. On it was a tin-plated flexible spout that was mottled with rust. Veldon picked up the can. Rudolph's eyes widened at the sight of it. He could tell by the way Veldon jerked it up that it was full. Rudolph knew it was from the lawn shed. Something had been planned.

"Winks," Votilinni said, "you know what da fuck ta do."

"Jimmy," Rudolph pleaded nervously, "you ain't gonna burn my place down, are you? I spent a lotta time designing..."

Votilinni whipped out the big .45 and shoved it into Rudolph's face, "Shaddup, you cocksuckin' sonofabitch. Whenna ya gonna learn to keep that fuckin' mouth shut?" As Votilinni said this a couple of dull, crunching sounds could be heard somewhere outside. The sounds were barely audible over Votilinni's voice. Rudolph backed against the wall, quivering with fear.

A couple of minutes earlier Tanya and Nick had run up the hill, toward the house from the edge of the woods. Tanya had slung her assault rifle over her shoulder and was unrolling duct tape on the way. Nick carried his assault rifle ready in one hand and his knife in the other. They laid down quickly in front of the basement window furthest from the house. The back wall of the garage was only twenty feet away. Tanya applied several pieces of the wide tape to the surface of the window glass. When Nick kicked in the window, the men in the garage heard the sound.

In the garage, Votilinni looked at Veldon and said, "It's probably Gary fuckin' around out there. The bastard is supposta' be checkin' the hangar an' shit around here." There was a worried look in Votilinni's eyes, "Get the fuck goin', you know what to do." Veldon, carrying the can, went around the vehicles toward the house.

Nick checked in around the gym with the flashlight on his rifle. He saw no one. It was a large area with a lot of equipment stacked near the walls. Tanya slid through the window on her belly. She hung from the windowsill and dropped quietly to the floor. Nick followed. Just as Nick was crawling in, Gary came up the hill at the far end of the garage. He saw Nick's head and quickly ducked below the hill. His pistol out, he crawled around the hill toward the front of the garage and crept up. He saw no one in the drive or entrance area. He quickly crept along the front of the garage. Votilinni saw him through the garage door windows and opened the service door.

"Get the fuck in here," Votilinni said. He noticed that the short blonde man's revolver was drawn.

Gary came in quickly. "Somebody's crawlin' in the basement window back there," Gary said frantically.

"Fuckin' sonofabitch, just what I figured," Votilinni growled.

Across the gym, in the corner, the door swung open and the bright flashlight on Tommy's rifle swept the room. "Barber here," Nick whispered hoarsely across the room. Grinke closed the door behind them. The four of them searched the gym quickly. Nick sniffed the air above the gray mats in the center of the floor. "They were here recently," he said, "at least Sally was." Nick could detect the scent of a person he had been physically close to in the past. Especially a woman he had been intimate with. "We'd better get upstairs fast," he whispered, "Nippy, you there?"

"Yes," Nick heard in his receiver.

"They aren't in the gym. We're going upstairs. You better come in. We may need reinforcements. Tanya and I will take the dining room and bedrooms to the right, that's probably where they are. Grinke, you check out the living room area to the left. Then come back to the other wing and back us up. Tommy, you check the pool area. It's central and you can coordinate all of our efforts from there." They went into the downstairs hall. Tommy crept up the steps to the pool, while the others took to the runners of the spiral staircase.

In the master bedroom, Ellie Winks Veldon slammed the door and walked around the large, round bed. Bones, having just consummated his rape of Sally, lay on top of her on the huge round bed. When he heard the man come in, he pushed himself off the bed quickly and picked up his pants from the floor. Veldon was in the far corner on the south side of the bedroom. He held up the gasoline can.

Sally was naked and helpless, spread-eagled to the bed with ropes painfully tight at her wrists and ankles. Her glasses had been knocked off and lay twisted in the pillows next to her head. She could see only the blurry image of Bones standing at the foot of the bed and another blurry figure to her right holding the red can.

Bones, standing there naked with his pants in his hand, eyed the can, "Whatta you gonna do, man?"

Veldon showed his teeth in an evil grin. His winking eyes narrowed. He sloshed the can out in front of him over the bed. Some of the liquid splashed across Sally's breasts. She winced at the heavy, sickening smell of the gasoline and looked toward Veldon, "No, please," she begged in an almost inaudible whisper.

Johnny Grimm had crouched and walked rapidly along the riverbank. He smelled the decaying flesh as he went by the ripped-up burial site of Rudolph's maid. He went on, but before he went as far as the edge of the yard, he stopped to peer through some bushes. Just as he did so, two figures came out of the trees into the yard. They were carrying rifles and wearing black leathers. The closer one was taller with long blonde hair and beard. He was at least one-hundred feet away. The man twenty feet beyond was shorter and heavier. He had long, dark brown hair and a scraggly beard. His gait was somehow familiar to Grimm. The two men ran up to trees in the yard, between the golf greens and peered around at the house.

From the pool area, Tommy also saw Nippy and Mac coming across the lawn. He saw them come out from behind the trees and then, he heard the rattle of a machine gun and saw them both go down in the lawn.

Johnny Grimm had panicked and opened fire. Tadd Nippy was hit on the right shoulder and the right side of the head. One of the .223 caliber bullets, spiraling by the time it reached him, smacked into the right side of his forehead. It rode along the surface of his skull, splitting the skin. He rolled to the ground. Grimm continued to fire at Mac. The man hit the ground and covered his head with his arms. Bullets slammed into the leathers for several seconds, then Grimm released the trigger. Crouching, he ran along the riverbank toward the house.

Tommy ran around the pool and opened a patio door. In an instant, he was out moving along the terrace. He could see Johnny Grimm's head bobbing along behind the bank.

Upstairs, Nick went immediately to the dining-room door. He swung it all the way open; it banged the wall. Instinctively, he moved away from the open doorway and aimed the bright light on his rifle into the faces of the two women at the table. He recognized Molly from photos he had seen. He assumed the other was Rudolph's girlfriend. "Hands," he said in a gruff whisper, "Let's see your hands!" The terrified women squinted in the light as he flashed it from one to the other. Slowly, they raised their hands. Satisfied they had no weapons, Nick ordered them to get under the table and stay out of sight. They complied without hesitation. He swung around and checked the hall, then stepped out, closing the dining room door behind him. As he did so, he heard the clattering of gunfire in the backyard.

TWENTY-EIGHT

Tanya had checked the kitchen and dining-room and then continued down the hall and checked the den. She was just coming out of the den when she saw Nick. She shrugged and shook her head. They could each hear voices coming through the door to the master bedroom at the end of the hall. There were two bedrooms to check on the way. Quickly, Tanya checked the one on the right and Nick checked the one on the left that Rudolph had been using. A moment later, they poked their heads and rifles out into the hall and then stepped out. Suddenly, one of the double-doors to the bedroom opened and Bones rushed out into the hall, his pants in his hand. He stopped abruptly, when he saw the two of them in leathers and holding assault rifles. The big naked man let out a yell and turned abruptly on his heel. He dove back though the master bedroom door, sliding in on the carpet. Nick got a glimpse of Sally on the bed and motioned Tanya to hold her fire.

In the bedroom, Bones kicked the door shut, frantically jumped to his feet and locked it. In the corner, Veldon held the gas can poised over the bed, ready to pour it on Sally. He looked at Bones and said, "What the fuck's goin' on?"

Bones didn't answer. He looked at Veldon momentarily, the whites of his eyes bulging in terror. Then he spun around quickly, frenzied, as though searching for something.

In the living-room Tough Tony Tosco had shimmied his sweat-lathered body into his clothes. He tucked in his white shirt and zipped his pants. He struggled into his shoulder holster and withdrew a small, switchblade from his pocket. He snapped out the blade and cut the ropes that held Christi's ankles to the couch. He heard a clatter out on the back lawn that could have been gunfire. He looked at the south glassed-in wall but it was closed up and the heavy drapes were drawn. He looked behind himself frantically, then he bent down and cut the ropes at her wrists. He grabbed her arms and stood her up. She was woozy, barely able to stand on her own. Tosco's eyes went to the hearth and the M-16 there.

Fritz Grinke had gone around the spiral staircase quietly searched the bar area. Then he went beyond and searched the guest quarters behind the fireplace wall. He came out and worked his way slowly back along the curving foyer wall toward the living room entrance. He heard noises. The barrel of his CAR-15 just below his chin, he peered around the doorjamb. There, he saw Tosco holding the tall, nude young woman. He could see no one else in the huge room. He recognized the heavyset gangster immediately even though the man's head was turned away. Grinke was filled with rage at Tosco. He decided he couldn't shoot for fear of endangering the Stordock girl. He decided not to allow Tosco to use her as a shield or keep her as a hostage, either. I have to separate him from the girl, Grinke thought. He decided to take the man by surprise.

* * *

In the master bedroom, the wild-eyed Bones fixed on a large, easy chair in the far corner, on the opposite side of the bed from Veldon. His pants fell from his hand as he ran to the chair. He grabbed it by the arms and picked it up. With a loud grunt, he coughed and threw the heavy chair, putting all the considerable resources of his heavily-muscled arms and legs into the action. The chair made a quick arc over bed. Veldon saw it coming and ducked back into the glass corner, cradling the gasoline can. It breezed by him rapidly and crashed through the glass panel to his right. It crunched on the stone patio below. Most of the panel shattered and splintered away as the chair went through. "You fuckin' crazy bas...," Veldon began to yell. Bones was already springing up onto the bed. His heel barely missed Sally's stomach as he bounded over her. Bones dived from the bed through the jagged opening in the panel toward the stone patio, one level below outside. Nick kicked the bedroom door open. It swung in and slapped the wall with a bang. Nick and Tanya burst into the room, just in time to see Bones' feet go through the hole. They swept the room with their rifles and, other than Sally, saw only Veldon. The red-headed man was rising with the red and yellow can held in front of him. His narrow eyes were filled with rage.

"You, out," Nick screamed at him waving toward the opening with the barrel of his rifle. Veldon shifted over in front of the hole, a look of terror on his face. He leaned out half falling, half jumping. Nick squeezed the trigger. A burst of gunfire went through the can. The momentum of the bullets forced Veldon and the can out the hole. Nick continued to fire, ripping the can open. Sparks from the rusty, steel can ignited the gasoline as Veldon tumbled through the air. He slammed the pavement with a thud next to Bones. Though Bones had held out his hands to absorb the shock, his head had taken some of the blow. He was dazed and just now rising. He looked back at Veldon groaning only a few feet away and was filled with horror as the man's gasoline-soaked clothes burst into flames. To his even greater horror, he realized that his own back was splashed with the flaming gasoline. He put his arms in front of him and saw that the back of them were in flames. He screamed in a high-pitched wail as the heat seared the skin on his arms and back.

"Watch the door," Nick said to Tanya. He had his knife out and quickly sliced through the ropes at Sally's extremities. The howling screams outside continued for several seconds as he worked. Then, as he lifted Sally from the bed, one pitch of screams died out, then an even louder, wilder shriek of pain began. He tried to lay Sally on the floor but she insisted on standing on her own. She asked for her glasses. Suddenly, Mac came in. Tanya had seen him coming down the hall and waved him in. He had not been seriously hurt. He did suffer stinging pain on his right side, from the bullets slamming into his kevlar-lined leathers. His chest was sore from the activity. Nick turned to him, "How's Nippy?"

"We were both hit goin' across the yard. Nippy got a crease in the forehead. Lotta blood, but I think he'll be ok. I dragged 'em into the showers by the pool and tied it up with a towel. Garcia went after the guy." The wailing scream from outside grew to a higher pitch now. "Jesus, what's that?" Mac asked.

"I'll take care of that. You take care of her. See if she can tell you where the girl is," Nick said. Mac took Sally from Nick's arms.

* * *

Grinke heard the horrible, high-pitched screaming and wailing from the other end of the house. He ducked behind the foyer wall just as Tosco turned back to look, his eyes bulging. "What da fuck's goin' on?" he said under his breath. Then he calmed down, as he realized Votilinni and Veldon were probably torturing Sally. After all, that had been the plan. The awful screaming, muffled by the distance, went on. Were they using a red-hot knife or even fire perhaps? he wondered. Diamond Jimmy, during amphetamine highs, had talked repeatedly of both methods, while the wacko Veldon cackled. Still, Tosco wondered about the gunshots out back. He turned back to Christi, "Hear dat ya bitch?" He shook her roughly, nearly snapping her neck. "I gotta good ideea dat's gonna be you inna few minutes." She kicked at him and struggled weakly. He laughed and held her away. Then, he looked at the weapon on the hearth again and decided to retrieve it.

* * *

In the master bedroom, Nick went to the window and looked out. Bones, thinking quickly, had dived into the yard and rolled in the grass. It had taken a number of turns in the smooth, damp grassy yard, but the awful flames eating into his back and arms had gone out. Now, he was running. He was more than halfway across the yard, headed for the forest. He looked back, stumbled into a red and white golf pin and fell onto the green. Nick looked directly down at the source of the screaming. Veldon had apparently come to, his clothes in flames, and stood up. As Nick looked down the man danced a macabre dance on the stone patio, his flaming arms out stretched. He stood in a ring of red-yellow flame and he himself was on fire from head to toe. He was blind and his face was burned black and melting away from his skull. The only thing Nick could see clearly was at the top center of the flames. It was Veldon's wide open mouth. The tongue was flicking like a snake's between the horseshoe-shaped rows of teeth. In the center was the black hole of the man's throat, the source of the terrible high-pitched siren wail of pain. Veldon fell to the stone. Nick looked back at Bones. The man had gotten up and was running again.

Nick raised his G11 rifle, switching on the laser sight as he did so. The straight red beam was dim in the bright sunlight, but Nick could see it. He drew a bead in the middle of the man's back and squeezed the trigger. The G11 issued a low rattling, whine. With bloody exit wounds popping on his chest, Bones went down on the green lawn. He was carried by the momentum of the small, high velocity bullets. He rolled to a stop again atop a green, his body twitching, his sightless eyes staring into the sun. The triangular flag at the top of the pin flapped above his head.

Below, Veldon's screams had turned to a low-pitched, shuddering gurgle. The flames had died down now. His blackened form twisted and jerked about on the stone surface. Nick aimed down and took his head off with a full automatic burst.

In the corner of the bedroom, Mac had found the robe that Votilinni had flung on the floor. He put it on Sally, located her glasses and replaced them. Then, he cradled her in his arms.

Nick heard Tommy's voice on the receiver, "Nick, I'm outside in pursuit of the wiseguy who shot Nippy and McGinnis. He's headed north along the river. You need any help in there?"

"In master bedroom. Sally's safe, but we haven't seen the Stordock woman. The rest of us are clear and accounted for now, except Grinke. He's at the other end of the house, but I haven't heard anything. Votilinni, Tosco, Rudolph and the bodyguard Gary haven't been seen. They've probably got the woman with them as a hostage. I don't think they're in the house. They might have all taken to the woods. I'll take Williams and Grinke and we'll check out the garage and the hangar."

Tommy walked through the trees near the west end of the house. He looked at the hangar and then up at the long garage, on the knoll in front of the house. "I'm along the river east of the runway now. I can see the garage and hangar. Doors closed, no activity."

"Good, stay there and cover us."

Grinke peered around the corner. Tosco's back was to him. Grinke then crouched and cradled his weapon. He charged Tosco's back like a halfback and jumped at the last second, just clearing the corner of the huge glass coffee table. Tosco had just released Christi with his right hand, his eyes still on the M-16. The full force of Grinke's weight drove his right shoulder into the larger man's back with all the force he could muster. Tosco hit the couch and rolled over it like a giant medicine ball, taking it over with him. Grinke braced himself and grabbed the weaving Christi. Tosco had the wind knocked out of him for a moment, but he never took his eyes off the weapon. His pudgy fingers reached to the hearth and the M-16 clattered as he dragged it off. Grinke shifted the staggering Christi behind him to protect her. She grabbed the back of his leather jacket to steady herself. Grinke got his CAR-15 rifle into position. He couldn't see Tosco, the man was hidden behind the massive white couch. He aimed the barrel over toward the fireplace in the direction where the man had gone over. For a heavy man, Tosco was able to move quickly when he had to. With the M-16 in front of him, he crawled around the end of the turned-over couch on his knees and elbows. He did not hesitate. He poked the barrel around, in what he thought was the proximate direction of Grinke and squeezed the trigger.

Tosco had flipped the M-16 to full automatic. In the curtained room, burned gasses surged like lightning out of the barrel. The weapon made a loud, popping sound backed by a low, grinding growl. The bullets slammed into Grinke's protected stomach. Still firing, Tosco pushed himself along the carpet with his feet, just enough so he could see his target between the couch legs. As he did so, the barrel of the gun walked up in reaction to the force of bullets and expanding gas leaving the barrel. He kept it aimed at the large, dark figure. Grinke staggered back, the wind knocked out of him, as the bullets slammed into his chest. He was unable to aim and return fire. Tosco held the trigger down and the barrel whipped up at an accelerating pace. The spinning bullets slammed into Grinke's face, as the reaction force rolled Tosco over on the floor. He released the trigger. Grinke's face was ripped open in a bloody furrow. He staggered back, then his legs collapsed and he fell back into a wide, white leather overstuffed chair. Christi, grasping the back of his jacket, was trapped under him in the chair. His arms flopped around and his body quivered in the throes of death as she struggled beneath him. Her right leg was hooked over the arm of the chair. Half of her abdomen up to her rib cage was exposed. Her face was behind his right shoulder.

The others in the master bedroom heard the burst of gunfire. Nick and Tanya went through the door and into the hall. They checked each room on the way, as they ran down the hall. They passed a still dazed Tadd Nippy, on his way up the spiral staircase, grasping the rail. The bloody towel was around his head down to his eyebrows. He had his .357 magnum revolver out. "Nippy," Nick said, as they went by, "cover the front door."

Tosco was on his feet now. He aimed the rifle toward Grinke, then positioned it low and to the left, toward Christi's exposed leg. He heard the quick footfalls in the hall behind him. He squeezed the trigger and the M-16 spit lightning again. The first bullets ripped into Christi's exposed lower abdomen. Spouts of blood and flesh appeared on her smooth flesh. Then, the bullets sprayed Grinke's chest and head as the weapon walked up to the right. Tosco spun to his right, the trigger still compressed. Whoever was coming was going to get it, he thought. He didn't care who it was. As he turned, a few bullets tore at the curtains and smashed through the far glass wall that overlooked the back yard. Then, they slammed through the exposed glass of the closer wall overlooking the pool area. Glass shattered at chest level, the top half of the large panel near Tosco falling away in large jagged panes. They hit the concrete at the edge of the pool with great crashes that echoed around the immense glass enclosure. Before he swung the rifle to the living room entrance, the clip ran out.

There was sudden silence as Nick and Tanya ran through the foyer. They each went to one side of the living room entrance. Holding his rifle in front of his face, Nick crouched low and took a quick look around the corner of the doorjamb. Tosco was just about to throw the useless rifle to the floor when he saw Nick. He flung the rifle toward Nick and it clattered against the jam. He would be defenseless for at least a few seconds, Nick thought as he came around the jam and sprung behind Tosco. As Nick quickly swept the room with the flashlight on his rifle, Tosco began to move quickly forward. Tanya came in, also checking the room. Nick saw Grinke's body and the naked leg protruding from below. He swung the barrel of the rifle in Tosco's direction. The heavy man was springing from the floor. This was obviously a desperate effort to escape. He was diving over the jagged wall of glass in front of him, down into the pool area. Tosco's left hand grabbed the sharp edge of the glass to help catapult him over. His head went down as his feet left the ground. His body rolled forward beginning a tumble. Nick squeezed the trigger. Tosco's great midsection was about to clear the jagged edge when the bullets snapped into his shoulder blades, forcing them down. He fell on the glass and teetered for a moment, the sharp edge having caught the top of his protruding belly. He appeared suspended in midair, his arms and legs flailing about as he see-sawed. Then, his body descended very slowly as the glass cut through him. The sharp edge went through his shirt and skin as he slid to the left, along the downward angle of the glass edge.

His head upside down over the pool area, Tosco watched as his own blood gushed forth and spilled down both sides of the glass. The sharp edge cut through the middle of his transverse colon and sliced off the back of his stomach. Accelerated by his own wriggling, the pane of glass then disemboweled him completely, carving out his entire midsection. He screamed and watched in terror and disbelief at the kaleidoscope on the other side of the glass. It was his own partially digested egg, potatoes and pasta mixed with dark, red spaghetti sauce, bright red blood and dark, greenish bile. This was followed by his purplish intestines sliding down behind.

From behind, Nick and Tanya kept their rifles trained on the man's buttocks as he slowly descended. His wriggling feet touched the living room carpet. Then his knees. Blood poured down the glass into a rapidly-growing red stain on the carpet at the base of the wall. Tosco stopped screaming, only because he had no more breath. The butt of the pistol in the shoulder holster hung down banging against his chin. He was still lucid, but only barely. His left hand had no feeling, it hung limply below his head. With his right he reached up and unsnapped the strap on the gun. It fell out into his quivering hand. He managed to get his finger into the trigger guard. He pushed the barrel of the .38 automatic into his right eye and squeezed the trigger. The left side of Tosco's head splattered into the air as the explosion of the shot echoed around the pool enclosure. His right hand fell limply down then stopped abruptly, swinging. The pistol swung with it for a moment, his thick finger stuck in the trigger guard. Then the weapon slid off and fell to the concrete below. It clattered in the broken glass on the concrete walk around the pool.

Nick stepped around and checked, then he looked at Tanya, "He's done for himself."

Outside, Tommy Garcia was watching the hangar and the house, from his position in the woods, near the east wing of the house. Suddenly, he heard shots behind him and bark exploded on the tree, next to his head. He hit the dirt and took cover behind a tree that was between himself and the river. He peered around the tree. Grimm was also peering around a tree, from above the bank, on the other side of the river.

Nick and Tanya went quickly over to Grinke's body. As Nick lifted the heavy corpse, he heard Tadd Nippy on his receiver, "Barber, this is Nippy. Hangar door opening!"

"Jesus," Nick said. Gripping the heavy body under the armpits, he rolled it to the side, so the chair arm would take the most of the weight. Grinke's split-open face was right under Nick's own face. His nostrils filled with the odor of burned flesh and mucus, intermingled with the iron smell of fresh blood. "Hurry up," he said.

Tanya pulled Christi out from under Grinke's body and laid her on the white carpet. Nick dropped the dead man back into the chair. The head lolled to the side chin up, as though he were taking a Sunday afternoon nap. Mac and Sally were at the entrance on the other end of the room. Suddenly, there was a hollow, whining scream and a loud pop and banging, somewhere out in front of the house.

Earlier in the garage, Votilinni had kept Rudolph under gunpoint, while he had Gary check around the outside. Gary had come back in the service door and reported he had seen no one. He told them that whoever had crawled in the gym windows must still be inside. Votilinni ordered a dash to the hangar. The three of them went out the service door of the garage and dashed down the hill to the hangar. They entered the service door in the front of the hangar and slammed it behind them. The sleek, cream colored Sabreliner jet stood in front of them. Beyond that, on the other side of the hangar stood a blue and white twin prop Beech Baron. Votilinni leaned against the wall gasping for breath. His face was pale. He held his pistol on Rudolph somewhat unsteadily now. When he caught his breath he said, "We're going ta have get the fuck outta here now. Whatta you fuckin' gotta do to get this goddamn plane going?" He waved the pistol toward the jet behind Rudolph.

Rudolph's mind was racing. Would it be better to stall until the FBI, or whoever was in the house, surrounded the hangar; or just fly out? If they closed in on the hangar he might be able to hide while Jimmy and his dumb bodyguard shot it out with them. Surely the two of them would be killed. On the other hand, Jimmy might just keep the gun to his head and use him as a hostage. He himself would probably be shot to pieces by either the gangsters or the feds in that case. The feds, whose wrath he had escaped only on the thinnest of legal technicalities thanks to high priced lawyers, had no love for him. They wouldn't give a second thought to shooting right through him to kill Votilinni, he figured.

"Answer me, cocksucker," Votilinni raged.

"Uh, I-I gotta get in the plane and check a few things, that's all, Jimmy," Rudolph stammered looking into the barrel of the pistol. "Then, we open the hangar door, pull out the wheel chocks and tow it outside." He motioned to the small, battery powered towmotor next to the wall.

"We're not towin' the sonofabitch out. You're going to fuckin' start it up in here and drive it out."

"What? Jimmy, I can't start those jet engines in here. It'll blow the whole, goddamn building apart. Maybe us too." Rudolph was sweating now.

Votilinni took a look out the window toward the house. He turned back to Rudolph and held the pistol out. The barrel nearly touched the big man's forehead, "Get around that goddamn plane and open the fuckin' door up now!"

Rudolph turned and walked around the plane, Votilinni following with the pistol pointed at the back of his head. Rudolph cleared his throat nervously and said, "Where we goin' Jimmy? If that's the feds here, they'll be waitin' for us in the Bahamas. An' that place in Canada. I don't have charts. I can't land this just anywh..."

"Shut the fuck up an' lemme goddamn think!" Votilinni had been worriedly thinking about their destination. "Maybe it ain't the fuckin' feds. Maybe it's just a bunch of goddamn, sonsabitchin' bikers goin' in your house to rob your fat ass an' fuck yer ol' lady. Then, the boys'll shoot the bastards and be out here to get us in a few fuckin' minutes." This was what Votilinni hoped, but he was very afraid it wouldn't turn out that way.

"You think anybody'd come to rob a house in the middle of the day, Jimmy?"

"Shut the fuck up an open up that Goddamn door, right now."

On the other side of the plane at the south wall, Gary had heard something outside. He opened the side window a crack and listened. "Hey Jimmy," he said in a loud whisper that echoed in the hangar, "somebody's screamin' out there. I hear shots."

With a shaking hand, Rudolph reached up and twisted the handle and got the door open. He pulled on the small, aluminum steps there and they flopped out, suspended by a thin steel cable on either side. The steps bowed under the strain of Rudolph's weight as he stepped into the plane. The plane itself tilted noticeably. He looked back at Votilinni nervously, "What about our women Jimmy?"

"Fuck the bitches. Just get in, you fatass bastard," Votilinni said.

Rudolph squeezed himself through the narrow door and then again, through the narrow opening into the cockpit. Votilinni stepped into the plane behind him. He turned to the door and said, "Gary, get those fuckin' chocks away from the goddamn wheels. Then, get ready ta' open the goddamn fuckin' door." In a moment, Gary was jerking on the chock ropes and flinging them away from the wheels. Then, he went to the side of the overhead door in front of the plane and stood with his finger poised in front of the green button that read, "UP".

Votilinni poked his head into the cockpit, the .45 pointed at Rudolph, "Get this goddamn piece of shit goin'. Now!"

Rudolph had switched on the electrical system and was checking the gauges. "I got just a few things to check, Jimmy. But we gotta tow it out!" he said, his voice becoming frantic.

"We're not towin' the fucker out. Get it started!"

"Oh Jesus," Rudolph moaned, "at least get the door open."

Votilinni turned back to the open airplane door and yelled out, "Gary, get that goddamn fuckin' door open now!"

Gary punched the button. The electric motor on the gear reducer above his head started with a whir. There was a clank as the heavy, metal door began to roll up on the axle up on the header above. The door clanked and squeaked and sunlight began to pour in under the rising door.

Votilinni nudged the side of Rudolph's head with the .45, "Start it now, motherfucker!"

The ignition was on. Rudolph pushed both starter buttons at once. The two jet engines began to spin with a low whisper that gradually pitched to a whine. The bottom of the hangar door was about four feet off the ground now. The jet fuel behind the engine compressors ignited and the whine of the engines built quickly to a scream. The thrust of the jets blasted against the back wall of the hangar with a whoosh. The aluminum panels bowed out momentarily, then peeled away from the building with an earsplitting pop followed by banging and crinkling noises.

Inside the house, Nick left Tanya with Christi. Sally and Mac ran toward the front door. The door was open. Tadd Nippy was there prone on the foyer floor. He was holding his .357 in both hands. As Nick approached, Nippy fired six times in rapid succession. Gary, still at the controls of the door was hit twice. Once in the right shoulder and then, in the lower back as he spun around from the first shot. Nick looked over the knoll. The hangar was more than one thousand feet away. Nippy looked up at Nick, "I think I got the bodyguard."

In the hangar the plane lurched forward with a jerk. Gary had fallen to the concrete floor, just beyond the wheels. He struggled to get up. Votilinni was looking out the door of the plane yelling to him, "Com'on, goddamnit." Gary struggled to get up from the floor. Votilinni looked down at the pool of blood below the man. Then, he looked into the blond man's face. Gary's eyes were pleading as he struggled on one arm, the other held out toward Votilinni. The roar and screaming whine of the jet engines was deafening. Votilinni aimed the .45 at Gary's face and squeezed the trigger. The man's head snapped back spattering tissue and bone. He fell sprawling on the floor. Votilinni was distressed at not having a bodyguard with him, but he decided a man so grievously wounded would not be of any use. And this one would never talk to the authorities. As the plane moved out into the bright sunlit day, Votilinni put the .45 on the carpeted floor and struggled to get the door shut.

Nick and Tadd watched from the front door, as the plane moved out onto the hangar drive and toward the main runway. "Hold your fire!" Nick ordered into the communications microphone in his mustache. "I've got to find out who's on that plane!" He ran back through the foyer and across the hall to the dining room. Molly and Shelly were huddled under the table. Nick crouched and looked under at

Shelly. "They're taking off in the jet. Is there a way to communicate with them?" Shelly looked at the big, threatening, leather clad man with long, black hair and bristling beard and mustache. She was wide-eyed and shivering with fear. "Answer me!" Nick said in a demanding voice.

"I-In the den," she stammered, "across the hall, the r-radio."

"Well, com'on," he said. She moved forward and he grabbed her arm and pulled her out. They went into the den and on a desk under the window was some radio equipment. "Can you raise him on there?"

She nodded quaking with fright, "I-I think so."

"Then sit down and do it! Ask them who's on that plane."

She sat down and switched on the set. She picked up the small microphone there and said, "Kenny, come in. Kenny, come in."

Rudolph had steered the nose wheel onto the main runway. The big, bright orange windsock to his left was pointing straight north. This meant he would have to go to the north end of the runway and turn to take off, into the south wind. Votilinni had closed the door and was just climbing through into the copilot's seat. The .45 was in his hand again. Rudolph heard Shelly's voice in his earphones, "I'm here," he said frantically.

Shelly looked at Nick. He waved toward the radio with the barrel of the assault rifle. "Who's on the plane?" she asked nervously.

"Just me and Jimmy." They both heard him reply.

"Who the fuck are you talkin' to?" Votilinni yelled. He jerked the headset off Rudolph's head and put it on.

Nick grabbed the microphone, "This is Nick Barber. I'm a federal agent. Stop that plane and get out holding your hands above your heads."

Votilinni laughed into the microphone. Nick realized the voice was different from Rudolph's. "An' just what the fuck you gonna do if we don't, prick?" He tried to sound like a man in control, asking a rhetorical question, but there was a tinge of real curiosity in his voice.

"I'm going to shoot you."

"Bull-fuckin'-shit."

TWENTY-NINE

Nick raced out and around the corner into the foyer. Mac was coming out of the living room entrance. "Votilinni and Rudolph are on the plane taxiing for take off. I told them, I'd shoot them if they didn't stop and get out with their hands up. Votilinni's on the radio and he won't comply."

"That's not surprising."

"You get in the den and keep giving him that same message. Maybe he'll listen to a ghost."

"You aren't really gonna shoot them?"

"I sure as hell am." Nick went toward the front door. He and Nippy watched as the plane bobbed down the runway. It veered to the left at one point. One of the wing wheels rolled on the grass along the edge of the pavement for a moment, then the plane steered back to the center.

Nick heard Tommy's voice in the receiver, "Nick, Grimm's gettin' away across the river. You need me to stay in position here?"

"No. Grinke's dead and the Stordock girl is wounded. The rest are neutralized, except Votilinni and Rudolph. They're on the plane. We'll take care of 'em. Go on after your man."

Tommy moved quickly toward the river using the evergreen trunks for cover. He sprayed the trees beyond the opposite bank with a burst of gunfire and then waded into the river. He swam across the deep center and waded quickly to the other bank. With stealth and using the trees as cover again, he climbed the hill on the east bank.

The plane was approaching the north end of the runway, nearly a mile from Nick and Tadd, who had stepped out onto the front lawn. The aircraft bobbed and weaved along as the overwrought Ken Rudolph frantically worked the throttle and brakes. In the den, Mac had grabbed the microphone and said, "Jimmy, this is Mac McGinnis. Do as they say. Give it up."

Votilinni recognized the voice he had known nearly all his life, "McGinnis, you fuckin' squealin' rat bastard. What the fuck are you doin' alive?" he screamed.

"They do make bulletproof vests, Jimmy," Mac retorted.

Sweat was pouring down Rudolph's face from the heat and from fear. As he worked the nose wheel around to turn the plane, he looked over at Votilinni. The man was white with rage as he screamed and spat into the microphone, "I'll get you yet, you fuckin' mick cocksucker! You'll burn like a goddamn fuckin' saint."

Nick leaned his assault rifle against one of the lawn chairs in front of the house. He walked out on the knoll and stood in the sunlight. Tadd, still dizzy from his wound, leaned against the front of the house. They watched as the plane jerkingly approached the end of the runway, far in the distance in the corridor, bordered by an expanse of green lawn and rows of evergreens on either side.

Tanya came out of the front door. "The girl," she said as Nick turned back to look at her, "she's in shock. Her nails and lips are blue. We have blankets around her, but it doesn't look good. Sally's with her, but..."

Nick reached in his pocket and fished out some keys. He threw them to Tanya. "There's a CIA medical kit in the left side cover of my motorcycle. Go get it. There's a small oxygen bottle and mask in there. I'll call for a hospital copter right away." She ran back in the house. Nick reached under his hairpiece and moved the switch to wide area communications mode. "Barnes, you out there? Dan Barnes, FBI, come in. This is Nick Barber."

After a moment Nick heard a reply, "This is Barnes. We're on the way. I'm in a van about fifteen miles south on highway 51. Chief Inspector Jeffery Gilbertson from Washington is in charge. He's coming in by helicopt..."

"I don't give a shit which one of your bureaucrats is in charge today," Nick interrupted. "We need a medical evac copter right now. The Stordock girl has gunshot wounds in the lower right abdomen and she's in shock. You copy?"

"Yes."

"Have them land on the knoll, directly in front of the house on the north side."

"Right. We have a couple of helicopters standing by at Tomahawk about sixty-five miles south. I'll get them in the air right away. Should be there within a half hour."

"That might not be good enough," Nick said. He thought he heard a scream in the background over the receiver.

At the end of the runway, Rudolph had completed the one-hundred and eighty degree turn. As the sharp nose of the jet turned into the wind, he pushed the throttle. Thrust thundered from the engines and the plane catapulted forward. He steered the nose to the centerline of the runway, and pushed the throttle smoothly forward, taking it to the limit. Nick and Tadd watched as the plane came toward them. It appeared to grow in size rapidly, as the roaring of the engines increased. Trails of black smoke poured from the engines back along the runway. The image of forested horizon behind the plane was distorted by the gases. Nick withdrew his HK G11 pistol from his jacket. He aimed it out in front of him with both hands. "Votilinni, you sonofabitch!" Nick yelled toward the plane. "You had your warning." He hopped forward threateningly, arms outstretched and waving the pistol up and down like a divining rod. "Stop," he yelled.

"Are you nuts, Barber?" Tadd Nippy said from behind, "You can't do anything with that pistol!"

Without looking back Nick yelled, "The answer to your is probably and you're wrong about this weapon."

Votilinni had thrown the headset on the floor. He leaned and looked out over the controls and squinted out the windshield at Nick. "That crazy fucker out there don't act like any goddamn FBI agent I ever saw," he yelled to Rudolph. Rudolph was oblivious to the comment. He was pulling back on the yoke, all of his efforts concentrated on the take off. The nose of the plane tilted up and a second later the wheels left the ground. Votilinni became exhilarated with the escape as they went airborne. "Mo-ther-fuck-ers," he screamed, "mo-ther-fuck-ers."

As the plane left the ground nearly a half mile away, Nick switched on the laser sight on the pistol. He kept it fixed on the belly of the plane. Rudolph kept the throttle on full and as the plane gained altitude and speed, he increased the angle of climb. The plane passed over Nick at five hundred feet, soaring upward.

Tanya had stopped to tell Sally she was going for the oxygen. Sally was laying another blanket over the shivering Christi. Tanya then ran out the back door of the living room on the east end, down the terraces and across the golf course lawn. She went through the trees and kneeled next to Nick's motorcycle. She turned the key in the lock on a plastic side door below the seat. She got her fingers around a gray plastic box and slid it out. The words "FIRST AID" were printed on the top.

The screaming jet climbed into the sky over the house. Nick pulled up a small, telescoping six-inch antenna on top of the pistol at the back, above the grip. An instant after he did so, the top of the plastic saddlebag on his motorcycle, back at the camp, snapped open. Tanya, startled at the sound, fell back into the dry brown pine needles on the forest floor. Nick held the pistol above his head with both hands, turning as he followed the plane. He kept the laser sight trained on the side of the fuselage. He squeezed the trigger slowly. A bright flash and a puff of smoke appeared before Tanya's eyes just above the plastic saddlebag. A streak of light brighter than the sun, stretched above her in the sky and she heard a shrill siren scream. Nick kept the laser sight on target. It was serving as a guide beam now. The wailing streak of light appeared, climbing from behind the house. The small missile curved into a perfect tangent with the laser beam and followed it into the side of the plane like a bullet. A blinding flash, then a puff of smoke, appeared at the point of impact. The smoke blew away quickly.

The crack of the explosion rolled about the grounds and forest like a thunderbolt, causing tremors. Slowly, the plane began to roll out of its upward vector. A two-foot wide hole had appeared in the skin of the fuselage.

The interior of the plane was filled with smoke and dust. Each of the men had lost their hearing from the shock-wave pressure of the blast. It had driven Rudolph against the yoke. Diamond Jimmy Votilinni was forced against the copilot controls, his eyes wide with terror. He looked out the windshield. The panoramic view of the bright, blue sky suddenly turned to green. As the nose of the plane dipped, only the forest could be seen. He screamed.

Nick targeted the beam on the hole and squeezed the trigger again. Tanya had scooted away on the pine needles just as another missile streaked out of the saddlebag. The faltering plane was nearly above her now. She looked up and saw the bright light streak toward it as she listened to the siren scream again. The missile disappeared inside the hole. Suddenly, the windshield of the plane, then several fuselage panels, blew out in a jarring explosion. The plane rolled overhead as it went into the downside of its arc-like path. It sailed down, spinning, nose first into the forest, south of the camp. The ground shook as the plane crashed into the forest floor. Tanya was up in a second and running toward the house with the medical kit.

Tommy had climbed the opposite bank of the river quickly. He made his way east using the trunks of the tall pine trees as cover. He came to a pond surrounded by sand. Across the pond, he saw Johnny Grimm peer out from behind a tree and take a shot at him. The bullet nicked the tree Tommy was hiding behind. He was about to drop to the ground and return fire, when he heard the jet soaring into the sky behind him. He turned and through the pine branches saw it gaining altitude in the sky. He watched as it was hit by the missile. He saw it go out of control, then roll and nose dive behind the treetops. "I'll be damned," he said aloud to himself, "it does work. Why risk my neck any more?" He laid his assault rifle on the ground and pulled his G11 pistol out of his jacket. He pulled up the small antenna and it snapped into place. He aimed around the tree.

Johnny Grimm had stepped out from behind the tree into the open. His suit was soaking wet. He was stepping backward as he squinted into the sky, where the plane had been. His mouth was agape and he held the M-16 rigidly in his hands.

Tommy sighted the laser beam on the center of the man's chest. "Drop your weapon and put your hands on your head," he yelled in a demanding voice.

Grimm looked at him and aimed his weapon as he screamed, "Fuck you."

They each squeezed triggers simultaneously. The M-16 rattled in Grimm's hand spraying the spiraling bullets in Tommy's direction. Tommy checked quickly to see that the beam was still on the man, then pulled his head behind the tree. He heard the siren scream behind him, as the missile came down seeking to join the beam. Tommy felt a numbness in his right hand. A bullet had scored his knuckles, as he held the pistol against the tree to steady it. The laser beam shifted down slightly as a result. The fins of the missile made a last, microsecond adjustment and followed the beam to the ground. Tommy flopped to the ground, his arms covering his head. The nose of the missile buried itself below the sand, several inches in front of Grimm's feet. Grimm had stopped firing and was turning to run as the ground below him erupted.

There was a giant flash of bright red-yellow light and a cracking, ear-splitting, boom rolled throughout the forest. The ground trembled and vibrating waves quivered on the surface of the pond. Grimm was blown twirling into the air in a pink cloud that was his own atomized flesh and blood swirling in sand.

Tommy looked up as the man's body slammed to the ground in a cloud of dust and smoke. He raced around the edge of the pond. The smoke and dust was settling as he approached. Tommy felt a great wave of relief from the tension of the battle and from his victory. He looked down at Grimm, what was left of him. His left arm was gone, only a shard of the humerus bone protruding from the ragged, bloody flesh at the shoulder. His legs had disintegrated. The lower trunk of his body was shredded at the pelvis and impacted with bloody sand. Amazingly, the man was still alive. His right arm waved about on the ground and his mouth opened and closed soundlessly. He stared up at Tommy.

"Like a land mine," Tommy said aloud to himself. Then he spoke to Grimm. "You hit me and threw my aim off. But then, close counts in missiles as in horseshoes." His right hand was numb and bleeding. He shifted the pistol to his left hand and raised it close to his face. He pushed the antenna back into the pistol with his chin. It clicked into place. There was an unintelligible sound from Grimm's mouth now. "Will I be kind today?" Tommy said. He aimed the pistol between the man's eyes. "Yes, I will." He paused for a moment, then squeezed the trigger firing a single shot.

Nick and Tadd heard the scream of the third missile and the explosion in the woods to the east. "Looks like Tommy's gunned his man down," Nick said as both of them stared in that direction.

Tanya rushed out of the house. "I think we're going to lose her," she said frantically.

As Nick followed her quickly into the house he said, "You give her the oxygen?"

"Yes, but it looks bad."

On the bloody carpet in the living room Nick knelt next to the wounded young woman. Sally was kneeling on the other side, holding the small, oxygen mask over the woman's nose and mouth. Nick put his fingers on Christi's forehead and pushed her eyelid with his thumb. Her pupil was buried up in the lid. Her lips were blue. Her body shook suddenly in a spasm. Nick shoved the blanket aside and took her wrist in his hand. It was cold. He checked her pulse and found it to be weak and erratic. He then removed the blanket from her abdominal area. There were two small, round entrance wounds there, the blood around them dried and dark. He felt around under her back at the right side, squeezing and kneading the skin there. Finally he said, "Heavy internal bleeding. The iliac artery must be severed. The copter should be here in twenty minutes or so, but she's not going to make that." He looked up at Tanya, "Go to the kitchen and get some pans of hot water, soap and clean towels; quick, warm water will do for a start." She was on her way in a second. He looked over at Sally, "There's a scalpel and a hypodermic syringe packet in that kit, get those out for me. And latex gloves. Give me a pair."

Sally reached down to the open med kit at her side. "What are you going to do, Nick?" she asked, a worried tone in her voice.

He straightened up on his knees, and took off the hairpiece and beard and threw them aside. He took off his jacket. "I'm going to do what I *came* here to do. If the bleeding isn't stopped, she'll die soon."

She handed him the syringe packet, the gloves and scalpel. He pulled some liquid into the hypodermic needle from a tiny bottle, then held the needle up and pushed a few droplets out with the plunger to purge it of air. He pushed the needle into Christi's right arm and emptied it into a vein. "Mild anesthetic and a muscle relaxant, hope it's enough." Nick said under his breath. "Mac, you hold her legs and Sally you hold her arms. Keep her from moving around. Tanya, the water?" She came in with a pan of hot water, a plastic container of liquid soap and some towels. Nick washed his hands and rinsed them in the water. He wiped them off with a towel and slipped on the gloves. "Get more."

With his left hand, he grabbed Christi's skin at the side of her abdomen and pulled it tight. He held the scalpel, so that the point of the blade protruded between his thumb and forefinger. He started an incision on her right side, just below the ribcage. Using his middle finger as a guide behind the scalpel, he continued the incision in a large, smooth arc out to her right side. As he did so, he moved his left hand on her torso, keeping the skin taut. The shallow incision and the thin scalpel allowed only a small streak of blood along the cut. He continued the cut arcing back toward the center of her body and stopping nearly at the pubis. Christi, unconscious, had moved only slightly in reaction during the process. Nick was sweating now, "Someone wipe my face," he said. Tanya reached over with a towel and soaked the sweat from Nick's face. He reached to the beginning of the incision and pushed two fingers through. He wiggled them slowly, splitting the incision open by tearing through the remaining fat connected below the skin. Keeping his fingers just inside, he moved them along it, breaking the layer of fat as gently as he could along the way. Fortunately, there were no serious bleeding points.

Tommy Garcia came into the room. His eyes went first to Tosco's body, sliced nearly in half, hanging over the glass. Then to Grinke, dead in the chair, then down at Nick, Sally, Tanya and Mac around Christi on the floor. Nick shot a quick glance up at him, as he continued to open the wound with his fingers. "Tommy, Christ, am I glad to see you. She's shot twice in the lower right abdomen. M-16 by our friend Tosco there. She's bleeding to death. I suspect the right iliac artery is ruptured. I'm going to try and clamp it. Get cleaned up and get down here."

Tommy threw off his jacket, hairpiece and beard, "Nick, I'm not going to be much good. My right hand's wounded and bleeding."

Nick looked to his right at Sally, who was holding Christi's arms. "Let Tommy take over for you. Go wash your hands and slip on a pair of gloves. Then get on the other side of her." She ran to the kitchen to wash her hands. Nick began to lift the flap of skin carefully, separating the layer of fat on the underside from the tissue below with his fingers. He then pushed his fingers into the flat, fibrous tendon sheet of abdominal muscle below and split it in the direction of the fibers.

Sally returned and knelt across from Nick. She slipped on the second pair of latex gloves from the kit. "Ok Sally," Nick said, "We've got to open a big hole so I can have a look around in there. Hold the skin and muscle apart. I'll split open the next layer of muscle. Then I'll cut through the peritoneum, the abdominal lining, and we should see the intestines." Following Nick as he worked, Sally's hands held open each successive layer. Finally, the intestines were exposed. "I'm going to go under the intestines. Very carefully, help me push them toward you, out of the way." Sally nodded. "Tanya, find the penlight in the surgical kit. Turn it on and stick it in my mouth. Then find the vascular clamps in the kit and get one ready to hand to me."

"What do they look like?" Tanya asked.

"Uh, like a small scissors." Nick grabbed the penlight in his teeth and aimed it into the opening. He slid his right hand down under the ascending colon on the left edge of the intestines and began to separate it from the tissue beneath. The lower parts of the abdominal cavity were filling with blood around his hand as he worked. Christi moaned and tried to shift around. Tommy and Mac held her. As Sally pulled the intestines over, putting pressure on them, the fetid smell from a perforation in the bowel wafted up. This was followed by the strong iron-tinged smell of fresh blood. Nick was feeling around below in the warm blood. There was the kidney and a mass of tissue and a myriad of arteries supplying the intestines and other organs with blood. "Damnit," Nick was saying, "I'm not going to be able to find that artery with all this blood." He looked at Sally. "Can you hold for a minute?" Sally nodded. Nick looked at Tanya, "Should be a piece of rubber tube in that kit." She immediately began to dig through the contents which she had spread on the floor. Nick reached into a pan of water and washed the blood from his right hand. The water turned nearly as red as the blood. Tanya helped him dry the hand and handed him a piece of rubber tube. Then, he lifted the skin below Christi's back and felt around for an exit wound. He found one of the two. Blood was seeping through. He opened it with his finger and pushed the tube through. He shepherded blood to the drain tube with the edge of his hand. "We need suction, we don't have it," he said to himself. "This is the best I can do." More blood flowed onto the already soaked carpet and was absorbed. Tommy reached over with a towel and wiped the sweat from Sally's face then from Nick's. With his right hand, Nick felt around in the tissue underneath. He found the lateral iliac artery branch. It was nearly one half inch in diameter, much larger than the other vessels. He ran his fingers slowly along it, wiping away the remaining blood until he could see the arterial blood pulsing forth. The bullet had torn the vessel, but not completely severed it.

"Ok, I've found the rupture. One clamp," he said. Tanya put it in his left hand. "Tanya, give me some light down here." She leaned over and aimed the flashlight down toward his hand. Nick "milked" blood from the artery, starting over an inch above the wound. This was to purge it of any air bubbles that may have entered and prevent embolism. Then he pinched it off.

This is starting to slip," Sally said suddenly. The intestines were beginning to come apart and slide between and behind Sally's fingers. "Hold it for a few seconds, Nick said. He opened the clamp and put it in place above the wound. The blood pumping directly from the heart, above the clamp, was stopped. " Sally struggled to hold the intestines together. They seemed to be squirming on their own. Just as Nick pulled his hands out of the cavity, the intestines filled it again. "Gently," Nick said. They tucked the organs back in place as best they could. Nick washed his hands and folded the semi-circular flap of skin over Christi's abdomen. "Tape," he said as he cleaned off the exterior of the wound with a wet cloth. He tore off pieces of surgical tape and put them across and along the incision. He looked at Tommy, "Breathing? Pulse?"

Tommy's ear was down near the breathing mask and his fingertips were on Christie's carotid artery at the throat. "Both weak," he said.

"The main bleeding is stopped. That's about all we can do here. We wait for the copter, now. Keep the oxygen on her." He looked into Sally's tired, blue eyes, "You did great work, dear." He looked around, "You all did."

"I didn't know you were a surgeon," Sally said.

"I'm not. But, they send us to school for damn near everything, at one time or another. We spend as much time in school, teaching and learning, as we do on the job. Right Tommy?"

Tommy, who was checking the oxygen mask on Christi said, "Yes, sir," absentmindedly.

"Actually, I haven't done anything like this for a long time," Nick said. "You alright, Sally?"

She sighed, "I'm a hell of a long ways from being alright. I'm going to wash up." She rose and began to walk shakily toward the kitchen, tightening the loose robe around her. Mac sprang up to help her.

Nick stood up and looked around. He walked over to Tosco's body and looked down onto the broken glass below. Tommy stood also and watched Nick leave the living room. He heard some crunching on the glass below, near the pool. Tommy went into the foyer just in time to see Nick come up the stairs, a bloody object in his hands.

"Major Garcia," Nick said looking at Tommy, "would you please go to the bar and see if there's some whiskey available? Bourbon would be good. Nick nodded toward the entrance to the bar.

Tommy came back through the foyer, an unopened bottle of bourbon in his hand. He went into the kitchen. Nick was there washing something off in the sink. "What's that?" he asked.

Nick dried the object off with a towel. He held it out to Tommy. It was a pocket package of Tiparillo cigars, unopened, still encased in cellophane. "Spoils of war," Nick said, "I saw it in Tosco's pocket. It must have fallen out when he shot himself. I hope it's waterproof."

Tommy looked at it. He scratched the cleft in his chin, "Bloodproof would be even better."

As Nick opened it, he said, "Why don't you fish a couple of glasses out of the cupboard?"

THIRTY

The chopping of a helicopter blade could be heard far in the distance. Nick and Tommy sat outside the front door in lawn chairs. Each had a lit cigar his teeth in one hand and a tumbler of bourbon in his hand. Nick took a pull of bourbon from the tumbler and put it down on the cobblestone patio. He balanced a pad of paper on his leg. He was writing. Tadd Nippy sat on the patio in a chair, warming his face in the sun. Tommy turned to him, "Why don't you lie down, Nippy? It's all clear now."

Tadd shook his head, "I'm ok."

A blue van came out of the woods kicking up dust. It drove below the knoll in front of them and began to come up the drive. Tommy waved it to a stop. The orange and white helicopter was just coming down to land on the knoll. "Lift for Life", was emblazoned on the side in bright blue. Nick looked up as it settled some fifty feet away, near the edge of the knoll. As the blades whirled to a stop, a man and woman with a stretcher and packs of equipment crawled out. Another man followed. Ducking low, they came toward the house. Tommy led them inside. Barnes, Pat Stordock, her husband and several agents came out of the van. Squinting into the sun, Nick looked up at them, the smoldering cigar clamped in his teeth. Below the knoll, another helicopter was touching down.

Dan Barnes looked haggard. Pat's face was streaked with tears, "My daughter, Christi, where is she?" she said in a near scream. Her husband was holding her up, his face streaked as well.

Nick stood up and held out a hand as though to calm them. "We did all we could here. They'll have to get her to a hospital, now." As he said this, two of the flight paramedics brought her out the front door on the stretcher. They slid her into the rear clamshell door of the machine. Pat ran over to her. Nick waved the other paramedic over. By now, a group of men in suits had come up the knoll from the other helicopter.

"Listen carefully," Nick said to the man. He nodded. "The woman took two .223 caliber slugs in the lower right abdomen. They both went through the intestine and exited the back." The harried conversation of the many people gathered on the knoll grew loud and Nick roared loudly, "Everybody shut up. I'm giving this man critical instructions to save this woman's life." He turned back to the paramedic. "One of the bullets ruptured the right iliac artery. I made an incision in the abdomen, opened it and moved the intestines. I purged the artery and clamped it above the wound. I then taped up the incision. This emergency surgery was done under less than ideal conditions so there is a danger of peritonitis. You follow?" The man nodded. Nick handed him a folded piece of paper, "Everything I just told you is written down here. Give this to the surgeon."

The engine of the Lift for Life helicopter engine was starting now. The man nodded to Nick and ran toward the machine, ducking under the blades. Within a few minutes, the helicopter was disappearing into the sky.

Nick picked up his bourbon from the stones and walked over to the group. He looked at Sally who was in bare feet and wearing only the blood-spattered bathrobe, yet she seemed in charge.

Agents had pulled Pat Stordock away from the stretcher as they carried it from the house. Now, she looked around the group, her eyes frantic, with fear and grief. "Can anyone tell me if she's going to be all right?" she pleaded.

Sally spoke up, "Her pulse and breathing are still weak. They're taking her to the hospital in Wausau. They should get her there in less than a half-hour. She's got a good chance, thanks to Nick Barber here." She motioned toward Nick. "Pray for her now."

Nick felt put on the spot, at a loss for words. "Uh, yes," he said looking at Pat, "I think she's got a good chance. Take Chief Inspector Stein's advice and pray for her."

Pat looked at Barnes and said, "Let's get to the hospital." She and her husband followed the tired Dan Barnes back to the van they had come in.

Sally spoke to Nick, "I'd like you to meet Jeff Gilbertson, one of our first class people. He's in charge of the operation."

A tall, thin man of about forty stood there. He wore a dark blue pin-striped suit, a white shirt and paisley tie, done in shades from subdued red to blue. His narrow face wore a non-committal expression. His medium length, dark hair was combed back and his eyebrows were thick and bushy. "Pleased to meet you," he said in a measured voice that was of radio announcer clarity. His eyes were on the ear on a bead chain, that had fallen out of Nick's gray, blood-soaked T-shirt.

Nick stuck his cigar in his mouth, reached out and shook Gilbertson's hand with a tight grip that was returned. Nick looked down and flopped the ear back under his shirt. "Little battle souvenir," he said. "Pleased to meet you. Anyone that Sally says is first class is the same with me." He took a pull from his drink. He puffed the cigar. "Little afternoon snort?" he asked Gilbertson.

Gilbertson frowned, "I don't drink on duty or off."

Nick wasn't surprised by this comment. "Good man," he said, "it's practically obligatory over at our agency."

"So I've heard," Gilbertson replied with a bit of sarcasm. "There's a fire to the south in the woods, you know."

"Oh, yeah. It's from that damned plane that crashed with Votilinni and Rudolph aboard." He looked at Gilbertson, "So, call 9-1-1".

"Very funny," Gilbertson said with no expression. "We've already informed the fire department and the Wisconsin Department of Natural resources. So, what happened here?" Another orange and white Lift for Life helicopter was landing in place of the one that had left.

"Well," Nick began, "there are two women inside you can arrest. Votilinni's girlfriend and Rudolph's, too. All the wiseguys? Well..." Nick drew his forefinger across his throat. He described the events briefly with Tommy's help, including the man cuffed to the tree on the entrance road. "Sally can fill you in on what happened before we got here," he added. A couple of agents were helping Tadd Nippy into the helicopter. Nick looked at Tommy, "Your hand. You want to go with him?"

Three U.S. Marine helicopters landed below the knoll. Well, Tommy, looks like our ride is here," Nick said.

A Marine Major in fatigues ran up and saluted Nick. Nick returned the salute. He explained to the officer where the two turbine-powered motorcycles were and told the man to get them loaded. The Major took a group and went around the west wing of the house. Nick turned to Gilbertson. "The other motorcycles, any of the equipment our agency supplied, we would like returned in good condition. We have to think of the taxpayers who foot the bill for all this."

"I'm glad to hear of your concern for the taxpayers," Gilbertson said. "But all these dead men?"

"The ones we killed were bad people. There are a certain number of bad, no, actually evil people in this world and there is only one answer for them."

"Your reputation for great capability precedes you, Mr. Barber. But, I didn't realize you had the ability to look into men's hearts and minds and divine the evil there."

"I don't. But didn't Socrates ask, 'What is virtue? How can we know it?' The same questions can be asked about evil. In some cases, it's just plain obvious. Prima facie. Retribution is required."

"Preferably after due process, in a court of law," Gilbertson retorted.

"Oh hell, it's our concern for the taxpayers again," Nick said, "The taxpayers of Illinois in this case. Not long ago, John Wayne Gacy was executed for torturing and killing thirty-three young men and boys in that great state. It took fourteen years until he was executed. Millions of dollars of hard-earned taxpayer's money went for his upkeep, trials, stays, appeals. You call that justice? In 1933, Mayor Cermak of Chicago was killed by an assassin's bullets that were intended for President Franklin D. Roosevelt. Giuseppe 'Joe' Zangara fired that shot on February fifteenth. You know when he was executed, Inspector?"

"Well, I know of the incident, but I don't know the specific date."

"He was executed on March twentieth, five weeks after the crime. Now, that was justice swift and sure. Our good citizens can't get it today, but it may return. Possibly, when the body counts left by people like Votilinni, Von Kloussen, Rashidii and Noska get high enough, the system will take control of the situation again."

"You'll have to stay for statements," Gilbertson said, changing the subject.

"No, we can't," Nick replied. "The press will be on their way. Tommy and I don't want our faces in the newspaper and on television. National security, of course. The rest of these folks can fill you in on everything you need to know."

"You tough bastards are afraid of the press, huh?"

"Definitely," Nick replied, "They could help destroy us individually and as an organization."

The marines wheeled the two motorcycles across the lawn and loaded each one into a helicopter. Nick and Tommy shook hands with Mac, Tanya and Gilbertson. Nick walked over to Sally and put his arms around her, picking her up from the patio stones. He kissed her full on the lips, then pulled away and whispered, "You want to come with us?"

She looked into his eyes, the glint of the western sun on her glasses. She whispered, "No, my job is here."

"He nodded and said, "I'll call you soon." He kissed her again and gently opened his embrace.

Nick followed Tommy to the waiting helicopters. A white van with "Channel 2", printed on the side was coming onto the grounds from the wooded drive. Nick reached the helicopter door and turned. He pointed at the van and yelled, "Saved just in time by the Marines!" The helicopter was already beginning to lift as he grabbed the hand bar and climbed in. The three olive-drab machines chopped their way into the bright afternoon sky.

PART FOUR
THE NEW KNIGHT

THIRTY-ONE

Friday, July 8, 1994

The dark sky over All Saints Cemetery in Chicago was foreboding with rumbles of thunder. The low, rolling dark green hills were studded with tombstones and monuments. The markers were white, black and all of the shades of gray in between like the undulating clouds in the sky above. Even the largest trees swayed in the cool brisk wind. The motion of their outermost branches and leaves seemed frantic and unceasing. Even the normally shrill, ubiquitous chirping and calling of birds was sporadic and subdued. The sun had not been seen all day and it had rained in the morning. Now it looked as though it was about to rain again. There was a large, open-sided white tent supported by a dozen white poles at the sides and corners with two larger, taller ones at the center. Taut ropes staked into the ground held the temporary structure in place. The scalloped edges up around the perimeter flapped noisily in the breeze. Folding chairs had been set up in rows under the shelter. They were full and people were crowded around the edges and flowed out into the open under the stormy sky.

At one end of the shelter was a black casket with gold handles and trim. It was draped with the red, white and blue flag of the United States of America. Next to the flag lay a single strip of white silk. The casket rested above a temporary blanket of artificial turf that covered the deep rectangular hole in the earth below. A priest in a black flowing robe stood behind it, facing the crowd. He was talking to a young man and woman, both dressed in black. They were Fritz Grinke's children. To his right, at the head of the casket, stood seven white-gloved officers of the Chicago Police Department. They wore dark blue uniforms trimmed with gold braid at the epaulets and cuffs. The traditional checkerband officers' caps were cocked on their heads at exactly the correct angle. Each held a rifle over his right shoulder. Directly across under the canvas roof, seven U.S. Marines in formal dress faced them. They also wore white gloves and dark blue uniforms. There was a row of brass buttons down the front of their navy blue red-trimmed tunics. On their heads, were the familiar white "jarhead" dress caps, the silver eagle and anchor crest at the front. Their rifles also at their right shoulders.

The front three rows of chairs were filled with Grinke's brothers, sisters, nieces, nephews and other relatives. His first wife, the mother of his children, was there with her husband of many years. The two rows behind them were occupied by dignitaries from the Chicago Police force and the city administration. The Chief and other officers were in gold-decked uniforms. Tanya Williams was there in full uniform. Other police administrators were there and even the Mayor of Chicago. Behind them sat an entourage from Washington, D.C. Nick Barber was there in his dark green marine officer's uniform, a silver star on each shoulder. Tommy Garcia was in his green army uniform, a gold oak leaf on each of his shoulders, his right hand bandaged. Even Joe Ronzoni had come to pay his respects. The CIA Deputy Director was in his dark blue U.S. Navy uniform. There were two silver stars on each of his gold-trimmed epaulets. The three sat in a row with their officers' caps in their laps. They wore dark glasses. There were rows of colorful medals on the left breast of each man. They all wore, on their left shoulder, the forward facing eagle above an argent compass rose framed by a shield, the logo of the Central Intelligence Agency. Joe Ronzoni had arranged for the Marines to be there since the operation had been, after all, directed by the federal government. And Grinke had himself been a Marine.

The priest waved his hands at the crowd to quiet them. He began, "Today, we lay to rest a brave man. A man who was honored and revered by his family, his friends and his government. Francis Grinke gave of himself for his fellow man as few have done. He volunteered for the war in Vietnam. As a young Marine infantryman there, a quarter of a century ago, he fought fierce battles gallantly for his country on the beaches, in the bamboo thickets and rice paddies of that far away land. He was decorated for his brave actions in Quang Tri Province...Pro Patria..."

Joe Ronzoni turned and whispered to Nick, "I hope this is therapeutic for you. I know it is for me." Nick, his head down, nodded slightly. "You put that silk on the coffin?" Joe asked.

Nick nodded and whispered, "He deserved it."

Joe frowned and shook his head in disapproval.

The priest continued, "...he returned to Chicago and bravely served the people as a police officer for more than twenty-one years. He loved his family and did the best he knew how for them. At the end, he died in the act of giving up his own life, in the line of duty, so that a young woman might live..."

The uniformed police officers and Marines raised their rifles to the gray sky. The cracks of the forty-two shots cascaded from the gun barrels and echoed off through the damp air.

Walter Peyton's America's Bar, downtown Chicago, 5:00 P.M.

Nick sat at the bar nursing a beer. He stared beyond the other side of the bar and past the tables along the front window. It was as dark as dusk outside, partly due to the buildings that walled the street, but also because the sun had not shown all day. The rain had started again. Driven by the wind, it splattered against the windows. The drops of water caught the subdued light from the red and blue neon signs inside the windows and scattered the colorful rays everywhere.

He thought back to his conversation with Joe, before the boss caught his plane back to Washington. The United States and Danish governments had held discussions with the Baroness Von Kloussen. She had agreed to accept a small percentage of anything found. They had opened up the hill and found a few items, some gold bars and several valuable paintings. Not what they had hoped for, but worth more than five million today. There must have been considerably more, but apparently, Himmler had moved most of it before the end of the war. There were clues as to other locations, Joe had told Nick, that would need to be investigated. Nick had stopped him and suggested that if another "vacation junket" was planned, perhaps Tommy Garcia could go. Nick saw Tanya coming toward him, a tall, young man on her arm.

Behind them was Tommy, then Sally and Mac. They had all agreed to meet for a drink. Nick slid off the barstool and saluted the group.

"This is John Turner," Tanya said, as she introduced him to the others.

"Oh," Nick said, winking at her, a mischievous glint in his eye, "is this the one whom you describe as not being 'not that heavy' with?"

Tanya smiled and leaned against Bill, "You remember everything, don't you? Now, you aren't trying to get me in trouble are you? Actually," she looked up at Bill, "it's getting heavier by the minute. But I'm afraid we won't be able to stay for a drink, another engagement, sorry."

Nick stood and gave her a hug. Then he backed away and shook her hand, "I was proud to work with you, Sergeant."

"And I with you," she said.

"I just wish Grinke..."

"I wish he could be here, more than anyone," Tanya said, "I lost one hell of a partner. He was rough around the edges, but he was a good man with a heart of gold. Hard to find here...or anywhere."

"Salute," Nick said, "Tanya, if you'd like to consider government service, give me a call. We're always looking for a few good men, uh, I mean...people." He laughed.

"I'll keep that in mind," she said. Then, she and Bill said goodbye to the others and walked away.

Tommy, Sally and Mac had ordered drinks. Tommy picked up the tab as the bartender served them. He raised his glass, "To Fritz Grinke, God rest his soul." They all clinked glasses and took a swallow.

"So," Nick said, "where do we eat? Anyone make reservations?"

"Well," Sally said in an apprehensive tone, "there's been a change in plans," she looked up at Mac and squeezed his hand, "ours, anyway. Mac has reminded me that our twenty-fifth class reunion for Lincoln High School in Grand Falls is tomorrow. He asked me to go as his guest. And well, I've been waiting for this a long time. He didn't invite me to the senior prom as I wished he would have." She laughed nervously, "Tonight is the kickoff cocktail party. We can still make the tail end of it, if we leave right away."

"Are you feeling ok, I mean after this week and all?" Nick asked, an obvious shade of disappointment in his voice.

"I'm fine. I'll admit I was more terrorized than I ever have been in my life. But I was safe in Mac's arms, when he helped me get my glasses back on."

Nick turned to Mac, "Are you sure it's safe for you to be in public? There might still be a few Votilinni hit men around."

"I'll be personally guarded by a top flight FBI agent, won't I?"

Nick nodded, conceding the point, "Well, have a good time kids," he said forcing a sad smile.

Mac and Sally finished their drinks and put their glasses on the bar. As they walked away waving, Nick said to Sally, "I'll call you."

She nodded and said, "Be sure you do." Then she turned and walked away with Mac.

Nick turned back to Tommy, "There's no other way to say it. I've been jilted for the mob. She ripped my heart out. And I," he poked his right thumb in his chest, "I was the one who cut her loose and told Mac to take care of her."

Tommy ordered them a couple more beers. He lit a cigar and offered Nick one, then lit it for him. Tommy blew a stream of smoke out on the surface of the bar, "I've been summoned to Washington. I'm being offered induction into an 'order' of some sort, Joe tells me. Very secretive. Can you tell me anything about it?"

Nick came out of his reverie momentarily. "I can tell you that I was among those who recommended you. But, I can't discuss it. The utmost secrecy is the nature of the beast in this case. I can tell you, however that if you accept entrance, you'll be perfectly free to tell any target you're about to neutralize all about it. As long as no one else can hear, of course." Nick chuckled weakly and returned his gaze to the rain swept window..

Tommy looked over at his preoccupied mentor. "She's just going to a class reunion with an old flame," he offered. Then he added hopefully, "Call the lady next week in Washington and things'll be back to normal."

"I'll give it a try," Nick said, "You know people do describe me as persistent and intense."

THE END
(Until the next crisis, anyway)

Mike Hatch is an adjunct faculty member at the University of Wisconsin-Oshkosh. He is a recognized management authority in the manufacturing industry. He has been a farmhand, migrant fruit picker, auto mechanic, race car driver, machinist, industrial engineer, computer programmer, business executive, university lecturer and management consultant. Mike has lived and worked in Wisconsin, Illinois, New York and Europe and has traveled in Canada and Latin America. He lives in Wisconsin with his family. *Take It To The Limit* is his Second novel, following *Horseshoes & Nuclear Weapons*, the thrilling account of a nuclear terrorist bombing. He is at work on a third.